Rising to the Occasion

Also by Linda Taylor

Reading Between the Lines
Going Against the Grain
Beating About the Bush

Rising to the Occasion

Linda Taylor

William Heinemann : London

Published by William Heinemann in 2001

1 3 5 7 9 10 8 6 4 2

First published in the United Kingdom in 2001 by William Heinemann

The Random House Group Limited
20 Vauxhall Bridge Road, London, SW1V 2SA

Random House Australia (Pty) Limited
20 Alfred Street, Milsons Point, Sydney, New South Wales 2061, Australia

Random House New Zealand Limited
18 Poland Road, Glenfield
Auckland 10, New Zealand

Random House (Pty) Limited
Endulini, 5a Jubilee Road, Parktown, 2193, South Africa

The Random House Group Limited Reg. No. 954009

www.randomhouse.co.uk

A CIP catalogue record for this book is available from the British Library

Papers used by Random House are natural, recyclable products made from
wood grown in sustainable forests. The manufacturing processes conform to
the environmental regulations of the country of origin

Printed and bound in the United Kingdom by
Creative Print and Design (Wales), Ebbw Vale

ISBN 0 434 00892 3

Acknowledgements

With enormous thanks to: All at Heinemann, especially Lynne Drew and Anna Dalton-Knott. Everyone at the Darley Anderson Agency – and a very big thank you to Elizabeth Wright for her hard work and support from the beginning. My good friends and my family for their solidarity. Debbie at the Golden Scissors for giving me an idea. Harry for being Harry and giving me some insights. Rachel and Jon, Gale, Rebecca, Ian, Chris and Rob – you've been wonderful. Thank you. Julie and Armin for unqualified support and encouragement, and incredible generosity. Margaret for introducing me to cricket way back when. The women's cricket team at MCO Oxford, where we had such fun playing, and the Internet cricket nuts and all the friends I've made through the game.

To the England cricket team, for cheering us up.

But especially my gratitude to my wonderful mum, who came through illness so bravely and continues to be my rock. I couldn't have done any of this without you. Thank you, Mum.

For Tris

Author's Note

In this novel an Ashes match takes place at Old Trafford. In fact, Trent Bridge has now been favoured over Old Trafford for the 2001 Ashes. All other details relating to the Ashes, the players and their actions are entirely fictional, and any mistakes my own.

I like dreams of the future better than the history of the past.

Thomas Jefferson

Chapter One

The sun was throbbing over east London, warming the late June air. Cathy left the throng of Hoe Street behind and sidestepped the kids wrestling with their bikes on the pavement. She couldn't wait to get home and change out of her suit.

She'd spent most of the afternoon locked in a stuffy meeting in Euston and the last half-hour in an even stuffier tube compartment. The weekend was supposed to start on Friday night. She tried to superimpose images of the coming weekend over her list of things to do on Monday morning.

That was the flip side of her recent promotion. It was difficult to leave it behind at the end of the day, or even the end of the week. A glimmer of a frown crossed Cathy's forehead as she unlatched her low gate and made the four strides that took her across the tiny concreted front garden to the doorstep. Then, while she sought her keys in the depths of her bag, she stepped back and gazed up at the façade of her house. She smiled. It was *hers*. It was much more enriching to think of the house as hers than to remember that it really belonged to the Woolwich and she was buying it back off them. She'd moved in about six months before and she still got a buzz every time she put her key in the lock of the front door.

It was an unexceptional red-brick terraced house, in

a long row where all the houses looked the same, with small bay windows and neat little porches. It was a quiet street, helped by being one way and endowed with sleeping policemen. The residents' cars lined the road on either side, the sound of groaning cars and buses from Hoe Street only drifting over the roofs in the still evening air and moving on.

Trying to push thoughts of work right from her mind, Cathy concentrated on the happy fact that it was the weekend, the summer had arrived with a passion and Jason was probably going to be back from his Paris trip some time on Saturday. Hopefully he'd come straight to her house, rather than stopping off at his flat first. That would give them a little more time together before he disappeared again. Perhaps they'd grab a meal out, or have a brainstorm about what colour to paint the living room, or possibly they'd just spread out on the sofa with a bottle of wine. Whatever they did, she'd missed him while he'd been away and was looking forward to seeing him. She worked her key into the lock and began to sing under her breath.

'Oh give me a home where the buffalo roam, and I'll give you a house full of—'

She pushed open the door. There was a loud clunk as the door hit something, followed by a sharp cry.

'Shit!' came a muffled voice.

'Jason!' Shock mingled with delight as Cathy spotted him on his knees on the hall carpet. He swayed backwards and forwards, clutching his nose.

'My God,' Jason whistled nasally. 'I know how the Serengeti feels in stampede season.'

'You're here!' Cathy exclaimed and threw herself at her boyfriend to give him a hug. 'What happened? I thought you weren't flying in until tomorrow?'

'We tied up the loose ends early, so I got back at lunchtime. I thought I'd put the chain on the door for you.' Jason held up the screwdriver as evidence. 'Then you can stop badgering me about it.'

'Then perhaps Melissa and Brian will stop badgering *me* about it,' said Cathy, referring to her adoptive parents and pulling a face. 'They think east London's full of gangsters and salivating dogs with spikes sticking out of their collars. They won't rest until I'm bound into this house like Houdini.' Cathy sank to the carpet with Jason to give him a kiss. 'Thanks for doing that. I never seem to have time to do fiddly things. I'm so glad you're here early. I've been thinking about all the things we can do this weekend. How was Paris?'

'The hotel room was fascinating,' Jason said ironically, dropping a kiss on to Cathy's lips. 'Hmn, that's nice.'

'Are you thinking what I'm thinking?' Cathy smiled suggestively.

'Well I *was* thinking of a cold glass of white wine, some French bread and some of that delicious cheese you love so much.' Jason grinned. 'What are *you* thinking?'

'You brought me back some Pont l'Eveque?'

'Of course. As if I'd dare come back from France empty-handed.'

Cathy put her arms round Jason and hugged him. His dark-brown eyes were still a bit watery from where the door had hit him in the face. He hugged her back.

'Thank you, Jace.' Cathy eyed the wonky chain hanging from the inside of her front door. 'You might as well finish the chain now you've started. I'll get us some plonk.'

Cathy danced through the living room, dumping her

3

bag and jacket, and into the kitchen. It was a long, bright kitchen with a big, square window facing the kitchen annexe of the next house. Cathy had visions of reinventing the whole thing in years to come, but for now the white floor tiles and white units were functional. She found a bottle of Pouilly Fuissé chilling in the fridge. There were a couple of bottles of red wine on the unit and a bag of goodies fresh from Paris. She spotted a *saucisson* sticking out of it and smiled. This was the bonus of Jason's trips away. He always brought back some mouth-watering souvenirs. For the moment Cathy didn't even mind that Jason had likened her entrance to a herd of buffalo. She was a nicely proportioned size sixteen and very happy about who she was, unless people sniped. Jason's teasing was only affectionate and made her laugh, so that was fine.

Cathy returned to Jason with cold wine for them both and perched on the stairs to watch him as he finished putting on her chain.

She loved the back of Jason's dark head. He had a little arrow of hair that tapered down the back of his neck. His skin was olive, his hair black, his eyes Spanish-brown. He was slim and fit without trying, which she envied but didn't try to emulate. He wasn't the slightest bit fashion conscious, but he had a classic way of looking smart, casual, or scruffy, without ever thinking about it. Today he was in jeans and a loose shirt, and Cathy took a moment to admire his rear view. He was five foot ten or eleven, but as Cathy was a modest five foot four, he always seemed satisfyingly tall too.

Cathy had first met Jason at work – at the business development company in Euston she still worked for.

He'd moved on, headhunted for the role he'd been dying to have – European Marketing Manager – in a firm based in the City. Cathy could still remember her first impressions of Jason, five years ago, when they were thrown together on a project. She'd been struck by how swarthy and handsome he was. So unlike herself, with her fair skin, deep-red hair, blue eyes. Cathy only had to look at a holiday brochure and she exploded with freckles. Jason could spend hours in the sun without even noticing that he was slightly warm. She'd speculated that he might have Mediterranean blood. In fact, Jason was European in taste, style and looks, but not in blood. It was just the way he was.

They'd worked together for almost a year before they'd started a relationship, and in that time Cathy had fancied Jason like fury. She still did. Watching him concentrating on screwing her chain into place, Cathy wondered if Jason missed her when he was away – at his flat, working hard, or off on his never-ending business trips – quite as intensely as she missed him. She wouldn't have minded an impulsive passionate reunion, but on the other hand it was lovely to drink wine, watch him and feel comfortable. Things would be passionate later.

'There. All done.' Jason took a glass of wine and drank from it. 'What shall we do this evening? I've got to be off again tomorrow, so let's make the most of it.'

'Aw, no!' Cathy felt her face fall. 'You haven't really got to go again tomorrow, have you? You've only just got back.'

''Fraid so. We've got to fly out to Amsterdam on Sunday morning and I really need to spend tomorrow night at my flat unpacking from Paris and getting

5

organised agian. Sorry, Cathy. So what do you want to do tonight? There's a great Fellini film showing in town. We could do that and a meal out?' Then he added, seeing Cathy's uncertain expression, 'A Stanley Kubrick video and I'll cook?'

Cathy swallowed back her disappointment. Just one night this time. She offered a tight smile. 'Sometimes I wish they'd never promoted you.'

Jason considered Cathy carefully. 'I know. And it's knackering, believe me. They expect me to be everywhere now.' He paused. 'But we've got tonight, so let's make the most of it. What would you like to do?'

'I don't mind,' Cathy said in a small voice.

'In which case,' Jason murmured, pulling her close, 'perhaps we should get a takeaway and have dinner in bed? What do you say?'

Cathy had been renting, until the lease on her flat in Stratford had come to an end and she'd found herself back in the flat-hunting loop, picking up *Loot* every day. She'd spent her time at work ducking under the desk to make calls to agencies, and her evenings steaming around on tubes and buses. It was a frenetic race to find a few square yards of concrete she could call home.

Then Melissa – her adoptive mother whom she'd always thought of as Melissa – had brought up the subject over lunch one Sunday and persuaded her to think about buying. Brian had gently added his agreement. It made much more sense than renting. Why throw money down the drain? Why not buy?

There were lots of reasons. Being broke was the main one. But Melissa had offered Cathy a small loan to put down as a deposit. She'd pointed out that if Cathy paid as much on a mortgage as she did on rent, she could afford a little place of her own, somewhere not very flashy. After a struggle with her conscience that lasted all of five minutes, Cathy agreed to be lent enough money for a deposit.

She had known, without asking, that Jason wouldn't want to buy in with her. He had a flat in west London – he was already paying a mortgage on that – and although they'd been seeing each other for four years, they were both fond of their own space. Now that she had a small house, however, Cathy was starting to feel that there would be enough room for them to live together and still have space. It seemed like the natural thing to do – if she could bring Jason round to the idea.

Her home was in a sprawling part of east London, lively, unaffected by trendy London life, and the Walthamstow street market was enough to draw her friends down for bargain-hunting binges. She was intrigued by the little shops, selling anything from saris and sofas to curry spices and bargain flights. It was an exciting place to be. Cathy loved the stringy lights over the Millennium Dome, the sharp, clean angles of Canary Wharf, the Docklands developments, the buzz around the regeneration of the area. It gave her a thrill. She was a part of something that was growing.

This was true of her work too. She worked with East End companies, trying to help them to get ahead. There was so much potential in the area, and every time she was part of a project that boosted employment and made a difference she felt that she'd really achieved something.

She was putting in a lot of work and she was doing very well for it.

Cathy lay beside Jason that night, full of wine, takeaway Chinese and squishy French cheese, and warm from their physical reunion. It was a hot night and they'd flung the duvet across the room. She squinted through the dusky orange light cast by the street lamps at Jason's back and curled herself into the back of his legs.

'Jace?'

'Hmn?'

'I don't suppose you'd like to spend a bit more time here?'

'Hmn.'

'I know we're happy the way we are. Just to say that you can. If you want.'

'Hmn.'

Cathy wriggled around on the cool cotton. She couldn't help feeling a bit peeved that Jason wouldn't answer. But after four years of their relationship she knew him very well.

Jason took time to get used to new ideas. When they'd first started seeing each other it had taken Cathy ages to persuade him not to sprint off after each night they'd spent together. He was busy, she knew that. Perhaps he was even a workaholic. Cathy was prepared to accept that too. But when Jason came to stay with Cathy he'd turn up with a handful of his own things and take them all away with him when he left.

A few times, when Jason was away, Cathy had wandered around her house, looking for signs of him. If it weren't for her kitchen, which he constantly rearranged so that he could cook, there'd be no evidence that he'd ever been there. No toothbrush, shaving foam, towel, loose change, or even a screwed-up hanky. Forensics would have to dust for fingerprints to prove that he'd ever visited. She gave it one more push.

'It's just that – you could leave stuff here, you know. If you wanted to.'

'What stuff?' Jason mumbled.

'Like – boxer shorts.' Cathy waited, holding her breath.

She felt Jason stir. 'Boxer shorts?'

'Yes. Just a pair or two. Somewhere.'

Jason turned over to lie on his back. 'You know, boxer shorts are fairly important to a man. I have to recycle them. I can't leave them as mementos everywhere I go.'

'Well, it was just an idea.'

Jason fell silent. A distant underground train rumbled and faded away. Before long, the wood pigeons camping out in the tousled sidings would stir and start whooping at each other – a reminder that summer was truly in full swing. Cathy flopped back into her pillows and stared up at the ceiling. That was enough mention of boxer shorts. Jason's voice had been quite tense in reply. It was best to forget it, for now.

'Thank you for putting the chain on my door. It was really sweet of you,' she cajoled.

'Hmn.'

'I love you.'

'You too,' he murmured.

She kissed the back of his neck and nestled against him.

*

9

Cathy was catapulted from drowsiness into sharp con-
sciousness again by the shrill of the telephone coming
at her in stereo. She sat up and peered at the radio
alarm: seven thirty in the morning. The sun was
already blazing through the yellow curtains. Her room
glared yellow wallpaper and lampshades back at her.
This was the only part of the house Cathy had got
round to decorating and yellow was her choice.
Everybody had something that gave their spirits a lift.
For some it was music, or scented candles, or paintings.
For Cathy it was yellow. It made her feel happy.

Jason draped an arm over his eyes. 'I bet that's your
mate Fiona in a boyfriend crisis.'

'No, I don't think so. I had lunch with her at work
yesterday. She seems fine. Who'd ring me this early?'

'Probably a wrong number. Just leave it.'

'No, I can't. What if it's an emergency?'

'Better answer it, then.' Jason rolled over.

Cathy padded out to the bedroom she'd turned into
a study. She shuffled past the boxes and heaps of files
she was intending to sort out one day and grabbed the
phone. 'Hello?'

'Cathy? It's Melissa.'

Cathy sat down and stared at the dead computer
screen on her desk. Melissa? At this time in the morning?
Melissa and Brian were usually in bed by eleven at the
latest. They were very early risers – but they knew that
Cathy wasn't. Something had to be wrong.

'Melissa? Are you all right?'

'Oh – it's just . . .' Melissa stopped. Cathy crouched
over the phone. Melissa was a creature of calm routine.
Something was dreadfully wrong. She licked at her dry
lips.

'What is it? Is it Brian? Has something happened?'

'Cathy, I've been playing this over and over in my mind. I don't know what to do. I want to do the right thing for you and I've decided this is the right thing.'

Cathy froze. 'What's the right thing?' she whispered.

'I'm so sorry to get you out of bed. It's just that I've been thinking about this all night. I've got to talk to you about it.'

It all sounded horribly ominous.

'I think you'd better just tell me what it is,' Cathy said quietly.

'It's – you see – it's . . .' Then Melissa blurted out the words that would change Cathy's life for ever. 'It's your grandfather. He wants to see you.'

'Grandfather?' Cathy perched on the edge of her chair, staring blindly at her wall. 'What grandfather? I haven't got a grandfather. They're both dead.'

Cathy was confused. Melissa's father and Brian's father had both slid philosophically away when she was in her teens. She hadn't had a grandfather for years.

'No, Cathy,' Melissa said in a quiet voice. 'I mean your real grandfather.'

Cathy shot down the stairs, through the living room and headed for the bottle of gin in the kitchen.

'Cathy?' Jason appeared behind her in his boxer shorts, his hair ruffled, rubbing his eyes sleepily.

'Want a gin?' She held out the bottle.

Jason screwed up his face in distaste. 'A gin? For breakfast?'

'I'm having one. Up to you.'

'Christ, Cathy, what's happened?'

'Nothing. Go back to bed. Sorry I woke you up.'

'Woke me up? You thundered down the stairs swearing at the top of your voice.' But he added gently, 'I was worried about you anyway, I didn't go back to sleep. You were on the phone for ages.'

Jason watched in amazement as Cathy splashed a small measure of gin into her glass. She added some tonic from the fridge, tossed in some ice, watched it fizz, then took a gulp. She stared at Jason with round eyes as the gin fired its way down her throat.

'Cathy?' Jason took a step towards her. 'Who was that on the phone?'

'That was Melissa.'

'Your mum? What was she doing ringing so early?'

'She had something' – Cathy stopped to take another sip of gin – 'that she just had to tell me.'

Jason took another look at Cathy's face, then reached for the gin bottle. He poured himself a more modest measure. 'Go on.'

Cathy stood silently for a moment, only the hum of the boiler and the soft tick of the battery clock on the kitchen shelf disturbing the air.

'I've got a grandfather,' she said. 'A real, live one. A proper one. Genetically speaking. Apparently.'

'What?'

'Exactly.'

'But hang on, Cathy.' Jason's eyes widened. 'People can't do that. I mean, they can't just get in touch with adopted relatives. There are laws against it.'

'I never thought of that,' Cathy said. She was still breathless. 'I wouldn't, would I? Both my parents are dead. Mum and Dad were, still are, Melissa and Brian, and my grandparents were their parents. All four of them. Now dead. Nobody has five grandparents, Jason. It's just silly.'

'But Cathy, how could he have found you, if it really is him?'

'Melissa said they'd had some brief encounter, when I was a baby, at the hospital. It wasn't supposed to happen, but he'd been there, looking at me or something. And he gave them a contact address. But this is the first I've heard of it. I'll find out more from Melissa later. Or maybe I won't bother,' Cathy said tersely.

'Wow.' Jason's eyes grew even wider. He sipped his gin thoughtfully. 'Wow. What a blast from the past.'

'And now . . .' Cathy swallowed down another mouthful of gin. It was making her feel ludicrously light-headed and a little sick, but it was better than shock. 'Apparently, he wants to see me.'

'Flipping heck.'

'My response was a little more forthright.'

Jason shook his head, dazed. 'I don't know, Cathy, it seems like a bit of an imposition. After all this time. I don't know how I'd feel.' He considered her carefully. 'How *do* you feel?'

Cathy gripped her glass tightly. How did she feel? Overwhelmed. Shocked. As if her world had been picked up like a paperweight, shaken about by a celestial hand and put back down again. But the words that came out were very ordinary:

'I'm extremely pissed off.'

'You know, you don't have to agree to see him.'

'Too right. I know that.' Cathy choked on her last mouthful of gin and thumped her glass back on to the unit. Her blood was boiling now. At the moment anger had become the triumphant emotion, though she hated

13

to think what she might feel once she'd had a chance to dwell on Melissa's revelation. 'I've got my life, right here. I know what I'm doing and who I am.'

'So,' Jason began hesitantly, 'your grandfather?'

'Can sod off. Let's go back to bed.'

Cathy had been about seven years old when she'd found out that she was adopted. She'd asked Melissa why she had red hair, when Melissa was dark, Brian was fair and the rest of their families were either dark, fair, grey, or bald. Someone in the playground had made a joke about the milkman and it had puzzled her. It had been an uneventful revelation, devoid of angst. Her blood parents had apparently both died and her adoptive parents wanted her as much as her real parents would have done. She wasn't abandoned, she was loved twice over, which was even better. That knowledge had grafted itself seamlessly on to her childhood experience. It was who she was.

Melissa and Brian had been attentive to her needs and she'd lacked for nothing. There were advantages to not having a brother or sister. She didn't have to fight for air space with a handful of siblings over the dinner table. Nobody could break her air-fix models of Henry the Eighth's six wives, or borrow her Plasticraft without asking. She became expert at beating herself at Kerplunk and read her way through the school library. Melissa would quiz her on her day at school, then Brian would repeat the exercise when he came home from work. They were always concerned with her progress, and her physical and material well-being. They were, in every sense, her parents and she loved them both as dearly as she knew they loved her.

It was a peaceful, organised household on the whole. Melissa was a Christian and believed that good behaviour was the key to happiness. She wasn't a fanatic and she wasn't a hypocrite. She didn't ram her views down Cathy's throat, but let her make her own way. She was a nice, solid woman; tall and upright with a firm figure, which had become a little fuller in middle age, and steady grey eyes. She held down a job at the local council, involved herself in community activities and charities, and was on the PTA of Cathy's school. In her own subdued way she loved life and loved people. The warmth inside Melissa wasn't the greedy, self-nourishing heat of a flame, rather an internal spiritual glow which people were drawn to. As a child, Cathy had felt comforted and safe whenever Melissa was close by. She was a strong woman and she had taught Cathy to be strong.

Brian played the guitar relentlessly, unhindered by considerations of accuracy or tunefulness. He'd been playing since Cathy was a child and he was still trying to perfect the chord of B minor. He helped out at the youth club and engaged in perennial debates with teenagers he found drinking, smoking pot, or stealing the pool cues. He had all the grace of a daddy-long-legs, which the kids mocked him for mercilessly. He passed it off with an affable wiggle of his head. It was Brian who'd sat patiently with Cathy for hours on end, playing childlike games with her, listening to her talk about her friends, her thoughts, her ideas. He was everything she could have wanted in a father.

Cathy had done the rounds of immature relationships, had been disappointed, had disappointed people back and had gone off to university. She'd made a bunch of good friends, most of whom she still saw, and had started work in Euston, where she'd met Jason. He'd invited her to a late-night showing of *The Thing* and that had been it.

So there it was: family and friends, a job she cared about and, now, her own house too. Cathy's life was full. She didn't see a crisis around every corner and tried to live a steady life. Jason did always say that underneath the even-tempered surface, Cathy was a volcano doing its very best not to erupt, but Cathy laughed it off. There were occasional ripples on the surface of her pond, of course, but she shunned any input to her routine that would cause anything more than a ripple.

But now the wind was getting up and there was surf on the waves.

Chapter Two

'Are you all right today?' Fiona's pale-blue eyes were rounded with concern.

'Of course.'

Fiona appeared round the low artificial wall that separated her office space from Cathy's in the vast open-plan room, as Cathy was replacing the receiver of her office phone. Had she just snapped at somebody? Surely not. She was very careful, always, not to let her feelings affect her work.

'You seem a bit – jumpy.' Fiona chewed the end of her pen, eyeing Cathy cautiously. The overhead striplights made Fiona's fine blonde hair look almost transparent.

Cathy took a steadying breath. 'I'm not jumpy. I've just been here since – quite early. I need a really big, strong coffee with a lot of froth on top.' Cathy stood up and gathered her handbag. 'I'll go and get one from Dom's. D'you want one?'

'*Quite* early?' Fiona smiled ironically. 'I was here at eight and the guys in reception told me you'd been in an hour then.'

'Well, maybe it was a bit earlier than I'd planned.' Cathy waited for Fiona to move out of the way so that she could slide out of her cubicle.

Fiona looked as if she wanted more of an explanation, one hand gently resting on the hip of her short, ochre skirt.

'Nobody speeds in to work on a Monday morning,' she said sagely. 'Not unless they're expecting a bonus and have to receive it in person. Or unless they've had a really crappy weekend.'

'Well, it was an odd weekend.' Cathy sighed. 'Do you fancy a chat over lunch?'

'Sure.' Fiona nodded. 'It'll be good to get out of the office. My eyes are turning into computer screens already.'

'How are the web pages going anyway?' Cathy asked.

Fiona was trained in IT, and her job mostly involved creation and design of websites for the companies they helped.

'Fine, fine. Paying the rent.'

Cathy's phone rang again. It was just as well she had got in early. Everyone seemed to expect her to be there and on top of things by the time they settled themselves into their chairs and took the first bite of their bacon rolls. She picked it up.

It was Mark, her immediate boss and one of the senior partners of the firm, asking her into his office to discuss the account of Havers Construction. Of all the clients she was involved with, Cathy liked Bill Havers most of all. Once a brickie, he'd built up his East End construction company with grit and the collective sweat of his family. She and Bill seemed to have clicked and she had some ideas she was very keen to put to Mark. Cathy looked apologetically at Fiona as she put her phone down again.

'Sorry. Mark beckons. I'll have to get the coffees later.'

'I'll get you one. And an eggy sandwich. I bet you

haven't had breakfast.'

Cathy paused as she struggled into her suit jacket to give Fiona a grateful smile. 'Thanks, Fi.'

Mark Lyme was in his early forties, angular, bespectacled and with a bad case of hair loss. He had an energetic manner and sharp eyes. He seemed to like Cathy and she thought he'd probably been instrumental in her promotion. She closed the door to his small office behind her.

'Bill Havers,' Mark began, indicating Cathy should sit on the swivel chair next to his desk.

'Ah yes, our Bill.' Cathy perched and smiled. 'I've been thinking a lot about this one. I've put together some ideas over the weekend.' She handed Mark the folder she'd amassed on Sunday. With Jason gone and her thoughts fluttering unsteadily over the idea of her new grandfather, she'd plunged herself into work with all the energy she could muster.

Mark picked up the folder and slowly leafed through it. He raised his eyebrows. 'You have been working hard, haven't you?' His eyebrows shot even higher as he scanned her report. 'Hellier's? What have they got to do with Bill?'

Cathy tingled with excitement. In all the work she'd done since her Economics degree at the LSE she'd got the greatest thrill from an idea that would actually do some good and she was especially proud of this one. She sat forward eagerly.

'I think we can put Bill in the way of Hellier's. The word is that Hellier's are going to relocate their European headquarters to London.'

'Really?' Mark's eyebrows were sliding over the top of his head. 'Hellier's are one of the top software development companies in Europe. Are you sure about this, Cathy?'

'Yes. At the last Docklands Business Club meeting I had a very interesting chat with Troy Vickers.' Cathy was careful not to sound too triumphant as she named the well-known architect. She did her best to attend all the networking functions and she was aware that Mark didn't. She didn't want to put his back up.

Mark clicked his tongue thoughtfully. 'You mean someone from Troy Vickers?' he asked.

'No, I mean Troy Vickers himself. He's been talking to Hellier's. They're definitely looking for an architect for their new development and they're definitely interested in him.' Cathy swallowed. 'Troy thinks they're very keen on the idea of government funding for converting a brown site.' The brown sites, as both Cathy and Mark knew, were the most crucial areas of redevelopment in east London. Once industrial, they were now a priority for rejuvenation and offered the most incentives in the way of government help. As Mark was still looking astonished that he hadn't heard about Hellier's plans, Cathy added, 'I gather it's under informal discussion already.'

'I see,' Mark said under his breath. 'And you're sure Troy wasn't just speculating?'

'There's nothing secret about Hellier's intentions.' Cathy tried to sound light-hearted. 'I'd heard it on the grapevine and there was another small reference to it in the *The Wharf* a week or so ago.' Cathy always scanned her local paper for ideas and opportunities that would affect her work. 'I've saved the article and marked it, there.' She pointed at her folder.

Mark ranged his eyes over the article. 'But what has

Bill Havers got to do with this?'

'Troy's keen to put in a holistic bid. He wants to offer himself to Hellier's with a construction company already in tow. Bill's an ideal candidate for that. It's just the break his firm needs and it'll create a load of employment opportunities locally. It's perfect.'

'I can't see a bigwig architect like Troy Vickers using a small building company like Bill's, Cathy.' Mark looked doubtful. 'It'll be up to Bill to lobby him, of course, if he wants to.'

'Well, that's the thing.' Cathy maintained an enthusiastic smile. 'Troy's keen to do as much for local employment as anyone. I think Troy would give Bill a fair chance to bid for the work and I really think Bill could do it.'

Mark was thoughtful for a moment, then he cleared his throat. 'Let me speak to Ruth. I was really hoping you'd be concentrating on the balance sheet and the market research. That's the top priority for you at the moment.'

'I've got that covered, there.' Cathy pointed delicately at the sheaf of papers. 'Here's the spread sheet and the report. I've flagged them up.'

'Hellier's are big brass, Cathy. I know Bill's company's growing, but I'm not sure he's ready for such a large contract. Any building company would give their eye-teeth to work with Troy Vickers on a Hellier's development. Bill would be up against the biggest and the best.'

Cathy took a patient breath. 'I know. But Bill's brought off the Docklands office complex without a hitch. Ahead of schedule and up to spec.'

'It's not a big site and it remains to be seen whether

there are going to be problems with it.'

'The work is all up to standard,' Cathy defended. 'Bill's far too sensible to take short cuts. His livelihood depends on it. I know he's trustworthy.'

'We can't put our heads on the block on a gut feeling, Cathy.'

'If you'd just let me put out some feelers—'

'Cathy,' Mark said patiently. 'Hellier's are massive and Troy Vickers is extremely influential. If there's any brokering to be done here, Ruth or I would want to handle it personally. You know that.'

Cathy opened her mouth and shut it again. If either Mark, a senior partner, or Ruth, the managing director of the firm, had bothered to get involved with business and social events in east London they might have had an inkling of the Hellier's move already. She counted to ten.

'Okay, perhaps you'll show Ruth my ideas.'

'Of course I will.' Mark sipped from a mug of coffee. Cathy stared at it enviously. She should have picked one up on the way in, but she'd been keen to polish up her report. Mark continued, 'And I'm sorry about the lack of office space. I'm afraid that unless someone bolts there still aren't any offices spare. Are you managing out in the goldfish bowl?'

'Oh, yes. No problem,' Cathy assured him. It didn't worry her a great deal that she hadn't gained a private office with her promotion. For the moment, at least, she was glad to work with the others and have Fiona close at hand. Since they had been working together they had become firm friends and Cathy sometimes wondered what she'd do without Fiona to help her see the lighter side of things, or drag her off for a reassuring gossip over lunch. Not having a private office did mean Cathy had to borrow one of the conference rooms for meetings, which was a bit of a pain, but in the meantime she just got on with the job.

'Great. So why don't you arrange a meeting with Bill anyway, Cathy? You and Bill seemed to hit it off. And have a look around the Docklands offices while you're about it. Even if we can't link him up with Hellier's, we should see how he's getting on.'

'I'd like to.'

'You arrange that. I think these old blokes like to see a feisty young woman about the place too. Makes a change for them.'

Not sure how to take that remark, Cathy made her exit, just spotting out of the corner of her eye that Mark placed his coffee mug on top of her folder as she left the room.

There was an intermittent beep that was driving him crazy. Nick threw his arm out of the bed. His fist hit several hard things. There was something tall which made a clunking sound as it hit the floor. There was a cylindrical thing which fell over and made a fizzing sound. There was a low, flat plastic thing. He thumped away at it. The beeping stopped.

'Oh God.'

The fizzing became a series of dripping noises. The overturned can of Stella Artois was emptying its contents over his bedside table and on to his carpet.

'Oh double God.' Somehow he'd knocked his bedside lamp on to the floor too. He wanted it all to go away. So he would make it go away. He closed his eyes again.

Some time later Nick was awoken by the ceiling falling in. When he opened his eyes, startled, he realised that the straining and banging above him was Terry, in bed with somebody. On Monday morning. Nick winced.

He sat and clamped his hands over his ears. The sight of his Pirelli calendar on the wall opposite soothed him. He'd left it on April as Miss April was so appealing. Fortified, he heaved himself out of bed and plodded to the kitchen to get a cloth.

His room was on the ground floor. There were three bedrooms upstairs, all taken by the others. He'd taken the downstairs room because it was bigger, nearer the kitchen and had the sun coming in in the morning. He liked that.

One of the many things he disliked about the morning was the state of the kitchen. Not that it wasn't always in exactly the same state in the evening when he got back from work, but by then he felt mellow and didn't mind so much. The draining board was stacked with unwashed plates. The sink was full of mugs, glasses and cutlery. The bin was spilling over. He made himself coffee, put two pieces of sliced white into the toaster and headed back to his room to clear up the beer.

He paused in the hall. The sun was filtering strongly through the coloured panes of glass in the front door. Perhaps the forecasts were right? Perhaps the early signs of a hot, dry summer were really going to develop into a heatwave? That would harden up the cricket pitches and mean a full summer's play. Nick passionately hoped so.

He peered into the living room. The ashtrays were

full, it was littered with beer cans and empty pizza cartons. Nick laughed under his breath. The dining-room chairs were still on the table from where Steve had shown them a balancing act. He hoped Steve hadn't broken his arm when he'd fallen off, but he'd find out when he sobered up. Stupid bugger.

Nick padded back into his room, gave an ironic round of applause to the final ecstatic yells coming from upstairs and got on with mopping up the Stella Artois. Then he threw on his towelling robe and sat down at the computer, lighting himself a cigarette. He headed for the cricket newsgroup. Catching up with the cricket news always gave him a boost before he headed off to work. One of the few good things about his job was that it was close, only a fifteen-minute drive. Another good thing was that nobody seemed to notice if he adapted his hours to suit himself. He worked late enough into the evenings, so he never attempted to get to the office much before nine thirty.

Nick rubbed at his chest and eyed Miss April again covetously while he waited for the messages to download. Nearly 200 new messages to the cricket group since yesterday morning. It was busy. The computer clicked him offline and he flicked through the messages eagerly.

There was the perennial debate as to whether Sachin Tendulkar was, in fact, God and a lot of ongoing comments about India's and Pakistan's latest performances. But Nick's spirits soared as he found the messages hotly debating the state of English cricket. The moments leading up to a new test series were always exciting, whether England were playing away or at home, but this year was special. This year was an

Ashes year and for the first time in ages, Nick felt in his bones that England stood a chance of winning. He swilled his coffee, sucked on his cigarette and closely read a debate entitled 'Will Hussain win the Ashes for England?'.

He scanned the names of the contributors who had left messages. There was Beefy again. He and Nick had been bantering with each other on this group for about two years now. Nick was impressed by Beefy. There were only a small handful of contributors to the group who managed to combine a wicked sense of humour with knowledge. Beefy was one of them. Nick read his message eagerly. He grinned.

Beefy was backing England to win the Ashes – an unusual stance, given his habitual dry pessimism. Nick was thrilled. He typed out a reply to Beefy's message, laced it with a fair amount of black humour and sent it off to the group. He guessed Beefy would come back on his remarks. They'd been sparking off each other for a while now and it was fun.

A row had started upstairs between Terry and the woman he was with. Nick rolled his eyes. Why did Terry try so hard? He'd enjoy his occasional encounters a lot more if he saw women as Nick did – delightful distractions from the daily routine. No woman had arrived in Nick's life recently who was interesting enough for him to change that routine. Perhaps one would, one day. Perhaps one wouldn't. For now, Nick was content enough with the life he had.

He sipped his coffee while he checked his e-mails. Beefy had mailed him too. He scrolled through the message, surprised by what he read: 'I've got two tickets for Edgbaston on Thursday. First day of the first

Ashes test. Would you like one?'

Nick pushed himself back in his chair, excitement rising in his chest. Edgbaston. First day of the Ashes series. Nick savoured the idea, a tingle running up his legs and along his back. He licked his lips. He'd have to take the day off work – but that wasn't a problem. He hadn't met Beefy before, but that made it all the more fun. Two lads having a laugh, a few pints and maybe going out to some bars in Birmingham later that night.

Nick laughed to himself. He'd been thinking about getting tickets, but he'd left it too late for the first test. That was a laziness that came from living only a mile from the ground. There was no way Beefy would know that. He typed back.

'Yep, I'm on for that. And you can crash here afterwards if you like.'

'The answer's no. I'm sorry, Melissa, it's how I feel.'

Melissa was still for a moment. Then she nodded. They were on the patio of Melissa's and Brian's home, the house where Cathy had been brought up. It was an unassuming, small, red-brick, detached house on a leafy residential estate in Woking. Cathy could remember when the apple tree on the lawn had been a sprig and the leylandii Melissa had planted along the slatted wooden fence were stunted bushes. Now the apple tree was wide and sprawling, the conifers looming. This evening Cathy sat back on the thin white bands of the wooden bench and assessed her stretched-out legs in the sun. She'd got a train straight down from work to sort this out. She didn't want it preying on her mind. Melissa stretched out her legs too, elegantly crossing one ankle over the other. Cathy peered at them.

She'd never have legs like Melissa's, long and slim. But it was no good being envious. She couldn't be buxom, with curves in all the right places (so Jason said) together with legs like chopsticks. She'd fall over.

She used to envy Melissa her height too. Being short, and full-figured with it, Cathy had suffered a painful adolescence. Ra-ra skirts had made her feel ludicrous. So instead she'd found her own way of dressing, slim tops, often sleeveless, skirts down to her shins, with a split. And she loved her jeans. She'd tried squashing herself into tight ones, until some guy at university had said her bum looked like two babies having a fight under a blanket. From then on she bought jeans that were big enough and didn't care that she didn't look like a model in them.

Cathy shaded her eyes with her hand and squinted at the clear blue sky. Everyone was predicting a heatwave this summer. In her linen suit she was feeling flushed, even though it was well into the evening. She fiddled with the St Christopher Melissa and Brian had given her for her eighteenth, peeped down at the white skin of her cleavage, wondering how long it would take to speckle over with fawn dots this year, then looked at Melissa again.

Melissa was in a wooden chair beside her. On her lap was an envelope, which had been opened. Her hands fluttered over it, then she stood up and poured them both another glass of chilled bitter lemon from the jug. Sometimes Cathy thought that Melissa had been shot straight out of Enid Blyton on an ejector seat and landed in Woking. When Cathy was a little girl, Melissa even used to make her own lemonade, though she headed a lot more towards convenience these days, now that she was working full time. Cathy had even spotted a bought pizza in a packet in the kitchen.

'I did wonder', Melissa ventured slowly as Cathy picked up her drink, 'if you might just want to read the letter.'

Cathy slumped against the bench.

'Melissa, if I read his letter I'm going to have a million unanswered questions in my head. There are lots of things I don't understand already. I'm just too busy. My life's full and it's happy. You and Brian are my family, I love you both. I don't want to know about him.'

Melissa raised a gently chiding eyebrow. 'I think he really is keen to meet you, Cathy. His letter—'

'Stop right there!'

Cathy got up and paced around on the patio for a bit, hoping it might settle her mind. Already she was being told things she didn't want to know.

'You guys have been everything to me,' Cathy appealed to Melissa. 'I don't want five grandparents. Don't you see? It's not normal. And I—' Her body tensed. 'I don't think he's got any right to suddenly appear like this. I'm not even sure if it's legal.'

'Cathy,' Melissa said softly. 'You've got every right to say no. But I think, for your sake, you should think about it carefully. I really don't want you to regret it later. I know you have a tendency for knee-jerk reactions, but in this case—'

'I do not have knee-jerk reactions,' Cathy barked hotly.

'I see that your temper's rising, young lady. That's something I haven't seen in you for a while.'

'It's not.'

'I think it is. Have another glass of bitter lemon.'

Cathy threw her hands in the air in a gesture of despair and sat down on the bench again. She'd guessed it would be a struggle. Melissa's Christian instincts were driving her to do the 'right thing'. She'd obviously made up her mind that this was right. From the open window, Cathy heard Brian strike up the opening chords to 'Sloop John B' on his guitar. She stared at the house blankly.

'He's not still trying to play that, is he?'

Melissa smiled back patiently, ensuring Cathy felt awful for saying something mean. Brian had been a kind and loving father. He'd given Cathy a lot of confidence in herself over the years.

'Cathy, you should know that your grandfather's been in touch, on and off, over the years. Just the occasional letter.'

There was a moment of calm. The sort of quiet that might occur as a meteorite whistled through the air on its way to make impact with the ground. Then Cathy's glass clattered back on to the table and she shot up.

'He what?'

Melissa cleared her throat and fumbled with the envelope on her lap. 'I didn't want to upset you and he seemed so – so distantly interested I thought it would be hurtful to you. The contact was sporadic and very vague. Only once every couple of years, nothing more. But he didn't want to see you.' Her eyes clouded with worry. 'I really do hope it wasn't wrong of me not to tell you.'

'You mean, he's been asking after me all this time? And I didn't know?'

'Well – yes. In a very abstract sort of way.' Melissa winced.

'But—' It was too confusing. Cathy scratched her head and pulled on a handful of hair. 'You'd better explain this to me. How can he have known where I was?'

Melissa looked strained, the muscles on her neck standing out. Her eyes were tortured. 'As I told you on the phone, he – he was there, at the hospital. He looked so fraught. It was just a chance meeting, one that shouldn't really have happened. We'd come to see you, while you were still in the incubator and there he was. I know perhaps I should never have done it, but I took pity on him. I – I took his address and told him I'd let him know how you . . . were . . . over the years. So I did. And after several years I realised that the last thing he would do was impose himself, so I let him know our address, so that he could make enquiries about you. Nothing more.' Melissa put up a hand as Cathy opened her mouth. 'I would never have brought him into your life. That's why you didn't know about it.'

Cathy was dumbstruck. Her emotions churned.

'What do you mean, he didn't want to see me?' she whispered.

'When – when you were eighteen.' Melissa struggled. 'I wondered if you should be told about him and offered the chance to meet him. I was just trying to do the right thing, you see.' She swallowed painfully. 'But he said no.'

'He didn't want to see me? Ever?' Cathy whimpered, allowing herself a moment of self-pity.

'No, dear. I'm sorry.'

'Oh – oh great.' In exasperation Cathy took off and did a circuit of the lawn. She plucked at a branch of the apple tree and pulled off a couple of leaves, ending up back on the patio, facing Melissa.

Melissa had turned very pale. 'I've done all the wrong things, haven't I?' she said sadly.

Indignation surged through Cathy's body, but stopped somewhere in her throat. Melissa's look of quiet despair kept her anger down and stopped it erupting into words she'd probably regret.

'Whatever has been happening in the past.' Cathy squeezed out the words breathlessly. 'And whatever's happening now is not going to change the way I feel. I have my family, I have a life, friends and a boyfriend. I love my job. Why would he suddenly turn up and want to mess it all up?'

'I see,' Melissa whispered with resignation.

'No, I don't think you do. I know who I am. Already, without any need for spare grandfathers. So he's probably getting on a bit, a bit mellow, thinking back over his life. Wants to chuck a glance at his granddaughter before he kicks the bucket? I really don't care. That's his problem. I don't know why he'd suddenly do this to me. He's obviously very selfish.'

'Oh yes.' Melissa was nodding.

Cathy was nonplussed for a moment. 'Well, there you are, then. Problem solved.'

'I'll, um—' Melissa stood up slowly and put the jug and glasses back on the tray, resting the envelope to one side. Cathy stared down at it. It was a crisp, creamy colour and long. Melissa's voice was soothing. 'I'll write back, then, and I'll tell him you don't want to see him. I don't think we'll hear from him again.'

Cathy felt queasy. For the first time she could see the scrawling hand on the front of the envelope with the address penned out. It was a bold hand, in black ink.

Unusual, as everyone she knew used biros.

'Just tell me this,' she rasped to Melissa. 'Which grandfather is he? Mother's or father's side?'

Melissa looked as if she was close to tears. She had turned horrifically pale.

'Mother's,' she said under her breath. 'And Cathy, I do think you should know that he's very ill.'

Cathy nodded, her face pinched. 'Jolly good.'

'I just think you should be aware that this might be your last chance to see him.'

'I know now. Thanks. Hope it's nothing trivial.'

Melissa nodded and headed towards the kitchen door with the tray. 'Let's go back inside, then, shall we?'

Cathy stood alone on the patio for a moment, her eyes filling with tears. She frowned severely. Where had tears come from? She swallowed them away again.

Her blood parents were anonymous to her. As a child she'd often pictured them. Her mother, regal and beautiful, gentle and kind. Her father, a top brain surgeon, probably. Handsome. Strong.

What she felt creeping up her stomach and into her throat was not sadness, it was fear. Her grandfather, who had known her parents as the real people they were, would just have to go to hell.

Chapter Three

Someone was pumping Capital Radio into the air. Mr Ali next door was getting cross with the children, who were beating each other's heads against the adjoining wall. Cathy peered at the view of her road from her bedroom window. The sky was a white glimmer and the air was clammy. The cherry trees stood, stagnant and green, like weed in a warm, still pond. It was going to be another bakingly hot weekend.

Cathy padded downstairs, picked up the mail from the doormat and headed for the kitchen with a yawn. She paused to appreciate her living room. She'd got it looking quite pretty now. She still had to paint it anything other than this dull pale-blue that the previous owner had inflicted, but she'd get there, in time. She wandered through to the kitchen.

She eased up the blind, flashing a smile through the window at Mrs Ali who was standing serenely at her kitchen sink.

The kitchen windows winked at each other across low fences – in Cathy's case a very low, decrepit fence held up by bindweed. She was getting used to these token neighbourly moments. This morning, conscious of wearing nothing but the skimpy French maid's outfit Jason had got her three years ago from Ann Summers, she waved at Mrs Ali's puzzled expression and gracefully pulled the blind down again. She could guess that

Mrs Ali was a little surprised to be met by the sight of a French maid with hair like a ball of orange wool that had been savaged by an army of kittens. Hopefully she'd rub her eyes and think she'd imagined it.

Cathy flicked the kettle switch and let out a contented sigh. Her physical life with Jason was still good. In their first year together it had been anytime, anyplace, anywhere, but although it was less impulsive now, they had plenty of good moments. And as this weekend Jason wasn't leaving until Sunday night, Cathy had felt more inclined to dig out the Ann Summers lingerie. She hummed, pulling out tea bags and tossing them at the mugs. She leafed through the envelopes. A bill, some junk mail, another bill. She slid them along the kitchen counter and fingered the last envelope. It was A5-sized and from Melissa. Curious, Cathy opened it. Melissa had written her a note and enclosed an envelope.

The forwarded envelope was addressed to her, Catherine Gordon, care of Melissa's address. The envelope was cream and slightly textured on her fingertips – probably expensive. The handwriting was scrawled and in black ink.

Cathy ignored the click of the kettle and leant back against the units, staring at the writing.

'Oh no,' she breathed.

There was no doubt. It was in the same hand as the letter Melissa had been cradling throughout her visit home. It was another letter, this time addressed directly to her, from her grandfather. Cathy turned it over and over in her hand. The kitchen was warm, but her skin prickled. She unfolded Melissa's note slowly and read it.

'Cathy, you don't have to read the letter, but I believe

this is your grandfather's final word to you. I have said I will forward it and nothing more. I hope I'm doing the right thing. With love, Melissa.'

The right thing. That was so typical. Cathy rubbed her palms on her French maid's outfit, took a deep breath and stuck her thumb into the back of the cream envelope. Once she'd torn open the top she put it down on the counter and looked at it from a number of angles.

She could call up to Jason and tell him. Or she could take it up there with the tea and they could sit and open it together. But it was addressed to her. There was something absurdly private about what might be inside. She could open it on her own. Or she could put it straight in the bin. Or she could set fire to it. But raw curiosity needled at her. What had her grandfather got to say to her? What was his final word, if this was it?

Cathy summoned up her courage, picked up the envelope and fished inside. She pulled out a couple of pieces of paper.

There was a note, folded over, in cream paper that matched the envelope. And there was a ticket. She glanced at the ticket. It was square, with some sort of pattern etched in the background and gave a number, a seat number or something.

None of it meant anything to her. Cathy painstakingly opened the note. Her pulse slowed. Now for the first time ever, she was reading words written to her by her own blood grandfather. Goose pimples rose on her arms. She swallowed.

'Dear Catherine,' she read in a murmur. 'Please be there. Frank.'

There was nothing else. No explanation, no excuses.

No acknowledgement from her grandfather that he'd been told (albeit by Melissa on her behalf) to bugger off and stay buggered off. There was a 'please', that was something, she supposed. But it was completely puzzling.

Cathy let out her breath and realised that she'd been holding it in. With a light head she made herself a strong cup of tea, piled plenty of sugar in it, then picked up the note and read it again.

'Be there. Be where?'

On a second look the ticket made a little more sense, but not much. The date jumped out at her. It was a Thursday, early in July. Hang on. This Thursday, this coming week. That was pretty much zero warning. And it was something at Edgbaston, the first Cornhill Test Match. England versus Australia. The Ashes series.

She stomped out to the hall and yelled up the stairs, 'Jace?'

'What's happened to the tea? Are the pickers on strike?'

'Jason, what's the Ashes?'

'It's what phoenixes come out of.' There was a pause. 'Why the hell do you want to know that?'

She heard his footsteps cross the bedroom floor. He stuck his head over the bannisters. His face was still plastered with bright-red lipstick. But her mind was on other things.

'The Ashes.' She waved the ticket at him. 'It says here the Ashes. At Edgbaston.'

He blinked at her. 'Where did you get that?'

'Someone sent it to me.'

'I thought I was the only exciting mail in your life.'

She stared back at him, not even managing a weak smile. She was too confused.

Jason looked thoughtful. 'Er – so who's sent you that?'

'It was – Frank's sent it.'

'Frank?'

'My grandfather, remember? His name is Frank. Apparently.'

Jason rubbed at his face, spotted the lipstick on his fingers and stared at it. Then he looked back at Cathy with an amused expression.

'What's so funny?'

'Your grandfather's what's funny. He hasn't got a clue, has he?'

'Why?' She strained her neck to look up at him.

'Well, if I were him and I were trying to win you round the last thing I'd do is buy you tickets to a bloody cricket match.' He shook his head. 'I've never known any woman show as little interest in sport as you. You can't stand it. It's hilarious.'

'Cricket?'

'Only the most famous cricketing battle in the world. England against Australia. They kick off this week. The Australians turn up, we go through the rigmarole of watching England lose, then the Australians go home again. It's great fun. So how many tickets did he send you? I could go and take a couple of friends from work. Shame to waste them.'

Cathy looked down at the ticket again. She'd vaguely heard of the Ashes, just never been interested enough to work out what it was.

'There's only the one ticket.'

'Really?'

Jason jogged down the stairs, cupping a hand over his genitals in an uncharacteristic moment of modesty. He looked at the ticket over Cathy's shoulder and then gently prised it from her fingers.

'Let's have a look.'

'Why do they call it the Ashes?' Cathy murmured.

'From the famous obituary notice in the *Sporting Times*. "In affectionate memory of English cricket which died at the Oval", some time in the late eighteen hundreds. Over a hundred years ago, anyhow. "The body will be cremated and the Ashes taken to Australia." Those pesky colonials. It was the first time they beat us at our own game in England. It was terribly shocking at the time.' He raised his eyebrows emphatically.

Cathy stared at Jason in surprise. 'How do you know that?'

'Man thing. I was at a boys-only grammar school, don't forget. We played a lot of cricket. You can't escape without knowing things like that.'

'So there aren't really any ashes, then?'

'Well, it sort of kicked off a running battle. We played them over there, they played us over here. At some point some old biddy burned one of the bails and put it in an urn. So that's what they play for.'

'Really?' Cathy couldn't help being amused.

'Well, it's a replica, really. The real one's in the Lord's museum.'

'So all this is about a little urn?'

'Hey!' Jason put on his Eric Morecambe voice. 'Don't knock Little Ern. Let's have a proper look at that ticket.'

Cathy peered at it too.

Jason made a noise of approval. 'First day. That's

always a laugh. And where are you meant to be sitting?' He flipped the ticket over and assessed a map of the ground. 'Third man. He obviously knows his stuff. Get a good view from there.' He handed the ticket back to her, his eyes smiling again. 'So he thinks you'd want to go on your own to a game you've got no understanding of and will inevitably hate after five minutes? What planet is this old git on?'

'I – Jason, I think he's going to be there too. I think that's what this is about.' Then she added, her stomach turning over, 'And don't call him an "old git" please.'

Jason raised his eyebrows. 'Well, I'm sorry. You called him a lot worse when you came back from Melissa's.'

'This is different.'

Cathy swept back into the kitchen to find her tea mug. Caffeine was what she needed. Lots of it. Why was it different when Jason slagged Frank off? She wasn't sure, but she was annoyed with Jason for jumping on her bandwagon. Frank was *her* grandfather. She could say what she liked about him. She had every reason to be cross with him for avoiding her for twenty-eight years, then suddenly appearing like Zeus on a thunderbolt and demanding instant attention. It was arrogant. But it wasn't for Jason to insult Frank. She felt Jason's warm palms on her shoulders and gradually relaxed back against him.

He nuzzled her ear and spoke softly into it. 'Cathy. Listen. He's left it mighty late to make an entrance. You said yourself. He's probably old, ill and scared and wants to have a look at you before he cops it. It's the arrogance of old age. You might have suddenly been run over by a bus, but he'd never think of that, would he?'

40

'What do you mean?'

'The point is, it might have meant something to you to meet him when you were eighteen, but what did he care? You don't need him now, do you? Eh?' He kissed her ear gently. 'Let's take our tea back to bed. You rub my shoulders, I'll rub your boulders.'

'I don't know. I think I need some serious retail therapy in Walthamstow market, topped with a large dose of the Sainsbury's wine department. And I might even let you drag me to a film with subtitles. Anything that takes my mind off things. I don't want to think about my grandfather.'

Jason wound his arms around her stomach and took the ticket from her hand. He tossed it on to the unit.

'There. Easy, see? You're not going to go. You said you were going to have lunch with Lucy from Hellier's on Thursday anyway and that's a big meeting for you. The last thing you need is to spend a day next to some old – gi— I'm sorry, *geezer* – in a boater, falling asleep under his newspaper while you do the honours with the thermos and sandwiches. He's trying to use you, don't you see? He probably needs somebody to wheel his catheter around the tea tent for him and thought you'd oblige.'

'Maybe.' She was deeply unhappy about the idea herself.

'And you hate cricket.'

'Probably.'

'You do. You said it was boring.'

'I just don't know what's going on. All they do is stand around scratching their crotches until someone gets out.'

Jason chuckled into the back of her neck.

He kissed her earlobe gently. 'Good. So let's carry on

41

the way we were and get the sparkle back into your eyes, shall we? Let's go to Sainsbury's and do a *Ready Steady Cook*. You choose the ingredients and I'll cook you a magical supper. Just make sure to include some fresh herbs for me to play with. Probably rosemary. With a nice bit of lamb. And maybe some red wine. And an aubergine. And possibly quite a lot of garlic. Not that I'm prompting you. Then you'll eat it and say, "Thanks, darling, that was scrummy." We'll watch a fantastic video that we miraculously found in Blockbusters and then we can go back to bed.'

She turned round in the ring of Jason's arms and touched his lips with a soft kiss.

'Thank you, Jace. I'm so glad you're here.'

The piece of toast that was heading for Nick's mouth fell back on to the plate. In one hand he held the TV's remote control. The Ashes were about to start and that meant that Ceefax had joined the cricket newsgroup as part of Nick's morning routine from now until September. After Ceefax he'd race out of the house, dive into his car and steam into Birmingham for work. He'd got the tea, got the toast and got mastery of the remote. He'd flicked on to page 340 for the cricket headlines and read it.

Gough ruled out of first test through injury.

'Oh *God!*' The toast flew across the room and hit the screen.

'Morning, campers.' Terry popped his head into the room. 'Just you? Letter for you.' He threw Nick an envelope. 'What's up? You're turning purple again. Must be cricket.'

'That bloody does it. Our best strike bowler with a

bruised bloody finger. What do they do to them in the practice nets, for Christ's sake? Hurl bricks at them?'

Nick managed all this without a glance at Terry. He stabbed at the 'next page' button.

Terry, slight compared to Nick's solid build and very bald compared to Nick's thatch of blond hair, slunk into the sitting room and perched on the arm of the sofa like Jimmy Somerville creeping into Arnold Schwarzenegger's private space. He picked stuffing absently out of a hole in the dralon while squinting at the screen.

'I thought Gough was a bowler.'

'He *is* a bloody bowler.' Nick paused to grit his teeth. Patience was not his forte. Explaining simple things, basic things that he'd had in his head since he was about eight years old was not fun, it wasn't entertaining and it wasn't rewarding. Especially not with Gough out of the side for this crucial first battle. He took a deep breath and continued in an elaborately steady voice, 'He has to bat as well, doesn't he? And the way he bats these days, he needs all the practice he can bloody get.'

'Right. I'm off then,' Terry said. 'Hope none of the team breaks a nail while they're ironing their whites. Don't want anyone else ruled out, do we?'

This morning even the Brummy lilt that usually rocked Nick into good humour was only jarring.

'Terry, have you ever actually played cricket, man?'

'Na, comprehensive boy, me.' Terry winked at him. 'We played "sniff the glue pot" oh and "pass the keys to the headmaster's Cortina". That was an old favourite. There wasn't really much room behind the boiler for a cricket pitch, if you know what I mean.'

'I was a comprehensive boy too.' Nick glowered at

him. 'I wondered if you'd ever faced a cricket ball.'

'Face to face, man to man, like? No, haven't done that. Bit of a wuss's game, really, isn't it?'

'Picture this. If Courtney Walsh bowled at you at ninety miles an hour on a pitch baked into concrete by the Jamaican sun it would be like trying to hit a cannon ball. You'd be standing there, with a couple of pads dotted about your body and a helmet on, praying to God that you actually saw the ball before it broke one of your ribs.'

Terry gave Nick a blank look, then walked away without another word.

Nick pursed his lips. Steve had already left and Graham was away this week. He had a few precious minutes alone in the house. They were few and far between, but when they came he relished them. He settled back on the sofa with his tea, wincing as an escaped spring stuck into his back and prodded at the remote buttons. He found Sky News. It was the sports news. He watched it warily, like a floored man awaiting another stab with a bayonet.

They cut to an interview with Nasser Hussain. Nick perked up a little. He'd doubted this man, two years ago when he'd taken over the captaincy of the England side from Alec Stewart. But after leading England to memorable victory against the West Indies and Pakistan last year, Nick was hoping that Hussain had the fighting spirit the England team needed to face the Ozzies head on. The Australians were a hard-nosed bunch, in every respect. From their infamous reputation for sledging – sliding insults to the batsmen to unnerve them – to the way they played the game. To win. No prisoners.

Hussain was standing with a young, fresh-faced

interviewer at the nets, his familiar heavy-lidded eyes
and strong cheekbones striking and uncompromising.
He wasn't smiling. He looked like Lee Van Cleef sizing
up the new kid in town before he went for his gun.

'Nasser, thanks for talking to us. The Australians
have had a pretty good warm-up to the Ashes; some
might say they've wiped the floor with the opposition
in the one-day games.'

Nick winced. Where did they get these interviewers
from? What the hell did the one-day games have to do
with test cricket? If he'd had any toast left he'd have
thrown it at the television again. Hussain's eyes flashed,
but he said nothing, merely nodded. Diplomacy. He was
supposed to be good at that too.

'And Steve Waugh's been quoted as saying he's
going to cut England down to size in the Ashes. Have
you got any reaction to that?'

A slight pause, a slight inclination of the head as
Hussain drew breath.

'We're ready for the Ashes.'

'What have you been doing?'

'We've been sharpening up our knives.'

Nick felt a chill of excitement rush through his body.
Hussain had narrowed his eyes and the interviewer
was stumbling over the next question, but that was all
Nick needed to hear. He hadn't felt that cold chill for a
few years – hadn't dared to feel it.

'Yesssss!' He thrust his fist into the air, stabbed the
'off' button, picked up the envelope Terry had tossed at
him and danced out into the hall. 'This time. This
bloody time.'

He needed music. Something thrusting, exciting. He
wanted to hold this moment. He dived back into his

bedroom and threw his piles of CDs around. They clattered round him. Where was it?

He found it amid the mess on his desk. Puressence. He'd play it in the car on the way to work. Nobody was going to get him down today.

He glanced idly at the envelope, ripping it open as he walked out of the front door with his briefcase and pulled it to after him. It was a note from Beefy. Nick stopped for a moment, his spirits plummeting. Surely he wasn't going to say he couldn't make it, was he? The match was in two days' time and Nick was getting really excited about it. He felt like a kid again, high on anticipation, picturing the scene, all the things that might happen, a friend to share the enthusiasm with. Tucked inside the note was one ticket. Nick quickly checked the stand, the number and nodded happily.

'Third man and about three back from the front. Perfect. You're a sound bloke, Beefy. I always knew it.'

He unfolded the note as he slipped his keys into the door of the only babe in his life to compete with Miss April, the red Toyota MR2 parked on the drive. He read:

'I'll find you there. I might be a little late. Beefy.'

That was cool. No fuss, no complicated meeting instructions. The sort of thing he'd expect from Beefy. Nick had a feeling he was going to like him even more once he'd met him. They obviously had a lot in common.

He slammed his car door, tossed the briefcase, note and ticket on to the passenger seat, fired the engine and screamed off through the quiet suburbs of Harbourne with 'Sharpen up your Knives' pounding in his ears.

*

46

Cathy prodded the spoon around in her cornflakes, feeling lonely.

It was a glorious morning. It was so lovely, she'd got up early even though she wasn't due to meet up with Bill Havers at the Docklands offices until nine. She had the windows open downstairs and the wood pigeons were whooping till they were hoarse. She found herself wishing again that Jason didn't always want to go off and spend most of the week in his own flat when he wasn't away on a foreign trip. You could never predict the moment when you'd suddenly want somebody to be with you so that you could share what was going on.

This morning was like that. The council had turned up early with a van to collect the old fridge, the broken bike and the moth-eaten sofa that she and Jason had managed to transport from the back garden to the front over the weekend. The weather was so wonderful that Cathy was starting to think about sorting out the garden. But when she'd opened the door for the council ready to point at her bits and pieces they'd gone.

'It is Walthamstow, innit?' The van driver had entered helpfully. 'Next time, stick it out the front, if it's still there the next day it's probably worth givin' us a ring.'

About ten minutes later the doorbell had rung and a woman in full purdah had asked her if she'd lost a canary.

Then, as Cathy was sipping her tea, she'd noticed that the front window of the house opposite hers was being taken out by a glazier, with a crowd of people observing. Several moments afterwards the same crowd of people painstakingly steered a coffin through the empty gap. She'd poked her head round the front door, curiosity too much for her.

Mr Ali had been standing outside his house too, watching. He seemed a very nice man: tiny, quite rotund, but with a very welcoming smile. Much like his wife. He'd grinned at her surprise.

'Asian tradition. We take the body out in the coffin. You can get the coffins in these narrow houses side-ways,' he explained. 'But they have to come out the right way up. You see the problem.'

'Ah. Yes, of course.'

Cathy had gone back to her cornflakes, wanting to tell Jason, finding that he'd already left for work so was on answerphone at home and not wanting to ring him at work this early in the morning to bother him with anecdotes about old furniture, canaries, or coffins.

So she put on the television and watched the breakfast news.

They were talking about cricket. Having been sent a ticket to some sort of big match, Cathy was slightly curious.

She perked up. There was somebody being inter-viewed who was quite hunky, with bright blue eyes. She learned his name was Gough and that he wasn't going to play in the match. He droned on about his finger for a bit and a few people in the studio assessed the impact of his absence.

As names were flung about, she realised her visions of middle-aged men in flannels with Brylcreemed hair were probably out of date. Cricket couldn't be like that any more, could it? Weren't nearly all sports now taken over by nine-year-olds on steroids? Cricket must have its share of young blood. Cathy paid a little more attention just in case. After all, most men looked nice in white. She could do with a boost.

There was a glimpse of a young hunk with blond hair and a huge body. Flintstone? She missed the name. Apparently he was a bit of a batsman and they all hoped he'd get lots of runs. The sight of his big, strong arms had cheered her up. Perhaps cricket wasn't so bad if you assessed it from a distance.

'I hope you all have a lovely time, get loads of runs and win. Sorry I won't be there,' she told the television flippantly. She glanced at her watch. Time to put a spurt on. She placed her bowl on the coffee table, picked up the remote and stopped with her finger poised over the 'standby' button.

They had cut to an interview with someone else. This man had strong features, with narrowed eyes and full lips. Cathy listened.

'What have you been doing?'

'We've been sharpening up our knives.'

A flash of blue eyes, a clenching of the jaw and he was gone. The closing commentary washed over her. She only caught 'England captain'.

Cathy shook herself and stood up. She hated sport. She hated the thought of cricket. The very idea was enough to send her back to bed. There was no way she was going to jump at her grandfather's sudden command. No way at all.

She marched back to the kitchen with her bowl, dumped it noisily in the sink and swung round. She stopped at the sight of the heap of her old mail. On impulse, she found the envelope from her grandfather and examined it again.

The postmark wasn't very clear, but it definitely said

'Oxford'. Cathy took out the note and reread it. Then she studied the ticket again. Now that she'd seen something on television relating to the event, the ticket meant more. The word 'Edgbaston' meant a cricket ground that millions would be focused on the day after tomorrow. The man with the narrowed eyes and strong features would be leading his team out on to that ground. It mattered to enough people for it to be on the news and she'd got a ticket.

Why did Frank want her to be there? Had it struck him as somewhere laid back where they could easily chat without staring at each other?

Cathy pictured elderly men snoozing, their hats cocked to stop their noses from burning. There'd be the occasional elderly lady in a print frock with sunglasses and a nose shield, doing a crossword. And didn't they keep stopping to have tea and cucumber sandwiches? It was all very Noël Coward. She couldn't imagine anything further from her daily life. She enjoyed rolling up her sleeves here in east London, helping real people out with real issues. Cricket, to her, was synonymous with vicars and teacakes. But all the same, she had a ticket.

She leant back against the cupboards, indecision and righteous indignation having a dogfight above her head. Did she have anything to lose?

Yes. Her peace of mind. Her dignity. Her moral stance. The chance to sound out Lucy about Hellier's. There was no argument.

'So, you lot, shut up,' she told the fighting forces in the empty space above her, before shooting up the stairs and dressing herself in the brightest suit she could find.

*

50

'That's what I've been telling Brenda and the boys. We know we've got to move with the times. And now, with your help, I reckon the future's looking pretty good,' Bill Havers was saying cheerfully.

Bill was giving Cathy a guided tour of the Docklands office complex. The smell of fresh paint and carpet glue hung in the air. Everything was clean, neat, new, ready for action. It sent a tingle over Cathy's skin.

They came to a halt in a small but light office overlooking the sludgy mudbanks of the Thames, with a wide view across the river. Bill propped open a vast arched window and the sound of bickering seagulls filled the air.

'Double glazed, you see,' he explained. 'But the windows open too. You imagine you're in one of these little incubation units working your socks off – you'd want to open the window sometimes, wouldn't you? So we talked it over with the architect. Traditional on the outside, all mod cons on the inside.' Bill's eyes sparkled as he watched for Cathy's reaction. It was clear he was very proud of the job his building firm had done. And rightly so.

'They're wonderful,' Cathy breathed. 'Little starter homes for new businesses. I love them.'

The offices had retained the outer shell of a Victorian warehouse, while offering every modern commodity inside. The furniture was solid and inviting, and the aspect was inspiring. In a small office like this there'd be space for three or four people to work. The complex had a reception to field calls and a mail service. On the ground floor there were retail outlets, also attractive and solidly built. All the complex needed now was people busting with ideas to come and fill it.

51

'I thought you'd like it.' Bill chuckled. 'Fancy putting your name down for one of these units, then?'

'Me?' Cathy looked at Bill in surprise.

'Well, gel with spark like you. I can just see you taking off on your own.'

'Oh, not me.' Cathy considered Bill's earnest expression. 'I'm happy where I am. I've had lots of ideas for going it alone, of course. Everyone does. But it's – well, I've just taken on a mortgage.'

'Hmn.' Bill's blue eyes were thoughtful. 'Let us know if you change your mind. I reckon these offices are going to go like hot cakes.'

'Maybe one day.' Cathy leant on the windowsill and inhaled the smell of the river. It was bracing. 'But I envy the guys who'll be moving in here. It's beautiful. You couldn't wish for a better start.'

She took another deep breath of London air and watched a barge drift up the Thames. Once these docks would have been spilling over with activity, before the demise of business in the area. Now, little by little, they were starting to spring into life again. If only she could get Bill and Troy Vickers, the architect, talking to each other . . .

But it wasn't in her control and it had all gone quiet since Cathy had given her folder to Mark. Cathy was planning to have lunch with Lucy from Hellier's tomorrow and very delicately sound her out, but she could justify that as partly social. They got on well. And if she found out anything, she'd put it straight back to Mark. She knew she couldn't do more than that at this stage.

'I'm really glad you like what we've done,' Bill said, as Cathy stepped back from the window and gazed around the office.

'You'll have to give Ruth and Mark a guided tour.' Cathy vowed to get the senior partners down to the complex, and soon. If they saw what Bill was capable of, Cathy was optimistic that they'd give him a real break.

'I prefer to deal with you, you know, Cathy,' Bill said, his big face flushing slightly. 'Don't get me wrong, Mark's a sound bloke and Ruth obviously knows her onions. But I can talk to you. You seem to know what I'm on about. It's instinct, in some people. I reckon you've got the gift. Tell you the truth, if you wasn't at that first meeting, I think I might have been scared off. You spoke a lot of sense. I thought I could work with you.'

'Thank you.' Cathy smiled with pleasure.

'That lunch they took me to, all olive oil and stuff. It's not my scene. I get a lot more sorted talking to you over a cuppa.'

'I prefer to do things over a cuppa myself,' Cathy agreed. 'I think that's why I love east London so much. I've never been one for designer lunches and wine bars.'

'You live in Walthamstow, don't you?' Bill said. 'Perhaps you'd like a night out at the dogs some time? I can book the restaurant. Prime seats, look right over the track.'

'The dogs?' Cathy was curious. 'I've never done that before.'

'Shame on you, gel, and just a spit from you too. If you haven't been to Walthamstow dogs, you ain't lived yet. You know Vinnie's got a dog that runs there. Fast little bleeder it is. Worth a few bob.'

'I'd love that.' Cathy laughed. So much for vicars,

teacakes, village greens and cricket bats. She could imagine that a man like Bill would splutter into his mug in horror at the thought of a cricket match. Her mobile suddenly rang from her handbag.

'Oh, I'm sorry. I thought I'd turned it off. Let me just sort it out.'

'You go right ahead and take the call,' Bill said with a wink. 'Then we'll go and grab that cuppa.'

'Thanks. I'll tell them I'll ring back.' Cathy poked a button on her mobile.

It was Lucy from Hellier's. 'Just to say that something's come up here and I can't make lunch on Thursday after all. I'm sorry about that. Can we do it next week some time?'

'Of course. I'll ring you later to sort it out.'

Putting her mobile back into her bag, Cathy turned to face Bill.

'So, Bill—'

'So. What do you reckon to the Ashes, then?' Bill asked, his thick eyebrows rising eagerly. 'We going to wop those Ozzie behinds, or what?'

Chapter Four

The alarm shrilled at five thirty. It was hardly light, it was hardly warm and hardly human. Cathy threw out a hand and banged the button. It stopped.

The sheets were smooth, the pillow soft. She hadn't told anybody that she was thinking of doing this. If she decided to wimp out nobody would ever know. Even Mark, who had been persuaded to allow her a day's leave given that she was owed so much, had no idea what she was really planning to do. Cathy opened her eyes and looked at the grey glimmer of the ceiling.

She had an hour to decide what to wear to meet Frank.

Twenty minutes later, after a shower and with a strong cup of coffee as support, Cathy threw everything in her wardrobe on to the bed. There were bright things, formal things, sexy things, casual things. What on earth was right for this?

She scrunched her wet hair in her hands and tried to think. It was forecast to be a scorcher today. So that meant she could toss the heavy things to one side. What did people wear to cricket matches? And this one wasn't just on the village green either. This was an international match. It had been on the news. She chewed her lip. The slinky dresses could go. They had to be worn with heels. She could imagine that high heels weren't very practical for trudging around a tea tent all day. Suits were out. Far too formal.

She was left with various pairs of shorts, blouses, T-shirts, some cotton trousers and her trusty Levis. She threw those around the room for a while. Time was getting on. Her train left from Euston at a quarter to eight. She had to get there and buy a ticket, and she'd be wrestling with a zillion commuters at the same time.

Attacking her hair with a brush under the dryer, Cathy was pleased to see it dried out straight today, down to her shoulders, thick, shiny and red. She wiggled her head and her hair obligingly bounced around looking vibrant. That much was great. But she was still in her underwear with no make-up on and she had fifteen minutes before she had to leave the house.

A quarter of an hour later, Cathy launched herself towards Walthamstow tube station in her bright-yellow suit and a pair of yellow high heels. Over her shoulder was her floppy leather bag with her make-up thrown in it. She'd have to do her face on the train.

The bustle of Euston Station woke Cathy up. She felt dreadful about scaring innocent people by walking about the concourse with a pale, unmade-up face, but she'd got her ticket to Birmingham New Street in good time. She grabbed a cup of frothy coffee and took it with her into the ladies, where she spent several minutes plastering make-up all over her startled features. She looked as surprised as she felt to find herself there.

She didn't look too bad once she'd finished. Her eyes looked bright, anyway, her lips and cheeks were charmingly flushed thanks to Max Factor and the yellow suit was striking. Frank would see straight away that she wasn't a slip of a girl. He'd see a young but competent woman and they'd meet on equal terms. They could take it from there. The last thing she wanted to look was vulnerable. Her nostrils flared as she inhaled, assessed herself in the mirror and went back to the concourse.

It was a Virgin train, a fast one she'd been assured by national rail enquiries (who'd also asked her what she meant by an oxymoron). She headed off for the platform, still outwardly confident, still apparently unmoved by what she was about to face. The journey was a buffer between the present and the future. The train would hopefully be quiet and she could read the paper in peace and organise her thoughts.

Maybe she'd be travelling with people who were also heading off to the test match and get a taste of her company for the day. She'd probably end up sharing a carriage with a couple of elderly men with their crosswords and sunhats. Perhaps she ought to read up on the sports pages. It would probably be a good idea to have a vague inkling of what was going on. It would give her something to say to Frank. She made her way to the platform.

She was hoisted in the air and carried along twenty yards in the arms of a nun.

'What the— ?'

'I'm really sorry, love,' one nun was saying, very genuinely. 'That's Martin. He gets a bit overexcited.'

'He doesn't mean any harm,' another nun said, jogging along beside them and pulling the arm of the nun who was carrying her. 'Martin! Put her down at once!'

Cathy felt her feet gently rested again on the floor. Life surrounded her.

'I'm so sorry, love, just instinct. You looked so gorgeous in all your yellow, like a great big primrose. I'm really sorry.'

Martin, the nun who'd carried her, was a good-looking man in his mid-twenties and well-spoken.

'Do you forgive me, Primrose? I was carried away by your beauty.' He sank to his knees and stuck his hand out to her like a supplicant knight. Cathy was surrounded by nuns, all young men, all handsome-faced and good-humoured.

'Please forgive him, Primrose.'

'Yes, do and we'll give you a beer.'

'That really was out of order,' a more serious nun said. 'Martin, you're a prick.'

'I know.' Martin sank his head to the floor. 'I'm so sorry.'

'No, I mean really apologise,' the serious nun emphasised.

Martin stood up and looked abashed. 'Seriously, I'm sorry if I offended you.'

Cathy's sense of humour surfaced. No, she didn't like being picked up and carried around by strange men. But there was an odd relief in being surrounded by men dressed as nuns. It was silly. It distracted her from what she was about to do.

'So do you—'

'Forgive him—'

'Primrose—'

'For being completely enraptured by you?'

'You are my sunshine,' a nun started, falling to one knee and throwing out his hands to her yellow outfit.

'My only sunshine,' another nun joined in.

'You make me happee –' the nuns chorused, even the

serious one. 'When skies are grey—'

Cathy laughed. Standing on a dingy platform at Euston Station with ten men dressed as nuns serenading her was not what she'd expected to be doing today. She felt important for a moment and other people on the platform were laughing too.

'You silly buggers,' she chided them. 'Get thee to a nunnery.'

'Your wish is our command.'

'So where are you lot going?' she asked, vainly attempting to be sensible.

'To see the bright lights of the Edgbaston cricket ground. They say we'll be so dazzled we'll be blinded for life. But we don't believe them.'

'No, we don't.'

'No, not at all. We believe we'll return with our sight intact.'

'Unless we hit the special brew.'

'But we won't do that.'

'Oh, no, no, no.'

'Not before eleven o' clock, anyway.'

They murmured in agreement, as if they all knew the script, and Cathy giggled at them. As a train rolled into the platform, her nuns began to stand up and shuffle around. It came to a gentle halt and they all stood back to let people off. Through the windows Cathy could see the faces of commuters straining to get to their London jobs. She felt a surprising surge of glee that she was heading out, with these mad people, whoever they were, to do something different.

'All right, stand back, lads, worthy people dis-embarking.'

Cathy laughed again at the serious nun. He was a bit

of a dish, with twinkly brown eyes. He winked at her.

'I never knew people like you went to cricket matches!' She smiled at him, her spirits up.

'Oh no?' He gave her a sardonic look and inclined his head down the platform. Cathy looked.

She just hadn't noticed. A bit further away was a small crowd of Ronald McDonalds. Just along from them were several Crusaders, complete with shields and tabards with stark red crosses. Dotted around them all were the people she'd expected to see with cool boxes, sunshades and hats. Some were older, some were younger and there were plenty of women among them. None of the sleepy crowd she'd imagined. Everybody seemed very much alive, whatever their age and Ronald McDonalds, Crusaders, nuns and ordinary people were mingling amiably together.

'See you, Primrose.'

The nuns started to edge down the platform to find an empty carriage.

''Bye, guys. Have a lovely day. And, hey – sharpen up your knives!'

'You into cricket, then?'

Her last comment seemed to have half the gang flocking back to her. She blinked at them, storing the research for future use. She should pass this on to her girlfriends. For a moment at least, she had the serious attention of a sizeable bunch of hunky young males.

'I heard –' She thought hard. What was his name? She couldn't remember. 'The England captain saying that. They'd better pull it off now. No good being all mouth and no trousers, is there?'

'Quite right.' Martin the nun looked as if he was about impulsively to rearrange his habit to demonstrate the point, but the serious nun was calling them down the platform.

'Oy! Will you lot give Primrose some space and get down here? There's plenty of seats.'

They swivelled obediently.

''Bye,' Cathy murmured to them again as they turned, regrouped and headed away down the platform.

It was then that she noticed that each and every habit had been cut away into a gaping hole at the back to reveal bright red silky knickers, bare hairy legs and Doc Martens. Even the serious nun was in the same ensemble. She could see it as he boarded the train behind his troop. Then she got on herself, found a seat with a majority of ordinary people and only one stray Ronald McDonald (who soon lost his nerve and went off to find the others) and settled herself down with the paper, unread, on her lap and a smile tugging at the corners of her mouth.

The great thing about living so close to Edgbaston, on the rare occasions when he did get his act together to go, was that Nick didn't have to get up at sparrow's fart, like most of the poor buggers who'd be turning up today. Not that he'd ever bother to go and watch Warwickshire, whose home ground Edgbaston was. Nick was a passionate, squirming, compulsive armchair sufferer.

Today was different.

Beefy had done him a huge favour. He'd wrested him from his foam-spilling, spring-firing sofa and got him out there where the action was.

Nick was grinning from the moment the alarm went

off. All the more so as he wrenched wide the limp curtains and saw the sun blazing over the neat front lawns of the street. The pitch would be dry. England only needed to win the toss and choose to bat. Rain might come later in this test and slow down the batting, so getting a high score today would be crucial. Nick's presence would influence the coin. Had he been at work, sneakily observing the proceedings on a corner of his computer screen, the toss would have been lost. But he, Nick, was going to be present and it was all going to be all right.

He flexed his muscles in the shower, sang loudly and bounced around the house at three times his usual speed.

'Hope it goes well for you, mate,' Terry said, slapping his arm as he headed off, toast crumbs dotted around his chin, for work.

'It will,' Nick told him. 'I shall make it so.'

He chose his clothes carefully. The black jeans had been unlucky before. He'd been wearing them at a crucial moment during the winter tour of Pakistan and he'd never forgiven himself. The faded blue Levis were untainted by disaster and they were clean and smelled wonderfully of soap powder. Vera, whom they paid to come in every Saturday morning to sort out the mess they all lived in, zipped through the ironing at a speed that Nick could only marvel at as a scientific phenomenon. Had Vera been alive in the Wild West she'd have been known as 'Vera "Fingers" Springer' with 'Wanted' posters plastered all over the place.

He found a pristine white T-shirt from the pile, flicked a speck of fluff from it and tucked it neatly into his jeans. Then he smoothed down his hair and packed his bag. He'd got some shorts, a magazine and some sun cream. He shoved them into his compact holdall. He thought of packing a jumper, or taking a jacket. But at nearly half past nine it was already very warm. And it wasn't really the done thing to turn up with lots of comfort factors. Not for the young, not for the boys.

So he picked up his holdall, threw it easily over his shoulder and headed out to ring a taxi.

Putting down the phone and waiting for the car to arrive, he stood very still. The fire of anticipation ran up his legs, through his stomach and down each of his arms. Goose-pimples rose on the flesh there. He saw them and his chest tightened.

He hadn't been this excited in ages. It wasn't until he was forced to stand still that he realised how long it had been. He flung open the front door, trotted down the short, steep drive to the road and stood on the path, looking up and down the road for the cab.

At Birmingham New Street Cathy piled from the train and went with the stream of supporters up the steps to the main area of the station. There was a newsagent's, a bar – and she spotted the Ladies. Her nerves beginning to flutter, she took herself inside to check that her eyeliner wasn't smeared all over her cheeks. She stood in front of the full-length mirror and studied her reflection.

She looked very – well, very yellow. That couldn't be a bad thing in a granddaughter. Better than black, at least. She was beginning to feel a bit formal next to some of the crowd she'd seen, but Jason had mentioned that these were good seats. A light suit was probably the right decision.

Cathy took a big breath for courage, stared at her own dilated pupils, then went back to the concourse.

Where to next? Perhaps the ground was within walking distance? The best thing to do would be to follow someone going that way. She couldn't see any of the nuns or Crusaders so she tacked on to the back of a pleasant-looking man clutching a cool box with one hand and a little boy with the other. The boy was swinging a child's cricket bat. They were both in sunhats, shorts and T-shirts. They looked purposeful. Cathy decided to follow them. They stopped at a kiosk, so she stopped too, a pace behind them. They bought some fizzy drinks and crisps. Then they went back along the concourse and into the newsagent's. She followed them in there and stood behind them while they looked at some cricket magazines and chose one. She shadowed them to the till. Then she followed them out of the newsagent's again, along the corridor that ran between the platforms and into a wide doorway. The pleasant man turned round and stared at her. He didn't seem so pleasant any more.

'Have you got a problem?'

'I beg your pardon?'

'This is the men's toilet. You can't follow us in here.'

He was gripping his son's hand protectively.

Cathy put her hands out in appeal.

'Oh God, no, I'm not after your son.' That didn't come out right. 'No, it's just that I'm lost.'

He was still frowning like thunder.

'It's – I saw the cricket bat,' she struggled, 'and the cool box and the sunhats and the cricket magazine. I – I'm looking for Edgbaston. I don't know where it is.'

'Ah!' His face cleared. 'Get a taxi. From the taxi rank.'

'Right, thank you!' She waved goodbye to him as he gathered his son and whisked him off into the toilets.

Cathy arrived at the taxi rank in time to see the last of her nuns' red knickers disappearing into a taxi. There was a queue, a multicoloured assortment of summer clothes, cool bags and boxes, holdalls and some Wombles. Joining the end of the queue, Cathy pitied the Wombles. They were going to bake in their furry suits with only their faces peering out. She was starting to feel very overdressed herself. There wasn't a single person in a suit and only a handful of the older men were in jackets. There were one or two ties, but those looked like club ties. The queue was moving swiftly, though, with a good circulation of taxis. She shuffled her way forward. Then a group in front of her turned as they were climbing into the next taxi.

'You're not going to the cricket, are you?' a jovial face asked her, with a query at her suit.

'Yes, I am, actually.' Cathy blushed.

'Want to share our cab?'

'Great, thanks!'

She squashed into the black cab along with two very British and good-humoured older men, and a young Australian couple in shorts and sandals. They were complete strangers to each other, but there was lively banter as they veered around roundabouts, gaining speed as they shot away into the unknown. Cathy peered out of the window at Birmingham. It was how she'd imagined it: full of roundabouts, flyovers and office blocks.

'You going to a box, then?' The Australian girl leaned down the row of bodies on the back seat and nodded at Cathy's suit.

'A box?'

'One of the hospitality suites,' one of the men explained. 'Corporate entertainment?'

'Oh. No, I'm not. I'm sitting in a seat. Somewhere.'

They all nodded.

'I'm meeting someone there,' she added, feeling a bit square.

'Never been to a match before, then?' The other British man smiled at her kindly.

'Now, how did you guess?' She managed a wry smile at him. 'I don't even like cricket.'

There was a shocked silence. Then her kind British man looked at her ruefully. 'Well, neither does my wife,' he said with sympathy, 'but she's never been to a game, so I maintain she's on very shaky ground. At least you're giving it a chance, aren't you?'

She nodded obediently and smiled. There really wasn't time to explain that being here had bugger all to do with cricket and everything to do with her curiosity about this old man who was her only living blood relative.

The Australian girl leaned over her boyfriend and grinned.

'It's all about overs,' she told Cathy. 'Once you've got overs, you've got cricket.'

'Okay,' Cathy said.

'We love it in Oz. Can't get away from it, really.'

'I see.'

'I play as well. You should have a go some time. It's so great.'

'Right.' Cathy smiled politely and nodded again.

Thankfully, at that point they started throwing names around which Cathy had never heard, so she could withdraw again. There was nothing worse than being told about something you had no interest in by someone with the fire of conversion in their eyes. At least Frank wouldn't try to convert her. Or she hoped to God he wasn't going to.

They'd been steaming through leafy suburbs for a few minutes, now, and Cathy was surprised that this was all part of Birmingham. It was very green and really pretty. The taxi swept down a wooded road then, before she knew it, they were being dropped outside the ground. They piled out and she added her change to the kitty.

'Have a lovely day!' The Australians disappeared.

'I do hope you enjoy yourself.' Her kind British man twinkled at her.

Then he and his companion disappeared too and Cathy was left standing on her own.

Barbara threw a dishcloth at Beefy, hissing at him. He crouched, narrowed his eyes, one eyelid twitching into an uncertain wink, then he spun round on the quarry kitchen tiles and hurled his bulk towards the cat flap. It clattered after him.

'Little usurper,' Barbara issued.

She surveyed the state of the kitchen. It was a spacious, airy room, like most of the rooms in the house, with leaded windows of neat square panes. A clematis, trained over the window from the porch, draped like a floppy fringe. Beyond, the cream gravel of the drive was bright in the morning sun. She twisted the window handle and wedged it open. The squawk of the magpies from the firs in the front garden filled the kitchen. She took a satisfied breath.

Then she set about the washing-up, screwing up her face as she scraped the remains of the stew she'd cooked for the two men from the plates into the bin. They'd only eaten half of it, at best, and at one side of one of the plates was a shiny patch of clean white where Beefy had been gorging himself when she arrived. Despicable creature. If she lived here he'd be the first thing to be consigned to the outhouse. Closely followed by the computer and the cable television, then Barry, the lodger. They were play-things, tacky amusements that Frank lavished money and attention on. It was an insult to him. He was betray-ing himself, at a time when he should be celebrating the fineness of his mind and his work.

Barbara suddenly froze in her scraping and peered into the bin. Poking a knife into the rubbish, she could see a pre-packaged food carton. She frowned, and picked out the box with two fingers: Chicken Jal Frezi. She dropped it back in again and allowed the plastic bin lid to slam into place.

So that was it. Barry was bringing home junk food and Frank was eating it. What was the point of her cooking good food for Frank and leaving it for him when she went home, if Barry completely ignored her efforts? She'd known, months ago when Frank had all at once announced his intention to let out one of the big back bedrooms, that it was a bad idea. When she'd met Barry, her fears had been confirmed.

Barry didn't speak properly. He used Tesco sham-poo, Tesco toothpaste and disposable razors. He never rinsed out the sink after him. He drove a string of fast cars, like shiny boiled sweets, that he borrowed from work. She was quite sure that he had never, ever read a book in his life. He was a bad influence on Frank.

68

Not to worry, she'd told herself. He'll leave. She'd given it three weeks, tops. But months later Barry was still there, ensconced in the house with his beer cans, Blockbuster videos, macho aftershave and packets of Chicken Jal Frezi.

Sometimes he brought friends home with him, all in denim jackets with bony legs and fly-away hair. They went up to his room and roared with laughter. She expected Frank to be furious, but he was too busy on the computer, or following some abstract tournament somewhere, to notice that his house was being ruined by the sights, sounds and smells of Barry and his friends.

And if Barry's smells weren't bad enough, his smalls were worse. He always managed to leave a pair stuck to the inside of the washing machine. They had things like 'Sex Beast' and 'Horny Boy' printed on them.

Frank was losing the plot. The one thing he should have been doing, the thing Barbara lost sleep over every night, was finishing his book. His biography of Alfred, King of Wessex, which was to be his final, triumphant statement to the academic world. They'd worked on it together for a long time. Or, at least, she felt her input had been crucial to it. Her job at the Bodleian Library ensured that she was useful to him still, as she had been useful to him for so many years.

First Barbara had been his student. Then she'd assisted him and done a little teaching herself. Then, as the years passed, assisting him had become a fuller job and she'd dedicated herself to it. Barbara had been Frank's right-hand woman for longer than anybody could remember. Since his retirement she had opted to work part-time at the Bodleian. And now he needed her more than ever, more than he knew himself. He was in danger and she was going to protect him. From himself, if she had to.

Barbara finished the washing-up briskly, dried and put away. Then she made tea in the pot and arranged a cup and saucer on the tray, with the sugar bowl, milk and a plate of digestive biscuits. She checked her watch. It was half past ten. Now was the right time to take in the tea. She only hoped she wasn't going to interrupt the toss.

Barbara picked up the tray and walked down the hall, her neat shoes falling softly on the row of narrow Persian rugs. She reached the door of the living room and put her ear to it. She could hear the drone of the commentary. Silently she pushed open the door and moved across the room. The sun blinds were down over the wide patio doors. The heavy curtains were half closed. The room was dim, the glaring sun barred entry. The rows and columns of his books, built floor to ceiling and wall to wall, were muted shapes. The only colour was coming from the huge television screen.

Frank's hands gripped the arms of his chair like white claws. She paused as she was about to pour his tea for him. She could see the bones of his knuckles straining against his thin skin. Under the light tartan blanket he'd draped over his knees his legs were trembling. His breath was coming in short, sharp rasps.

Fear surged through Barbara. She peered around the wings of Frank's armchair. His cheeks were shallow and pale, his eyes moist and glassy.

'Oh!' Her breath shot out of her like a bullet. 'Oh, my God! Frank!'

She shook his arm roughly.

He jumped round, fixing her with wild eyes.

'What the bloody hell is wrong with you, woman?'

'You're –' Barbara clasped at her chest, her heart bursting. 'Are you all right?'

'Of course I'm bloody all right.' He contorted his face at her in desperation. 'What did you think? That I'd kick the bucket here? Now?' He threw out his white hand to the television to make his point. 'Today?'

She shook her head, flustered.

'I – you looked so—'

He narrowed one eye at her.

'Did you think I might die before I'd given you a credit in *Alfred*?'

'Frank!' Barbara scowled at him.

'I'm telling you this.' He jabbed a finger at her. 'You're not having my bloody ashes until these bloody Ashes have been won. Is that clear?'

'Frank, I don't want your ashes,' Barbara stated primly and poured his tea. 'It's just that for a moment there you looked, well, in a state.' She planted the teapot firmly on the tray and marched back to the door.

'Of course I'm in a state!' Frank leant round the side of his chair and stared at her as if she were an idiot. 'We've won the bloody toss!'

She shut the door on him and went back to the kitchen, where Beefy had brought her a frog.

People milled everywhere, laughing, chatting, clutching Union Jacks, or Australian flags. There were blokes with painted faces, bunches of young women striding along in skimpy summer clothes, plenty of men in straw hats and blazers too. Cathy had lost her nuns, but the Crusaders were in evidence and it looked like

71

they'd met up with another faction of the army. Every few yards there seemed to be a tiny roadside stall selling something. There were banners strapped to posts along the pavement, marking the event. A large piece of floppy cardboard was pressed into her hand by somebody handing them out. She took it, as everybody else seemed to be taking one, and turned it over. There was a large '6' on one side, a '4' on the other. She'd seen shots on the telly of people waving these things when someone hit the ball. Where to now?

Cathy reached an admission gate, presented her ticket, pushed her way through a turnstile and entered Edgbaston cricket ground.

She couldn't share the excitement of the others, but it was difficult not to be swept along by the buzz in the air. She still couldn't see any grass at all. The backs of the high stands formed an oval boundary. To see the pitch and maybe sneak a look at Frank, she'd need to take one of the staircases that led up from the concourse she now ambled round. There were beer stands, souvenir clothing stands, hot dogs, teas, signs to toilets and everywhere Australian and English supporters bantered with each other. The crowd was robust, happy and very big.

Kick-off was at eleven, according to her ticket. She was in good time. Now she had to calm her nerves, try not to think about catheters and get to her seat.

Nick had arrived early. He hated lateness, in himself or anyone else. Beefy was coming from Oxford and the least he could do was be there to greet him. He leafed through *Wisden Cricket Monthly* while he was waiting.

He loved this part of the day. He'd made it to one or

two test matches before and he'd worked out that being there early was fun. He could lounge in his seat before the place filled up, appreciating the emerald smoothness of the rolled pitch, the openness of the ground, the increasing warmth of the sun, the growing hum as spectators arrived and found their places.

It was an atmosphere of building anticipation. There was none of the quickfire adrenalin of a footie or rugby match, no slap-bang-wallop, right boys, there's the door. And there wasn't the frosty hush associated with a tennis match. True, it annoyed him like hell if he sat near jabberers. But the subdued mumble of conversation, a bit of humour, that was all part of it.

There were big replay screens fixed high on either side of the ground. No sound would come from them. None of the jarring razzmatazz of baseball, or ice hockey. One-day cricket was going that way, but this was *test* cricket. This was the real thing. He squinted at the scoreboard and imagined how it might look at the end of the day. England 350 for – one wicket? He chuckled under his breath. Perhaps he could bet Beefy a pint on the likely score by stumps. Where was he?

The Eric Hollies stand on the other side of the ground looked to be almost full by now. The Barmy Army was there in force. Nick could see a number of nuns. Not very original. The last test match he'd been to – a few years ago at Trent Bridge – must surely have had the most Nelson Mandelas ever to be collected in one place on the planet. A troop of Crusaders paraded round the stand waving cardboard swords covered in tin foil, to resounding cheers.

Nick grimaced. The cheapest seats were in that long, broad stand and there were plenty of fanatical cricket fans, but always one or two revellers who started on the beer at eleven and were giving the world a view of their backsides by five. He didn't mind a laugh and a few prats dressing up as rabbits, but the Mexican wave got on his nerves. He didn't want anything to distract too much from the cricket. But looking kindly at the Crusaders for a moment, Nick decided they were much more pleasing on the eye than his computer screen at work. And the home-made helmets were quite good. He allowed himself a smirk.

Nick swivelled on the plastic seat and looked back up the low tiers to the nearest entry points, wondering if Beefy was going to walk in at any moment. He didn't even know what sort of bloke he was looking for. But the seat next to him was still promisingly empty, so there couldn't have been any major balls-up. Beefy must be headed that way and he couldn't wait to talk to him about the toss.

Nick turned back to the pitch and gazed over it happily. How about that for a bucket of Four-X? Winning the bloody toss? Hussain was now in Nick's good books, at least until he came out to bat and tore his nerves to shreds. It was a beautiful batting track. Dry, flat and England should be able to fill their boots with runs. In his mind was a seductive whisper, 'Remember the Ashes '97?' Hussain had scored 207 on this very pitch. It had been magic. Except, of course, that England had gone on to lose the Ashes that year.

Nick pulled himself up sharply and slapped his hands on his knees. No negative thoughts. Not allowed. It would influence things. Only positive . . .

He turned in amazement. A woman dressed like a squashed daffodil had just sat down next to him.

Chapter Five

Cathy felt completely stupid. A suit was the wrong thing to have worn. Nobody in this stand was in a suit. One or two smart frocks on the older women, but nothing like she'd gone for. The younger women were in jeans, shorts, or sexy little cotton dresses. Most were already rubbing sun cream on to bare legs – something she couldn't achieve through a pair of sheer tights, even if she'd remembered to bring any sun cream. She was standing out like a lighthouse each time she clacked up and down the stone steps in her heels, frowning at her ticket and frowning at her supposed seat. Doing that, and being bright yellow, was getting embarrassing. She'd already gone back and asked the steward at the top if she was in the right place twice. He gave her a pained look when she caught his eye again.

So instead, she took her ticket, her big leather bag, her floppy piece of cardboard and her bright yellow-ness to the seat which tallied with the details on her ticket and sat in it.

Instantly she felt, rather than saw, the hostility coming from the man next to her. It was like being microwaved. Cathy didn't feel very civil herself.

She hadn't been able to see anybody in the vicinity of her seat who could even faintly resemble a grandfather of hers. There seemed to be a huge clump of younger men and a lot of mixed groups in that area. The only men she could see of advanced age were with other friends and chatting among themselves. By the time she'd hovered over her seat a good few times, then sat in it, she'd have thought that anybody who was Frank would have looked her way with some purpose. Nobody did.

Secondly, she didn't feel civil because the man she was now sitting next to was about as approachable as a bouncer. As she was trying to get her leather bag under her seat, he'd had to shift his legs a bit to give her some space. They were very long, very solid legs and he hadn't said 'Oh, sorry', or even 'Bit cramped here, isn't it?'. Any sort of inane comment might have made her feel better, but he'd just shifted his legs tensely, then sat still again, his hands slapped over his knees. She felt like a bloody nuisance.

What she'd expected when she got here she couldn't say. But she had been quite sure that her seat would be next to Frank's. Apparently it wasn't. On one side was the aisle, on the other was Action Man. She'd hardly had time to appreciate how neat the pitch looked, how incredibly green the grass was, how small the ground seemed once she was in the stand and how she'd always thought from clips on the telly that the seats were stacked high, like tower blocks, all around the grass, whereas in fact the stands were low, spreading and very open air. In fact, as she'd arrived at the top of the steps and looked over the scene she'd been struck by how pretty it all was.

She sat still. Waiting.

What the hell was she was waiting for? Her neurons sparkled like Christmas tree lights. There was only one logical solution: Frank was late. This twit next to her was in the wrong seat. She relaxed a little, pulling at her St Christopher with relief, and turned to him carefully.

'Excuse me, do you have the right seat?'

He turned to her. His eyes were light-blue, not warm, very distancing. They were set in a forbidding face with a strong nose. He had blond hair, cut very short round a solid head. Her first impressions were dead right. He would look perfect in combats lying across a plastic tank with a miniature grenade in one hand.

'Yes.'

'Oh.' She faced the ground again, her thoughts churning. Then she said, very politely. 'Are you sure?'

His eyes narrowed a little, as if trying to work out which of the two she was: deaf or stupid.

'Yes.'

'Oh. I see. Thank you for your time.'

Rude git. He hadn't even done her the honour of getting out his ticket and showing it, which would be a way of reassuring her. He'd also made it clear by his tone, if she hadn't got the message from his microwaves, that he was mightily peeved to have her sitting next to him.

'That's good, then,' she said.

He was silent.

'Wouldn't want to be in the wrong seats, would we?' She tugged on the chain round her neck in agitation. She hadn't bargained for a no-show on Frank's part. What on earth was she supposed to do now?

'Are *you* in the right seat?' he said, surprising her.

She gave him a very straight look. If he wasn't going to flap his ticket around, neither was she.

'Yes,' she said firmly.

'I see. Thank you for *your* time.'

'It's my very great pleasure.' She nodded at him. 'There is nothing more satisfying than assuring a complete stranger that I know my own mind.'

Cathy stared out over the pitch again. So far, nothing was happening. No sign of anyone playing cricket. But by the big clock she could see it wasn't quite eleven o'clock yet. She was starting to wonder whether Frank had arranged some sort of fanfare to greet her by way of a surprise. What the hell was the point of all this?

But then a thought hit her with a force that made her stomach lurch. Frank had never said he would actually be here. It was her assumption. After all, that was what he'd told Melissa he wanted to do: meet her and talk to her. Why would he suddenly spring out of nowhere with a burning desire to buy his completely unknown granddaughter a ticket to a cricket match? Could Jason have been right? Could Frank really be under the misapprehension that if he treated her to a day out on her *own*, to an event she had no understanding of, she'd be thrilled to bits?

Cathy giggled. It relieved some of the tension. In herself, anyway. The man next to her flicked a magazine with what she could only assume was irritation.

It had to be funny. She couldn't look at it in any other way. If he wasn't here and if it was some sort of absurd joke on Frank's part – or, to be kind, even if it was his very misguided notion of her idea of fun – then all she had to do was get a taxi back to the station, get on the train and go home again.

She was comforting herself with that thought when another idea came to her. What if Frank hadn't been able to get two seats together? That meant he could be damned nigh anywhere in the whole ground. The only way she'd find out would be if she stayed in her seat and waited for him to come and claim her. At some point.

78

Cathy heaved an annoyed sigh. She'd made the trip out of curiosity. As a tactic, Frank's cryptic approach had worked in getting her inside Edgbaston cricket ground. But from here on, she thought she had every right to feel let down.

Melissa's and Brian's love and attention while she was growing up had stopped her from feeling that she was unclaimed baggage. In fact, she'd gone years at a time without even thinking about her blood family. But now, here she was and her own grandfather, from her own family who years ago had somehow failed to claim her, was making her feel exactly like that.

Cathy didn't want bitter feelings to eclipse the majestic blue sky, the powering sun, the wonderful newness of the experience. But she could feel her blood rising. Then the man next to her turned to her again. She felt his eyes boring into her. She swivelled and stared straight into his face.

'What?' she snapped.

He was smiling. A strange, slow smile, as if he knew the punchline to a secret joke. He had raised a finger and was wagging it knowingly at her. It was very odd.

'You', he said, 'are beefy.'

Cathy glared back at him. Stony eyes, as best as she could muster. A thread of flame licked its way through her body.

'And you', she said back to him, 'are ugly.'

He blinked at her. She maintained a level, ungiving stare.

'You're not beefy, then?'

She felt her jaw drop. 'And you're not ugly? When was the last time you were unlucky enough to be facing a mirror?'

His eyelids flickered. She was glad of it. Not so tough after all.

'You're definitely not beefy,' he said.

'But you', she assured him, infuriated, 'are most definitely ugly.'

'Thank you.'

'It's my pleasure.'

She'd made him back down. Quite right. She was who she was, what she was and nobody who wasn't very close to her, not for years and years, had made any sort of crude reference to the fact that she wasn't, by the wildest stretch of the imagination, Kate Moss with an unfortunate case of water retention.

'I thought you were someone else.' His voice arrived again in her ear.

So he was the 'dead but won't lie down' sort. She could handle that.

'I didn't think you were someone else. Only wished it,' she muttered, just loud enough for him to hear.

'I meant', he said slowly, 'that I'd hoped I'd be sitting next to somebody else.'

Cathy powered him an evil look.

'I'm so sorry. Obviously Melinda Messenger has stood you up and you feel a bit miffed. But once I've gone you can give Caprice a buzz on your mobile, apologise for it being short notice and she'll be with you in two ticks. Just put up with me, if you will, until I can look at my timetable and work out when the next train leaves.'

She grappled with the floppy bit of cardboard on her lap with the '4' and '6' on it, and attempted to reach her handbag. A corner of the card stuck up her nose.

'Hold this.' Unceremoniously she dumped the card

on his lap.

He sat with it passively. She was aware that he was watching her. His voice, the last thing she wanted to hear, probed at her ear again.

'I'm not sure what I've said but I think I've upset you.'

Cathy pulled her bag back on to her lap and gave him an arch look. 'How on earth could you upset me? I don't even know you.' She fumbled in her bag and found her timetable.

'But you've just arrived and now you're leaving,' he persisted. It didn't sound as if he cared a bit. It was just an observation. Cathy flipped through her timetable, her nerves standing on end.

'It's upside down,' he commented.

'Thank you, I know that.'

An announcement filled the ground through the loudspeakers that were placed around the ground. The Australian team were apparently coming out. Cathy glanced up. The entire stadium was clapping. Out there, in the middle of the dazzling green scene, there were a group of white people bouncing out of the little pavilion and heading for the middle of the ground. It captured her attention for a moment, then she went back to her timetable. The applause died down.

'You're not really leaving, are you?'

Cathy slapped her timetable on her lap and turned to settle this matter once and for all.

'Look, whoever you are—'

'Nick.'

'Whatever. This has nothing to do with you. Please will you mind your own business?'

He shrugged at her as a response.

'Thank you.' She widened her eyes at him and went back to her timetable.

'I'm just surprised you'd come all this way and not even wait to see the first over.'

'You'd be amazed,' Cathy muttered.

'Obviously not a cricket fan, then.'

'Not at all,' she replied with great pride.

'That's a bloody shame. You've got a great seat and you don't even know it.'

'Absolutely. I'm a very sad case. But I can console myself with the knowledge that today I met an even sadder case than me.'

How dared he call her beefy? Now Cathy felt she could be as rude as she liked. The loudspeakers jumped into action. Cathy grudgingly peered up from the mystifying train information booklet on her lap. Two batsmen were being announced and were met not only with applause, but with rampant cheers from some parts of the ground. She squinted at the two white figures waving their bats around and homing in on the centre of the ground.

They took their positions, one at each wicket. Then the crowd suddenly rippled into life. Cathy leaned forward. A long, lanky man was racing towards the middle. The crowd accompanied his run with a call like a revving jet engine, that built up to a crescendo as he bowled the ball.

There was a clunking sound. The sharp sound of the ball on wood cut through the buzz of voices as the stumps flew into the air and were dispersed some-where behind the batsman on the grass. There was a stunned hush. Even the batsman seemed confused. He glanced behind him at the smatterings of what used to be the wicket, then turned and began to walk back slowly to the pavilion, pulling off his gloves and shaking his head. As he did, the lanky bowler was surrounded by the rest of the Australian team, who slapped him on the back and turned to face the replay screen in glee. Parts of the stadium were in uproar.

'Fuck,' came the fierce ejection from beside her.

Behind her she heard a breathless 'Shit' and an 'Oh my God' from the seats in front.

The Australian flags were hoisted high and swung with verve. Cathy bit her lip anxiously, infected by the sudden black cloud of despondency that had descended on her portion of the ground.

'That, in case you're wondering, is a bad thing,' came the tense voice of the man beside her.

'I guessed as much.'

'Stupid *bastard*!' he muttered under his breath. 'Still McGrath's bunny.' Cathy glanced at Action Man. He pulled a face of pure despair. 'He gets him every bloody time. I don't know if I can watch this.'

'Who was that?' Cathy mouthed.

'Atherton,' he gritted back and apparently decided not to discuss the matter further. He clamped his hands over his knees and set stony eyes on the pitch.

Cathy decided that maybe she'd sit still for a tiny bit longer. She thought she'd heard the announcer say Hussain was coming out next and, if she remembered rightly, that was the same guy with the narrow eyes she'd seen being interviewed on the telly. He looked crisp and fresh against the green. Like a little white cue ball rolling over an oversized snooker table. And she was starting to appreciate how good these seats were. As he took position in the middle, next to a set of stumps, she could see very clearly that he had an utterly gorgeous bum.

'That's—' she stopped herself in mid-question.

'Our best hope,' the voice beside her finished.

'I mean, that one's the captain,' she mumbled without looking round. 'It was a statement, not a question.'

'Oh, I see,' he replied opaquely. 'Thank you for informing me.'

'Anything you want to know, just ask,' Cathy retorted. She bit her lip again.

'No doubt you think he's got a nice bum,' Action Man said. She bristled at his tone. It wasn't friendly. It was patronising. She was going to deny it, but thought of a better option.

'Hmn.' She peered out over the pitch in concentration. 'Yes, it's not bad. Not an ounce of fat on him and he's so beautifully dark. I love dark men. Can't stand blond ones. All bleached eyelashes and pasty faces. Like little pink pigs.'

She went back to her timetable. The blond man next to her wasn't pasty, she'd noticed that much. In fact, his skin was an intriguing shade. Almost golden – she'd have thought that if she was being kind. But he was blond and he obviously had an ego like a solar system, and he'd got a kick out of insulting her for no reason. She was satisfied to note that he ran his hand over his hair: a man caught in the unconscious act of preening. It meant he was unsure of himself. Cathy was gratified.

She glanced up again as the bowler ran in to bowl for the second time. The Australians whooped. The English held their breath. There was a resounding 'tonk' as the ball hit the captain's bat. It flew through the air, was dived on by two fielders who both managed to miss it and shot out to the boundary rope.

84

The applause was deafening and followed by excited chatter. The ground buzzed like a hive.

'That's a good thing,' the man – what was his name again? Nick – informed her as he clapped. His eyes had taken on a sparkle.

'I know that,' she snapped back. And to make the point she grabbed back her piece of cardboard and waved it in the air.

Nick took it from her hands, turned it round and gave it back to her.

'That's four runs,' he informed her. 'It's only a six if it doesn't touch the ground before the boundary.'

'All right,' she said testily. 'I don't want a lecture.'

'I'd be the last person to offer you one,' he replied flatly. 'And I thought you were leaving.'

'I am,' she assured him. 'But I wasn't going to leave before the first over, was I?' She mocked him. 'And in fact I've sat through two overs, so now I can go.'

He examined her as if she were, as he'd originally thought, extremely stupid.

'That wasn't two overs. That was two balls. An over consists of six balls.'

'Well?' Another heat bubble emerged from Cathy's simmering pot.

'So,' he said steadily, 'if you were going to watch the over, you'd have to watch another four balls. That's all.'

'Well, I—' Cathy thought erratically. 'I'm only going to sit here until the person I'm meeting shows up. Overs have got nothing to do with it. Then I'm going.'

'You're going when the person you want to meet shows up?'

'No,' she said icily. 'I'm going as soon as I know he's not going to show up.'

'You're not confident he's actually here, are you?'

'Well.' She yanked on her St Christopher. 'Well, I just don't know.'

'You're quite sure you didn't take the wrong turning for Ascot?' Nick eyed her suit and heels with a glimmer of humour. He seemed happy with that put-down and turned back to face the pitch.

Another ball was bowled. The crowd whooped again. This time the ball didn't go so far and the batsmen ran backwards and forwards. Twice, Cathy counted. She picked up her card and waved it defiantly, with the '6' proffered outwards. Nick gave her a very blank look.

'What are you doing?'

'I'm waving my card.'

'Yes – but why?'

She put on a prissy face. 'Because, they've got six runs. Four and two others. That makes six.'

He shook his head at her.

'You only wave that thing if someone hits a straight six. And anyway, there were three runs.'

'There were two,' she contradicted him. 'I counted.'

'The ball was bowled wide. That's an extra run, but Hussain hit it and they ran two. They've got seven now.'

Cathy opened her mouth as she sought out the scoreboard and closed it again when she saw that the home side had a total of seven runs.

'Well, there you are. It just goes to show how stupid this game is. If they make it impossible for anybody to understand then it's no surprise that nobody likes it.'

She sat tensely, biting back her disappointment in Frank, as the full crowd sang and cheered. Perhaps it wouldn't be accurate to say that nobody liked the game. In fact, everybody at the ground seemed to be having a fantastic time.

Cathy felt her shoulders droop and allowed herself a moment of quiet, sad contemplation. She stared down into her lap at her timetable. Why had she been so utterly, miserably stupid as to show up today? She could have been at work, steaming on with her projects and following up things she had to do. She should have ignored Frank. Whoever he was, he was definitely a sadist. She was suspicious of him before, but now she had good reason to be very angry with him. He'd set her up and she felt stupid. She even allowed herself a private wobble of her lower lip.

'I came alone because I was meant to be meeting someone,' Nick said, giving her a strange look. Cathy wondered if he'd seen the lip wobble. 'I don't know where he is either, if that makes you feel any better.'

'Thank you,' she said in a tight voice without looking at him. 'It doesn't.'

'And McGrath's just bowled a no-ball, which gives us another run.'

'I don't really care.'

'I just thought you might have wondered why everybody cheered.'

'No, I didn't.'

'Suit yourself.'

Was that another dig at her finery? She squinted at him, but he seemed to be concentrating on the game.

There was another raucous cheer. She swivelled to counter Nick's comment before he'd even had a chance to make it. His lips had parted. She frowned at him thunderously.

'If you're about to explain that we've got seventeen and a half runs now due to the Silly Midriff taking a direct hit in the googlies and taking into account the perfect pitch and the long division of the tangent of the pavilion to the bat, then just forget it.'

He closed his mouth. His lips tightened, but she couldn't tell if it was in humour or annoyance. Then he turned away again.

Cathy fell silent, fingering her timetable, vaguely watching the activity out on the pitch. Intermittent loud cracks from the bats seemed to signify that a ball had been hit hard. The score crept up, the crowd roared with delight, while she sat, dazed, in her own world, the sun beating down on her, thinking hard.

Nick couldn't quite get to grips with what was going on. Beefy had never stated that the seats were together and he *had* said something along the lines of 'get there, I'll find you'. So he must have got himself a seat somewhere else and in a matter of time he'd arrive and introduce himself. But it was annoying not to know where Beefy was. Nick hated not being in control of a situation.

If Atherton hadn't gone first ball, perhaps he'd feel more generous. But right now Nick needed somebody to empathise with his frustration. He wanted to share the tenuous hope that Hussain and Trescothick were going to knock those smug smiles off the Ozzie faces. They looked as if they might. But all he had for company was the yellow woman.

For some reason he'd even started explaining the laws of the game to her. He, Nick, who never explained anything to anybody. But he felt a prick of pity for her. Somebody had stood her up, or at least put her in a situation where she didn't know what was going on. That wasn't fair.

There was a brief, insane moment when he'd thought she must be Beefy. After all, lots of people posted to the cricket group under nicknames. How was he to be sure Beefy wasn't a woman? He'd even felt really tickled by the idea that she might have been teasing him, but it had all fallen pretty flat.

She'd gone quiet for about an hour after her last outburst. He'd actually found her monologue funny, but he wasn't going to show her that. She seemed uncomfortable, shuffling stuff in her handbag and playing with a timetable. She wasn't his type of woman looks-wise, although he wasn't exactly sure what his type was. He spent his more amorous moments picturing women with perfect figures, young, nubile – and friendly. But he had to admit that the yellow woman had pretty eyes. Very pretty, in fact. Dark-blue and intense. And an appealing face. Her lower lip was soft and would have been very kissable if it weren't in such a defiant pout most of the time. And, of course, he couldn't help but notice that she had a full figure. Her hair was very distinctive. He could tell it was naturally red. It was too dark and strong to be a tint. That was all just an arm's-length impression. And that's where she'd stay, at arm's length.

So what he really needed to do, as soon as possible, was to work out what had happened to Beefy and set about finding him. In his holdall he'd still got the envelope that the ticket had arrived in. Beefy's letter was in there too. He zipped open the bag, found the envelope and pulled out the letter. He read it again.

*

'Excuse me?' Cathy pointed. 'Can I see that?'

'See what?' She noticed that Nick held something defensively to his chest, but she was indicating the magazine he'd put on the floor. He followed her finger. 'You want to look at *Wisden*?'

'If you don't mind. If I'm going to sit here and wait, I might as well have something to read.'

Nick handed it to her. 'It's a cricket magazine. If you don't like cricket I doubt you'll find it engrossing.'

'I'll look at the pretty pictures, then.' She gave him a short smile.

Cathy rubbed her nose and the sensitive skin around her breastbone. The temperature was rising steadily and the sun was blazing right at them. There wasn't any shade to be found in this stand. Peering down at her chest, she saw it was turning pink already. She hunched her jacket around herself to close the gap.

She flipped through the glossy pages without interest and glanced at her watch. It was time for a tea break, surely? Giving Frank one last attempt at goodwill, she imagined it might just be possible that he would come and find her at the first natural break. Whenever that was. Perhaps it was considered rude to walk about when the cricketers were playing? The stewards seemed to hold people back from the steps when batting was in progress.

'Excuse me?' she asked pleasantly. Nick looked fazed at another interruption. 'I just wondered when the tea break was?'

'They'll stop for lunch at one.'

'One?' She squinted at her watch. 'But that's—'

'Oh, *shot!*' Nick was on his feet, the whole crowd around her had risen and were applauding and whistling. She stood up too, ready to turn to Nick and ask him where people went for lunch. Anything that might give her a final chance to find Frank.

Nick was gazing into the air. Everybody's necks were craned. They were all like extras in *Armaggedon*.

She looked up too. A tiny speck was sailing above them, just a little black dot against a canvas of deep blue. Cathy's mouth dropped open. Was that the ball? God, it was high. No wonder they were all so amazed. She continued to stare as it seemed to hold its position in the sky, levitate for several seconds, then began to drop steadily.

'Crumbs,' she whispered.

It gained speed, plummeting downwards. Cathy blinked at the growing black dot. Was it her imagination, or did it seem to be directly overhead?

Time seemed to stand still. The ball grew in size.

'Catch!' somebody yelled from behind.

Cathy gaped. There was nowhere to dive to. Her bag was blocking her legs on the aisle side and Nick was in her way on the other. She could see that he was flinching, his hands rising above his head.

'Oh God!' Cathy squeaked, just managing to throw herself on to her seat and wave her arms above her head defensively before she was hit on her hand by something like a cannon ball. 'Argh!'

Cathy rolled off the seat, over her bag and on to the concrete aisle. She stuck her arm out in the air like a limp flag. Around her, she could hear a combination of gasps and cheers. She stuffed her head between her knees. Her finger felt like it had been attacked with a sledgehammer.

She was aware that a steward was crouching next to her. An older man in a straw hat touched her shoulder

91

tentatively and asked if she was all right. Then Cathy heard Nick's voice.

'Well, you can console yourself that Devon Malcolm couldn't have handled that catch any better.'

Cathy shot up her head and glared, her eyes bleary. 'It's not funny. Do something!' she gasped.

'No first aider's badge, I'm afraid.' Nick gave her an inappropriately playful look. 'Unless you want me to go and nut the bloke wot did it.'

Nick seemed to be a looming skyscraper with a blond balcony running round the top. Then he squatted down and his face crept closer to hers. He whispered to her.

'Smile. You're on Channel 4.'

'Piss off!' she hissed at him.

'My, you did hold back on your language earlier, didn't you?' But the smile he gave her was sudden and kind. In her agonised state she couldn't help noticing that it had shot him from bouncer to yowzer in two seconds. Then his lips straightened and he touched her arm gently.

'They're going to get the St John's Ambulance guys for you. Can you move it?'

'Move it?' she growled at him. 'Why the hell would I want to move it? It feels as if someone's tried to amputate it with a blunt saw.'

Nick tutted. She was gratified to see that he flinched a little when he saw the floppy state of her hand.

'Catching it would have been a better option. You'd have made a guest appearance on every Rory Bremner cricket video from now until eternity.'

She glowered at him, biting back hot tears of self-pity and shock.

'I thought the ball was made of rubber,' she blurted.

'I knew it was going to hurt, but not this much.'

'Rubber? Oh, you mean like those little power ball thingies?' Nick sucked in his cheeks as if he wanted to laugh.

'Don't laugh at me,' she instructed.

'Okay, I'm sorry.' He pouted. 'I'm glad it was you who copped it instead of me. A foot to the right and I'd have been lobotomised.'

'That might have been a good thing!' she bit back at him.

'Now, now. I take it you *are* left-handed?'

'No I'm –' Cathy stopped to screw up her face and flinch as another bolt of pain shot up her arm. 'I'm bloody not.'

Nick shook his head with some sympathy. 'You're a bit buggered, then, aren't you?'

Cathy felt her head spin, then focus again. She wasn't imagining it. There was a TV camera being thrust in her direction from a mobile cameraman.

'Who the hell are you?' she wheezed.

'Sky Sports,' Nick murmured in her ear.

She realised that Nick had now sat down next to her on the shallow stone step and had laid a hand very lightly on her shoulder. She stared straight into the lens of the camera.

'Frank, you bastard!' she issued. 'This is your bloody fault!'

'Sh.' Nick patted her arm. 'You're honoured. Sky usually only film women at cricket if they're not wearing bras.'

'That's very comforting to – to know.' Cathy's vision became extremely blurred.

'Is your left hand okay?' Nick's voice enquired softly.

'Yes. Just about.' She felt something being put into her left hand.

'Here. You can hold this, then.'

'What's that?' She closed one eye to focus on the cardboard scorecard.

'It was a six,' Nick whispered into her ear. 'It's okay to wave that now.'

Chapter Six

'What a bloody brilliant day!'

Barbara flinched as Barry crashed into the kitchen. She was putting the last sprinkles of freshly chopped parsley on to the shepherd's pie she'd made. She didn't fail to notice that Barry was carrying a Sainsbury's carrier bag and that the corner of a pizza box was sticking out of the top.

'Whoops, sorry, Barbara. Thought you were Frank.'

Barry pulled an apologetic face. At a mere five foot eight or so, with black hair and brown eyes that looked, on a first glimpse, warm and friendly, she might have mistaken him for a nice person. But his hair was dishevelled and, as he dumped the plastic bag carelessly on the floor next to the fridge, she heard the clunk of beer cans against the tiles. Without a doubt there was the scent of beer on his breath already and it was only eight o'clock.

She'd seen the car skid into the drive. Barry seemed to relish the opportunity to practise his emergency stops on the gravel. It was a little blue car tonight, bright, shiny and cheap-looking, with a low bonnet. It looked like something he'd found in a cereal packet. Barbara felt her heart sinking as she watched him pull carelessly on his tie and loosen the top buttons of his shirt. His skin was becoming chestnut-coloured from the sun and she could see a couple of dark hairs from

his chest as he yanked open his collar. It made her
recoil.

Barry grinned at her impishly.

'Did you watch it with Frank?'

'Did I watch *what* with Frank?'

She hacked at some celery and piled it into a bowl,
not wanting to look at him any more.

'Did you watch the *cricket* with Frank, Barbara? I
thought we'd had it when Athers was out first ball, but
what a fantastic recovery!'

Barry seemed to have missed the edge in her voice
completely. It was no doubt why Frank found him such
easy company. He was unchallenging, as empty vessels
normally were.

'No, Barry, I have been to work this afternoon. I have
also managed to come back, prepare a meal for you
both, sweep the drive, hoover the hall and remove all
your shaving clippings from the bathroom sink.'

'Great!' Barry pulled a can of beer from his bag and
flicked the ring-pull. He beamed at her. 'All this and
you don't even get paid for it. Frank's lucky to have
you as a pal. You're a star, Babs.' He winked at her.

She widened her eyes at him. She was not a woman
to be *winked* at. She wasn't one of his little tarts from the
Cowley road pubs, or the nightclubs, or wherever it
was he picked up his insignificant women.

'And I managed all of that, miraculously, without
needing the fortification of alcohol.' She cast a prim look
at Barry as he took a deep swig of his beer.

Barry raised his fine, dark eyebrows as if he was
impressed.

'It'd be more fun doing it when you were pissed,
though, wouldn't it?' He sniffed. 'I popped in to the

Philosopher and Firkin after work to watch the end of the day's play on their big screen. The atmosphere in there was amazing! I really think we might pull this one off. Two batsmen with tons to their names, in one day. Flipping amazing!' And he was off again in a free-flow of pure enthusiasm.

Could a person really be this dense? Even a man? Even a man called Barry? He seemed to have no idea whatsoever that she hated him and everything he represented.

'I'll go and take Frank a beer, then. I take it he's watching the Sky highlights?' Barry yanked a four-pack from the bag, looped his finger through the plastic and swung the cans.

'Frank is in his room, yes. But I think he'll be taking some time to work on his book this evening. He won't want any beer.'

'I'll ask him if he wants one. If he says no, I'll bugger off and sit in my bedroom. Okay?' Barry chortled. It seemed that he was laughing at her.

Barbara tensed. 'And' – her voice sounded brittle, but she had to make her point – 'the doctor has said that he's not to drink too much on his pills. That, at least, you might respect.'

Barry put up a hand. 'I respect that.'

Barbara pinched her lips together. He was a cocky little character. His voice was chirpy, his face was chirpy, even his body was chirpy. As he moved away, his neat bottom seemed to swing at her. She could envisage the 'Horny Boy' pants clinging to him.

'I've made a shepherd's pie,' she called after him.

'Great. We'll have that later. Whoops!' She heard him skidding down the hall on the Persian rug and hitting the walnut table with a dull thud. 'You've been polishing the floor again, haven't you?'

Another chortle. Didn't anything get him down? His head appeared around the kitchen door again. He grinned rakishly.

'It's hard to get used to.'

'Style always is,' she retorted coldly.

'Where I was brought up all the floors were lino. Easier to clean, see? And Penny insisted on wall-to-wall shag-pile, so I just used to walk around in my socks.'

'I can imagine you were the ideal husband.' Barbara wanted him to go away. Why did he insist on coming out with such inanities all the time? Didn't he understand the value of a thoughtful silence? She had no interest at all in his failed marriage, other than the fact that it had led him, at thirty-whatever-it-was, to be living a second adolescence in the back bedroom. She wished Penny had glued him to his damned shag-pile. It would have kept him away from her.

'Are you going to bother to eat the shepherd's pie, or can I assume it will go the same way as the lamb stew?'

He looked confused. 'What way?'

'Straight into the cat?' Barbara maintained an expression of calm enquiry.

'Oh.' Barry pulled a face. 'Sorry, it's just that we had some tea last night before we found the stew. But we did have some before bed. It was scrumptious.' He grinned and was gone again.

She heard him making his way down the hall carefully. At least he bothered to tap on Frank's door before erupting into the room with his beer twirled round his fingers.

The cat flap moved. Barbara swung round and

glared at it. Beefy's front paws appeared. He could sense she was there, she was sure. He had frozen with his ginger stumps on the doormat. Little by little, the flap was nudged upwards as Beefy edged himself delicately further into the kitchen.

'Don't – you—' Barbara crept back. The cat was getting its revenge. It was personal. It knew all about her fear of frogs. That could be the only reason . . .

Beefy's head slowly emerged, followed by his body. He slinked on to the doormat. Then, gently, he dropped the little brown frog he had been carefully carrying home in his mouth. It wriggled.

Barbara screamed and shot away. Down the hall, skidding on the mat and ricocheting from the walnut table, she found herself at the door to Frank's room. She burst inside, gripping at her chest.

'I – I —' she panted.

Frank was clutching the remote and showing something to Barry on video. He was nudging the picture forward frame by frame.

'What do you make of that, then?'

The picture was frozen on a shot of somebody lying on the ground with an arm in the air. All Barbara could make out was a yellow blur. Her pulse was firing like a machine-gun. Beefy could be taking the frog anywhere for her to find later.

'Frank!' she barked. 'That cat has brought in another of those things.'

The picture disappeared suddenly and the screen went black. Frank leaned round the wings of his armchair.

'Will you not creep up on me, woman? Do I get no privacy at all?'

'I didn't creep,' she said reasonably. 'I came in very

quickly. And if somebody doesn't make that frog disappear then I will make the cat disappear.'

Frank squinted at her. So he wasn't used to her having emotional outbursts, but maybe it would do him good to see that being upset was within her range. She was frequently upset. She just chose not to let him know about it.

'I'll deal with it. Don't you worry about it,' Barry said soothingly, getting up from the sofa. 'At least he doesn't eat them,' he added with a reassuring smile at her as he left the room.

Barbara stared at the back of Frank's armchair.

'I'll – I'll go now, then,' she told the chair.

Frank responded with a careless wave of his white hand.

'I want his address and I want it right now!'

Cathy gripped a pen in her left hand. Her index finger on her right hand was bound up in a thick bandage and the rest of that hand still felt numb. The phone was wedged under her chin. She lowered her voice. It wasn't ideal to make this call from work, but Cathy felt that it couldn't wait. 'Please, Melissa.'

'Oh, are you going to write to Frank after all?' Melissa sounded pleased. 'I do think that's the right thing to do.'

'Write to him?' Cathy said under her breath, ducking Mark's gaze as he strode past with his tie flapping over his shoulder. 'What would I write with? My nose? I told you, my finger's fractured. I have a cotton stump for a right hand. All I can manage with my left is a bit of spirograph. I've had to tell everybody at work I had an accident with a wallpaper brush. Nobody believes me.

Frank's completely buggered up everything for me and I am going to bloody well tell him so.'

'Cathy, I'm not sure—'

'You must be in a hurry to get to work, surely?' Cathy pushed. It was nearly a quarter to nine and Melissa would be about to leave the house. 'Just give me the address and you can get going.'

'Perhaps we should talk about it later?'

'The address,' Cathy demanded. 'Now.' Then, aware that she was snapping, she added a tense, 'please'.

'Well.' Melissa sighed. 'Well, all right.'

Cathy waited, tapping the pen on her desk and darting her eyes around the office to make sure nobody was watching her. The pen was difficult to control, even for impatient tapping purposes and flipped out of her hand. She scrambled to the floor and picked it up again.

'Have you got a pen?'

'Yes,' Cathy issued.

Melissa read out the address.

She had to repeat it five times so that Cathy could scrawl strange shapes with the pen. When she'd finished, it looked like a telepathy test.

'Thanks. And his surname?'

'It's – it's Harland.' Melissa sighed once more. 'Cathy? Do be careful, won't you?'

'Careful? Like, "Don't sit under falling cricket balls?" I can do that sort of careful.'

'No, I mean, just look after yourself, won't you, dear?'

Cathy was only half listening to Melissa. She prodded at the keyboard and ranged through her e-mail messages, wondering how long it was going to take her to reply to them with the wrong hand. She didn't want to hear Melissa's protestations any more. Her mother's role as mediator was over. From now on, Cathy was going to deal with Frank Harland direct. For the moment, Cathy was too infused with indignation to be gentle with Melissa, even though a nagging voice told her that Melissa and Brian might need to hear some reassurance from her. But Melissa had urged Cathy to respond to Frank's approach. Now she was going to do exactly that.

'Don't worry. He's the one who's going to need armour, not me.'

Cathy put the phone down quickly as Mark strode back again, casting her a glance. She smiled at him and fixed her eyes on her computer screen. After she was sure he had gone, she sat back in her swivel chair, heaved an unsteady breath and closed her eyes.

It had started to get worse yesterday, when she'd been dragged away by the St John's Ambulance man. She'd left a shoe on the aisle and had been hoiked out of the stadium limping like Quasimodo. She'd been sat in the mini-ambulance, where she'd been poked, prodded, sprayed and attacked with bandages. Then Nick had appeared and handed her the yellow shoe with the quip, 'Cinderella, I presume?'

She'd jammed her foot back into her shoe as elegantly as possible, given that her stockinged foot was black with dirt and wet around the sides from stepping in a pool of spilt beer.

Then they'd all decided she needed an X-ray.

Nick had got her bag and her cardboard scorecard and brandished them at her. It seemed he was determined to come with her. So the St John's people had agreed that they could take off in a taxi on their own, as she was nowhere near death. They gave her a couple of painkillers and off she went.

It was all a blur. The taxi shot around Birmingham; she arrived in a casualty department somewhere, but she had no idea where. She waited, was X-rayed, told to her horror that she'd suffered a slight fracture to the index finger, but that it wasn't serious and that sensation would come back soon. Then she was bound up and they stuck what looked like a condom over it to keep it dry.

When she'd returned to the waiting area from her ordeal, Nick had been there, tapping his rolled-up cricket magazine against his leg. Then a bizarre situation had ensued where he seemed to want to drive her back to London.

Cathy felt that he'd been quite kind enough and appreciated him waiting while she was analysed, but was absolutely not going to get into a strange car with a strange man and be whisked away. Especially a man who seemed to be finding the whole thing funny. She had a return ticket and the fact that she had a sausage roll for a finger on one hand didn't stop her getting a train. Besides which, there was nothing stopping Nick from going back to the ground to enjoy the rest of the day.

Nick insisted, then, on seeing her to the station. They got a taxi back to Birmingham New Street and she paid. That had turned out to be something of a fight as she and Nick both attempted to squash fivers into the taxi driver's hand.

After winning that struggle Cathy got out, muttered

a few words of gratitude at Nick and hobbled off in her yellow heels, clutching the cardboard scorecard, which Nick had insisted she should take as a souvenir. She'd never felt more humiliated in her life.

That was the end of her Edgbaston adventure.

By the time she'd got home, Cathy felt tired and dizzy and her feet were killing her. She'd got into the house, grabbed a glass of wine and tried to ring Jason at work. But she was told he'd been hauled away on a trip to Düsseldorf and was likely to be gone for several days. Cathy's heart had fallen even further at that news. He was usually so wonderful at taking care of her when she wasn't well. So she gave up and even though it was only late afternoon she'd taken a couple of painkillers and retreated to bed.

She'd woken up early the next morning and made her way straight in to work. Then she'd rung Melissa.

Cathy slipped Frank's details into her handbag and tried to fix her mind on the day's events. It wasn't easy. She was hurt that Jason had slipped off on another foreign trip without even telling her he was going to be away. It was Friday today and if Jason weren't abroad somewhere they would expect to spend the weekend together. Did he think she'd just assume from his absence that he was out of the country? He hadn't even left her a message. And they'd been planning to see a film that weekend. Cathy didn't want to see it with anyone else. She always loved the way Jason got so animated when he dissected the films they saw. They'd usually go for a drink afterwards, and Cathy would watch him, his brown eyes luminous with ideas, the thoughts tumbling from his lips. At some stage he'd take her hand and implore her to see his point. It always made her laugh. Then maybe they'd get a late meal out and a cab back to her house, his arm round her, her sleepy head on his chest . . .

Cathy interrupted her own line of thought. She'd been looking forward to the weekend, but it seemed that Jason had taken off without even thinking about it, and it was disappointing that he hadn't touched base with her before he'd left. How did he know that she was all right? Or even still alive? What if she'd been in an accident and was squashed somewhere on a motor-way? He'd never know. Or what if the ball had landed on her head and wiped her out, just like that? Would Jason think of the unexpected? How could he be so very sure that when he came back to see her each time she'd always be exactly the same Cathy that he'd so confidently left behind?

He couldn't know and he shouldn't be so sure of himself, Cathy decided, the hurt swelling in her heart. Trying to type e-mails with her left hand was making her more unhappy. In fact, when she added it all up, she realised that she and Jason hadn't spoken to each other for several days. In that time anything could have happened.

In fairness, anything could have happened to either of them, but at least she'd bothered to ring his work and find out that he'd taken off for Düsseldorf yesterday. Unless he was doing it in the back of a hearse the evidence was that he was alive.

Whereas *she* had a story to tell. The England captain had fractured her finger and if that wasn't worth a phone call, nothing bloody was.

*

'Blimey, this doesn't half look like you, Cathy.'

Cathy paused as she was halfway through reception on her way back to the lift with her takeaway lunch of a chicken tikka bap, a packet of crisps and some hot coffee from Dom's. Nita, the receptionist, was bent over the desk with Lionel, the doorman. They both seemed very engrossed.

'What's that?'

Nita held up the back page of the *Sun*. There was a picture of a woman in yellow, pulling an agonised face and holding up an arm. Fortunately the picture was very blurred. A small headline read, THIS MAIDEN IS BOWLED OVER!. Cathy stared at it in horror.

'You've got a suit just like that too,' Nita mused, taking a bite out of a sandwich. 'You've got a double.'

The *Sun*? The *SUN*?

'Must get back to work.' Cathy sped to the lift, her lunch gathered to her chest, her face burning.

'Still,' Lionel continued to Nita, 'it was a damned good shot. Watched it on the highlights. He's the man to win back the Ashes, that Hussain. You mark my words. And it looks like this match is in the bag for us. Doubt it'll run the full five days. I betcha it'll be over by Sunday.'

Cathy stabbed at the button again. Her own image plastered across a tabloid was branded into her retinas. As long as nobody else saw it.

'Hmn. He's nice-looking,' Nita's voice came. 'Says here he scored a hundred and seven. That's good, isn't it? If we're going to win, I suppose it might be worth watching.'

The lift arrived and Cathy dived into it. Her pulse steadied as she reached her floor, found her way back

106

to her desk and settled herself again. Frank bloody Harland. He had a great deal to answer for.

Her phone rang just as she was taking a bite of her bap. She picked it up, swallowing quickly. It was Bill Havers.

'Thanks so much for all the paperwork you've sent me. I was wondering when you'll be free for that trip to Walthamstow dogs. And hey, you should have a look at the back page of the *Sun* today. There's some gel who got whopped by a cricket ball. She's the spit of you. It'd make you laugh.'

Cathy's bap dangled limply from her good hand. She made an arrangement to meet up with Bill again, trying to sound cheerful, and rang off.

Fiona rolled herself round the corner of the cubicle on the wheels of her swivel chair.

Cathy glanced at her, unable to keep the unhappiness from her expression.

'You haven't been reading the *Sun* as well, have you?' she asked.

'Why would I do that?' Fiona pulled a face. 'Have you got a minute?' Cathy nodded. Fiona continued in hushed tones, 'Guess who's left with no notice and guess who's taken over his office?'

'No idea.' Cathy shook her head, still preoccupied with tabloid headlines.

'Gus Forester's out, of his own volition so rumour has it, and Lisa Spencer's in.' Fiona widened her eyes and flicked her blonde hair. 'Thought you were next in line for an office?'

'Oh.' Cathy felt her spirits flatten even further. A flicker of annoyance went through her body, but there was so much to think about at the moment. One thing she'd never done at work was rock the boat. It was an ethic Melissa and Brian had instilled into her. Effort will be rewarded, in time. But Cathy couldn't help feeling peeved.

'Why don't you ask Ruth what's going on?' Fiona quizzed, raising her eyebrows.

'I'd rather not.' Cathy frowned. She was hoping to hear back from Ruth on her suggestions for Hellier's at any time. It wouldn't be a good idea to march up to her and make a fuss about not getting an office.

'I think this has more to do with Mark's extra-curricular activities with Lisa than it has to do with merit.' Fiona's delicate face was unusually sombre. 'I just think you're really good at what you do, Cathy and it doesn't seem fair. Lisa's crap. She doesn't deserve an office all to herself.'

'Heck, it's only an office. There'll be another one along soon. I do a lot of work at home anyway. I've got lots of space in my study,' Cathy assured her, pushing back her hair from her warm face. She winced as her finger got caught up in it.

'Couldn't you get Jason to help you with the decorating?' Fiona eyed Cathy's bandaged finger sympathetically. 'He's a big strong bloke, isn't he?' She raised her eyebrows suggestively and Cathy couldn't help smiling. 'Okay,' Fiona admitted, 'you know I think Jason's gorgeous and I'm dead jealous. But things are going really well with David, so I promise I won't flirt with him. For now.'

Cathy was cajoled back into good humour by Fiona's eye roll. In fact, Fiona had never flirted with Jason, even in her single moments and despite the fact that Cathy knew she fancied him rotten. There was a mutual trust within their friendship that was very special. 'I wouldn't mind Jason doing my decorating . . .' Fiona teased on.

Cathy laughed aloud. 'Well, I wouldn't mind him doing mine either, but he'd have to be in the country first.'

'Away again?' Fiona looked sympathetic. 'I'm going to have words with that man. He mustn't neglect you. You two are great together.'

'When we *are* together.'

Cathy's phone rang. She wrinkled her nose at Fiona, who rolled away on her wheels. Cathy picked up the phone.

'Jason!' Cathy's spirits rose at the sound of his voice. Jason might have deserted her, but this could be a sign that he was on his way home. In which case, Cathy decided, she would forgive him anything. And she had so much to tell him. 'You won't believe what's been happening.'

'Sorry, Cathy, it's just a quick call.' Cathy could hear plenty of bustle in the background. She squashed the receiver to her ear. 'We're having a lunch break.'

'Oh,' Cathy said. 'Lots of meetings?'

'Loads. I'm stuck in Germany for the weekend. I've really got to be here – they all expect it. I don't think I'll make it back until the middle of next week. I just wanted to let you know in case you expected me tonight. I'm sorry about the film and everything. Is that okay?'

Cathy buried an inward sigh. No it wasn't okay, but there was bugger all she could do about it.

'I guess so.'

'I had a strange call from Paul as well. You remember Paul? We had dinner with him and his girlfriend Theresa that night in—?'

'I remember Paul,' Cathy cut in with bad humour, thinking of how she could have been killed by a cricket ball and Jason would never have known.

'He reckons he saw your picture on the back of the *Sun*.'

'He rang you just to tell you that?'

'No, he rang to tell me that he'd faxed over some things I needed, then added that.'

'Ah.' Cathy's head drooped.

'Did you go to Edgbaston after all, then?'

Cathy took her time to reply. Jason was so distant. He wasn't dashing back to see her this weekend. She was missing him horribly already. He didn't care. It made her feel churlish.

'Yes, Jason, I went,' she said sulkily.

'Oh, right. Was that picture really of you, then?'

'I'm afraid so.'

'Paul said there was some guy with his arm round you – not your grandfather I take it?' Jason gave a low laugh. But it was a subdued sound.

'No, that was someone else who was just there to help. Frank didn't even turn up.'

'Oh, he didn't?' Cathy could hear voices in the background. It sounded as if people were talking to him. 'Look, Cathy, I've got to go.'

'But I'm fine,' Cathy said testily. 'Despite my fractured finger, so don't you worry about me. I'll also get over the huge emotional upheaval of going to meet my grandfather and him not even being there. So don't you lose any sleep over that either.'

'Cathy? I've really got to go now.' Jason obviously hadn't heard a word she'd said. 'Everything all right with you?'

'Yes, fine. Why wouldn't it be?' Cathy swivelled on her chair, suffused with discontent.

'Look, I'm sorry but I'm only really touching base next week, then we've all got to go to Boston to do some things with the computer guys. I'm really sorry about this, but there's not much I can do. There's a lot of pressure on me to oversee this stuff personally. Damn, I must go. I'll try to talk to you again when I can.'

'Right. Well why don't you just wait for me to want to talk to you, Jason? That'd make a change, wouldn't it? 'Bye.'

Cathy put the receiver down first. Then she stared at the phone woefully. Jason was under pressure. He sounded tired and on edge. But she'd been too unhappy herself even to say 'take care'. All in all, everything was going wrong. That was fine. All she had to do now was buy up every copy of the *Sun* in England, throw a bag together and take herself to Oxford.

It was about time Frank Harland came face to face with the damage he'd done.

Nick punched off an e-mail to Beefy from work:

'Where were you, mate?'

He pulled at his tie and swung in his chair. He did a complete spin, his head back, watching the strip light overhead rotate, then stopped again. He added:

'Sorry I didn't catch you. Maybe you tried to find me around lunchtime? I had to take some woman to hospital who'd got hit by the ball. Maybe you saw it? Oh, how I laughed. I wasn't back in the ground till about three. Hoped you might appear later. Lemme know what happened. I owe you for the ticket. You'll need to send me an address. Great day, wasn't it? It was such a damned relief to get away from this shitty job and the cricket couldn't have been better. Thanks again for the ticket.'

Nick sent it off, closed the e-mail screen and pondered the match again. His thoughts flew back to the yellow woman. Cathy, she'd said her name was. She had an attitude on her. He'd taken great pleasure in knocking her down a bit. But she'd been fun to be around too. She was unusual. Different from the women he usually met.

Nick stuck his Bic into his mouth and chewed on the pen top. He spun round again. One of the advantages of being the sole IT manager in this poxy company was that he got a room all to himself. The other advantage was that nobody else knew diddly squat about computing. That meant he could roar at them from his chair as they ventured their heads round his door and, most of the time, they went away again. All he had to say was 'I'm in the middle of something really complicated. Do you mind?' complete with a cold stare and they quaked. That meant he could get back to following the test match.

It was sobering to be nearly thirty and to find that what he loved and what he did for a living weren't in any way related. All Nick could do was sneak a tiny TV programme on to his computer to give him a boost at work. Sometimes he wished with every fibre of his being that he'd thrown himself into cricket at school. He'd been good, then. A medium-fast bowler and a hefty bat. Maybe, if he'd trained really hard, he'd have been good enough for the county trials and maybe he might have been picked. And possibly, in his dreams, he might have played for England one day. Then, when he'd retired from playing he could have been a commentator, like Jonathon Agnew, or Mark Nicholas. Now that was the life, spending your life following matches. Nick heaved a sigh.

Or perhaps if he'd trained in a different area of technology he could have become a Sky Sports cameraman. He'd get to go to all the games and follow every ball avidly. That'd be a job to die for. Nick went off into a reverie, sucking on his biro. The pen top flew into his mouth and hit his palette. He jumped to his feet and spat the pen out. It ricocheted off the computer screen.

'Ugh.'

Sandra appeared in the doorway. She was in a very short skirt today and beneath the white blouse was the very obvious outline of a black bra. Her hair, dry through constant efforts to bleach it, was nipped back. It actually looked nicer than usual. She was probably forty, divorced and alone from what Nick could make out. She made no attempt to hide the fact that she appreciated male attention. She quirked an eyebrow, indicating some papers she was holding.

'Delivery. Downstairs. About six thousand boxes of computer equipment blocking reception. Here's the paperwork.'

Nick gave her a thunderous look. 'Don't people realise I'm programming up here?'

'If they do, they don't seem to care. Tough life, isn't it?'

Sandra walked in and dropped the papers on to his desk. Her eyes caught the computer screen and, more specifically, the little box in the corner where he'd fixed up a TV link. She tutted.

'Really tough.'

113

'I'm testing a program.' Nick gave Sandra a hapless shrug. 'How else am I meant to test it?'

'I wouldn't know.' She stalked away. 'My little girly brain wouldn't be able to understand even if you explained it.'

Nick put out his hands in appeal. Just because he'd once said that women and computing didn't mix.

'Are you harking back to that comment again?'

'What comment?' Sandra stopped in the doorway and gave him a Lauren Bacall look.

'That thing I said in the pub at Reg's birthday drinks.'

'Oh, the women-are-thick comment?'

Nick chuckled, twiddling his biro between his fingers. 'Now you know that's not what I said.'

'Oh, no, you're right. It was that women were too thick to use computers. Quite different. Silly me.'

'Sandra, I was only saying that I thought men and women had different strengths. You drew the rest of the conclusions yourself. And' – he raised an eyebrow at Sandra – 'I'm entitled to my opinion.'

'Yes, but the problem is, Nick, you think everyone else is entitled to it too.' She smiled sweetly.

He laughed. It was difficult not to laugh when Sandra was so good at bantering.

'Well, what can I do? I know what all the women here say about me.'

'You think you know that?' Sandra pushed her tongue into her cheek. 'You *are* sure of yourself, aren't you?'

Nick felt a moment of doubt. He blinked at Sandra.

'Let me guess. They think I'm a grouchy, miserable old git who doesn't go on the pub outings. I don't join in the fun as much as I should, but that's because these buggers make me work long hours.'

'Well, I'm not sure grouchy and miserable is spot on, but the general opinion is that you're in need of some light relief.'

'Light relief?' Nick queried, colour rising in his cheeks. He wasn't sure if he needed that clarified or not.

'Oh yes.' Sandra shot a look at Nick's thick arms, visible as he'd rolled up his thin cotton shirtsleeves. 'What you need is a damned good—'

'Thank you, Sandra,' Nick interrupted quickly.

'Big boy like you. Isn't right that you should be alone,' Sandra almost whispered.

Nick turned his attention back to the computer quickly. He enjoyed parrying with Sandra, even flirting with her, but he didn't intend to do anything about it.

'Downstairs. Boxes. Reception. Move.' Sandra gave Nick a short smile. 'Before Ernie fires you. And don't be such a wimp about it. It's not as if you're a seven-stone weakling, is it?'

Sandra looked him up and down – all six foot three of him – and met his eyes obliquely. Then she disappeared down the corridor.

Nick flicked the biro from hand to hand, then threw it at the waste-paper bin. It clanked off the side and rolled across the floor. He checked the screen once more for the cricket score, then strode from the room.

Chapter Seven

Driving to Oxford was not an option. Cathy had sold her car to contribute to the down payment on the house. It had been a priorities thing at the time. Nearly all her work was local, in easy travelling distance by tube or bus. When she was straight, she was planning to buy another car, but for now it meant public transport.

She'd get a train. That was simplest. That way she could pick up a taxi the other end and be dropped right at the door.

Right at the door.

Cathy paused at the threshold of her house with her big leather bag stuffed full of some things in case she needed them – a bottle of Coke, magazine, make-up bag, hairbrush, throw-over cotton sweater just in case it got really chilly, change of shoes, Aftersun for the stinging chest, Frank's letter and the half-ticket she had left and *The Beach*. She'd owned it for three years and she had to read it some time.

Mr and Mrs Ali were bundling the little Alis into the car as she passed. She waved her bandage at Mrs Ali. Mrs Ali gave her a broad smile and said, 'Oh hello!'

That was what other people did. They had families and on Saturdays they got into cars and went some-where. They got stuck in traffic jams, got cross in packed supermarkets, shouted at the children, shouted at each other and all came home crying. It was normal.

As she paced the pavement out towards Hoe Street and onwards to the tube station, Cathy wondered for a moment why she didn't do normal things too. But it was difficult to envisage a normal family life when your boyfriend was hardly ever in the same country. Didn't Jason ever think about where they stood and what they might do next? Why did Cathy feel as if she was the only one who bothered to ponder such things?

She loved spending time on her own. Like Jason, Cathy needed her own space to refuel, to think, to be creative, to follow up ideas from work, to come up with new ones. But was it completely impossible to do that in the same house as somebody else? Especially a house which, although it was little, had three bedrooms? If that was too claustrophobic for Jason, couldn't he build himself a shed in the garden and go and sit out there? As it was, when they did see each other Jason was only on flying visits. He had none of his own things around him. She couldn't really say to him, 'Okay, I've got to go off and do some work in the study for four hours now. You just amuse yourself gazing at my fixtures and fittings.'

On the other hand, at least Jason had fun in her kitchen. He'd sort of annexed it. If Cathy so much as moved the cheese grater a millimetre to the right, or used up a clove of garlic when he wasn't there, Jason noticed. He brought wonderful delicacies back from his trips and had a great time working out what to do with them. It was always a treat for Cathy to be presented with one of his gourmet meals. And that did mean that as long as he was concocting something in the kitchen they both gained a bit of space without having to be fifteen miles apart.

But *today* . . . Well, today Cathy would have liked Jason to have been with her, in some form, as she made her way to her grandfather's house. She was sure that she wouldn't have felt quite so rattled with her boyfriend by her side.

But on the other hand, perhaps this was something she was always going to have to do alone.

It was a sweltering train journey from Paddington. Cathy got stuck in a seat on the sunny side of the carriage and was barbecued all the way there. There were warm gusts blowing in from the tiny windows, but it was still too hot in jeans and a loose white sleeveless top. It was a tiny train, with short chippolata carriages, and full. Apparently every foreign tourist in the world had chosen today to nip off to Oxford for a bit of sightseeing. There was a constant babble of conversation, which ensured that neither the magazine nor *The Beach* got opened. Cathy stared at the gaping green fields and bushy hedgerows instead, until she got off at Oxford and followed a caterpillar of people over a bridge and into the station.

It was a small station with a strong smell of stewed coffee wafting over from a sandwich bar. Cathy paused to think, rubbing at her neck, her sunburned chest and her hair.

It was funny that when she'd arrived in Birmingham, her nerves jumping at the thought of seeing Frank, dolled up in her suit and heels with perfect make-up, she'd really cared that her grandfather's first impressions of her should be good. Now, she didn't care. She wasn't trying to impress him. He'd stood her up and she'd had a disastrous day, thanks to him. Frank would have to take her for who she was. No frills. No fancy bits. Even so, Cathy dived into the loo and brushed her hair.

Peering at the mirror, she could see little beads of sweat on her face. She dabbed them away. Then, abandoning all hope of glamour, stuck her condom-covered finger out of the way and splashed her face with the lukewarm water that came out of the cold tap. Her eyes blinked back at her like starfish. The thick hair round her neck was making her feel hotter. In a defiant gesture she scrabbled around in her make-up bag until she found a broad hairclip, gathered her hair up in a bundle behind her head and snapped it into place. Now she felt cool. She didn't look cool, but she no longer cared.

Outside the station was a set of wide steps and beyond she could see a taxi rank. There was a small queue. Cathy joined it.

While waiting, she found the piece of paper where she'd written down Frank's address with her left hand. She squinted at it, turned it round a few times and finally made out some words. The Woodstock Road. She had no idea at all whether that was close or not, but the postcode was OX2, which might suggest it was fairly near the town centre.

As for Oxford itself, she'd never been and she didn't have any real interest in it. While the Japanese tourists directly in front of her in the taxi queue were clutching guidebooks and pulling faces at each other, Cathy felt completely unmoved. Even when they fell into the next black taxi with such enthusiasm that one of them got his camera caught on the door handle she remained calm.

Then it was her turn and when she read out the address to the taxi driver he merely nodded and waited while she climbed in the back.

Well, what did she expect him to do? Turn round and in a thick West Country accent declare, 'You don't want to be going there, my pretty. People goes there and they never comes out again.' Or, 'Frank Harland's house? He's a laugh, that man. Love him, we all do.' Or, 'I knew it! The minute I laid eyes on you, I thought, "Frank's granddaughter. Has to be." Chip off the old block.' And in any case, her driver's accent was more likely to be Gujarati. So Cathy sat still in the back, feeling like a pork pie on a conveyor belt being yanked further and further towards the bit where the plastic exploded from a machine and suffocated it to death and spoke not a word.

When the taxi drew to a halt in a wide, leafy road which looked as if it must be rather expensive and wasn't ten minutes' drive from the station, she sat, superglued to the back seat.

The driver pulled open the dividing window.

'This is where you wanted, no?'

'No.' She swallowed.

'No?'

'I mean, yes. Sorry.' Cathy sat, paralysed. The driver waited.

'You want to get out, no?'

'No.'

Her driver turned round to implore her with soulful brown eyes.

'Please, will you pay me? Today is a busy day. I can make some good money if you get out.' He put a little emphasis on 'get out', but he'd done it very politely.

'Yes, sorry.'

Cathy scrambled out of the taxi. She paid him, adding a pound's tip out of sympathy and he shot away. She was left standing on a pavement, surrounded by lofty evergreen and deciduous trees, with a thick scent of mown grass settling over her like dew. Peering furtively around, she could see that there were a number of huge, craggy buildings. They were all set back from the road. There was a bed and breakfast, one had a sign outside proclaiming a language school, most of the houses looked as if they had been converted into something. Between some of the thickets and bushes were tantalising glimpses of the driveways of residential properties.

Cathy took a deep breath. She wandered along the pavement, ignoring for a moment that she had been set down outside Frank's house. Further up there were house names peering from rhododendron clumps, from under conifers, or not visible at all. It was a busy road, near the town centre (probably walking distance, in fact) and yet it was green, peaceful and spacious. In short, she could tell instantly that these houses cost a bomb.

Bracing herself, she hoiked her bag on to her shoulder, turned on her heel and walked briskly back to Frank's house. The front was hidden from the road by a dense row of conifers. A gap in them showed a curve into a wide gravel drive. The house had a number, not a name, and it tallied with the one Melissa had given her.

So all Cathy had to do now was march confidently up the drive and throw a brick through the window to announce her arrival.

*

Barbara was in the dining room. Papers were in neat, segregated piles in front of her, at far left the most recent research notes from the British Library yet to be incorporated. Next, her own research notes from the Bodleian. To the right of that, half-drafted letters to a number of publishers, seeking permission to quote from their works. Next, a copy of a letter from Frank to a fellow academic assassinating his theories. The extremely insulting reply was balanced on top. Far right, letters from Frank's publisher politely requesting some feedback on the current progress of *Alfred*. Barbara added the letter she'd opened this morning to that pile.

She settled herself in the dining chair. The dining room was the best room to work in now. Frank never entertained, not any more. Frank's room, where his books were ranged around him, had gradually turned into an entertainment centre. First he'd bought a powerful computer with an Internet connection when he realised that the other academics were out there debating hot issues in cyberspace, though from what Barbara could see, ever since he'd discovered the Internet he seemed to use his computer to talk about anything other than Anglo-Saxon history.

As Frank's heart condition had got worse, he'd started to focus his daily activities on that one room. He'd bought a bigger television, then he'd got himself hooked up to cable. For the cricket, obviously. She couldn't quibble with that, having orbited this passion for all her adult life. But all his paraphernalia was there, dotted around his armchair, all contained safely within a world that was becoming smaller.

It was something Barbara had seen in her father

before he died. A spreading house had imploded around him until he'd actually had his bed in the living room and only ever left it to use the toilet. She'd seen a progression in Frank. In the time she'd known him he'd gone from a flat, to a small house, to a large house and now he seemed to be reverting gradually to a bedsit. But at least he still defiantly used his bedroom. She wasn't sure how she was going to feel once he retreated into a few square feet of space.

Laughter and hoots throbbed through the adjoining wall. Barbara stared at the silky beige bands on the wallpaper, at the framed etchings on the wall. What was going on? From the duet of cackles she could guess that England were doing well. An involuntary smile tugged at the corners of her mouth. She could picture it. The tournament being fought out to the bitter end. They came out in their armour, they faced the assault, they won the day. In her mind cricket was infused with the jousting tournaments of medieval literature. Where else did a woman look for a brave knight in the modern world? When she got home, she'd catch up on the score.

The doorbell chimed.

Barbara edged back her chair. If Barry flew out there to answer it she'd know he was expecting more of his skinny friends. Not a crowd of men in there all howling in response to every shot, please. She prayed silently that she wasn't going to have that inflicted on her while she tried to work.

Frank and Barry yelled again. She could hear Barry laughing. Frank went into one of his long coughing fits. They didn't seem to have heard the door.

Barbara tutted and made her way out to the hall. It

was mercifully cool and dark, the sun throwing its strong waves at the back of the house. There was a muted shape beyond the coloured panes in the leaded glass. She opened the door.

A young, short woman stood there, in jeans, with a clean, pleasant face. Her hair was very red and scraped back unpretentiously. Barbara would have smiled, only she didn't smile very often any more.

'I – excuse me.' The woman cleared her throat and took her bag from one shoulder and moved it to the other.

'Yes?'

'Is this Frank Harland's house?'

'Yes.' Barbara stiffened slightly. What did she want?

'It is?'

'Yes.'

The young woman seemed to fidget a lot. She put her bag down, picked it up again, hunched her shoulders, straightened them, then fixed Barbara with a blue-eyed stare.

'Can I see him, please?'

Something in the tone put Barbara on her guard. It was direct, strong, assertive. And the eyes were very intense. Her goodwill faded.

'I'm afraid he's busy at the moment. Can I take a message?'

'He is actually here? At the moment?'

Barbara's stiffening turned into rigor mortis. Something was whispering to her that this woman was an intrusion. Perhaps a student. Perhaps an academic groupie. He'd had one or two in the past. But this girl seemed too agitated to be a groupie. Barbara raised herself to her full height. It diminished the girl even more.

'May I ask who you are?'

'Who are you?' the other responded simply.

Barbara bristled. 'If you don't mind, *you* are the stranger at the door.'

'Oh, yes. Of course. I don't mean to be rude.' The young woman let out a long breath and rubbed at her face. 'I'm sorry. I'm his granddaughter.'

The crows cawed in the trees. The young woman's knot of red hair and invasive eyes blazed at her.

'I'm sorry,' the voice came again firmly. 'I said, I'm his granddaughter. May I see him, please?'

Barbara stared.

She was face to face with her nemesis.

In fairness, Cathy reasoned, it was a bit of a shock statement to make on someone's doorstep after twenty-eight years. But she was surprised when the woman who'd answered the door fainted clean away. She fell to the ground in an artistic heap of blouse, skirt and sensible shoes, and lay there looking white.

'Oh dear,' Cathy uttered under her breath, crossed the threshold to stand on the hard wooden floor of the hall and squatted down to pat the woman's shallow cheeks. 'Hello? Are you in there?'

The eyelids twitched. The brown eyelashes, devoid of mascara, fluttered open and a pair of pale-grey irises looked back at her.

'Thank God for that!' Cathy breathed, getting on to her knees so that she could prop this person into a sitting position. 'You gave me a hell of a shock.'

'I gave *you*—' The woman puffed as if she'd just run for a bus. She struggled as Cathy's hands held on to her elbows for support. 'I'm perfectly all right. There's no need to make such a circus out of it.'

'No. Well.'

Cathy stood up slowly and allowed the older woman to do the same in her own time. She patted at wings of greying hair around her head and fussed with her blouse. There wasn't a speck of dust on it. Whoever did the hoovering around here was very good at it. Now that the woman was on her feet again Cathy felt tiny. The older woman wasn't exactly a giant, but she was tall and straight with firm cheekbones. Cathy watched curiously as she wobbled a little and held on to a small table to steady herself. Then she took a deep breath and stood stiff and upright, as if nothing had happened.

There was a long pause. Cathy waited, biting her lip. It was an airy, cool hall, with several doors leading away from it. To the right, it seemed to run into a corridor. She could hear the muted sound of men's voices from somewhere.

'I – it sounds as if my grandfather's got company,' Cathy ventured as politely as possible.

The woman stared back. Her hands flapped around her sides, over her blouse, rearranged her waistband. It was as if she didn't know what to do.

'I'm sorry I gave you a shock,' Cathy continued vaguely. 'Are you Frank's wife?'

A strange look came over the woman's face.

'No. Indeed I'm not.'

'Oh. I'm sorry. Nobody said anything about a wife. I hadn't really thought about it, but when I saw you—'

'Professor Harland is not married,' the woman barked at her.

Cathy cleared her throat. She could still hear noises and a sudden shout of laughter. It sounded like a young man's voice. They were obviously oblivious to her arrival, anyway. She could stand in the hall with the incredible fainting woman all day, but it wasn't what she'd come for.

However, it was like getting past Cerberus to hold a conference with Hades.

'I'm Cathy.' She shifted her bag on her shoulder and put out her hand.

'Yes,' the woman said, looking startled.

'And you are—?'

'Look, I'm sorry to have wasted your time, but it's quite impossible. I will tell the Professor that you called and no doubt he can write to you if he wishes. I'm sure he won't—'

The door directly ahead flew open, causing the woman to jump in the air. A man rushed out who bore more than a passing resemblance to Gary Lineker. He was in a T-shirt, baggy shorts, bare legs and trainers. He screeched to a halt, a dented empty beer can in one hand. Cathy's spirits cautiously nosed upwards. His eyes were smiling. He looked unlikely to faint at her arrival. He was too robust, albeit in a diminutive way. He looked straight at her and grinned.

'Hello!'

She allowed herself to smile back. The woman reached round and slammed the door shut behind him.

'Please, Barry. Doors.'

'Right. I'm just getting a refill.' He looked at Cathy quizzically. 'Are you staying? Want one?'

'Barry!' Barbara yelled, taking them both by surprise. Barry blinked black eyelashes from one woman to the other.

'Okay, Barbara,' he said with comically pursed lips.

'I'll just disappear.' He swung away down the corridor and out of sight.

Cathy heard a fridge door opening. She gave the woman called Barbara a square look.

'If you don't mind Mrs – Barbara – I've come all the way from London. Do you think you could possibly tell Frank that I'm here?'

Barbara stared for a moment longer. There was no doubt now in Cathy's mind that what was radiating from her was raw hostility.

'Please?' she added, her voice breaking into a plea.

'Wait here!'

Barbara puckered her lips, then slid into the room that Barry had come out of. She shut the door firmly behind her. Cathy let out a long breath. What was that all about? Barry seemed to be hiding in the kitchen. She could hear him singing.

The sound of raised voices issued from behind the door. A man was shouting. Barbara's voice sailed back in, she assumed, a series of retorts. She couldn't grasp what they were saying. Her nerves, which had steadied when Barbara had hit the floor, woke up again and jangled around.

Barry's head appeared round the corner. She couldn't help smiling at him again. He was brown all over, like a compact, shiny chestnut.

'What's a nice girl like you doing in a place like this?'

And who would he be? A friend? Barbara's son? A nephew or great-nephew? Could he even be a relative?

'Who are you?' she hissed at him.

'I'm the lodger,' he hissed back. 'Who are you? You look vaguely familiar.'

'Oh.' Not a relative. That was a shame. He looked

like he'd be a fun one to have. 'I'm the granddaughter,' she said and wanted to laugh.

'Oh fuck,' he said, his eyebrows shooting up his forehead. 'Oh double fuck. I'm going to go upstairs and hide under the bed.' He disappeared.

She was just wondering whether he really meant it when the door ahead opened and Barbara came out, smoothing her hands over her skirt.

'He'll see you,' she said curtly and marched away to another door further down the corridor, opened it, went inside and slammed it shut.

'Well hoo-bloody-ray,' Cathy whispered under her breath, staring after Barbara in confusion.

But now she was left with the deed itself.

Cathy inched towards the door. It was ajar and she stuck her nose tentatively through the gap.

The room was darkened, apart from a huge television screen at one end belting out colour. It was showing cricket. There was a sofa stretching under a window where the thick curtains were pulled. Further up the curtains lengthened to the floor, probably concealing french doors. She could dimly make out a lot of books on the walls and there was an armchair, its back to her. She could see a hand on the arm.

Cathy took a deep breath. She stepped into the room and nudged the door closed behind her. The hand didn't move. So he obviously wasn't going to jump up and greet her. She could always hope the shock of her arrival had killed him.

But as her eyes adjusted to the light she realised the hand was very pale and thin. He was definitely old. How old she still didn't know. She stood still, breathing softly. It was a very strange feeling. For the first time in her entire life she was in the presence of somebody she was related to. Her own grandfather. Cathy swallowed.

'Are you here?' A thin voice drifted over the back of the chair. It was a cultured voice, but weak.

She cleared her throat. The commentary to the cricket was snapped off, leaving only the picture blazing. The room was eerily quiet.

'Come here, woman! I can't see you!' he shouted suddenly.

Cathy pursed her lips. The sudden volume provided just the spark her box of fireworks needed. To think that looking at that pale little hand had almost made her feel profound about their meeting. She dumped her bag on the floor and strode across the room, swivelling as she reached the TV set to make sure she completely blocked the screen. Then she faced Frank with her hands on her hips.

'Don't talk to me in that tone of voice. Who do you think you are?'

'Aha! There you are.'

He seemed undaunted by her blast.

Cathy saw a small, thin creature with a blanket over his knees despite the heat. His hair was white and soft, wafting randomly about his head like candy floss. In the half-light his eyes were bright. Cathy had wondered if she would see some striking physical ressemblance. A shock of red hair, perhaps. The same ears, nose, or mouth. But as her grandfather scrutinised her, a long finger probing his chin as if it helped him think, he looked just like Digory's Mad Uncle Andrew. Terrific, she thought.

'I've got some things to say to you,' she declared before she could lose her nerve. Her feelings were swaying dramatically.

'Ah yes, I thought you might have.' He wriggled in his chair with pleasure, as if he were settling down to an omnibus of the *Antiques Roadshow*. 'Please, be my guest.'

'You—' Cathy stopped to take a fortifying breath. 'You've got a bloody nerve. All this time I've survived without even knowing you exist. Then you appear like a bloody genie. You demand attention and ignore Melissa when she tells you I want to be left alone. If that isn't boorish enough, you send me up to Birmingham, of all places, on my own in the expectation of meeting you.'

'Go on.' Frank blinked back at Cathy. He offered no defence. Cathy cleared her throat emotionally and continued.

'You stood me up. I had a horrible day and it was a damned cruel and insensitive thing to do.'

Frank peered at her. He rubbed his hands together.

'Did you enjoy the cricket?'

Cathy glared back.

'What?'

'The cricket. If you take all your misfortunes out of the equation, did you or did you not enjoy the cricket?'

Frank pulled back in his chair, even his slippered feet seemed to pull away from her, like a mischievous child who'd just confessed to putting the mouse in the teacher's lunch box.

'Did I – what?' she spluttered, dazed.

'Both Hussain and Vaughan got centuries. We hammered them. They'll never catch up now.' Then he giggled and put a hand over his mouth. He watched her, his eyes lively.

Cathy shifted from foot to foot, placing one hand, then the other on her hip. She wasn't sure what she'd expected. To make her point and then storm away, perhaps. Or, if Frank was more robust, a bit of a row and then to storm away. But he seemed so unmoved by her seething emotions that she was completely thrown.

'You mean, you're choosing to ignore absolutely everything I've just said to you?'

'Well, sort of.' Frank pulled his blanket up to his chest. 'Or rather, yes.' He ducked under his blanket. He peered over the edge. Then he tossed the blanket back to his lap. 'Oh, come on, woman. It was a day in a million. All that drama. I saw you on the highlights. You're not telling me you're ever going to forget it.'

Cathy's jaw dropped.

'You saw that?' She was confounded. Frank hadn't turned up to meet her, but he'd seen her on the television? Stunned, Cathy managed to iterate, 'How did you know it was me?'

'Photographs,' Frank said. 'Melissa sent me photographs of you. Last one was your graduation, granted, but you haven't changed much and it was the right part of the ground. It was most definitely you.' He nodded at her bandaged finger and pulled a rueful face. 'That wasn't my fault, though.'

Cathy expelled a long breath. Another followed. She paced backwards and forwards in front of the television, not failing to notice that Frank ducked his head to one side to check the score. She planted herself full in front of the screen again.

'How *dare* you?'

'I dare.' Frank pulled a strange face at her.

'I'll have you know that my picture was in the *Sun* because of that bloody ball.'

'That can be the only justifiable reason for appearing in the *Sun*. If you'd been featured in that rag for any other reason I'd have disowned you.' Frank contorted his face in thought. 'But the circumstances are mitigating.'

'What – what sort of creature are you?' Cathy's breathing became shallow. She was torn between bursting into tears of frustration and yelling at Frank. He seemed completely incapable of reacting to her dismay. 'You deliberately led me to believe that you wanted to meet up with me at this cricket match. Didn't it occur to you that I'd be hurt? Or confused? Or even angry? Didn't it even enter your selfish head that I might not want to sit at a cricket match on my own all day? On a working day, for that matter?' She added in an aside, 'Not that you'd be interested in what I actually do.'

Frank thought about it, his finger poking his cheek.

'Yes, all those things crossed my mind. But I assumed you'd be fascinated by the experience and come here and tell me all about it afterwards. Which, if I'm not mistaken' – Frank raised his white eyebrows ironically – 'is what you're doing.'

'And that's what you wanted?' Cathy rubbed her head, hoping everything was suddenly going to make sense. 'For me to come here and tell you what happened?'

'Yes!' Frank splayed out a hand. 'By Jove, I think she's got it.'

133

'I don't understand.' Cathy was annoyed to hear the emotion choking her voice.

'Oh, sit down, you must be tired after a long journey,' Frank exclaimed.

Cathy frowned down at the strange figure, twisted in his chair. She had no idea at all how to handle him. Any expectations she'd had of what her grandfather might be like were completely shot to pieces.

'I don't want to sit down.'

'Please? You're blocking my view. I can't see the score.'

Cathy stared at Frank in despair for several moments. Then she drifted over to a lengthy sofa under the curtained windows and sat on it. She continued to stare at him.

'You had no right to make any assumptions about me,' she told him, recovering a firmness to her tone. 'You don't know anything about me at all.'

'You are very much as I'd expected.' Frank scratched at his mop of white hair. 'You look like your mother, but I knew that anyway. There's more Harland in your spirit than I'd anticipated.' He tutted and seemed to lapse into thought. 'That could make things tricky, but it can be overcome.'

Cathy took a deep, tremulous breath. When she spoke again she was annoyed to hear that her voice shook.

'Please don't ever mention my mother in that cavalier fashion again.'

There was a long silence. Frank played with the edge of his blanket. Then he peered at Cathy thoughtfully.

'Quite right. That was out of order.'

The silence continued. Cathy looked down at her

hands and fiddled with the rubber sheath protecting her bandaged finger. She didn't want to yell just at the moment. It was all too surreal and the sudden mention of her blood mother had knocked her sideways.

Frank cleared his throat.

'I haven't offered you tea. I've been rude. I'll arrange things.' She glanced up in time to see Frank throw back his head and yell, '*Barbara*! Damn that woman. Don't tell me she's gone home in a huff. *Barbara!*'

'It's all right, really,' Cathy insisted, astonished at her grandfather's insistent yell. Surely he didn't usually use that tone to Barbara?

'Where is she?' Frank muttered, raising his voice to a shout again, 'Barbara! Come *here* at once!'

'What is she, your slave?' Cathy ejected. Her self-pity was momentarily stifled.

Frank stared at Cathy without comprehension. It seemed to be the first time that she'd said something which had surprised him.

'Barbara and I understand each other. *Barbara! Get in here!*'

'Good God.' Cathy stood up. 'I think I could make us both tea, if you tell me where things are.'

'Catherine.' Frank waved a bony finger at her. 'I would advise you not to go anywhere near the kitchen. Barbara is very territorial.'

Cathy frowned, as the door flew open and Barry's cheery face appeared.

'Hi, folks. Everyone still alive?'

'Barry,' Frank said with exaggerated patience. 'Please will you ask Barbara to make us tea and bring it in. If she would be so very kind.'

'Barbara's gone home,' Barry said with a rueful look.

'Beefy was sick in her gardening shoes and she sort of stormed off. I'll put the kettle on for you both, shall I?'

Chapter Eight

Cathy couldn't work out which was the more surreal: the fact that she was sitting on the sofa in her grandfather's house with a cup of tea in one hand and a ginger cat the size of a small lion on her lap, or that in the other hand she was holding a letter of apology from the captain of the England cricket team.

She glanced at the letter again, still ready to believe that it was a prank. But it was headed authentically and signed with a decipherable squiggle and, while not a rapturous piece of prose, was short and genuine. Apparently it had been sent to Frank's address once her seat number had been identified.

'You've got to give the man credit,' Frank was saying. 'He's a gentleman. That must put him up in your estimation, eh?'

Cathy sat with her cup of tea and letter, pinned down by the cat, and wondered which she could unload herself of first. She really wanted to walk about so that she could maintain her indignation, but circumstances had conspired to fix her adamantly to the spot.

'Thank you for giving me this. But it's not really relevant to anything.'

'How can it not be relevant to anything?' Frank sat up tensely, his blanket clasped round his waist. 'You'll go to Lord's now.'

Cathy blinked back. Every time she felt she had a

tenuous grasp on what was going on, Frank said something to throw her off balance.

'Lord's? Why would I want to go there?'

'You must! You have to!'

'Frank,' Cathy said, trying to keep a hold on her slippery thought processes. 'This isn't what I came about. None of this. Not Edgbaston, not the cricket, not my mutilated finger. None of it matters in the slightest.'

Frank's eyebrows rose slowly. His cheeks grew pink.

'I don't understand what you mean!' he exclaimed, his voice squeaking in frustration. 'How can it not matter? It's integral, don't you see? You must do this for me. How else—' He stopped abruptly, drew a rasping breath and erupted into a violent coughing fit.

Cathy sat, feeling like a wisp of paper trapped under a concrete paperweight. She wriggled, wondering if she should dive into the kitchen and get Frank a glass of water, but Beefy opened an orange eye, glued it to her and launched into an extended purr.

Frank waved his hand dismissively.

'I'm all right!' He took a noisy slurp of his tea.

Cathy's concern was overtaken by wonderment that Barbara, whoever she was, could put up with this constant maverick behaviour from Frank. Sour as Barbara was, Cathy felt a prickle of pity for her. While Barry and Frank seemed to get on very well, Cathy was sure that the real responsibility for Frank's welfare fell into Barbara's lap. Barry had disappeared jovially, swinging a beer can. He'd fixed them both tea, making the effort to use the nice cups as far as she could work out, but hers was swimming with tea leaves. She was fairly sure that Barry didn't double as Florence Nightingale when the need arose. That duty would no doubt fall to Barbara.

Cathy looked at Frank again, wondering how she could be related to such a man. What *was* the point in her being here at all? She'd been in Frank's house for over an hour now and getting her feelings through to him was like trying to drill for oil with a banana. She shuffled herself forward on the sofa, earning eight needles in her thighs as Beefy decided to grip on to her lap for dear life. She tried again.

'The point is this, Frank. Now that I'm here, with you, there are things I'd like to know about you – about my family. And I would have thought there are things you'd like to know about me.'

Frank nodded idly, his eyes once more on the television screen. He hadn't gone so far as to put the sound back on since she'd arrived, but he didn't seem in any danger of actually turning the cricket off.

'Or is that too much to ask?' Cathy ended faintly.

'Good God, *no*!' Frank declared, his hands flying out to grip the arms of the chair.

'No?' Cathy allowed herself to be marginally heartened.

'They're bringing on Flintoff!' Frank twisted round to face Cathy in anguish. 'At this stage. What in hell's teeth is going on? They can't do that! Let the man bat, by all means, but don't hand him the ball!'

Cathy stared at Frank, at his glaring eyes and red face. His hair had now levitated from his head and was pointing upwards. She could almost count the strands. To her dismay, she felt hot tears fill her eyes. Before she could stop it one had escaped and dribbled down her face to her chin. It hung there for a moment, then plopped on to Beefy's head. He wiggled his ears in response.

Frank screwed up his face. 'Are you crying?'

Cathy leapt to her feet. The cat flew across the room, her teacup and saucer clattered to the floor and rolled away. Gripping her letter of apology from Nasser Hussain, she waved it at Frank.

'Yes, I'm upset. Because of all the things I'd expected, I didn't think seeing you would end up being this humiliating. You don't seem to have the slightest bit of interest in me at all.'

'Humiliating?' Frank's voice was high. His eyebrows were now forming a zigzag across his forehead. 'I'm not humiliating you! I'm educating you. Can't you tell the difference? How did you ever get a first in Economics if you left all your lectures in floods of tears?'

Cathy stifled a sob. 'How did you know I got a first?'

'Because I asked and I was told.'

'You asked?'

'Yes!' Frank stated, as if it were obvious.

'Well. That's the sort of thing I thought we would talk about. For example. And lots of other things.'

Frank blew out, his lips vibrating like a trumpeter's who'd had the instrument whisked away from him.

'I *know* all about you. I know you enjoyed your degree. I know where you've worked since and what you do. I know that you are clever, focused and sharp.' He put up a finger to make his point. 'You're lucky. That's where you take after me. I know you're a humanist – with parents like yours, it's not surprising really – and you're very motivated. You're more fired up by the idea of doing something useful than getting rich. Which, as it so happens, I admire. You live in a cheap and unfashionable part of London, and you've got a boyfriend who won't marry you. So what on earth is there left to talk about?'

Cathy gaped, her hands dropping to her sides. She knew her mouth was open, but she didn't have the strength to shut it. Frank gave her a demanding stare.

'Have I missed anything out?'

'You – you've missed a few things out.' Cathy swallowed, gathering her courage. Frank was looking like Mad Uncle Andrew again. 'You don't know how I *feel* about anything.'

There was a long pause. Frank sniffed, rubbed at his hair and sent it swirling in the air like wisps of smoke.

'Yes I do!' he finally declared in frustration.

'Like – like what?' she challenged, venturing to put a hand back on her hip.

'I know how you feel about me. That's one "what" for you!' Frank pulled a strange face. He sucked in his cheeks in an overt attempt not to laugh, then dissolved into cackles. He put his face in his hands, chuckling. 'Oh yes, I do know that much.'

Cathy's chest was tight. Standing there, breathing shallowly, she wondered if she was going to have a panic attack after all. She took a long, slow breath to calm herself. How could this strange old man know what she felt about him? She had no idea – absolutely no idea at all – how she felt about him herself.

'I want you', she began steadily, 'to tell me about my parents. I want to know what you know.'

'Oh, dear God.' Frank slumped in his chair, peering down at his knees disconsolately.

'Well, what did you expect?' Cathy fired at him. 'A nice cup of Darjeeling and a civilised debate about the weather? You're my real grandfather, for God's sake. You know things. Things I have no other way of finding out.'

'And this is what you want?' Frank suddenly hoiked up his head. 'You want me to shout facts at you? Like this?'

'If we have to shout,' Cathy shouted, 'then we'll shout!'

'I will not shout about things that are disturbing to me!' Frank bellowed back. 'My heart can't take it. You may despise me, but don't ask me to do this. Not like this.'

'It's all I want from you.' Cathy was hollering now. They seemed to have rocketed off into a dimension of their own, far away from the peaceful cricketing scene on the television, or the dishevelled, academic calm of the big house. 'If you don't give me facts, I'll leave!'

Frank's eyes widened, so that his face looked tiny.

'And if you leave, what will you have achieved?' He gripped his chest. 'Oh, it's no bloody good. I'm going to have to ask you to get my pills.'

'What?'

'My – pills,' Frank emitted, his face tightening and turning a terrifying shade of mint green.

Cathy took one second to assess the situation, then flew across the room to touch his arm. 'Where are they?'

'Kitchen. Drawer next to – fridge.'

'What the bloody hell are they doing in the kitchen? They're no use to you out there.'

'Barbara brings them in. With – tea.'

'From now on, you keep them with you, all the time.'

'Just get the sodding things and stop being so cantankerous, will you, woman?'

Cathy narrowed one eye at Frank. For a moment, there, he'd seemed perfectly robust again, but she couldn't tell. She sped away to the kitchen, rummaged in the drawer, found a brown plastic bottle and dashed back to Frank's room with them. Beefy followed her both there and back and settled down on the carpet by her feet, staring up at her quizzically.

'Here.' She opened the top for him and handed him the bottle. Frank took one pill and swallowed it with an overtly noisy gulp. He took another sip of tea.

'Thank you.' He settled back into his chair, looking ruffled.

'Are you all right now?' Cathy asked, hovering over the chair. She couldn't help being concerned. That was only normal. If a complete stranger suddenly gasped out 'Pills!' at the bus stop, she wouldn't just carry on sorting out the change for the fare. It didn't mean she was softening towards him.

'I'm all right,' Frank said gruffly. 'I'm always all right. It's such a bloody damned nuisance, that's all.'

'What's wrong with your heart?' Cathy asked tentatively, creeping back to the sofa and sitting down. Beefy immediately descended on her lap like a deflating airship.

'He likes you,' Frank observed, ignoring Cathy's question. 'That's unusual.'

Cathy was going to persist with her questioning about Frank's heart, but it struck her tangentially that Frank had just paid her a sort of compliment. Via the cat. She looked down at the orange furry beast with a little more curiosity.

'Why is he called Beefy?'

'He's named after England's finest test cricketer this century,' said Frank, continuing with a sign, as Cathy gazed back blankly, 'Ian "Beefy" Botham.'

'Oh.' The cat nuzzled a wet nose against her fingers. Beefy. It took her back to the grotesque insult Nick had thrown at her at Edgbaston. Perhaps it had been his idea of a joke. It still wasn't funny, even if he had been thinking of Ian Botham at the time. But she'd asked Frank a straight question and for once she'd got a straight answer. In the midst of all the fraught exchanges, a sense of truce floated between Cathy and her grandfather.

'Catherine.' Frank broke the silence in a croaky voice. 'I'm going to have to rest. Your questions have made me feel quite ill. Do you mind if you go now?'

Cathy looked up sharply. Just as she'd thought it was starting to go well he'd done it again. Bowled her a beamer – that's the expression Jason would have used and although she didn't quite know what it meant, she now knew what it felt like to be on the end of it.

'You want me to go?' she asked in a small voice.

'Yes.' Frank nodded, yanking his blanket up around his chest decisively.

'Now?'

'Yes.'

'Back to London?'

'Where you go is naturally immaterial to me. The effect on my blood pressure will be the same whether you go four hundred yards down the road or to Kowloon. However, if it's more logical for you to go back to London, then by all means do.'

Cathy stood up, her face reddening. Just for a moment she'd been lulled into thinking he was showing some interest in her. Even, at a push, some concern. But she felt toyed with and abandoned. Beefy plopped on to the sofa and sat looking disgruntled.

'Back to your boyfriend who won't marry you,' Frank finished in a bored voice. 'And don't forget your letter. You should get it framed.'

'Okay, now listen.' Cathy pointed at Frank, her patience stretched. 'You don't know anything about Jason, or my relationship with him. That is a no-go area for you. Do you understand?'

'Yes, yes,' Frank muttered.

'I said, do you understand?' Cathy repeated grimly.

'I said yes!' Frank pulled a naughty face. 'Now stop telling me off and give me some peace. You can come back next week.'

Cathy moved to the door, stunned. She'd felt a little like this when she'd come off the flume at Chessington World of Adventures. She turned the door handle as if she were drifting through a dream sequence.

'I won't be back next week,' she said, more to herself than to anybody else. She picked up her bag, hooked it over her shoulder and left the room with her letter, scrunched up at the edges from where she had gripped it so hard.

Cathy leant back against the door once she had closed it behind her and gazed around at the hall. All kinds of paintings crowded the walls, faded Persian rugs were laid over the polished old wooden flooring. Any moment, now, she'd be able to move. Then she'd go.

A figure loomed down the hall and arrived in front of her. A pair of warm brown eyes peered into hers curiously.

'Are you all right?'

'No,' Cathy said.

'I've never seen anyone look more in need of a drink in my life. Am I wrong?'

'No,' she said again.

'Then let me take you down the road for a pint. I guess it's on your way back anyway?'

Cathy nodded, too dazed to do anything else, and followed Barry across the hall and out of her grandfather's house.

Barbara was still shaking. She'd had two brandies and they weren't small ones, but the jitter was still in her arms and legs. She sat at her kitchen table, pretending to read the Saturday *Guardian*.

She abandoned the paper, edged a little more brandy into her glass and wandered from the kitchen through to her small living room.

It was a compact house, one of the smaller terraces on Osney Island. But she'd bought it years ago, before house prices rocketed in that little patch of quaintness. The Isis flowed along the railway line and down one side of the houses. A small network of streams circled the development, leading it to be known as an island, but it was urban and only saved from the growling traffic on the main road leading up to the station by a shallow stream that provided a buffer.

She took the bottle and her glass to the low, carved table beside her preferred armchair and picked out Klaeber's edition of *Beowulf* from the bookcase. She sat down with it in her lap and opened it, sipping her drink once more and blinking strained eyes at the print.

She started again from the beginning, muttering the Anglo-Saxon words under her breath.

'*Hwaet we gardena in geardagum, theodcyninga thrym gefrunon—*'

Barbara let the book fall to her lap. She gazed up at

her ceiling. The melodious sounds pained her. Why was she doing this to herself? It was a form of self-flagellation. A way of punishing herself again, for not being good enough, not clever enough, not funny enough, not beautiful enough. Somehow not ever, ever enough.

Even as she gazed at the plaster swirls on her ceiling, she could see herself as an eighteen-year-old girl. She was back in the beamed tutorial room – the hushed reverence that cloaked the group as Frank Harland opined, strode, twisted, exclaimed. The smell of an old building, musty yet alive and growing, like moss. The way that her eyes followed him, as if they were stuck to his form without hope of release. She wasn't the only one. She was one of many who dreamt, squirmed and aspired to hold his attention. Then his pale-blue eyes were strong, flashing with ideas. His body was grace-ful, when it wasn't caught in animated explanation, or criticism, or exasperation. She'd thought he was like a Nordic god: blond, petulant, aggressively outwitting his opponents.

Barbara closed her eyes and licked her lips. The brandy tasted acidic on her tongue. *Beowulf.* The period of her enlightenment. The vision changed from a breathless group of overawed students, to a red-haired young woman with fiercely intense eyes, standing on her doorstep.

She smiled humourlessly. Well, it wasn't really *her* doorstep. She didn't own it, she patrolled it. How old would that woman be now? Late twenties? Barbara did a fuddled calculation, picking off her fingers, getting it wrong and starting again. She dribbled more brandy into her glass and tried once more. Probably twenty-eight or twenty-nine. Barbara pictured herself at that age. Not assertive, not fiery, not demanding. Hopeful and patient, yes. Biding her time, yes. Now she was over fifty. She was still biding her time.

But now? Now that this had happened? How much longer did she have time to bide?

'If I may say so, you look like shit.'

Barry chuckled as he put two pints of Varsity down on the wobbly circular table and shifted his stool so that he was opposite Cathy.

She was glad to collapse on a benched seat. She was knackered and bemused.

'I feel—' Cathy paused. She wasn't sure how much Barry knew of her situation. 'A bit worse than that.'

She gave him a slight smile. She was grateful for being dragged off for a drink. She guessed Barry had asked her down to the pub more to have a sociable beer with somebody than because he wanted to hear her ramble on about herself, but it didn't matter. She didn't want to go straight home and she needed some fortification. Barry had led her along the Woodstock Road until they'd found this pub. Not exactly towny or gowny, but a mixture of the two. It had rowing blades and college crests fixed up along the wall and a gregarious jukebox.

'Frank's a great bloke,' Barry said definitively, offering her a cigarette from his packet. She shook her head. Barry lit one for himself and exhaled, nodding. 'He really is. I think people get him wrong all the time. But he's been so good to me.'

Cathy took a big gulp of her beer, swallowed it and let the sensation sift through her body. Then, when she was ready, she thought about what Barry had said.

'He doesn't strike me as so great, but I've got my own reasons for feeling that.'

Barry put his elbow on one knee and eyed Cathy speculatively.

'The thing is – I know a bit about this.'

'You do?'

'Well, let's just say I've followed some of the story so far. I knew that he was getting in touch with you. He told me about it.'

'Did he.' Cathy was unimpressed.

'And I did say that I thought it might be a bit complicated. I sort of warned him.'

'You did?' Cathy took another sip of beer.

She wasn't usually a bitter drinker, but it was going down well. It was still a hot afternoon, although it was edging towards evening, and a long drink was just what she needed. She looked at Barry again. There was something incredibly appealing about him, but she couldn't pin down what it was. It was as if he were smiling all the time, even when he wasn't. His body language smiled. She began to relax in his company.

'I'm sorry,' she said warmly, 'I sound really snotty. Tell me about it.'

'Well, the thing is, I had a bit of a funny upbringing myself. My mum ended up on her own, then she remarried, but he was a complete bastard. And the upshot is, I got sent off to a sort of cheap boarding school. Nothing posh about it. More like a home for waifs and strays, really. Lino and washable wallpaper everywhere. And it took me ages to sort things out with my mum. So I know families are weird.'

'Mine's not weird,' Cathy asserted. It had seemed normal to her, up until now.

'Well – and tell me if I'm out of order, because I know it's all very private – I do know that you were adopted and didn't know about Frank. He told me that much.'

'Okay. You're not out of order so far.' Cathy grinned at him. In fact, it crossed her mind that if Barry weren't here to talk to, she'd be heading home, with the prospect of an empty house to greet her. She'd be able to ring Fiona tomorrow, but Cathy knew that she'd be out with her new boyfriend, David, tonight. It was actually very comforting to be here, in the pub, with Barry, while the sensations were still new and confusing.

'I know Frank. And I know blokes. We're not like women, you know.' Barry laughed. 'I mean, we're no good at talking. About anything, really. Not the sort of stuff that women natter about all the time.'

'Natter?' Cathy frowned. Barry had just earned his first black mark.

'You know what I mean.' He gave a lopsided smile that made her forgive him instantly. 'You gals just open up and off you go. It's normal. I don't think Frank's ever been able to do that. I don't know that for sure, but it's just my instinct.'

'So, Barry.' Cathy sat forward and gave him a somewhat ironic look. 'What do you think he feels that he's unable to express?'

'A real—' Barry paused, puffed on his cigarette and downed half his pint in one go. 'A real – need.'

'Need for anything in particular?'

'Look. He's ill. More ill than he lets on. Barbara's always there, but they only communicate by arguing. She seems to get a buzz out of being there, he seems to get a kick out of pissing her off. Don't ask me why.'

'She wasn't pleased to see me,' Cathy contributed.

'She's never pleased to see me. Don't take it personally. She's really possessive about Frank. From what I can work out, she's known him for ever. He's sort of – her thing.'

'Curious.' Cathy nibbled her lip. 'I wonder how that all came about.'

'That's too complicated for me. But one thing I do know about Frank is that he loves his cricket.'

Cathy sat back, disappointed. She'd been hoping for a flash of insight.

'I think I've worked that much out for myself,' she said drily.

Barry pursed his lips, tapping his cigarette on the ashtray in concentration.

'It's more than that. He needs it. It drives him. It gives him a – I don't know – a structure. A reason. It's got a timetable. There's always something planned for the future. He can look ahead to the next fixture and depend on it. He can . . . can mentally engage with all the fluctuating things, while all the time he knows the essence of what he adores isn't going to go away. It's always changing, but it's always the same. It's fascinating but at the same time it's completely reliable.' Barry pulled an embarrassed face. 'I'm sorry, I'm talking utter crap. It's not coming out right.'

Cathy took another mouthful of beer.

'Are you sure you're not talking about your own feelings?' she parried.

'I mean' – Barry's eyes took on a twinkle – 'that it's the complete opposite of a woman.'

'No! Cathy defended. 'That's not fair. A woman can be reliable and fascinating at the same time.'

Barry shook his head as a reply, his face creasing into a smile.

'Only a woman could think that.'

'So – well, it's a lost cause, then. If a woman can't be reliable without losing her fascination, then what hope is there for long-term bliss?'

'None.' Barry's smile widened into a grin. 'But we can have lots of bits of short-term bliss and enjoy them to the full. Then, if you string them all together in the end, they add up to the same thing.'

It was hard to be annoyed with such a statement when Barry's good humour was cascading over the table like a big, warm wave. Cathy couldn't even be sure that she disagreed with it – based on her experience so far – and she'd be on shaky ground bringing Jason into the debate. She wasn't even sure if she and Jason ever got to the point of relying on each other. They'd come close, perhaps a year ago, before Jason had been promoted, but now it seemed they only spent a day or two together at a time. The thought brought back a longing for Jason. Why wasn't he here today? She didn't want to think about that right now. She drank some more beer instead.

'Well, your theories are interesting,' Cathy said lightly. 'Truly, I'm riveted. A real, if unwelcome, insight into the male brain. I've got two points to make, though. One, you can't speak for all men. At least, I hope to God you can't.' She pulled a face. 'Two, what the hell has this got to do with Frank?'

'I'm not really sure. But I get the feeling he's been messed around. He shouts a lot. Bluffs a lot. He likes scaring people. I think it's a defence thing. Like you get with small blokes.' Barry winked suddenly. 'I mean, smaller than me. Or rejected men. Or something like that. Oh hell, I don't know what I'm saying. Another drink?'

'Cricket fanatics are all just a bunch of heartbroken men? Is this the key?' Cathy drained her glass and held it out to Barry for another. 'My God, I've cracked the Enigma code. Men and sport. It's a substitute for intimacy. It's as simple as that. Is that what you're saying?'

Barry cocked his head and scrutinised Cathy very closely. It wasn't an unpleasant experience. She even found herself smoothing down her hair.

'You are a phenomenally sexy woman,' he said bluntly. 'Same again?'

She blushed furiously, but maintained eye contact, determined not to be seen as a pushover.

'Certainly,' she declared, standing up and taking the two empty glasses from Barry's hands. 'But it's my shout.'

Nick stumbled in from the pub with Terry and Graham. They all headed for the living room to put Ceefax on and catch up with the sports news. Nick wrestled Terry for the remote control. He knocked the landlord's sixties-style standard lamp over. It fell with a dull thud and a small tinkle.

'Light bulbs. Add to shopping list.' Graham fell on to the sofa sideways.

'Cricket first,' Nick told Terry, raising a fist and putting on his best menacing face.

'Piss off. Footie first.' Terry grabbed back the remote.

'Christ, you've got no sosti . . . soflistication. Don't you realise we won a test match today?'

'No.' Terry waved a drunken finger, sliding on to the

floor. 'Not won yet. We have to come out and bat again tomorrow.'

'It's won!' Nick exclaimed. Nobody, not anybody was going to stop him now. 'They can't pull it back. Tomorrow's just a pleasantry. Normality. What do I mean? Formality. That's it.'

'You're talking shite, man.'

'I know I am. But we've won the first test. The rest, my dear, is simply a normality. Bastard colonials. We'll send them packing. I'm starving. Where's the phone?'

Nick flopped over the phone and dialled, on autopilot, the local Tandoori restaurant. He made every effort to sound sober and polite. Terry rolled on the carpet, sniggering.

'You' – Nick pointed at Terry sagely when he rang off – 'are a bastard. So look at the footie. I'm going to read my e-mails while I wait for the curry.'

Nick swayed into his bedroom and crashed into his chair. He thumped at the keyboard until he'd got a response.

His mouth drooped. Receiving one message of one. Didn't anybody else love him? Sods. He didn't love them either. He put a hand over one eye so that he could focus on the one e-mail that was there. It ranged up and down in front of his eye. Oh wait, he'd got it. Beefy! The invisible bloke. So he'd deigned to mail back at last.

Nick flicked through the mail, his head swaying heavily backwards and forwards. He'd read it again tomorrow. Then he'd make proper sense of it. But what was his bastard excuse? Bastard.

'Nick,' he read aloud, reaching for a beer that wasn't there. 'I can't apologise enough. I came to look for you, but it must have been when you were out of the ground. *Mea culpa*. Let me make it up to you. I've got tickets for Lord's.'

Nick paused as his chair tipped over and deposited him on the floor. He crawled back up to his knees and carried on reading, his attention grabbed.

'Can you meet me at Lord's instead? Should be a great match.'

Nick screwed up his face, closed both eyes, opened them again and tried to focus on the last line.

'I've got your address – I'll send you the ticket. This time let's not sod it up.'

Nick rolled over on the carpet. He kicked his legs up into the air and did the bicycle exercise, giggling.

The door flew open and Terry peered in.

'You all right, mate?'

'I tell you something,' Nick hiccuped. 'This summer's turning out to be a real corker.'

Chapter Nine

'How did it go, darling?'

'Oh, Melissa. Hello.' Cathy held the phone to her ear, snuggling into Jason's chest.

She and Jason had been sitting on the sofa, talking, on an evening in the week when Jason had made it round to Cathy's with his suit carrier and a cleanly ironed shirt ready for the next day at work. She'd been delighted that he'd decided to stay over midweek and go straight to work from her house. It didn't happen very often these days. But as he'd been out of London so much recently and had no idea when he'd be called away to one of the company's offices abroad again, Cathy guessed even Jason was realising that they needed a night together. At last, Cathy had been able to spill out her thoughts about her meeting with Frank to Jason and he'd listened sympathetically, mostly, although he seemed to be of the opinion that Cathy was likely to get hurt if she even considered seeing Frank again.

But it was easier to talk to Jason about her grandfather than it was to attempt to discuss him with Melissa and Cathy found herself regretting that she'd impulsively picked up the phone. Jason had even said softly, 'Why don't you leave it on answerphone? It's so good to see you tonight, let's shut the world out.' But Cathy had felt a needle of defiance. She couldn't just

156

pretend the world didn't exist when Jason was there. She needed the world to exist for her when he *wasn't* there too and that meant not dropping out of sight from her friends the moment he arrived.

So she'd picked up the phone and now she sought vainly for the right words to say to Melissa.

How might Melissa be feeling about Cathy's jaunt to Oxford to meet up with a real blood relative? Betrayed? Worried? Or was she calm about it? And if Cathy were to tell the truth, that she'd found her own grandfather to be a monster, she'd be voicing a very private thought, one that would deny the thread of curiosity she felt about him. It seemed that whatever she might say would be disloyal, to Melissa and Brian, or to herself.

'He – um – well, it wasn't that eventful.' Cathy stopped awkwardly.

'I have worried about you, dear. But then I thought I'd let you contact me – but it has been over a week now. I don't want to pry, I just want to be sure you're all right.'

'I'm all right.' Cathy said. Then, as Melissa waited, she went on, 'He's not what I thought he'd be.'

'Do you think you might see him again?' Melissa asked. Her voice seemed only concerned. There was no edge to it.

Cathy felt crowded by conflicting emotions. She couldn't talk to Melissa about it – or didn't want to – yet. She was still too unsure of how she felt herself.

'I really don't know.' Cathy sighed, realising that she couldn't just be evasive. 'Look, Melissa, you and Brian both know how much I love you. Frank's . . . well, let's just say I don't think he's going to be a part of my life.'

157

'Oh dear, it's not that I want to hear you say that. Please don't think that, darling. I want you to be happy.'

Biting her lip, Cathy pushed the emotions away. She said tensely, 'It's just that Jason's here and we haven't seen much of each other recently. I couldn't ring you back another time, could I? Perhaps later in the week?'

'Jason's with you? Oh, I'm so pleased.' Melissa's voice brightened. 'Do give him my love, won't you. Brian's found a recipe for him, something with seafood that he spotted in a magazine. Shall I send it to you, or will you both be down soon?'

Cathy closed her eyes.

'Send it, that'll be lovely. I – I'm not sure when we'll make it down. Jason's away a lot on business and I've been hellishly busy too.'

'Oh, don't feel pressured, dear. Just whenever you want. We'd love to see you both. But you are making time for each other. That's good. I do so like Jason. Quite a catch, you know.'

Cathy glanced at her 'catch', his eyes closed in exhaustion, his long black lashes casting shadows on his cheeks, his lips warm, his face relaxed as he drifted into sleep beside her on the sofa. Yes, he was a catch. One that was working so hard that he didn't seem to have time to be caught.

'I'll call you later in the week, then, Melissa,' Cathy ended softly. 'Love you both.'

After she'd hung up, she moved the phone carefully back to the coffee table and gazed at Jason for a moment. His breathing was slow and steady. He was out for the count. She slid back on to the sofa beside him, gently lifted his arm and placed it round her

158

shoulders, then settled back against his warm chest.

'My mum sends her love,' she whispered.

It was only a question of curiosity, Cathy told herself as she got off the tube at St John's Wood. That was all it was. A natural human instinct. There was nothing weird or bizarre about it. She certainly was not, as Jason had so sweetly put it, 'like a dog running into a fist'. It was simple. Frank had begged her to do this. She had decided to do it. That was her choice.

The tube rattled away and Cathy flowed with the crowd up narrow steps, surprised to see the police out in force controlling the cheerful gathering but at the same time realising that there were a great many people arriving and the tube station was tiny. This time Cathy couldn't see anybody in fancy dress, but she could imagine that pink furry ducks wouldn't go down very well at Lord's.

The sunlight dazzled her as she was swept out of St John's Wood Station with the crowd. She smoothed back her hair and allowed the fresh morning heat to beam on to her face. The stream of pedestrian traffic headed one way, down a narrow leafy road. There were the same distributors of Channel 4 '4' and '6' cards, and a bubble of excited conversation. Bare legs were out in force and the searingly hot early summer had ensured plenty of tans. Even her own legs were now going slightly beige and her breastbone was speckled with fawn freckles. She set her sunglasses on her nose and peered ahead.

It was a Saturday. Cathy had found out now that test matches were played over five days and at least Frank seemed to have acknowledged that she did actually

159

need to work in the week. Maybe Barry had worked on him, or perhaps Frank had bought the ticket a while ago and it was just luck. Anything was possible.

Cathy hadn't spoken to Frank, or Barry, since her visit to Oxford a fortnight ago. Since then, her feelings had been see-sawing. She was still filled with confusion over her encounter with Frank. The reality of her grandfather had been so far removed from anything she had imagined. But her outing to the pub with Barry had mellowed some of her feelings. Afterwards, as she'd mulled it over, she'd decided that Barry was a truly nice guy. And if he was nice, and liked Frank, then perhaps Frank wasn't as much of a monster as he'd appeared to be. The thought had crept up on her more and more as the Saturday of the Lord's test match approached.

She'd stayed in the pub with Barry until nearly closing time and got very nicely pickled. They'd talked about all sorts of things, especially Frank. It was only after she'd been poured on to the train home, waving through the window at Barry grinning at her from the platform, that she'd actually realised that she'd never mentioned Jason. It hadn't really come up. Barry had been so busy smiling at her, and being funny, and saying uplifting things, that she hadn't thought suddenly to insert, 'I have a boyfriend and his name is Jason.'

In fact, if Cathy was honest with herself, she'd been flirting a little bit. Only a little bit, but she'd really needed a silly five minutes. Or a silly three and a half hours. Anyway, it had ended up being fun.

So when she'd received a letter through the post several days later in Frank's distinctive scrawl, instead of cowering from it, she'd opened it with curiosity and had been surprised to read these words from Frank:

'I implore you to go. As you know, I can't. My doctor will not allow it. Please feel it for me. I need you, not to be my eyes and ears, but to be my heart.'

He'd enclosed a ticket for the second Ashes test match at Lord's.

Cathy had been stupidly touched by his simple letter and had wandered around her house with blurred eyes, moved to think warm and affectionate thoughts. Barry had told her that until Frank's heart had become so weak he'd always attended each and every test match that England played at home. This year he couldn't, and it meant so much to him. This year, Barry had said, England actually stood a chance of winning the Ashes and Frank wouldn't be there to see it. It had broken his heart.

Perhaps, if she strained really hard, Cathy could try to see it from Frank's point of view? Barry's asides and funny observations had helped. She was never going to understand the idolatry they both shared for a game and its players, but if she really concentrated, could she see how Frank might want her – his own blood relative – to go and feel what he couldn't feel through a flat, cold television screen?

In a way, she was taking a zigzag route to where she wanted to be, but if Frank dictated that it must be a zigzag, then it seemed she had the choice of going along with it, or having nothing at all.

And Jason was away again this weekend. It had been wonderful to see him in the week, but early the following morning Jason had taken a call on his mobile. After he'd rung off he'd ruefully admitted that he had to return to Paris to oversee a crucial stage in the project there. Cathy knew that she could have reacted more sympathetically. He didn't look too happy about the prospect himself. But Jason had whizzed away, taking all his possessions – including boxer shorts – with him as usual. As a consolation to herself Cathy had barked out, 'Well you'd better not show your face here again unless you're weighed down with Beaujolais.' She'd only regretted her outburst once she'd heard the front door close behind him and was left in a silent house with visions of Jason's apologetic, tired eyes haunting her.

So on Saturday, because it was a glorious day, because Cathy was curious about it all, because Fiona had plans of her own, her other friends were busy and she didn't fancy shopping alone, she'd made a decision, which resulted in her trooping down the road with a flood of cricket fans to watch the test match at Lord's.

No way was she going to tip up in a suit and high heels again. This time she was comfortable in loose khaki trousers, a snug vest top that clung to her curves and made her feel feminine and a linen shirt to chuck over the top. She also had sun cream in her bag, a huge bottle of Coke and the latest copy of *The Wharf* to browse.

Lord's cricket ground loomed up to her right as Cathy progressed along the pavement. There were more men in suits at this match: the MCC members Jason had talked about. Their red and yellow ties were distinctive. They seemed cheerful on the whole, certainly not the snotty-nosed brigade she'd always assumed them to be.

Cathy still didn't really care too much if it snowed, or

if the entire England team suddenly went down with mumps. She was Frank's roving reporter. But the excitable mood of the crowd was infectious. She knew that England had won the first match convincingly and that there was a buzz in the air about it. And, of course, she'd heard of Lord's. She'd never thought for one minute she'd see the inside of it, but here she was.

She pushed her way through the turnstile and into Lord's cricket ground. Then she stood inside, on the concourse and for the first time felt a tingle sprint up her spine. There were adults, children, men, women, sensible people, daft people, England and Australia supporters all mingling with animated faces. She was a part of something big. Perhaps this time she might really enjoy it. And, she thought optimistically, wiggling the finger that was now out of bandages and healing nicely, hopefully this time she wouldn't be assaulted by any famous sportsmen.

She would do her best to be Frank's 'heart' and take her feelings back to him. Maybe, just maybe, if she showed her grandfather a little goodwill, he would show her some goodwill in return.

Nick was glad to get inside the ground. Now he was away from the London throng and especially the underground. Birmingham was big, but it was predictable, he knew it well and he could drive around it with one hand on the wheel and the other on his mobile phone without so much as a heart murmur.

The underground was something else entirely. In the past he'd visited friends in London whom he knew from university and they'd all carted themselves about en masse as a drunken troop. They'd done the 'Circle

Line' expedition, which involved getting off at every single stop and having a drink. That was a lark. It wasn't, though, much fun travelling around London on his own. It was faceless, hot and busy. It made him feel vulnerable.

But once Nick had got beyond the turnstile, and could all but smell the linseed oil on the bats and the rolled grass of the pitch, he felt much more comfortable.

He stopped at a stand to buy a hot dog and a cup of tea, and gazed at the lively throng. There were signposts to the Lord's museum. He'd have liked to have taken a trip round it, but with a match on there wouldn't be time. He absorbed the atmosphere and felt his skin prickle with anticipation.

He was actually here, on the hallowed ground. Lord's, the home of cricket. With a quarter of an hour to spare before play started he could stand still and watch the goose-pimples rise on his arms. A crowd of young women laughed past. He pretended not to watch them. Two of them looked his way. He merely raised an eyebrow, which seemed to make one of them giggle. They moved on.

Sandra had been flirting with him strongly on Friday. She'd put her fingers on one of his arms and squeezed. Her eyes had flashed at him and she'd told him he was a hunk. Just like that. It had been a very nice ego boost, but he'd have to be careful not to give Sandra the wrong signals.

He'd stopped in at the gym on the way home and paid for membership. He'd been meaning to do it for ages. Last night, before he'd gone to bed, he'd looked at himself in the mirror wearing only his boxer shorts. The way he saw it he was never going to be handsome, but there was apparently something about him that some women liked. That was nice to know. He was six foot three and solid, with a broad chest, big arms and big legs. None of the men in the family had ever been fat. They'd all worked too hard for that. But they'd always been strong. He just took it for granted.

He pushed thoughts of women from his mind. Cricket was becoming more popular among women – he'd noticed the change since he was a fanatic as a child – but a day out at a test match was still, in his mind, a day out with the boys. He couldn't wait to meet up with Beefy and get stuck into batting averages, dubious leg-before-wicket decisions and the ongoing match-fixing debate.

He crammed the last lumps of the rubber hot dog into his mouth and took his polystyrene tea cup with him to the steps leading up to his stand. Beefy would probably be a big bloke too. Unless he was being ironic. But even so, he wouldn't adorn himself with Ian Botham's nickname if he was a shy, retiring violet. Today, they'd have a riot.

Nick broke into a grin as he showed his ticket to the steward at the foot of the steps and plodded upwards. England were one–nil up in the series. The Australians were off their guard. The match had started on Thursday and two days in, England were in a good fighting position. The Australians had batted first and set a challenging total, but last night Trescothick, opening with Atherton, had come in to bat and blazed away as if he were facing the Stow-on-the-Wold Under Tens. All England had to do was bat all day and get a high score in reply. That would set up a fantastic match, worthy of Lord's.

What he wouldn't think about today – what he refused to think about – was the curse of Lord's. The fact that England often failed on this, their most historic home ground. That wasn't a thought that was even going to be passingly entertained.

Nick was smiling all the way to his seat.

He found it was an aisle seat again. He peered around for signs of Beefy, a frown settling over his brow. He checked the ticket, the seat number and, just for the sake of argument, confirmed to himself that he was in the right stand. He sat down. He looked at the person next to him.

She had red hair brushed back, thick and glinting in the sun. She was wearing sunglasses. She was leaning back on her seat, fanning herself with a newspaper and staring straight ahead.

The first thought that went through Nick's head was that he hadn't laid eyes on such a gorgeous woman for a very long time. The second thought was that the last time he had laid eyes on a woman who looked like this was at Edgbaston. And the third thought was that this was the same woman.

'What the fu—?' Nick's voice trailed away.

Cathy had turned to him and nudged her sunglasses halfway down her nose. She was blazing at him with her intense, dark-blue eyes. He swallowed and continued to stare, words not arriving to save him. She blinked back at him, frowning.

'*You?*' she exclaimed.

'It's . . . um . . . It's Nick,' he said pointlessly. He was sure that she would remember his name.

She nodded back.

'Cathy,' she said faintly.

'Yes, I remember.' He cleared his throat and tapped his knee in agitation. 'So . . . erm . . . So Cathy. What are you doing here?'

'I'm – I'm here to watch the match.'

'Yes. Me too.'

They nodded at each other. She took off her sunglasses as if she wanted to look at him properly.

'It really is you, isn't it?'

He nodded dumbly.

'Well – how . . . how about that.'

'That's . . . erm . . .' Nick raked a hand through his short hair. 'That's odd.'

'Yes. Yes, it is.'

'So, how's your finger?' Nick asked. It was buying time. Something was more than strange about this, but one of them had to admit it. He wasn't going to lose his cool first.

'Oh, it's . . . um . . .' Cathy waggled it to demonstrate. 'It's fine. Nearly.'

'Good, good.'

'So,' Cathy continued, expelling a long breath. 'So what made you pick this seat, then?'

'This one?' Nick looked at the number again to reassure himself. 'Well, I didn't pick it myself.'

Cathy nodded slowly this time.

Like him, Nick thought, she was trying to solve a puzzle but finding that all the bits were missing.

'And you?' he asked with fake joviality. 'I thought you couldn't stand cricket!'

'Well, I can't, really.'

'But you're here – and – how did you come to pick that seat?'

'Oh, I didn't,' she said.

'You didn't either?'

'No.' She shook her head at him.

'Are you – are you meant to meet that boyfriend again? The one who stood you up at Edgbaston?'

'Boyfriend?' Oh, that wasn't my boyfriend. That was somebody else. But no, I'm not meeting anyone here. I've come on my own.'

'Oh. Oh, I see. Right.' Nick thought hard. 'I'm supposed to be meeting someone here. Like I was at Edgbaston. Only he never showed up.'

'He didn't,' Cathy said.

'Nope.'

'Well.' Cathy shifted herself in her seat, took a swig from a Coke bottle and looked at him again. 'Well, this is a coincidence, isn't it?'

She went quiet on him, putting her sunglasses back on and staring at the pitch. Her body was perfectly still, as if she was thinking so hard she couldn't move.

Nick shifted to face the emerald turf. He took a sip of his warm tea, his brow furrowed like corrugated iron.

'Look,' he said finally. 'Can I ask you again. Are you Beefy?'

Cathy rotated her head slowly to face him. This time there were no histrionics, he was relieved to see.

He continued quickly, 'I was supposed to meet somebody called Beefy, but I don't know his real name. It's a nickname. If it's really you, can you own up? Because I'm mightily confused here.'

'Beefy?' Cathy's mouth opened while she thought. Nick tried not to stare at her lips. He'd forgotten just how soft and appealing they were. It was very distracting. 'Beefy,' she said again, more firmly. 'You mean, Beefy Botham. England's finest test cricketer this century.'

168

'Well.' Nick raised his eyebrows. 'I wouldn't agree that he was the finest. Of the last three decades maybe, but if you include the whole century—'

'The only Beefy I know is a cat,' Cathy stated.

'Really?' Nick's face fell.

Cathy swivelled round in her seat. She looked right at him, her face gaining animation.

'Yes, Beefy is a cat. A fat, ginger cat.'

'Right.'

'A cat' – she stuck out a finger – 'owned by my grandfather.'

Nick nodded, trying to keep up.

'Your grandfather's got a cat.'

'Yes. And my grandfather bought me this ticket.'

'That's very familial of him. But a bit odd, seeing as you don't like cricket.'

'Yes. Exactly.' Cathy broke into a smile. Nick found his frown disappearing.

'You've got a nice smile,' he said.

Cathy stared at him and her smile suddenly dropped. Nick felt his face burn with embarrassment. How on earth had that come out verbally? He'd thought it, then suddenly, slap bang wallop, it was out there. He buried his nose in his polystyrene teacup and faced the pavilion with the twin towers. After an uncomfortable pause, Cathy spoke again.

'Nick? How do you know Beefy?'

'It's . . . um . . .' He fumbled with his cup. What was he going to say? Over the Internet? I've got an Internet friend whom I trust and who keeps not turning up? I'm a sad bastard with no normal friends so I need to find them over the Internet? She'd stereotype him instantly. What would it be suggesting about himself? I'm a stupid bugger? I haven't got a life? Please feel free to scoff at me? He cleared his throat noisily and said nothing.

'The point is, you've never met him, have you?' Cathy continued.

'Not yet.' Nick tried to say it in a deep, commanding voice. He sounded like James Earl Jones. He tried again. 'No, I haven't actually seen him yet. We only know each other – over the phone – so far. We talk a lot. About work. That sort of thing.'

Cathy nodded. He glimpsed her face. She seemed unfazed.

'You've never spoken to him on the phone, have you?'

Nick pulled a disbelieving face at her.

'Yes. Often.'

'Okay and he's – you'd say, how old?'

'You know, average-ish sort of age.'

'U-huh. And what does he do?'

'Do? What do you mean, "do"?'

'You're squirming.' Cathy laughed at him. 'Is he in the same line of work as you, for example?'

'What, computers?' Nick pulled an uncertainly negative face. 'Nah.'

'You're in computing?' Cathy showed real interest for a moment, but as Nick was thinking of replying she waved her hands. 'Never mind. Just tell me what Beefy does.'

'He's – just freelance. Nothing special.'

'Nick.' Cathy rested a hand on his arm. He looked at it. Her fingers were neat and clean, not sharp and painted like Sandra's. They sent a frisson over his body. Sandra's touch hadn't done that. Her dark-blue eyes were probing his. 'You know Beefy over the Internet, don't you?'

He shook her hand off his skin, pretending to sit up straight and rearrange himself in his seat.

'Cathy – I don't see where you're heading with this. It's an almighty coincidence, I agree. But stranger things have happened.'

'There's nothing strange about this.' Cathy smiled at him warmly. 'I think this is all about Frank. As they say, "one coincidence is a misfortune, two seem like sheer carelessness."'

'I don't know anyone called Frank,' Nick said factually, watching her mercurial changes of expression with growing fascination. 'And anyway, they don't say that.'

'No, they don't. But they should.'

'I – um – I'm sure when Beefy turns up, we'll see this is just a strange . . . a strange thing that's happened twice. That's all.'

'Nick,' Cathy said patiently. 'If you'd spoken to Beefy on the phone, you could never have thought I could be Beefy, could you?'

He looked at her helplessly. Her expression wasn't exactly pitying, but he'd been caught out by steely logic.

'No,' he answered in a small voice.

'Right. In which case my guess is that I know exactly who your "Beefy" is. His name is Frank Harland. He lives in Oxford and he's got a fat ginger cat. He's my grandfather. He's got a computer, he's mad about cricket and I happen to know from a friend of his that he spends a lot of time on the Internet. He's up to something. I don't quite know what it is, but I'm sure as hell going to find out.'

171

Cathy sat back. God bless Barry. She'd flown in and out of her grandfather's house with all the concentration of a bluebottle. She'd never have noticed the computer at the back of the room, or have had any sense of Frank's love affair with the Internet if Barry hadn't tried to sell it to her as a plus point.

'Frank's more in touch with the world than you think,' she could recollect Barry saying, somewhere around the fourth round, at which point she'd been swaying happily on the bench. But she'd remembered him mentioning that Frank's ability to experience things was now channelled through wires: through the television and through the computer. That had been the flash of understanding she'd experienced when Frank had implored her to be his 'heart', to feel what he couldn't over the electronic media he clung to.

Seeing Nick again was a shock. There was no other way to put it. It hadn't been particularly pleasant or unpleasant. It was just that his had been the last face she had ever expected to set eyes on again, and assuredly not in the seat next to her at Lord's, and absolutely not with the same set of confusing circumstances facing them both. There could be no other explanation. Frank was caught up in this, that was for sure.

The teams were coming out, and Cathy instinctively clapped along with the rest of the crowd as they filed out of the pavilion and through an opened gate that led to the grass. First the Australians, spilling out on to the pitch athletically, followed by the two England batsmen. She'd looked at a paper so that she knew, at least, that England would be batting today. The rest was a mystery, but Frank would be given facts through his television. If he wanted feelings, he could already have 'it's a very beautiful place' for starters; 'I've seen the famous Old Father Time weather vane, but it's small and stuck on the top of my stand, so I had to strain my neck to look at it' and he could also have 'I don't know why I'm sitting next to Nick again'.

Cathy gave Nick a sneaky look and studied his profile. Then she edged her eyes down his neck, his shoulders and over his body. She turned back to face the pitch quickly. Her first impression in Birmingham had been that Nick looked like someone who wrote with his fist – and didn't necessarily remember to put the pencil pointy side down. But now she noticed that he had a strong profile and his skin was even more golden than it had been two weeks ago. His hair was honey-coloured. And she'd noticed that his blue eyes, while still not overtly friendly, had a sleepy look about them. He was actually quite sexy.

Cathy frowned at herself, fiddled with her newspaper and took another sip from her Coke bottle. And now she was sitting next to him again and sure that he was somehow linked with Frank, there was nothing else for it. She was just going to have to get to know him a whole lot better.

Chapter Ten

'I can't believe this.'

Nick was almost in tears. Cathy was clutching her plastic pint of lager and she didn't want to believe it either. Not for her own sake, but for the sake of everybody who cared.

'I think I understand what's meant by an England collapse now,' she whispered.

There was no response. Around her the crowd were silent. It seemed as if most of the packed ground had been muffled and gagged. From several isolated quarters extended songs and cheers rang out. The Australians were gloriously happy. She could see a few blow-up kangaroos that had apparently been sneaked into the ground being waved in the stand opposite.

Cathy slid a look at Nick. He was pale. It was now mid-afternoon and things had taken a disastrous turn for England.

She and Nick had got through the day so far by chatting intermittently about various things, including what Frank might have to do with their strange seating arrangement, but all in all they'd concluded that they'd both have to ask Frank about it. At least Nick now seemed to agree with her that Beefy and Frank just had to be the same person. She insisted on it, even though she was still completely bemused and even speculated that Nick knew something she didn't. Several times she'd caught Nick frowning at her too, as if wondering whether she knew more than she was letting on. In between their respective musings, Cathy had found herself swept along with the match.

The ground was beautiful. At either side of the red pavilion were stocky towers and she could see the little balconies where the players wandered out from time to time to watch. Nick had pointed out the Natwest Media Centre to her, a structure that looked as if it had been beamed straight in from a *Star Trek* convention. It was low, wide, with a row of windows gleaming in the sun like a toothy grin. She could understand why it was known as 'Cherie Blair's smile'.

Stuck, as they were, together, she and Nick had formed a convivial bond. They'd had a hamburger at lunchtime and in the afternoon tea interval Nick had asked Cathy if she wanted a drink. By that time England had 140 runs and four batsmen were already out. Nick had explained that as long as Stewart could stay put they could steer their way through.

Now, two pints later, Stewart had gone. Cathy had seen him caught, which was gratifying as some of the other dismissals had been so quick she hadn't even seen them and the replays on the screens hadn't made them seem any clearer. Now the bowler had changed and a big man with bleached hair was flipping the ball from hand to hand in anticipation of his turn. The crowd sat silently as Flintoff came out to the crease.

'Oh God.' Nick thrust his hands over his eyes suddenly. 'I can't bear to watch. I can't do it. If you threw a piano at this guy he wouldn't be able to play it.'

'Sh.' Cathy patted his leg. 'I'll watch for you.'

'Okay.' Nick's voice was a husk.

Cathy glanced at him. This was no show. He was strained around the jaw and his fingers were white. Thank God she'd never become passionate about a sport. It looked like agony.

'All right,' she commentated softly as Nick put his head in his hands and refused to look up. 'That guy's sort of skipping in to bowl and he's bowled and—' She stopped. Even she could see what had happened there. And the clatter had resounded around the ground. 'And the little sticks have gone all over the place.'

'Oh God!' Nick looked up to watch the replay on the screen. 'The flipper. Bastard Warne and his bastard flipper.'

He put his head back in his hands and stared at the floor.

'Um –' Cathy wondered how she could make the best of this. 'But – but hang on, there's another batsman coming out. So that's good.'

'Uuh.' Nick let out an extended groan.

'So—' Cathy waited while the new batsman settled himself. 'Okay, so the bowler's running in again and – oh look, this is good – they're running. Oh. One of them's running. The other one didn't run. Oh, both the batsmen are at the same end. Is that good?'

'Argh.'

'It's not good, is it?'

In fact, Cathy could tell by the groans from the crowd and the way that the Australian team were leaping up and down that two batsmen being at the same end was not good. She bit her lip. What was odd was that she was starting to feel bad about it herself. She hadn't thought she'd care, but her heart was sinking further and further into her shoes.

'Oh dear,' she said quietly. Nick still didn't look up. He took a very large swig from his plastic pint, almost finishing it in one go, and muttered to her.

'Shane bloody Warne's on a bloody hat-trick. Bloody sod. Expect the Ozzies to go wild at this point.'

They did. Behind her there were mad cries of expectation. Around the ground, small flags and kangaroos were flung in the air.

Trying to be fair, Cathy could see how exciting it must be for them. She put her mouth close to Nick's ear, as he still resolutely had his head in his hands and was staring down miserably at the concrete.

'What's a hat-trick?'

'Three wickets in a row.' Nick really sounded as if he were going to break into sobs at any moment.

'Right,' she said brightly. 'Well, let's hope not. So—' she waited for the next batsman to face the big, blond bowler. 'So Warne's bowling and – oh, this is good. This really is good. You can look now. The batsman's hit it really hard and up in the air and it's flying across the ground and—'

She stopped. The Australians in the crowd went absolutely manic.

'Caught,' Nick said.

'Yes. Somebody caught it,' Cathy confirmed quietly.

'Oh. Oh my God.' Nick gulped.

'So – does that mean he got his hat-trick?'

Nick's body straightened. His face was sombre, his nostrils flaring as only those of a man hiding excrutiating pain can. Then, to Cathy's astonishment, he stood bolt upright and clapped loudly and solidly, in big hearty claps, not little feathery ones. Cathy looked about her. The immediate crowd surrounding their seats were England supporters. She had no doubt about that. But every single person, without exception, was on his or her feet giving the Australian bowler a standing ovation for his achievement.

Stunned, Cathy also rose to her feet and clapped. The ground rippled at first then stand by stand, every individual in the ground stood and clapped. The ripple became a crashing barrage of noise that thundered through the ground. As Cathy realised that the entire Lord's stadium, regardless of allegiance, was congratulating this man on doing something special, she felt a strange lump lodge in her throat.

She had never felt anything like it. Even the cacophony at Edgbaston when she'd known England were doing very well was nothing compared with this. You'd expect supporters to yell when their own side were on top. But to cheer and applaud and to support a player who was cutting through your hopes like a hot knife through butter?

Without even realising she was doing it she touched Nick's arm and squeezed it. She leant her head towards his as they continued to clap and the bowler in the middle of the ground raised his hands to the crowd in acknowledgement of their salute.

'I have to write this down. For my grandfather. I have to write down how I feel. I understand why you have to be here now.'

Nick turned his head slowly to look at her. He had to look down, both standing as they were, from his height to hers. He had tears brimming in his eyes.

Cathy caught her breath. This big toughie with the hard shell was *crying*? His eyes seemed suddenly sensitive, and generous too.

'It's not often you get to see a hat-trick,' he said emotionally. 'And it's a bloody fine thing. I've never even watched one live on the telly before. I can't believe I've been here today to actually see this.'

Her eyes filled up too as a response. It was so silly. Why should she care? But the crowd were still standing and still applauding. She was part of something very special and it made her feel alive.

'I'm glad I'm here too,' she said.

Then Nick suddenly bent his head and kissed her.

As the crowd settled and sat down again, creating a murmur of conversation that filled the ground like the arrival of the killer bees, Nick was still kissing her.

Then finally the ground became quiet again with an expectant hush as the next England batsman wandered out on to the ground, like a hamster being fed to a gladiator armed with a net, spear and nuclear warhead, and Nick was still kissing her.

Cathy pulled away as somebody behind her said 'Way-hey!' at the same time as an irritated voice complained, 'Oh, for God's sake sit down, will you?'

She sat down rather too quickly and stared at Nick breathlessly. He stared back at her. They blinked at each other. Cathy's legs were burning, her stomach was somersaulting, her throat was dry and her thighs – her thighs were just melting in anticipation. She had never felt a sexual chemistry like it. Her entire body felt as if it had done a Whirlpool spin cycle. She felt the heat on her face, the ripples over her skin, and all she wanted to do was to pull Nick with her under the seats and carry on with what they'd started.

Cathy tried to look away, but she couldn't. She knew that she was definitely staring. But Nick's pupils had enlarged too, overpowering the pale-blue irises.

For a long time neither of them spoke. Cathy looked away first, confused. She tried to focus back on the pitch, but it seemed now that the batsmen were just trying to defend themselves without doing much. She cleared her throat.

'Gosh,' she said. It sounded as if she'd been inhaling helium.

'Would you like another drink?' Nick asked in a gentle voice.

'Yes please.'

She knew her face was glowing like a hot coal as she handed him her plastic glass.

'I'll get you another.'

'Thank you.'

She caught his eye again and once more she was dragged into a suffocating, throat-clamping spiral.

'Would – would you like to go somewhere to eat after the match?' Nick asked.

She nodded.

He looked back at her tensely. Then he smiled. She felt like an ice cream dissolving on a hot pavement. She smiled back.

'I'll get the drinks, then,' he said.

Cathy waited until she was sure Nick wouldn't be looking, then she twisted in her seat and watched him walk away – up the wide steps, along the top of the stand. He strode confidently, or at least, if he wasn't confident he sure as hell looked it. His back was wide, strong, solid through his T-shirt. His jeans fitted him perfectly. He did have an extraordinarily good figure. She even felt something odd twang inside her – a little like Brian's attempt to do a fiddly bit in the middle of

'Sloop John B' – seeing that Nick's ears stuck out a bit from the back. It wasn't a sense of 'oh no, there's a naff bit there'. It touched her, not with pathos, or pity, or revulsion, or delight, but just because from the back with his ears sticking out he looked human. Almost vulnerable. Certainly reachable. There was something about ears that brought out the humanity in everyone. She turned back to face the pitch, pondering.

Nick had very short hair. Jason's hair was thick, black, not floppy in the Hugh Grant speech-impediment sense, but soft and downy. It was completely different. Jason had that little arrowing bit of black hair that went down the back of his neck. He didn't even know it was there, but she liked it. Even when they had a row and he turned away from her, she'd look at that bit of hair and soften towards him. With Nick, it would probably be his ears.

But she hadn't kissed anyone else since she'd first started seeing Jason.

She'd let Nick kiss her and she'd kissed him back. For the moment she was too stunned even to feel guilt. Jason was hundreds of miles away. Emotionally, she felt as if he had shot through a wormhole recently and ended up light years away from her. She felt a wave of guilt, but it peaked, then subsided. Her attraction to Nick was suden and daunting. It was like an electric shock. She couldn't have ancitipated how it would make her feel, but it left her frazzled. No other man's kiss had ever made her feel this way.

Cathy ran her tongue over her lips. They tasted odd. Of someone else. But nice. Another ripple ran over her legs and up her stomach. Nick was strange. He had an indefinable northern accent. He was a 'bloke', in a way that none of her male friends or boyfriends ever had been. He was tough and inscrutable. He had a cruel sense of humour that more than once had made her want to laugh really loudly. He was blond. He was huge. He was completely different from anyone that she had ever met in her life before.

For the first time Cathy could understand why opposites were supposed to attract.

Barbara was distraught. Indignation had mushroomed into anger, betrayal and despair. And the most dreadful thing about it was that Frank could see it all, as if she were one of his ancient manuscripts, opened up and displayed in a glass case for him to peer at.

'I want to know what this all means.' Barbara refused to leave the living room even though Frank was ensconced in his armchair with the cricket splashing green and white images at them both. She was standing to one side of the television. Even in the state she was in, she would never dream of blocking his view at a crucial time in a match, or asking him to put the television on 'mute'. He had, however, done her the courtesy of nudging the sound down a little so she didn't have to yell above it.

'I'll tell you again, then.' Frank's voice was croaky. His eyes were slightly bulbous. She knew that meant he was stirred up too, but this time she'd been the one doing the stirring. That made a change. 'It doesn't mean anything to *you* at all!'

'How can you say that?' she appealed. 'You told me nothing about getting in touch with Catherine. You hid it from me. You went behind my back and connived.'

'Connived?' Frank screwed up his face. 'Connived

with whom, for God's sake? She's my blood relative. I don't have to *connive* to have contact with her. And' – he pointed a sharp finger – 'I certainly don't need your permission for any dealings I have with her.'

'Barry knew who she was. You told him what you were doing and you didn't have the decency to tell me.' As she spoke the words, Barbara felt the knife twisting inside her. 'Do you know what he told me they did? They went to the pub and got drunk together. They left you and got drunk. Did you know that? That they were laughing at us, behind our backs?'

Frank pulled a face of mock horror. He put his hand over his mouth.

'They went for a beer? Oh, my God. What did the police say?'

To her exasperation, Barbara felt a tear edge its way down her face. She swallowed hard.

'There's no need to make fun of me. You've made very sure that everybody else does. Your personal input is hardly necessary.'

Frank pushed his blanket off his knees. He looked at it, on the carpet. It was like a toddler throwing a beaker on the floor to see what would happen. Barbara stood rigid and didn't react. He squinted at her irritably.

'Nobody mocks you, you stupid woman. Why would they? I can't understand you at all.'

'She – I didn't recognise her,' Barbara mumbled. 'I wouldn't have recognised her at all if she hadn't told me who she was.'

'So?'

'So, I was shocked and she saw that I was shocked. It's your fault that I lost my dignity in front of her.'

Frank heaved a huge, impatient sigh.

'Barbara, let me explain this in words of one syllable as you seem to be having a problem getting to grips with the basics. Catherine has no interest in *you* at all. She didn't come to see *you*. She didn't even ask me who *you* were. She came to see *me*. This is my house, and she is my flesh and blood, and Barry is my lodger, and everybody has a right to be here. Everybody – it seems – apart from you.'

His pale-blue eyes glittered at her. Then he turned his attention back to the television.

Barbara stood, feeling as if she were tied to a mast and had just been delivered forty lashes. She was smarting, stinging, an agonising pain churning inside her. But she couldn't move.

'What—' she started to whisper. Her voice was small against the low tones of the commentary. She tried again. 'What about *Alfred*?'

'*Alfred*?' Frank stared back with wild eyes. '*Alfred* is *dead*!'

Barbara felt the blood drain from her cheeks. In the warm room she was suddenly icy cold.

'*Alf—Alf—*' She couldn't get the words out. An enormous sob was working its way up her throat. '*Alfred* – is – your life.'

'No, Barbara. *Alfred* is *your* life.'

'Please, Frank, don't do this,' she begged him.

'You want to get credit for *Alfred*? You finish the bloody book. You put it together, write it and publish the sodding thing. I no longer care. I have far more important things to do now.'

'B-but Frank.' Barbara was really feeling panic rising within her now. 'Y-you just don't mean that.'

'I don't?'

Frank suddenly hauled himself out of his chair. He grabbed the arms and pulled himself round, then lurched across the room to the door, shouting over his shoulder, 'Follow me!'

Barbara stumbled after Frank, clutching at her blouse. Great waves of fear were crashing over her. He led her along the corridor and into the dining room, where all their research papers were stored.

'No—'

His movements were erratic, his white hair dishevelled. It was terrifying. She'd seen him angry too many times to count, but she'd never seen him like this. Frank crashed the door against the wall and headed for the table.

'Now, Frank, don't do—'

Frank swept his arm over the waxed sheen of the table top. The papers that she'd carefully arranged exploded around the room. She watched them float and fall, like confetti caught in a hurricane. He struggled to the shelves and pulled out the files, hurling them across the room at her. Papers flew out. He took a box file and cast it at the long french windows. It crashed against the glass.

'Do you see?' he shouted at her, his eyes like fire. 'This is a demonstration of me no longer caring, for those present without the imagination to picture it. Here we are.'

He stabbed at the keyboard of the word processor she used to write his letters, where she had faithfully recorded every detail of their research.

'No – Frank!' She ran at him and tried to pull him away. He shook her grasping hands off his body.

'*Alfred* is mine. I made it and can destroy it.'

'Stop it!' she shrieked but cowered back against the shelved walls as he peered at her, his finger now held over the 'delete' button like the Sword of Damocles.

'Shall I?' He grinned at her. 'I don't care if I do. Do you?'

'Yes!' she breathed, her heart leaping in her chest. 'I care. And you care. You're just having a moment of madness.'

'Oh! Diminished responsibility. I have a witness. Thank you so very much. Now I have my defence in hand, I can go right ahead.'

His eyes held hers for a moment longer, then his finger descended on the key. The computer groaned. Barbara stared in horror.

'Let me see. Do I really want to delete the folder "*Alfred*, research notes from the British Library" and all its contents?' Frank fondled his chin thoughtfully. 'Yes, I do believe I do.'

His finger hit a key and Barbara slid down the wall. She sank to the floor.

'There we are.' Frank slapped his hands together. 'A job well done. I'll leave the other computer files for the time being as I wish to go back and watch the England cricket team humiliate themselves at Lord's without any further interruptions.'

Frank leant hard against the corner of the desk for a moment, breathing heavily. His cheeks were flushed, his eyes unnaturally bright. He seemed to gather his strength, then he walked slowly across the room. Papers crunched under his slippered feet.

Barbara crouched in silence, her soul bruised and battered. Frank stopped at the door. He said quietly:

'Let yourself out when you've finished.'

He closed the door slowly. It clicked shut. Barbara sat as still as a rock. A moment later his etching of Winchester Cathedral slipped from its place on the wall behind the door and hit the floor, the glass cracking from side to side.

'It's a remarkable thing' – Cathy fumbled with her keys to the front door, giggled and dropped them; she scooped them up carefully – 'that you can dislike someone one minute and like them the next!'

She gave Nick a dazzling smile. He smiled lop-sidedly back at her.

'Y'know,' he said, helping her get the key into the lock, 'I could still go and sleep on the platform. Just because I missed my train doesn't mean you have to take pity on me.'

'No, I know.'

They fell into the hall. Cathy somersaulted straight over her briefcase and hit the floor. Nick closed the door behind them. She sat up, laughing again. She couldn't remember the last time she'd laughed so much. Most of her mascara had disappeared by now, she'd been busy wiping it away. Not that Nick was Paul Merton and Steve Martin wrapped into one wholesome package, but he was funny. And she was high and light-headed, even though they'd splashed out on a gorgeous curry. They'd both been a bit too high-spirited to eat much.

'Let me help you up.'

'Thank you.' She stuck out her hand.

He hoisted her up as if he were pulling up a dandelion. She felt as if she'd flown several feet in the air before she landed safely.

'Good Lord, you are a strong'un, aren't you?' Cathy observed with a raised eyebrow. She careered through to her living room and waved to Nick. 'Come on in.'

Nick followed and looked around.

'Is this all yours?' he asked.

'Yes.' Cathy threw out her hands happily. 'All of it. Lovely, isn't it?'

Nick scratched his head. He was scanning the pictures, the furniture, the ornaments, the flowers, the array of tropical plants on one window ledge, the bookcases, the books squashed into every possible space and even the carpet, the rug and her lamps.

'How – how did you do all this?'

'Drink?' Cathy went into the kitchen and hunted around. She found a bottle of Julienas she and Jason had been saving to have with their next Sunday roast together. In fact, given that they hadn't had a Sunday roast together for ages, and she had no idea when Jason would be around to share one with her in the future, she decided to open the bottle. She grabbed it and a corkscrew, a couple of glasses, and floated back to the living room. Nick had perched on the edge of the sofa. He looked distinctly edgy.

'What's the matter?' she asked him, dangling the glasses upside down.

'It's this, all of it.' He seemed a bit flushed. But there'd be no surprise in that as they'd done their best to drink London dry between them.

'What about it?'

'It's very – grown up.' He blinked at her.

'Beg pardon?'

'Well, the blue in the rug matches the picture frames. And the lamps match the curtains.'

Cathy hiccuped, put the glasses down carefully and wrestled with the corkscrew as she looked about her own house. She wasn't even sure if he was paying her a compliment or tossing her a casual insult.

'Ah.' He scanned her line of videos. 'You've got *Spinal Tap*.' His eyes lit up as he pulled it out and turned it over. 'Brilliant. I must get this on video.'

Cathy sank to her knees next to the coffee table and splashed wine into the two glasses.

'We can watch it if you like.'

Nick still seemed puzzled by something. He took the glass she offered him and drank from it. He looked around again.

'I don't suppose I'd be allowed to smoke in here?'

'Sure.' Cathy struggled up from her knees. 'Some of my friends do. I didn't realise you did.'

'Well, I don't much. I'm trying to give it up. But you know what it's like with a drink.'

When Cathy came back from the kitchen with an ashtray, Nick was looking at the label on the bottle of wine.

'See?' he said, turning his blue eyes on her.

'Yes,' she said stupidly. 'I see it. What about it?'

'I don't know anything about wine. I don't drink wine. I wouldn't even know whether this was better for stripping paint or drinking.'

'Have you tasted it?'

'Yes.'

'And what's your' – she flopped down again; she really was wonderfully drunk – 'conclusion.'

'It's very nice.' Nick smacked his lips to make the point.

'So – it'd be a bit of a waste to strip paint with it.'

Cathy grinned. 'Shall we put this vid on, then?'

He nodded, so she crawled around on the floor until she'd got the video into the machine and juggled with her various remote controls to get it to start. Then she hovered, wondering where to sit. She could flop on the floor again. Or sit on the sofa by the opposite wall. It was only a small room and you could see the television easily from both sofas.

Or she could sit next to Nick.

The thing was, after they'd come home on a tidal wave of silliness it had now gone rather quiet. Something was bothering Nick, but she couldn't work out what it was. And she was starting to feel a bit bothered herself about having this great big hunk of a man in her house. Not that she thought for a minute that he might be a lunatic. Which sounded a little odd, as she didn't know him very well. She felt completely safe around him. There was something about the way he'd been saying things all evening that made her feel that what she saw was what she got. Jason would find this an amusing situation, given that she'd nagged him to put the chain on the door. There was little point in having a chain if you were going to invite men who looked like bouncers right into your house. The thought of Jason on his knees, putting the chain on the door for her, made Cathy feel uneasy. It was just as well she was legless and her thoughts were merely a blur.

Nick looked up at her and smiled.

'Come and sit next to me.'

'Oh.' She thought about it for two seconds, then descended on to the cushions by his side. He put his arm round her shoulders. It was a bit forward, she supposed, but it felt very nice, so she didn't say anything.

Other than their astonishingly sudden kiss at the cricket ground, they hadn't done anything else intimate, other than looks, blushes, a bit of preening on both sides and lots of vibrations of curiosity throbbing between them. When Nick had suddenly leapt up in the Indian Restaurant near St John's Wood, thrust out his wrist (which Cathy hadn't failed to notice was the girth of an oak tree) and indicated his watch, exclaiming, 'Oh shitty death. I'm going to miss my last train,' she'd said lazily, 'Don't worry, I've got a sofa bed. You can crash on that and take off tomorrow if you like.' She'd maintained a firm and fair face, just to make sure he didn't think that he was on a promise. A possibility, perhaps. But definitely not a promise.

And now, here she was, clutched to him on the sofa, with Nigel Tufnell proclaiming at them from the video and Nick chuckling under his breath, and she realised that she wouldn't have that much longer to make a decision. Where was this all going to lead? And when it did, what was she going to do about it?

'You're very stiff,' he murmured to her.

Cathy wriggled from under his arm and reached her glass of wine. She was going to quip, 'I was just wondering whether you were too,' but she bit her tongue. It was probably better not to be too provocative until she'd thought about it all a little more. What on earth would Jason say, if he could see this? What would he feel? What did *she* feel? She had absolutely no idea.

'Cathy.' Nick took his attention from the screen and looked at her searchingly. It struck her once more what lovely eyes he had and how different they'd been at Edgbaston: so cold and guarded. Even when he was teasing her his eyes had been distant. Today, most of the day, they'd been quizzical. Softer. Sleepier. Warmer. Now, he looked thoughtful. 'Cathy, I want you to know that I'm quite happy to sleep on the sofa. I just want you to relax.'

'I – it's all right.'

Now she felt confused. They looked at each other and she felt the ripple of attraction run through her again. What was it about him? When he said 'I' it came out as 'Oy'. Nick was nothing, nothing at all, like anybody she'd ever been attracted to before.

'This –' Nick pushed his hand through his hair. The blond strands were flattened for a moment, then sprang up again. 'This doesn't make any sense to me. But – I'm glad I'm here. If that doesn't sound too rubbish.'

'Oh dear,' Cathy said, heat firing through her.

'What?'

'I'm going to kiss you.'

She did. His lips were amazingly soft. He seemed to hold himself in check for a few moments and then his arms were suddenly clamped around her, lifting her up. He stood up, holding her like a doll in his grip and, kissing her gently, lowered her to the floor again.

She gasped at him breathlessly, 'Nobody has ever, ever done that to me before!'

She could feel her eyes shining. Too much wine. Too much fresh air, no doubt. Her skin was still smarting from the sun on her flesh all day. Her cheeks felt red and scoured. Whatever had brought this feeling about, it was utterly exhilarating. She'd been thought of as a dumpy girl all her life. No man would ever have tried to lift her up without cracking some sort of joke. Even Jason made jokes about it sometimes, which she laughed about with him. But this man had suddenly made her feel like a tiny, delicate object. She looked at her fingers interlacing with his. His hands were large and tanned. Her stomach quivered.

Before she could say anything else, Nick had kissed her again. His body felt hot. As he held her tightly, crushing her mouth, she realised too that behind his cool exterior was a pelting furnace of passion.

And at that last thought her knees threatened to buckle completely and leave her on the floor.

'Christ Almighty, Cathy, you left the keys in the bloody door! What's the point of—'

Cathy sprang away from Nick. Nick stood, his arms stuck out where he'd held her, like a rugby player practising a ballet pose. Cathy hurtled round to see Jason in the living-room doorway.

He had a cardboard box of wine in his arms, her keys balanced on the top and he was staring from Cathy to Nick in complete disbelief.

Chapter Eleven

Jason put the box with the wine in it down on the carpet so suddenly that it was as if he'd dropped it. The bottles rattled. He pushed the loose sleeves of his shirt up his arms. The sight of the sprinkling of soft, dark hair against his tanned skin buckled Cathy's stomach. Then Jason pulled his sleeves down again, stood stock still and looked at Cathy. It was as if he didn't know what to do. Her mouth dried up in horror.

'What – ?' Jason attempted in a pale voice. Then he cleared his throat and began again. In that moment his brown eyes seemed enormous. Cathy felt helpless to do anything about the pain she could see there. 'Cathy, who's this?'

Cathy's first instinct was to say, 'This isn't what it looks like.' But she couldn't. It was absolutely what it looked like. What's more, she felt faint at the thought of what Jason might have seen had he walked in an hour later. And that would have been even more what it looked like.

Cathy had no idea what to do next – no more, it seemed, than Jason or even Nick did. They all stood silently, engulfed in an atmosphere which was as thick as smog.

But speared by the hurt she could see in Jason's face and unable to explain herself properly in Nick's presence, Cathy acted purely on instinct. She became defensive. And there was a genuine shard of indignation inside her. Hadn't Jason disappeared again this weekend, off to Paris? Hadn't he told her he'd be away for the entire weekend? She never quizzed him about his activities when he was away from her. Why should he suddenly arrive at her house with no warning and expect to be welcomed like the prodigal son? It was as if he lived there. Which would have been absolutely fine, if he did live there and were around to do all the caring, supporting and listening that somebody who lived there might have done. But he didn't live there and these days he wasn't a particularly frequent visitor.

So instead, realising that she had to do something to break the silence, Cathy found herself saying, 'Jason, how can you just walk in here like this? Are you trying to catch me out, or something?' to Jason and watched his chin drop in surprise.

'Your keys were in the door,' he said eventually. 'Anybody could walk in here.'

'Thank you for pointing that out,' Cathy said haughtily, edging over to the box and snatching her keys from the top. She crept away from Jason again.

'So – ?' Jason looked straight into Cathy's eyes. He seemed alarmingly quiet, but he appeared to have no intention of storming out. Cathy almost wished he would. It might ease the nauseous feeling in her stomach. 'Cathy? Is this what happens when I'm not here?'

'Don't be silly, Jason,' Cathy snapped, her voice sounding strained even to her own ears.

'You're drinking the Julienas.' Jason looked at the bottle unhappily. 'The one we were saving. And you're sunburned. Your nose is bright pink.'

Cathy swallowed. 'I went to Lord's today,' she said.

Jason nodded. Behind her, Cathy was aware that Nick was still standing motionless and silent. But Jason hadn't once attempted to look Nick in the eye.

'I guessed as much. And this – is this the guy with his arm round you in that picture in the *Sun*?'

'We were in the paper?' Nick muttered almost to himself.

'Not now, Nick,' Cathy stated. 'Jason, that's a coincidence. We happened to be sitting next to each other at both matches.'

Jason looked bewildered. And no wonder, she reasoned.

'That *is* a coincidence,' he said and for the first time Cathy heard the edge in his voice.

'Really, I have no idea why that happened. It's something to do with Frank, but we haven't worked out what yet. Then Nick missed his train back to Birmingham,' she rattled on. Nick said nothing. Cathy could almost feel his height and bulk casting a shadow across the room. 'And because he's stranded in London, I offered to put him up on the shofa bed. Sofa bed, I mean.'

'You're drunk,' Jason observed.

'Yes.' Cathy felt she couldn't really deny that, although Jason's arrival had certainly started the sobering-up process.

'I came straight here from the airport, Cathy.' Jason had lowered his voice, as if he was speaking to Cathy intimately and Nick couldn't hear. 'I brought you the wine. I—' He stopped and Cathy saw his Adam's apple rise and fall as he swallowed. Then Jason looked at Nick. Cathy watched in dismay as his dark eyes flickered with emotion, but his voice was steady. 'I think one of us had better leave, don't you?'

Cathy glanced at Nick cautiously. He looked very calm. But she guessed that at that size there wouldn't be many men who could be a threat to him. And she could only imagine, although she couldn't know it, that he'd been in one or two rough pubs in his time. He'd probably dished out his fair share of bruises.

After a peaceful assessment of Jason, Nick returned his gaze to Cathy.

'If you'd like me to leave,' he said in a quiet voice, 'I'll leave.'

'Where will you go?' Cathy asked logically. 'It's nearly one o'clock. The tubes won't even be running from here this late.'

Nick shrugged. 'I'll sort something out.'

'Why don't you do that, then,' Jason suddenly erupted at Nick. Cathy was surprised. Despite the differences in their height and size, Jason didn't seem in the least daunted by Nick. He'd been avoiding his eye until now, yes. But Cathy could guess that was for emotional reasons, rather than instincts of self-preservation. She hadn't seen that look of defiant confidence on her boyfriend's face for a while – in fact, probably not since they'd worked together, when she'd admired the way he carried himself in meetings. But then, Jason probably wouldn't have had reason to display his quiet courage to her in the last couple of years. Nothing had happened to provoke it in their personal life. Until now.

So Cathy found herself sandwiched between two men who were – well – behaving in an extremely manly fashion. In an odd way, under the circumstances, she felt her admiration for them both rising. But something had to happen to resolve this. It was awful, and even if Jason's stance and voice were in every sense commanding, his eyes were still round with the hurt he felt.

'I'll certainly leave if Cathy asks me to,' Nick said evenly.

'How about if I just show you to the door?' Jason replied, equally calmly, direct to Nick, with a look on his face that indicated that he was considering doing just that. And suddenly realising that if she didn't do something quickly, there was going to be blood on the carpet, Cathy asserted her presence.

'Now, Jason, stop this!' Cathy raised her voice. 'I wasn't expecting you. You told me you'd be in Paris until early next week, so I made other plans with my weekend. You know I don't just sit here in – in cold storage – when you're not around, waiting for you to turn up again. I've got a life beyond you, which is just as well as you are never bloody here. And Nick, nobody is going to ask you to leave, because you've missed your train and you've got nowhere to go. So can we just get out of this horrible mess, please? It's a misunderstanding, Jason. Nick has to stay here, but there's nothing for you to be worried about. It's going to be completely innocent. Please, Jason, believe me.' Cathy appealed to him, her heart turning over as he looked back at her with pure sadness in his eyes.

'You'd like me to leave?' Jason asked simply.

Cathy chewed her lip until it hurt. Causing Jason pain was unbearable to her. But he had caused her pain recently, she tried to rationalise. She'd been going through a major upheaval in her life – finding out about her grandfather, visiting him, wanting to talk about it, needing reassurance, advice, a helping hand, a shoulder, a friend. Jason had caught up on her news in the moments he'd spent with her, but it just wasn't the same. She'd felt alone with her problems and for the moment she was prepared to think that the flicker of anger she felt towards Jason was entirely deserved. He always assumed so much about her – that because he was content with the state of the relationship, she was too. But she wasn't content with it. She was disappointed and, recently, she'd felt let down. And here was Jason again, making grand assumptions about Cathy: that she would be in when he arrived with his bottles of wine and would welcome him back to the hearth with nothing but joy. He had no right to assume that. He was being arrogant. Yes, she decided, Jason was being arrogant.

Above all, Nick was in her house. It was late and she couldn't throw him out on the streets. And she had to find out what Nick's connection with Frank was. She couldn't alienate him, or leave him stranded in London with nowhere to sleep. It would be cruel.

She had no choice. It was a case of last one in, first one out.

'Jason, I'm – I'm sorry,' she managed uncomfortably. 'Please can we talk about this tomorrow.'

Jason nodded, but it was horrible to see his expression harden.

'I've never been unfaithful to you,' he said. 'I just thought you might like to know.'

Then he turned and walked out of the room.

Cathy's eyes fell on the soft little arrow where his black hair tapered into his neck. She wanted to call him back and change her mind, but she still had Nick in the room and she didn't know what else to do. She couldn't imagine that she could put one on the sofa and one in the bath, seeing as neither of them probably wanted to head for the bed any longer. So she stood, feeling dreadful, until she heard the front door close behind Jason.

Nick sat down and took a swig from his wineglass.

'Your boyfriend.'

Cathy sank into the sofa opposite Nick. She didn't want to sit too close to him now.

'Yes, my boyfriend,' she breathed. 'Oh God.' She let out a long sigh. 'Oh bugger.' And as she was about to voice 'poor Jason' she realised that it was a sentiment Nick might have very little sympathy with, given that she'd kissed him quite willingly. She held the thought inside her.

Poor Jason. Guilt now drenched Cathy from head to foot. How completely, absolutely awful for him. She could picture him, sitting in his car, probably still stunned by what he'd seen, starting the engine and taking a lonely drive home to his flat. She eyed the box of wine near the door, where he'd left it. It tortured her further. She imagined for a moment how different things might have been if she'd been at home, alone, at gone midnight and Jason had surprised her by coming home from Paris early and bearing the present she'd demanded. She wondered what sort of warm welcome she would have given him. Perhaps he would have stayed with her all day Sunday and they might have eaten that Sunday roast together, the one they were saving the Julienas for. Cathy peered at the bottle unhappily. Then she cautiously raised her eyes to Nick's.

He'd obviously been watching her. Had her emotions been displayed on her face? His eyes were quizzical, as if he wasn't sure what he was allowed to say. But then he obviously decided to trust his own judgement. To her surprise, he let out a low laugh and his face gained a cheeky look.

'Whoops,' he said.

'Yes, whoops indeed,' Cathy agreed, unable to share Nick's apparent sense of mischief.

'How long have you been going out together?'

'Oh. Um.' Cathy felt slightly embarrassed. 'About four years or so. We knew each other for a while before that. We used to work at the same place. It's where we met.'

'Phew!' Nick finally lit the cigarette he had been fingering and tutted. 'Long time. Why no marriage?'

'Marriage? What's that got to do with it?'

Nick shrugged. 'I just thought it was normal in people of our age. If you're sure enough about someone to go out with them for years on end you get married, don't you?'

'Well—' Cathy floundered. 'Why would you?'

'Why wouldn't you?'

Cathy grabbed her glass, sipped some wine and assessed Nick carefully.

'That's a very traditional attitude.'

'I guess I come from a very traditional world.'

'Let's talk about that instead.' Anything, anything at all to take her mind off Jason until she could speak to him again.

'Let's talk about the picture in the paper.' Nick was grinning. 'I hope you kept a copy.'

'I most definitely didn't.' Cathy raised her eyebrows

and tried to switch the conversation back to Nick. 'I'd rather talk about you for a moment. Where do you actually come from? I can't pin down your accent.'

'Generic North.' Nick laughed again. 'Bit of Yarkshire. Bit of Newcastle. Bit of Birmingham. Believe me, I do my best not to pick up the Brummy accent, but it's hard when you live and work there.' Cathy nodded, her feelings beginning to steady. It was easier to talk to Nick about Nick than to talk to Nick about Jason. That was impossible now. Her guilt was bad enough. 'And you're a softy southerner, from a family of academics.' Nick gave a long, low laugh, gazing around Cathy's living room again. 'What am I doing here?'

'I'm not from a family of academics,' Cathy defended.

'You said Beefy – sorry, Frank – had been a professor at Oxford. That's pretty damned academic. And something about your mum having been at university too – and you're some sort of economist. Must be in your blood somewhere.'

'Ah, no. My mum's—' Cathy paused. Did she really want to spill the beans all over Nick's lap? Well, she guessed that their moment of passion had truly been thwarted, so she might as well. 'My mum's not really my mum. So it doesn't run in the family.'

'Ah,' Nick said. He looked at her more warmly. 'Were you adopted?'

'Yes.'

'Ah,' Nick said again. He smoked his cigarette quietly for a moment. 'All the bits start to fall into place. That's why you don't know Frank.'

'That's right.'

'And he definitely is your real grandfather.'

'Yes. That time I was telling you about, when I saw the cat and had a row with him. That was actually the first time I'd met him.'

'Ah.' Nick grinned at her. 'Well, thank you for joining the dots for me. It's all been a bit mysterious. I think I've got the picture now. In fact, as I've been talking to Beefy over the Internet for some time, I probably know him a bit better than you do.'

'Yes,' Cathy admitted. She turned her glass round in her hand. She could still see the back of Jason's head flashing through her mind. She wanted to pick up the phone and leave him a message for when he got back to his flat, but she couldn't do that in Nick's presence. It didn't help her muddled feelings to have Nick proclaiming that he knew her own grandfather better than she did. Even if it was true. She felt very confused.

'Top-up?' Nick held out the bottle.

'Oh, I don't know. I think I've had enough.'

'Okay.' Nick poured himself another glass anyway. 'You have worked out, haven't you, that your grandad wants to get us together?'

Cathy held out her glass to dodge the issue. 'Actually, I will have a top-up. Just a tad.'

Nick obliged, giving Cathy a very direct look. Despite her rumpled feelings it sent a bolt of physical attraction through her again. But she didn't want to answer his question. The idea that Frank was for some bizarre reason trying to match the two of them up had played on her mind all day.

Nick chuckled. Cathy was starting to realise that he laughed a lot when he was relaxed. A far cry from her first impression of him. But then, he had more reasons to relax now than she did.

'Let's try that again,' Nick said, unfolding himself back on to the sofa once more. 'Have you any idea why your Frank is playing Cupid?'

'I don't know that he is,' she retorted quickly. 'He might have all sorts of reasons for getting us both tickets. I'll have to find that out from him.'

'Hmn. We're both single, both the same sort of age—'

'I'm not single,' Cathy said quickly.

Nick raised an eyebrow. 'Are you engaged?'

'No!' Cathy looked at Nick as if it was a silly question.

'Well.' Nick shrugged. 'Call me a traditional bloke, but any woman who's not engaged, or married, or maybe these days living with someone, is basically fair game.'

'Fair game?' Cathy ejected. 'You make it sound like the hunting season.'

'Well, isn't it?'

Cathy stood up, swayed a bit and waved her glass.

'It might be like that oop North, but it's not like that down here. I think – I think you're much more traditional than me. I think the women you've been around are probably much more traditional than me or any woman I know. I think we come from different worlds, Nick.' To her irritation, he nodded at her in emphatic agreement. 'This is – this is London.' She frowned at herself. There was proof that she was indeed still drunk. She sounded like a World Service announcer. 'Here, we don't marry people. We hang around each other for a few years and think about it a lot. In my language, you are single and I am not.'

Nick pondered her outburst quietly. He muttered agreeably, 'Red hair. I'd pretty much worked out you

204

had a streak of fire in you.' Then, when she stared at him aggressively in response, he cleared his throat and said, 'Cathy, has it occurred to you that as from tonight you might actually be single, even in your language, too?'

'That', she said archly, 'is something that I don't think I'm going to discuss with you.'

'All right.' Nick pursed his lips amiably.

'And now', she declared, 'I'm going to go and get you some bedding and I am going to my bed and you are going to yours.'

'I'd never imagined it would be any other way.' Nick stood up and tucked his T-shirt into the waistband of his jeans. 'I'll carry the bedding. Where is it?'

'I'll – I'll get it.' Cathy was thrown by the fact that they were now both on their feet and only a yard from each other. It took her straight back to their passion before Jason had lunged in. Her stomach turned over at the thought. If it hadn't been for that interruption, they would have progressed from downstairs to upstairs. She knew it. Nick knew it. 'You wait here!' she instructed.

Cathy scrambled up the stairs. She yanked on the airing-cupboard door and heaved out the spare duvet, sheets and pillows. She bundled them up in her arms and edged all the way back down the stairs with them.

When she got back into the living room, Nick was sprawled out lengthways on the sofa. His eyes were closed. She could be sure he wasn't asleep, but he looked very serene.

She dumped the bedding on the floor. 'It's all there,' she said.

'Thank you,' he murmured. He opened his eyes lazily and looked at her. 'Goodnight.'

'Goodnight,' she blurted, her pulse fluttering, and legged it out into the hall, pulling the door firmly closed behind her.

Cathy tiptoed downstairs in the morning wearing someone else's face, the hammers of a thousand cave-dwelling dwarfs beating at the inside of her skull. She hesitated in the hall, then tentatively pushed open the living-room door.

The sofa was devoid of Nick and there was a neat pile of bedding on the carpet. Apart from one cigarette end in the ashtray and the two empty glasses there was no sign that any of it had ever happened.

'Jason, we need to talk.'

'I don't see that there's anything to talk about.'

'Please, let me in.'

Cathy had managed to get as far as Jason's flat door, as one of the occupants of the block had been leaving as she arrived, had recognised her and held the front door open for her. She'd climbed up the fire escape staircase, avoiding the lift as the laws of science dictated that a hangover the size of China could not be fitted into a lift the size of a shoebox. Then she'd banged on Jason's door, swigging from a bottle of water in an attempt to rehydrate, and finally he'd opened the letter box and peered out at her.

Now she was on her knees, pleading with the bit of him she could see through the letter box. He didn't seem to want to meet her eye. His eyelashes looked blacker and thicker than she'd remembered. Even the tiny bit of him she could see was handsomer than ever before. She felt utterly wretched, stupid and guilty.

And most of all she realised with an aching desperation that she didn't want to lose him.

It was only as she'd lain in bed that morning, sweating heavily due to a combination of environmental temperature, hangover and memory of the night before, that she'd started to picture how Jason must *really* have felt and how utterly miserable his drive home must have been.

He had arrived impulsively at his girlfriend's house – his girlfriend of four years, at that – armed with the wine he'd been instructed to return with. Cathy had given him a spare set of keys for the house when she'd first moved there – why was it so unreasonable for him to assume that he could just walk in? Hadn't she implicitly invited him to do just that? On arrival, Jason had found his girlfriend in the clutches of a complete stranger – and then she'd thrown him out, while the stranger stayed. No wonder his expression had been so forbidding as he'd finally turned to leave. She was only now starting to imagine just how devastated he must have felt. He had been utterly, miserably betrayed by Cathy's behaviour.

And what was chewing Cathy into shreds in the clear light of day was the knowledge that she had taken a terrible, unaccountable risk. She loved Jason, really loved him. She hadn't realised just how much until this awful morning when, sick with hangover, she'd opened her eyes in bed and the memories of the previous night had stampeded over her. She loved her boyfriend. And she had probably lost him.

She loved the way Jason laughed, the glow in his eyes when he was enthusing about one of his passions. The films he was desperate for her to share with him, or new recipes he wanted her to taste. The way he smelled – his aftershave, his sweat, his maleness, even the slight waft of the washing powder he used in his machine at home – drew her to him. The dark shadow round his chin in the evening that was rough to the touch and moulded his face into an image of masculine sensuality. The fact that they could talk about anything at all that occurred to them both and it would become interesting. The way a sudden idea would bring his expression to life and the way she could never predict what his opinions would be, but loved to hear him outline them, clearly, rationally, intelligently. The way he could make her laugh by a surprising turn of phrase, or a tangential thought, and then would watch her reaction with pleasure. The way he would suddenly reach out and touch her, with a softness in his dark eyes that had always whispered a reassurance that he loved her too. And the way he kissed her, with gentleness at first, but with an insistence that teased them both into passion.

Cathy's regret had mushroomed into aching despair then complete desperation that morning. She had to try to do something, anything at all, to put it right. And quickly. Rather than ring him, she'd thrown herself into a cool shower, dragged on some shorts and a cotton top, and legged it right over to him on the tube. The air was still, her palms were damp, everything smelled of roasting tarmac and she had a lovely gingham pattern on the back of her bare legs from the seat in the tube, but she was determined.

'Fine,' Cathy said, squeezing her face up to the letter box. 'If you won't let me in, I'll talk to you right here. I am so, so sorry that you saw what you did.'

Jason cleared his throat.

'It's all very confusing,' she stumbled on. 'But please let me explain. Frank sent Nick tickets to the matches. Next to mine. I didn't arrange to see him there. He was just – there.'

'And why would your grandfather, insane as he is, do something like that?'

'I don't know. I honestly don't know. I'm going to see him to find out.'

'And Frank instructed you to snog him as well, did he?'

Well, at least Jason hadn't let go of the letter box, which was a good sign.

'No, of course not. That was just silly drunken behaviour. It wouldn't have gone any further than that.'

She was lying. She hoped Jason wouldn't be able to hear it in her voice.

'You're lying.'

'Not really.' Cathy squirmed. She sat back on her haunches and looked up to the strip light running along the corridor ceiling for inspiration. 'Jason, haven't you ever done anything really stupid?'

'No.'

'What, never?'

'Not in the way you mean, no.'

'Haven't you ever, ever had an unfaithful thought when you were with me?'

'No!' He half laughed, but it was from indignation rather than humour.

Cathy was so confused. Why couldn't Jason have told her these things in a nice way, over dinner and a bottle of wine? It would have been so reassuring in the long periods they spent apart. She'd have held such words to her like photographs. She racked her brains for some way to appeal to him.

'Yes you have. You've got *Working Girl* on video just so that you can replay the bit where Melanie Griffith's nipples show.'

Jason sighed heavily. 'I have never snogged Melanie Griffith.'

'But you would.' Cathy pushed an eye against the letter box. 'If you got drunk with her on a hot day and lost your mind for a minute, you'd snog her.'

'How can you compare that gorilla to Melanie Griffith? If I wasn't so pissed off I'd laugh. I thought you had a modicum of taste.'

'It's not about taste,' Cathy asserted, ignoring the fact that the occupant of the opposite flat was coming out. She could hear the jangling of keys behind her. 'He was just there, that's all.' And Cathy added, in flash of self-defence. 'And you're never there.'

'I spend as much time with you as I can. I'm hardly ever in my own flat these days.'

Cathy's stomach turned. For Jason, spending as much time with Cathy as he could only meant that it was the time he allocated to their relationship. It didn't mean that it was enough time for their relationship – any relationship – to survive. He was forgetting about his trips away, the long hours they both worked, her evening meetings with local businesses, his unpredictable schedule. Yes, she was busy too, but even when she was at home Jason was hardly ever there.

'You're never around any more, Jason. You weren't there when I needed your moral support. I'd have loved you to come to Oxford with me to see Frank. But I had to do it on my own. This is a difficult time for me and I really need your help.'

Cathy shot a glance over her shoulder. A woman in a slinky linen dress with heeled espadrilles was attempting to lock her door, but taking her time over it. She had long black hair swinging to her waist. Cathy bristled. Jason had never mentioned a gorgeous woman living in the flat opposite him. She lowered her voice.

'Let me in, Jason,' she issued at him.

'Hi, Jace!' the woman called loudly, tossing a bag over her shoulder and looking right through Cathy to the letter box.

'Oh, hi there, Candida!' Jason called in a brightly polite voice.

There was a silence while Cathy waited on her knees for Candida to spontaneously combust.

'I'll bring the glasses back when I see you later!' Candida called again, a little too sweetly. Cathy ground her teeth.

'Sure thing!' Jason obliged in return.

Candida clacked away down the tiles and pressed the button to call the lift. She didn't so much as give Cathy a glance. Cathy sank to her bottom, feeling podgy, ginger and plain by comparison. The lift arrived and Candida stepped elegantly into it. She caught Cathy's eyes briefly as the doors closed. The look she gave her was one of cool confidence. As soon as she was sure the lift had departed Cathy hissed through the letter box.

'Who was that?'

'Candida,' Jason said, failing to elaborate.

'No, I mean, who is Candida?'

'My neighbour.'

'What did she mean about the glasses?'

'She borrowed them.' Jason seemed determined to be cryptic.

'Well,' Cathy simmered. 'It's not surprising you don't want to leave your boxer shorts at my house then, is it?'

Cathy glowered at Jason through the letter box. He looked straight at her. There was a glint of humour in his eyes. Or it might have been sadism.

'It's just as well I didn't. How would you have explained them to Nick?'

'Please, Jason. I've said I'm sorry. It won't happen again. I was lonely and confused and he knows Frank in some weird way and I wanted to get to know him better. I need to put all the pieces together. Please believe me. He slept on the sofa bed last night and I didn't even see him this morning. It was innocent. Don't you see?'

'I see that you wanted a quickie on the side and me to forget about it.'

'No!' Cathy pulled herself up on her knees and sprawled against the door, shoving her face as close to the gap as possible. 'I don't. You've just been so – so distant. I didn't know where we were going. And—'

Cathy paused. She knew what she was about to say could be committing relationship suicide, but her brain was still adled, her emotions were running high and the thoughts suddenly formed themselves into words.

'I mean,' she asserted, 'we've been seeing each other for four years, for God's sake. We're both grown-ups. Why haven't we got married?'

'*What*?'

'Well, it's what normal people do. I know what

you're thinking, "Why should we?" and all I'd say to that is, "Why shouldn't we?" It's what people who like each other do.' Cathy appealed to Jason with her eyes and said in a more demanding tone, 'Jason, will you marry me or not?'

There was a long, forbidding silence in reply. Then Cathy leapt in the air as she heard keys jingling behind her again. She swivelled round on her knees.

There stood Candida, right behind Cathy, with a newspaper under her arm, smiling at Jason's eyes through the open letter box. She stooped slightly to show off a tanned, firm cleavage.

'Seven o' clock do you, Jace?' Candida queried with icy calm.

'Yes, that'll be fine,' Jason called back.

Candida swept into her flat and slammed the door, in a lively, robust and sexy kind of way. Cathy cringed in horror. She hadn't heard the lift, or the clacking heels. She'd been so obsessed with her own thoughts. Now the sexy Candida had seen Jason's sweaty, unappealing girlfriend making herself even more unappealing by asking for his hand in marriage through the letter box.

Which would only have been ninety-five per cent excruciating, if Jason hadn't replied with a very meaningful stony silence of complete rejection. Cathy's humiliation was quite complete. Her face, still glowing and weather-beaten from the previous day's exposure to the elements, now burned.

'What are you doing with her at seven o'clock?' she blurted at Jason through the door, close to tears.

'Candida's coming round for supper.'

Cathy's lips wobbled.

'What are you cooking for her?'

'Roast red pepper and chorizo soup with seafood pasta.'

'Oh.'

A sob shot up Cathy's throat. She burst into tears of exhaustion and despair.

'You said you'd never been unfaithful to me.'

'I haven't.' Jason paused, then added, 'Yet.'

'You're not allowed to touch her!' Cathy cried desperately.

'Go away, Cathy,' Jason said coldly.

With that, he flipped the letter box down and she heard his footsteps as he walked away from the door.

Cathy wrenched herself up and blundered away, taking the stairs down and stopping halfway to have a very good cry. She wiped her hands over her face.

There was nothing she could do. She had been caught red-handed and she had no moral high ground. If only she hadn't been so desperately drunk the night before, maybe she would have handled things better. She could have ensured that Jason hadn't felt humiliated and rejected. She could have chucked Nick out and left him to find a bed and breakfast some-where. After all, Nick was a grown-up. Even more physically grown-up than any man she'd ever known before. The muggers would have run away.

What would happen with Candida tonight? Jason had seen Cathy snogging. Did that mean that he'd have a snog to get his own back? Or would he raise the stakes? I'll meet your snog and I'll raise you to a snog and a grope. Would it be her turn next? I'll meet your snog and grope and raise you to a snog, grope and some nipple chewing. Where would it end? She wanted to run back and shout through the door, 'The maximum pot's a snog!'

What made it worse was that Barry's cheerful summary of women was now bouncing through her head on a spacehopper. 'See what I said? Fascinating. That's the key.' If Candida was anything, she was fascinating. Cathy, red-faced and smarting from her rejected proposal of marriage, was not fascinating. She'd put all her cards on the table – or in this case, posted them through his letter box – and Jason had turned up his nose at them.

Cathy sobbed quietly to herself all the way back on the tube. She lurched home from Walthamstow Station and down her leafy road.

Mrs Ali was in her front garden, delicately clipping at her yew hedge with the shears. She met Cathy with a friendly smile.

'Hello! Are you liking your new home?'

'It's – it's bleak and empty!' Cathy managed and shot into her house.

Chapter Twelve

'You are a plonker,' Fiona said, delivering a vodka for herself and an orange juice for Cathy back to the table they'd commandeered in the corner of the pub.

It was Monday evening and Fiona had insisted on taking Cathy for a drink straight from work. As Cathy had been too despondent to think of a venue, Fiona had decided they'd better head for the Goose and Granite near Walthamstow tube. That way, Cathy only had to amble home on foot and Fiona could get back on the tube and to Highbury easily. And, Fiona had observed, Cathy didn't look as if she had much nervous energy left inside her. A five-minute walk home from the pub was probably about all she'd manage that evening.

The pub was relatively quiet and the tables were large and spaced well away from each other. Here they could talk privately with some comforting bustle around them. But Cathy was too numb really to take in her environment. She sipped her orange juice, chewed on a chunk of ice and considered what it felt like to be a plonker.

'Thanks, Fi. I know that.'

'Jason was a babe, you know,' Fiona said ruefully, slipping off her jacket and fiddling uncomfortably with the silver bracelet round her tanned wrist. 'I don't want to make you feel worse, but he was a corker. You do know that all your friends fancied him, don't you?'

Cathy looked at Fiona miserably.

'Thanks.'

'Even Ruth fancied him.' Fiona nodded. 'After the Christmas dinner last year, she said to me, 'What's Cathy's boyfriend's name again?' with that sort of look in her eye. You know, that mid-life crisis look she gets sometimes.'

Cathy gave Fiona a glare.

'It isn't particularly helpful to know that the whole world, including the MD of the company I work for, was in love with my boyfriend.'

'Well, in lust, at least.' Fiona took a sip of her vodka. 'I know, I'm supposed to tell you he was a bastard and to forget him. The trouble is, he really wasn't a bastard.'

'Just tell me he was a bastard,' Cathy urged. 'Please.'

'Jason was a bastard,' Fiona iterated obligingly. 'Forget him.'

'Thank you.'

'But he *was* a bastard in one respect,' Fiona reasoned, softening her gaze. 'He wasn't around for you. And frankly, girlfriend, he got what he deserved.'

Cathy glanced up from her unappetising fruit juice in surprise.

'Do you really think so?'

'Yes,' Fiona confirmed. 'You're a babe too. And he took you for granted. His mistake. I expect he's regretting that now.'

'I don't think so.' Cathy pursed her lips. 'There's that bitch-woman across the corridor to distract him for starters. Then, after Can-dee-dah, he can work his way through the rest of the female population. According to you.'

'Hey,' Fiona said softly, touching Cathy's hand. 'He

won't do that. He's just not that type. He never strayed when you were together, did he?'

'No, but—' Cathy stopped herself. Why was she so sure? She had no idea. But she was sure, and when Jason had told her he'd never been unfaithful she'd known it to be the truth. The knowledge that Jason had been trustworthy whereas she'd been the one to stray, just made her feel worse.

'So this Nick character must be a bit of a hunk, then,' Fiona went on. 'Perhaps something will happen with him?'

'Oh Fi,' Cathy pleaded. 'I don't want to do anything with Nick. Thinking about other men just makes me feel awful.'

A thoughtful silence fell between the two women. Fiona sipped at her vodka steadily and tutted to herself.

'Well, Cathy, I see it like this. Either you get Jason back, or you try to move on.'

'I won't get Jason back,' Cathy said in a small voice. 'Let's not even go there, Fiona. It's so wretched. He was so cold, so hard when I saw him on Sunday. He's never been like that with me, ever, not in four years. I've blown it. I know it. I wouldn't dream of speaking to him at the moment. I said everything I could think of, even that stupid proposal – and he practically laughed in my face.'

Fiona sighed sympathetically.

'All right. Then it's my duty, as your friend, to tell you that there are plenty more fish in the sea.'

But the thought of fish only brought back painful memories of Jason's passion for seafood. Cathy let out a soft whimper.

'I mean, look over there.' Fiona nodded towards the bar. 'At least three, no four, men of our sort of age. All presentable. They could be lovely. For all you know, this was meant to be. There could be somebody out there right now, waiting for you, who's perfect for you. And don't you dare say that Jason was perfect for you. If he's not coming back you can't wallow in misery. I won't let you.'

Cathy tried to smile.

'Thanks. Let's talk about you and David instead.'

'No, let's not.' Fiona laughed to herself. 'He was messing me about, excuses not to meet up, all those uh-oh warning signs. So I ended it before he could.'

'No! This weekend?'

'Yep.' Fiona seemed undaunted. 'Come on, Cathy, it was only a couple of months. I hadn't really got attached to him. I don't mind being single and just enjoying myself until something turns up. I'm really not bothered.'

'You aren't, are you?' Cathy studied Fiona's face in fascination. 'I wish I could be like you, right now.'

'Well, you can't. Four years is a bloody long time. I mean, some marriages don't last that long. When I split up with Rob after three years together I was gutted. In fact, the whole family went into mourning, which made it worse. They knew him so well, you see, and we'd lived together and everything. My mum said it was like losing a son-in-law. God, it took me a year to get over it. But that was – what – three years ago? I really did get over it and for now, I'm just happy being me.'

'Just happy being you,' Cathy echoed under her breath.

'Yes. And that's what you're going to be. Happy being Cathy Gordon. You can't beat yourself up about this any more. If you can't put the clock back you've got to live with it. You've got a full life, you adore your job, you've got some good friends and you and I are going to go out and set the town alight.' Fiona laughed as Cathy slumped her elbows on the table with a look of pure exhaustion. 'All right, not tonight, maybe not this weekend, but we will. And you'll wonder what you were so upset about.'

'Maybe,' Cathy said doubtfully.

'You'll see,' Fiona reassured her with a smile. 'The last thing you need right now is loads of people making sympathetic noises. It'll just make you feel worse.'

'Oh Cathy, I am so, so sorry.'

Cathy cradled the phone to her chin as she lay, tired and deflated, on her sofa. She and Fiona had parted company by half past nine, Fiona noting that Cathy was far too bushed to make any more sense, and should just go home and put herself to bed.

Once she was home, Cathy had felt desperately lonely. The box of wine that Jason had brought was still sitting near the living-room door, where he'd put it down. Cathy hadn't been able to bear moving it. So she'd phoned Melissa. But hearing the genuine unhappiness in Melissa's hushed tones once Cathy had imparted the news that she and Jason were no longer together was threatening to rub salt into her raw wounds.

'You know how much we liked Jason,' Melissa said gently. 'But if this is what you've both decided, you know I'll stand by you, don't you? You must have had your reasons. If there's anything I can do, let me know.'

'Thank you,' Cathy breathed, warmed by her mother's support.

'But I am so sorry. Oh dear.' Melissa went quiet for a moment and Cathy lay silently, tears brimming in her eyes. 'Oh, what a shame.'

'Well.' Cathy dashed the back of her hand against her eyes. 'It's not as if we were married or anything.' She could hear the tightness in her voice. A lump of emotion was caught in her throat and choking her.

'No, dear, marriage really isn't the thing these days, is it? But four years, darling, it's a very long time. If you had been married you wouldn't be allowed to throw it all away on one misunderstanding. When I was young the whole family would rally round. People would make sure you'd tried everything, they'd talk to you, make you talk to each other. It was different then.'

'Well this is – is now.' Cathy struggled. 'And nobody's going to rally round. It just wouldn't make any difference. Jason's going to live his own life from now on and I'm going to live mine. And that's – that's it.'

'Oh my poor girl. I wish I could take your pain away,' Melissa said, so softly that Cathy began to cry. She cried and cried, while Melissa stayed on the phone and let her.

Then, finally, Cathy felt more peaceful, her body too tired to produce any more tears.

'Thank you,' she whispered to Melissa. 'I think I can sleep now. I love you.'

Cathy threw herself into her work. She didn't have the courage to ring Jason. She didn't want any contact with

Nick, who'd unwittingly been the catalyst of their separation. For the time being she just wanted to try to remember what it was about the life she'd created for herself that was so wonderful.

She even did her best to shove Frank to the back of her mind. She wanted to know why she and Nick had both been sent to the two test matches by him, but with the working week so desperately busy and her romantic life having collapsed in a heap, the last thing she wanted was to expend emotional energy she couldn't spare on a cryptic and irascible old man. Cathy still felt that Frank was somehow manipulating her. It was when he had arrived in her life, like the wicked fairy being lowered into a pantomime on a wire, that things had started to go wrong. Hadn't he been the first one to tell her that she had a boyfriend who wouldn't marry her? It had never occurred to her before. Since then, every bugger she met seemed to be reinforcing the fact. Now she'd ascertained it for herself. It was as if it were up on a poster in every tube station in London. She couldn't go anywhere without being aware of it.

So instead of moping around, Cathy got up early and went to bed late, filling every hour in between by making phone calls, visits, banging off e-mails and following up her contacts.

She tried to catch Mark at work to ask him about Hellier's again. Surely he'd have spoken to Ruth about it by now? But Mark seemed rushed off his feet too. Cathy managed to trap him in the corridor one stuffy afternoon in the week.

'Mark! I just wondered if you'd had a moment to talk to Ruth about my ideas?' Cathy widened her eyes eagerly, hoping to keep his attention.

'Ah, yes.' Mark loosened his tie. There was some problem with the air-conditioning which meant that everybody was hot and slightly on edge. There was a dewy film over Mark's bald patch. 'Ruth's been away, so we've only had a chance to bring it up in principle, but she's got your brief and we'll get back to you on it.'

'I just wondered if there'd been any feedback already,' Cathy persevered. 'With the board meeting you had on Monday—'

Mark was distracted by his mobile phone going off.

'Right. Sorry, Cathy, I've got to take this in my office. I'll get back to you on it when I can.'

And Mark disappeared, pulling his office door closed behind him, leaving Cathy to plod back to the goldfish bowl in search of a plug-in fan to cool herself.

Cathy took Bill Havers up on his offer to visit Walthamstow dogs. He insisted that the outing was on him and Cathy was really looking forward to a night out doing something completely different. They sat in the restaurant at a long barlike table, which looked directly over the track. Bill treated her to steak and chips, and insisted on covering her first few bets, which the startlingly efficient waitresses collected from them as they sat, delivering the winnings back on a saucer. Cathy relaxed, enjoying the bustle of the event, the boisterous audience, the informality and the fascination of entering a foreign world. It was a lively, and very welcome, distraction.

As Cathy sipped at a glass of wine, straining with excitement to watch the dog she'd backed for each race, it struck her that this summer was turning out to be a time for new experiences. Being at a dog race was as different from a cricket match as she could have imagined, but the thrill of experiencing something new was the same. If someone had told her a couple of months ago that this year she'd have been introduced to both cricket and dog racing, she'd have shaken her head with disbelief. But here she was, in the thick of a bakingly hot summer, being educated in cricket, dog racing and grandfathers. With the benefit of wine and Bill's lively company, Cathy was amused by the thought. It was a release, to have a bit of respite from her routine and to be able to drag herself away from the gloomy feeling of missing Jason. It put her on a high. It was a high she hadn't felt since her day out at the Lord's test match – even though England had gone on to lose the match horrendously badly.

She mentioned the cricket to Bill and he pulled a face.

'Bloody England. They win the first match by a mile and lose the next by an innings. Tossers. Build us up and bring us down, they do.'

'How many matches are there, then?' Cathy asked. 'I keep thinking the Ashes is all over, then they start talking about the next match.'

Bill laughed. 'Five this year. Edgbaston, Lord's, Old Trafford, Headingley and the Oval.'

Cathy nodded. It wasn't exactly *The Lord of the Rings*, but there was a hint of legend about the names.

'Why?' Bill gave her a funny look. 'You haven't got into cricket, have you?'

'No.' She waved her steak knife emphatically to reassure him. 'But I ended up going to the first two matches by accident. Someone else bought the tickets.'

'Bugger me. You never did!' Bill seemed impressed.

'You're a corking gel, you know that. Your boyfriend must be dead chuffed. You don't get many women showing an interest in sport.'

Cathy decided to pass on the subject of her boyfriend. It sent a quiver of adrenalin over her stomach and visions of Candida unwinding her espadrilles and unstrapping her strappy dress all for Jason's benefit.

'The thing is,' Bill continued unaware, 'it's all about character, innit? You only know what you're really made of when the odds are stacked up against you. That's how we've all survived in the East End. You never know what life's going to throw at you next. It's how you deal with it that counts.'

Cathy gazed at Bill, sipping her wine, thinking how right he was.

'These dot com Jessies', he went on, and Cathy smiled to herself having heard this particular rant before, 'want a fast buck, everything handed to them on a plate, without doing a hard day's work in their lives. What do they know about running a business from hand to mouth? Bloody nothing. But you' – he pointed at her – 'you're not like them. You're a grafter with a damned good head on your shoulders. You'll go all the way.'

'Oh, I'm just—' Cathy blushed.

'No, no. Listen to me.' Bill drew on all his East End bluster and Cathy sensed that he wouldn't be contradicted. 'I know a rising star when I see one. I notice things, see? Your e-mails. I notice the time you send them. Six in the morning, after midnight, any time of the day. You're committed. See my point?'

'I think you're saying I need to get a life.' Cathy laughed, slightly perturbed at the evidence of the hours she was working.

'You've got a fine one ahead of you, gel.' Bill nodded several times to emphasise his point. 'We don't let people in lightly down here. You might have worked that out for yourself. But you're one of us now. And why? Because you don't roll over at the first obstacle. You don't go round it, or over it. What do you do?'

Cathy shook her head, unsure.

'You go right through it, gel, and that's what makes you one of us. You don't lie there counting the things what's piling on top of you. You deal with them. You're a survivor.' Then Bill grinned at her disarmingly. 'You must meet my missus soon. You'll get on like a house on fire.'

'I'd love to.' That was the biggest compliment Bill could pay her and Cathy knew it.

'You know' – Bill lowered his voice – 'I wouldn't ask Mark or Ruth round to my place. No offence to them. But you know what I mean.' Cathy absorbed the remark with a rueful smile. Bill went on, 'Nah, there's something about Mark. Nice geezer, don't get me wrong. But he can smell the money.'

'What do you mean?' Cathy sipped her wine, eyeing Bill curiously.

'I mean, you're in it to help people. You really care. I can tell that. But that Mark. I dunno.' Bill shook his head thoughtfully. 'He gets into bed with the big guys, the ones with the big bank accounts. I heard on the grapevine he'd taken Harry Cooper out to dinner. Expensive dinner.'

'Harry Cooper?' Cathy frowned. 'Managing director of Cooper's Construction?'

Bill's thick eyebrows both shot up as he nodded.

'And who else d'you think was there? Troy Vickers.'

Cathy put her wineglass down, her thoughts churning at the mention of the architect. She was the one who'd told Mark that Troy was looking for a construction company to work with him on the Hellier's project. Mark couldn't have – ? No, surely not. He wouldn't have taken her idea, substituted Cooper's for Bill's growing firm and gone ahead to broker a deal?

'But Cooper's are huge and successful already,' she found herself saying faintly. 'They're not local to east London. And they bring in labour from all over the country. They don't recruit locally. It doesn't do anything to create employment here.'

Bill refilled Cathy's glass and then his own. He carefully put the bottle down on the table again.

'Is this about Hellier's, Cathy? I'd heard all the rumours. Do you know anything about it?'

Cathy stared back at Bill's honest face, her loyalties torn.

'I'd heard that Hellier's were thinking of coming here, but I – I really don't know why Mark held that meeting. There could be lots of reasons,' she said, hoping that was the truth. Mark couldn't possibly have gone behind her back to deal with Troy direct, with an established construction company that would do nothing whatsoever for the regeneration of the area? The thought made her heart somersault with dismay. There'd be more money in it for the company, but they were supposed to work in business development and Bill's company was ripe for development. Harry Cooper was already at the top of his tree. This wasn't all about profit. Was it?

'All right, gel. You don't have to say any more,' Bill said and flicked the event booklet open to the page listing the races. 'So what do you reckon for the nine o'clock? I'll go for "Laughing Girl".'

At nearly midnight Bill dropped Cathy off outside her house.

'I want to thank you for everything you've done for us, Cathy. I thought I could keep on doing things the old way and I hate to be told. God knows, ask my wife, I can't be told. But things was knocking on my door, things that wouldn't go away. And you've helped me see that change is a good thing. You're a real star.'

'Thanks, Bill.' Cathy almost choked on her words. She'd spent her own life resisting change. She was even resisting it now, shunning her grandfather, too afraid of what she might hear to speak to Jason, avoiding Nick, trying to maintain her routine, keeping quiet about her knowledge of Hellier's out of loyalty to her boss so that she didn't rock the boat. But Bill was smiling at her earnestly. He trusted her to do the best for him.

'It's a bloody shame you don't want one of them Docklands offices. We could fit you up, you know. I know blokes who can provide anything you'd need. We look after each other here.'

Warmed by Bill's kindness, Cathy swallowed. She took a deep breath and wondered if what she was about to say was the riskiest thing she had ever done in her professional life.

'Bill, there's a meeting of the Dockland's Business Club on Friday. Er, were you thinking of going?'

'God, yes.' Bill smacked his forehead. 'I'd clean forgotten. You know I try to go to those things if I can.'

'Well, er' – Cathy reached for the door handle – 'I

think you should go to this one. There will be some . . . people there you should talk to.' Bill nodded, looking slightly confused, but Cathy was opening the car door. 'Just promise me you'll be there. It could be the most important thing you've ever done.'

Cathy said thank you again for a lovely evening and dived out of the car before Bill could quiz her any more. She waved at the back of his car and found her keys.

She let herself into her house and slammed the door behind her, leaning back against it. Her body was tingling with an odd mixture of elation and anxiety. Bill's confidence in her was awesome. She didn't feel that she was rising to the occasion at all. She felt more as though she was floundering like a novice swimmer who'd been thrown in the diving pool. She hadn't got anywhere with Frank yet, she'd had a pointless grapple with a guy she hardly knew and she'd lost her boyfriend. Now it seemed as if her immediate boss had taken her ideas and used them for the least moral aim she could think of. She felt like she had one wooden leg that had been nailed to the floor while the other went round in circles.

At that moment, she had every sympathy with the England cricket team. She could just imagine how they felt.

'Aw c'mon, let's go clubbing,' Graham started on again.

Nick swilled his beer around in his glass. When were the guys going to get it into their heads that he hated clubs? He gave them enough hints.

'Can't.' He indicated his faded jeans. 'They'll never let me in wearing these.'

'What's the matter with you tonight?' Graham

punched his arm playfully. 'You're dead quiet. Are they working you too hard?'

'Yep, of course.' He grinned.

Four of them had gone to the pub together. The lads had insisted on drinking centrally. In the centre of Birmingham the weekend started on Thursday night. There were also places where the weekend started on Monday night, but after falling asleep on the loo at work a few too many times in his mid-twenties, Nick avoided those now.

The guys had said they wanted to view the totty from a good vantage point. Tiny dresses and exposed legs were in, and as the heat was still rising there were tans and cleavages to be spotted in all directions. None of them would go along with Nick's suggestion of a quiet game of pool in the local.

Now they'd lost Terry and Steve, who'd headed off to the other side of the bar in pursuit of two Australian women. Nick and Graham were perched round a high table which encircled a pillar, although Nick was finding it hard to keep Graham's attention. But he was too tired to do anything other than sit and drink. He was putting in long hours. He hated his job and he was also confused about things he'd rather not be thinking about.

'In the summer, a young man's thoughts turn to love.' Graham whistled under his breath as a group of young women came into the packed pub and pushed their way to the bar.

'And in autumn, winter and spring in your case,' Nick observed.

'The sap is rising,' Graham told him, preening his crop of black hair and readjusting his T-shirt. 'You don't want to miss out, do you?'

'Actually, mate, I'm just knackered. I think I'll call it a day.'

'Not a chance. You're not leaving me here on my own.'

'Sorry.'

'This isn't still about England losing, is it? Why bother caring? Australia's the best side in the world. We're pretty much the worst. What the hell did you expect?'

'We are *not* pretty much the worst,' Nick defended.

'C'mon. I'll tell you a joke to cheer you up.' Graham chuckled. 'What's the difference between an England batsman and Houdini? An England batsman gets out more easily.'

'Har har.'

Nick curled his fingers into his palms. This was just the sort of doom-mongering that he couldn't stand. The tabloids were the same. A fortnight ago they were full of praise for England's efforts. Now, after one more match, they were hissing and spitting at them like resentful cats. All he wanted was for someone to share his optimism.

But Nick was also confused that his memory of the test match was combined with images of Cathy. He could see her eyes dancing with humour, the way her mouth curled when she made a wry remark, the way she moved and the exact tone of her laugh. When Graham had asked him what he'd thought of Stewart's edge to first slip, Nick had remembered the kisses and then had had to concentrate to bring all the cricketing detail back to the front of his mind.

He'd been wondering all night what Cathy would think if she could see him now, out with his mates.

Drinking beer, hanging out in the cattle markets. Cathy probably never went to bars like this. She was too solid. Not at all boring – she'd proved that – but wholesome. She'd probably take one look in the door and leg it as fast as she could. What she'd think of Graham he could only shudder to think. Big, with an untamed beer gut and overburdened with hope when it came to women.

What women couldn't tell when Graham came out with his ludicrous patter was that he was as bright as a button, employed by one of the top software IT companies and the most loyal friend you could ever ask for. But Graham looked like a Millwall nightmare and that's what Cathy would see.

That Saturday night with Cathy had been haunting Nick all week. He'd managed to laugh off her boy-friend's sudden arrival at the time. Jason was just the sort of guy he'd picture her with. Good-looking, smart, well-spoken and obviously not short of a bob or two. Not that Nick was short of cash any more. He was making a mint and hardly spending any of it. But his family had never had much money, which meant he'd never been brought up with matching lamps and curtains, stylish pictures on the walls, silk cushions. And the thought of reproducing that comfort in the shared house was laughable. They were all fond of the sofa that ejaculated springs into your back, the fact that the landlord wouldn't care about the cigarette burns, the lack of incentive to wash up, the piles of empty pizza cartons. It was how they were. Even making the comparison with Cathy's house confused Nick.

Jason had turned up like the Milk Tray man: 'and all because the lady loves a dozen bottles of good French red'. Nick wasn't ready to shower gifts on any woman.

It was like a snowball. Once you started it rolling, you'd be struggling to keep up with efforts to please her – whoever she was. He'd once turned up at a girl's house after the pub had closed with three of his mates and half a dozen bottles of Newkie Brown. They'd even bought her a kebab, but she still refused to come to the door. She'd told him she wanted him to be impulsive, so he was trying to prove that he was. She never spoke to him again.

'Hello? Anyone in there?' Graham waved a hand over Nick's eyes.

'Sorry, mate. Just thinking.'

Graham grinned wickedly.

'I bet I know what you're thinking about.'

'I bet you don't.'

'You still won't tell me where you were on Saturday night. You looked like death when you piled in on Sunday. I reckon you were kept up all night.' Graham rolled his tongue in his cheek and wiggled his eyebrows suggestively. 'I bet you were thinking about what you were doing all night.'

Nick chuckled. Graham's persistence was always funny after a while.

'I was thinking about Beaujolais, actually.'

'Oo, well ex-cuse me!' Graham gave a belly laugh. 'Right. Like I believe you.'

'See?' Nick spoke mostly to himself. 'It's impossible. Why even think about it?'

'Hey – hey, ladies!' Graham caught the attention of two young women sauntering past them. Nick sighed into his T-shirt. They'd been through this routine so many times before. 'How would you like to bring your drinks over here and join us?'

Nick could hardly bear to watch. They were maybe twenty-three or twenty-four, both attractive, lithe, in heels and nice dresses, and they didn't look stupid. He knew what would come next. Graham would overdo it, the women would give them both withering looks, maybe even make some comparison of their faces to backs of buses, then continue on their merry way.

Graham was already shrugging haplessly.

'It's all right. You have a nice night. You can get used to being put down, as the vet told the dog.'

The woman with the long fair hair looked at her friend, who was darker, with fluffier hair that exploded round a nice face, and they seemed to reach a decision without saying a word. How did women do that? Nick had always wondered. They ambled up to the table, which was high with teetering chrome and padded leather chairs placed round it, drew out one each and sat down.

'So what have you two got to say for yourselves, then?' The dark-haired woman fixed Nick with a cautious look, then gave him a slight smile. He blinked back. He'd been looking forward to a quiet night with the boys, or a night on his own with the television. The last thing he'd expected was to have to make conversation with a strange woman.

Graham jumped in his seat, knocked over his pint glass and swept it up again quickly, succeeding in only spilling half of it across the table. He slid off his chair and swamped the spillage with paper napkins.

'Right then. Right. So I'm Graham and this is Nick. And can I get you a drink? You've just got one. That's fine. So, here we are. What are you doing out tonight, then? I mean, we should start with your names, really.

Then we'll talk about something else.' His face had gone from pink to purple in two seconds.

'I'm Hannah, this is Mel.' The dark-haired girl laughed at Graham, but it wasn't an unkind laugh. Nick noticed that Graham was running his hand nervously over his hair and wished he'd stop because he was making them look like a couple of berks. Then he realised that he'd been doing it himself too.

'Hi, Hannah,' Nick said casually, not in the mood, but not wanting to be rude.

'Hi,' she said and smiled at him again.

Hannah wasn't beautiful, or striking, or unique in any way. But she had a friendly, pretty face. It wouldn't be nice to head off home now and leave her feeling rejected, and anyway, out of loyalty to Graham, Nick felt he should hang round and not break up the group.

They all bantered together. Once or twice Graham caught Nick's eye and he returned the glances obliquely. Nick's mind was being dragged back to Cathy all the time, but he made the effort.

Hannah worked for a travel agency. She shared a house with Mel, who was a nurse, and another woman who worked in a solicitor's office. She was pleasant company. It was easy to smile, nod, throw in a caustic remark to make everyone laugh. Hannah even gave him a coy glance and said, 'You are funny.'

Cathy wouldn't have said that. She'd have come back with something that made him laugh too. Conscious that he was tying himself up in knots, Nick decided to put Cathy right out of his mind and have another beer.

Cathy's heart was pounding as she wove her way through the animated crowd amassed in the town hall.

Every so often she waved a hand, or stopped for a quick chat with the many people she now recognised from the local businesses. But she had one man fixed in her sights.

He was of medium height and portly build, with fine white hair caught back in a ponytail and a thick, cascading beard. He was dressed, as ever, in casual clothes, today in baggy linen trousers with a tunic that came over the belt. He looked like an artist, but Cathy was aware that beneath the bohemian exterior was a brilliant mind. His confident, cultured voice caught the attention of those who passed. He was an important man and he knew it. But Cathy also knew that Troy Vickers was a man with humanitarian instincts. She was counting on it.

She grabbed a cool glass of white wine for support and took a deep sip from it as she pushed her way towards him. Bill Havers hadn't spotted her yet, but she was filled with relief that he had come. He was standing in a small group, only a few yards from Troy, but possibly hadn't seen him, or perhaps didn't know who he was. Cathy wasn't sure that Bill would have recognised him on sight. But that was where she came in.

She'd known for sure that neither Mark nor Ruth would be here tonight. Apart from the fact that Mark never bothered to get involved in evening activities and Ruth rarely seemed to have the time, they had both been away from the office ever since Cathy's evening out with Bill. Cathy had been frustrated to find them absent – she very much wanted to ask Mark about his private dinner with Troy and Harry Cooper – but in some ways it alleviated her guilt for taking this step without their authority. All she was going to do was introduce Bill and Troy to each other. It would be impolite not to. Nobody could blame her for that.

Just as Cathy was wondering how on earth she was going to enact the introduction, her plan began to work like a dream. Bill saw her and immediately moved her way. They were now only a yard from Troy himself.

'Cathy!' Bill enthused, slapping his hand into hers and giving it a firm shake. 'Great to see you here. You must meet Mick. We've worked together for years. He's just getting us both a drink.'

'Lovely,' she said breathlessly, her eyes darting to Troy, who at that moment was gazing round the room, looking for somebody to speak to next. 'And there's someone I'd like you to—'

She held her breath as Troy began to move her way. Was he going to walk straight past? Her pulse drummed in her ears. But suddenly he stopped, gave Cathy a very open stare and then broke into a genial smile of recognition.

'Cathy Gordon? I do believe we've met before. Troy Vickers.'

Cathy heard Bill choking with surprise beside her. She shook hands with Troy and fixed Bill with a confident smile.

'Bill, I don't think you've met Troy Vickers yet? May I introduce you to each other. Bill Havers of Havers Construction, Troy Vickers.'

'I know all about you, Mr Vickers.' Bill went bright red as he shook Troy's hand. 'I admire your work very much.'

'Thank you,' Troy said. 'And please call me Troy.'

'Bill's company built the new Docklands office

complex that you might have heard people talking about,' Cathy said warmly. 'I think the retail outlets have all been snapped up already and the offices are going like hot cakes.'

'Is that so, Bill?' Troy's pale-blue eyes brightened. 'And you're a local man, are you?'

For a moment Cathy wondered if Bill was going to blow it. His eyes were bulging, his face puce. It was as if he had suddenly realised what an opportunity he was being faced with and desperately wanted to run away and plan what to say. But the moment was now and Cathy urged Bill to take it. Then, to her relief, Bill cleared his throat, stood up straight and spoke clearly.

'Yes, I'm East End born and bred. Seen a lot of changes round here in my lifetime and now things are looking up for us local businesses. We know the area, we know the people. We know who needs the work. It's a promising time for us all.'

'Yes, that's very interesting.' Troy nodded. 'Perhaps you could tell me a little more about your company? Forgive me, I have a card here. Please take it.'

Cathy silently exhaled the breath she had been holding as Troy and Bill exchanged cards. Bill had begun to talk about his business in detail. Cathy pointed delicately at the other side of the room, even though neither of the two men noticed.

'Oh, I spot someone,' she whispered and slipped away.

It was Barry on the phone.

Cathy was taken completely by surprise. For a moment she couldn't work out how he had her number, then she remembered giving him a card with

238

her contact details on it. But it was strange to be phoned by the Frank camp. So far the only communication had been via crisp, enigmatic notes in Frank's inky scrawl. She couldn't imagine Frank using the phone. Ringing someone up was far too mundane for him. Just as Digory's Mad Uncle Andrew would never have picked up the phone and enquired after someone's health before going back to the attic to be mad again.

But Cathy had also almost succeeded in pushing Frank right from her mind. She'd been too caught up with the complexities of work to try to unravel whatever weird plan he was putting into action. She'd arrived back at her house this evening, glowing from the image of Troy Vickers and Bill talking animatedly to each other, and all she had been envisaging for the rest of her Friday night was a glass of wine, a pizza and *Frasier*.

So when the phone had rung after she'd only been on the sofa for about ten minutes and she'd heard Barry's tense voice, Cathy had been completely taken aback.

'How are you?' Barry asked.

'Fine,' Cathy bluffed. 'And you?'

'Great. Everything's great.'

'What's wrong?'

She heard him take a deep breath.

'I don't know where to start. Everything's gone tits up.'

'For you?' Cathy could guess that Barry would rather enjoy everything going tits up in his life. But she shook the thought away. He sounded agitated.

'No. It's Frank.'

Cathy's skin went cold. She felt prickles run up her back. It was only after the call that she'd thought back and realised that she'd been scared to death at this point.

'What's happened?' she demanded.

'Barbara's gone. They had some sort of row. She's taken all the files, the books, the stuff they were working on. He's been hunched up in his chair for days. I can't make him eat properly. He's strung out and the doctor's increased his dose.'

'Dose? The dose of – his heart pills?'

'Yeah. He's like, white. He's so tense. I keep expecting to find him sitting there, watching telly, dead.'

Cathy felt this wasn't a good time to point out that Frank couldn't be simultaneously watching the telly and dead. She tried to think.

'What happened? With him and Barbara?'

'No idea. Not really. He won't talk about it apart from to yell things and then go quiet again.'

'So no change there, then,' Cathy muttered. She went on, 'So – when you say Barbara's gone, what do you mean? She never lived with you, did she?'

'No, but she's gone. I mean, she doesn't come round any more.'

'Since when?'

'Since Saturday. I haven't seen her since then.'

'Well, I'm not surprised, Barry.' Cathy's relief that Frank hadn't actually had a heart attack made her callous. 'I couldn't believe the way he behaved towards her. And you said that was normal, so my guess is she's snapped. As I would. I'm only surprised it took this long.'

'Cathy, I rang you because I didn't know who else to call.'

Cathy pondered, clicking her tongue in her teeth.

'Has Frank actually tried to contact Barbara?'

Barry guffawed.

'No way. He's not going to do anything about it. He spits venom if her name's mentioned and I have a feeling this is a permanent thing. Just by the fact that she's always here, every day, whatever he does to her, and now she's not here at all. And she's taken so much stuff. I don't think she'll be back.'

'So – what has it got to do with me?'

Even as she asked the question, Cathy sensed that it had a lot to do with her. She bit her lip.

'It's like he's just sitting there, waiting for death. The bloody cricket didn't help. It's like he's got nothing left.'

'Barry, I don't see how I can possibly help. Just me being there put his blood pressure up. He told me. You know that.'

'Yeah, but.' She heard Barry light a cigarette. She guessed he must be allowed to smoke in his room. She couldn't imagine that he was calling her from downstairs, where Frank might hear. 'He's asked me, a couple of times, if I've heard from you.'

'He has?'

'Just if I've seen a letter from you, or if there've been any calls. Or if you've contacted me. I think he really wants to see you.'

Cathy took a sip of her wine while she thought.

'Barry, what if I don't come? Frank's been messing me about like you won't believe.'

'I know.'

'No, you don't know the half of it. He's manipulating me in some strange way and he's got no right. Maybe

241

it'll do him good to spend some time on his own with nobody to bully. Why should I care?'

'Cathy,' Barry said carefully, 'I honestly think he's going to die soon. Barbara used to warn me about him, that he was fragile, and I just laughed it off. But I can see it now. I keep expecting him to be dead the next time I see him. That's the best I can put it. I've never been round death before, but it's like it's turned up already and it's just sitting there, waiting for him.'

Cathy's pulse slowed.

'I just thought I should tell you,' Barry said. 'I'm the only one here now who knows that you care. I thought – what if you never got to see him again? Someone had to tell you.'

Cathy set her glass back on the coffee table clumsily.

'I'll be up tomorrow.'

Chapter Thirteen

Barry had told Cathy about a coach that ran a regular and quick service to Oxford. He'd said it was comfortable and easy to find at Victoria.

Cathy found the Oxford Tube stop at Grosvenor Gardens, behind Victoria Station. It was a smart red double-decker coach with tinted windows. It was packed with day trippers – but on a Saturday at peak summer holiday time this was inevitable. Cathy slid beside a tourist, opened a book and pretended to read it.

As the coach veered up the M40, she felt the knot in her stomach beginning to unravel. She knew it would form again when she turned up on Frank's doorstep, but for the moment she gazed over the green fields and made the most of the respite.

She took the coach all the way to the Oxford bus station, looking properly at the town this time as the coach swept through. This was where her grandfather had paraded as a young man. Barry had told her all he knew – which wasn't much – but her imagination filled in the gaps. Which of the creamy colleges, luminous today in the sunlight, would he have frequented? Where did he teach? Did he go to the pubs, eat at the restaurants, entertain the crowds with his knowledge and wit? Or had he been a grumpy little sod whom everybody hated?

Cathy guessed that Barbara might know. Barry hadn't known much about Barbara's friendship with Frank, but it seemed that it spanned many years. The only way Cathy was going to find out some facts, and bury the fantasies, would be by talking to Frank. And she had to do that, if possible, without killing him off.

She took a taxi again and arrived on the doorstep.

The house was quiet. The windows in the kitchen were closed, although if anything it was hotter today than when she'd visited before and then they'd been open. But Barbara wasn't present any longer and Cathy realised that it made a big difference. She took a deep breath and pressed the domed button of the bell.

She waited. Eventually a shadowy figure appeared behind the coloured glass panes and Barry materialised as the door was yanked open. He grinned at her warmly.

'Hiya!' he chirruped.

'Hi!' Cathy smiled back and was for some reason hit by a blushing attack. It wasn't until she was face to face with Barry again that she started to wonder exactly what she'd said in the pub and how flirty she might have been. Since then, she'd lost Jason and that made things very different. Flirting was no longer fun and aimless. If she was truly single, any flirting from here on would be meaningful. It was best to knock it on the head. Which was a shame, as Barry was lovely.

'It's great to see you again!' Barry insisted, giving every impression of being absurdly delighted.

He was in jeans and a vest top. He seemed bronzer-skinned, and darker in eyes and hair than Cathy remembered. He'd obviously been enjoying the sun. He looked like the sort of man you might find emptying fish out of a wooden boat on a beach in the Bounty adverts, almost exotic.

'Fucking hot, isn't it?' Barry laughed. Cathy crossed 'exotic' from her mental list. 'You'd better come in, then.'

Cathy stepped into the hall and instantly felt chilled. Barry closed the front door behind them and she had the feeling you have when you suddenly walk into a museum on a hot day.

What was odd, though, was that she felt the absence of Barbara. Not just because she knew she wasn't there, but because her first visit had created a mental picture of a household in action. Barbara was a part of that, fainting fit and all. Her neat shoes and A-line skirt had somehow fitted in with the surroundings.

Cathy crept over the polished wood floor and the faded rugs – noting that they were askew and that nobody had straightened them – as if she expected Barbara to pop out of one of the doors at any minute and glare at her. It was a bit like a friend holding a party on a weekend when the parents were away. You could temporarily assert your presence, but you didn't want to leave any evidence of it. It was somebody else's house.

'Frank's really bad,' Barry said, dropping the level of his voice. 'I'm so glad you came.'

'Any sign of Barbara?'

'None. Like I said, I think it's permanent.'

'Did you tell him I was coming?' Cathy watched Barry's face for a reaction. She hadn't thought to say 'Warn him' or, equally, 'Don't tell him, let's make it a surprise.' Either way, she'd made up her mind to come and that was that.

'I was going to this morning, but he was in such a foul mood I left him to it.'

'Right.'

Now Cathy wished she'd given Barry a firm instruction to warn Frank. She didn't know what to expect.

'He'll be pleased,' Barry told her. 'And in any case, he must have really liked you to have asked after you again. He doesn't like many people.'

Cathy tutted. 'He likes you.'

'Yeah, but that's because I don't argue with him. It's a man thing. We just take each other for what we are, watch the cricket, you know. It's easy. Men usually do get on, even if they don't like each other very much. It's different with women.'

Cathy could have countered with a few neat examples. Football hooliganism and wars for starters, but this was not the time to have a heated debate.

'Okay.' She put up a hand. 'Don't start on that again. I've had enough nightmares since you last gave me your list of man things.'

'Well, I'm glad you brought an overnight bag. I put some sheets in one of the spare rooms for you,' Barry said, his voice dropping even lower as they approached the door of Frank's room.

'Overnight? I'm not staying overnight!' Cathy protested.

'Oh, I just assumed. It's a big bag.' Barry nodded at her bag. 'Don't tell me, you've got everything in there including the Holy Grail and Lord Lucan, but you never thought to bring a toothbrush.'

'Oh, these are just . . . journey-type things.' Cathy glared at her leather bag indignantly. In fact, she had stuffed in a change of underwear, her toiletries bag and a clean top just in case. But she wasn't going to commit herself.

'Right. Well. Okay, see how it goes. Good luck. I'm going back to my room to fiddle about. If you want to come up, it's up the stairs, straight down the corridor, the one facing you.'

'Okay.'

Barry gave Cathy another smile, then disappeared. She watched his bare feet pad away. As he did, a large mass of orange fur swaggered down the hall towards her. She watched it cautiously, then, as it stopped at her legs, sniffed her, looked up and gave her a plaintive yowl, she dropped to her haunches and stroked Beefy's head.

'Hello, you,' she whispered. Beefy rattled a purr back at her. 'You are being fed, aren't you?'

The cat wound itself to and fro round her legs like a Slinky. She'd picked up from Barry that Barbara hated Beefy, so surely she hadn't been relied on to feed him, as well as do everything else? She decided Beefy didn't look hungry. Hot, yes. As she stooped, Beefy decided to lunge at her. Cathy had never been lunged at by a cat before and her first instinct was to scream – which she stifled – before she realised that it was an affectionate lunge and the cat was intent on being carried over her shoulder.

A minute later, when she'd gathered herself, Cathy tapped on Frank's door and walked in, with Beefy slung over her shoulder, rubbing a wet nose and feathery whiskers against her neck.

'Frank?'

The curtains were closed, even though the television wasn't on. Cathy had to blink several times to adjust to the gloom. She could see the back of the winged

247

armchair and one hand resting on the arm. She edged the door closed behind her, trying to ignore the fact that Beefy had now decided to chew her hair, and cautiously made her way round the armchair to stand in front of the television.

Frank looked three times smaller than when she'd last seen him and he'd been tiny then. He'd shrunk under his blanket, so that just his feet and hands stuck out. Over the top was a bent head. She thought he might be asleep.

'Frank!' she said more assertively.

His head jerked up. He focused on her and pulled back in his chair.

'Catherine!' he said.

'Frank,' Cathy said again, not knowing what else to say.

'Catherine!' Frank repeated, shuffling under his blanket. He seemed stunned.

It was like a scene from *Rocky Horror*: 'Doctor Scott!' 'Janet!' 'Brad!' 'Rocky!' 'Dr Scott!' Somebody had to say something more meaningful.

'I'm here to see you,' Cathy said as meaningfully as possible. Beefy leapt from her shoulder, amazing Cathy by not creating a crater in the floor as he landed, and decided that he'd jump into Frank's lap instead. Frank instinctively put out a hand, which Beefy headbutted. Frank didn't take his eyes from Cathy.

'Well, I can see you're here and I'd assume it's to see me,' he barked at her.

'Well . . . there you go.' Cathy decided she'd stay reasonable for as long as possible. 'I thought I'd come and tell you about Lord's. A strange thing happened to me there. I thought you might want to hear about it.'

'Well, you weren't hit by an England batsman swiping anything for six this time,' Frank muttered acidly. 'Were you? Useless bloody lot. I don't know why I bother.'

Cathy thought for a moment.

'Why *do* you bother, then?'

'What on earth do you mean, woman? What are you saying? Let's not bother because it's too difficult? Just like a female brain. It's tricky, run away. God, you don't need to tell me about that.' Frank wiped a hand over his face. Beefy had slumped in his lap.

Cathy considered her options.

For one thing she could see how frail her grandfather was. Like Barry, she'd probably passed his illness off as inevitable, enduring, part of who Frank was. But now she could understand why Barry had rung her. In the space of only a few weeks he'd taken on the aspect of a small skeleton with a bit of skin wrapped round it.

She'd thought she'd be gentle with him. But his vituperative spirit seemed to be unaware of the state of his body. Now she decided suddenly, his use of the word 'woman' providing the catalyst to set her temper alight, that she wouldn't be so gentle after all.

'Right, that's it!' she said.

Cathy strode across the room and hauled the curtains wide open. There was a lot of curtain, over double french doors and windows either side. She yanked the heavy material right back so that the room became ablaze with light. Beyond, for the first time, she got a view of the garden. It was wide, long, studded with trees and huge shrubs. The lawn was vast and utterly beautiful. At the end, Cathy could see weeping willows. The sudden brightness of the image was numbing. It was like walking out of a cinema.

'What are you doing?' Frank croaked at her irritably, leaning over the side of his chair.

'We're going outside,' Cathy said.

'We're – what? No we're bloody not.' Frank shook his head.

'Yes we bloody are.'

'I said we're not.' Frank raised his voice but his body shied back into his chair as Cathy strode round it.

'We're going to pretend, just for a while, that we're normal people. We're going to sit in the shade of that laburnum out there. There's a bench, some chairs and a table. That's where we're headed. And I'm going into the kitchen and I'm going to make us a cool drink. It's simple. We're going to sit outside, in the air, drinking our cool drinks and we're going to talk. Are you with me so far?'

Frank's eyes gleamed back at her. For a second he looked like C3PO, all eyes and skeletal head, with a busting intelligence that got on everyone's tits.

'Why are you bossing me about?' he asked, his voice wavering.

'Because' – Cathy took a shallow breath – 'because, Frank, if I don't, then nobody else will.'

Frank glowered back at Cathy resentfully. In response, Cathy went back to the french doors and twisted the handles. She opened them wide. Instantly the heavy scent of summer flowed into the room. Beefy bounded from Frank's lap and edged out on to the terrace. He sat down and washed himself.

'Come with me.'

Cathy put out her arms to Frank. He waved her away, his face contorting into distaste.

'What are you going to do? Carry me out there?'

'If I have to, yes.'

'Oh God.' Frank hid his face with his hands. His voice was broken. 'Oh God, it's come to this. Now I feel like a baby again.'

'Will you just stop feeling so bloody sorry for yourself?' Cathy snapped at him. Frank's hands dropped immediately. He stared at Cathy in astonishment. 'Yes, I mean stop all this me, me, me bollocks. And I mean *bollocks!*' she yelled, getting great pleasure out of ejecting the word into his face. 'I'm going to help you outside. If you don't need my help, then don't make a West End play out of it, just say, "It's okay thank you, granddaughter, I can manage." That shouldn't be difficult for a man with such an impressive command of vocabulary as yourself. And then, when you're comfortable outside, I'll make us some drinks.'

'You can't speak to me this way,' Frank attempted. Then he spluttered and said crookedly, 'My pills!'

'We'll take your pills out with us.' Cathy put her arms out again, this time not in a coaxing gesture but in one of intent.

'You wouldn't get away with this' – Frank wagged a thin finger – 'if Barbara were here. Oh no. She'd rip you apart like a terrier.'

'Don't kid yourself,' Cathy gritted back.

'Oh, she would. She hates you, you know.'

'Not, apparently, as much as she hates you,' Cathy bit back, her arms still outstretched to the recoiling figure in the chair.

'She only hates me because of you!' Frank retorted, sticking out his chin like a child in a playground battle. Cathy sucked in her cheeks.

'I'm not interested. The difference between us is that I'm not interfering in your private life.'

Frank laughed. He laughed and laughed, his finger poking at his chin while his feet disappeared right up behind the blanket. He curled himself into a ball.

'That's funny. The idea that you don't interfere in my private life. You know, Melissa told me once that you had a good sense of humour, but that's the first time I've seen it.' His face collapsed into a scowl. 'I'm not going outside.'

'Yes, you are.'

'No, I'm not.'

'Frank, which word didn't you understand? If I have to carry you out of this foetid hole that you've created for yourself I'll bloody well do it.'

'I'd like to see you try.'

Cathy took a breath, then stuck her arms into the blanket. Within was a small frame. She wasn't tall, but she was firmly built and she had decided in that moment that if it took a concerted search through the *Yellow Pages* and an emergency call to the local JCB hire, she was going to get Frank out of his chair. She scooped him up, blanket and all. In an ambitious manoeuvre she also decided to pick up his plastic bottle of pills in one hand. But then she'd always been someone who'd try to clear the table with one tray stacked up like a mountain range. Cathy began to stagger towards the french doors with Frank in her arms.

'You're completely barking mad!' Frank issued into her ear.

'Well,' Cathy puffed, 'if I am, then I inherited it from you.'

Desperate not to trip and kill her grandfather by

collapsing on top of him, Cathy edged her way outside, ignoring Frank's wriggles, which were only faint anyway, and they emerged into the garden. She stepped carefully over the terrace, down some steps and on to the lawn. At this point she lost the bottle of pills. It bounced away. She peered to one side to see Beefy patting it happily across the lawn. Lurching on, Cathy hauled Frank's body the last few feet towards the shade under the laburnum, the world dancing in front of her eyes.

'I . . . think . . .' she huffed, her body buckling, 'I'll put you . . . down now.'

Frank was, to her surprise, silent. He was probably in shock. She allowed him to slide out of her arms. His slippered feet found the ground. Before he could run away, she propelled him down on to the slatted bench, which was completely shaded. She swept up the blanket from the grass and, her limbs still shaking from the effort, tossed it over him. It wasn't a very accurate aim and it covered him completely. For a moment he looked like a child at Hallowe'en pretending to be a ghost, with a sheet draped over his head and legs sticking out at the bottom. But he pulled at it and his head appeared.

'Now.' Cathy bent over to regain her breath. Sweat had broken out on her neck and face. 'I'm going to make us a drink. And if you move, I'll—'

'You'll what?' Frank said, but his voice was a whisper.

'I'll – I'll bloody well kill you,' she answered and marched back into the house.

*

253

Cathy came back with two glasses of Red Bull, watered down, with added ice. It was all she could salvage from the fridge. She hoped Barry wouldn't mind if she stole his drinks – she couldn't imagine for one minute that Barbara had left them. The last thing she or Frank needed was an adrenalin rush, but she'd said she'd come back with cold drinks and it was either that or water. She wasn't going to lose face at this point.

To her relief, Frank hadn't moved. He was pretending to be fascinated by something at the end of the garden as Cathy set the glasses on the table and settled herself in a seat.

'The river's down there, you know,' he told Cathy. She took this as a good sign. She'd expected a rant.

'Is it?'

'Yes. And I've got a little boat moored by the willows.'

'Have you?'

'Yes. More of a coracle than a floating palace, but a little boat all the same.'

Cathy took a sip of her diluted Red Bull. A rush was what had given her the strength to heave Frank out into the garden. She hoped she wasn't going to get an additional one.

'Do you ever use it?'

Frank looked at Cathy squarely and pulled a face.

'Don't be ridiculous.'

'When did you last use it?' Cathy substituted, realising that she might have phrased her question better.

'Oh.' Frank gazed off into space, then rubbed agitatedly at his forehead. 'Oh, a while ago. I've lived in this house a good few years, you know.'

'Is it fun? Boating on the river? I've never done it.'

'Yes, it's fun,' Frank said severely. 'Of course it's fun. Why do you think people do it? It's great fun. Not as much fun as hiring a punt and taking it out with a group, but it depends, of course, on your company.' He turned to stare at the willows again. 'You know, that smell. Of the river bank. It does take me back.'

Cathy froze. It was like coaxing a stray cat. This was the moment where you had a fistful of treats in your hand and the cat was tentatively walking towards you, more focused on the treats than on the fact that as much as you wanted to give something to the cat, you wanted something back. You wanted the cat to make you feel loved. Cathy held her breath, watching Frank's distracted expression.

'What was it like here, in Oxford, when you were younger?'

Frank twisted his neck and stared at Cathy.

'I was younger five minutes ago. What on earth do you mean? Oxford changes, but the places that do change aren't relevant.'

'I'd be so interested to hear about what you did when you were a young man.' Cathy cupped her chin in her hands to show her interest. 'Really. I wish you'd tell me.'

Frank looked away to the willows, he gazed up to the sky, he looked back to Cathy and back to the willows again. He started to cackle.

'Oh no, I don't think you do want to know.'

'Yes, I do,' she insisted, feeling her spirits dive again. She hadn't heard that evil cackle for all of an hour and it had been blissful.

'No, you don't,' Frank said factually and took a sip

from his drink. 'And why are you sweet-talking me anyway? I thought you'd come here to bully me.'

Cathy sat up straight and placed her hands in her lap.

'Well, I did come here wondering about a few things.'

'Yes?' Frank squinted back, his eyes like pale-blue slits.

'Just some things I thought you could help me with.'

'Oh, for God's sake!' Frank flailed on his bench. 'A moment ago you were heaving me round, now you turn into a wittering mess. What's happened to you? Speak sense, woman, if you can.'

Cathy pursed her lips. The birds clamoured round her. The garden was beautiful, the setting idyllic. But a sheepshank knot had arrived in her stomach. A little late and apologetic, yes, but it had arrived and she decided she wasn't going to put up with it.

'All right, Frank. You're blunt to the point of rudeness – something I guess you see as a quality – so let me be blunt back. Melissa told me you're my mother's father. I want to know about my mother, about your reason for contacting me, why you've sent me to cricket matches and why you're trying to set me up with Nick. I'll sit here and wait while you answer.'

Frank eyed Cathy brutally.

'You want those in any particular order?'

Cathy shook her head. 'You just go right ahead. I think I've got the nous to work out which answer might apply to which question.'

Frank fluttered his eyelids mockingly.

'You are so bright.'

'Just do it.'

'Well, let me see.' Frank poked at his face with his

256

finger. 'Your mother was a perplexing woman, I contacted you because I felt like it, I sent you to cricket matches because I wanted to and I put you with Nick because he's good company.'

The reference to her mother meant Cathy was now fixed to her chair like a waxwork. The rest of the reply, including the casual admission that Frank was manipulating Cathy's contact with Nick, was temporarily forgotten, although she would remember it later.

'My mother was perplexing?' Cathy echoed faintly.

'Oh yes. In every way. She had no faculty for reason.' Then Frank opened one beady eye ironically. 'I guess it skipped a generation.'

'How – how did she die? I just . . . I want to know everything now. I mean, I know it was a car accident, but please tell me. Anything you know.'

'It was just an accident.' Frank's face was black. This time Cathy could see the sadness was genuine. She slapped herself mentally. She should remember that although she was talking about her mother, Frank was remembering his own daughter. Her feelings weren't the only ones being raked over.

'I'm sorry, Frank. I know this isn't easy for you either.'

Frank put his hand over his face.

'It was just a twist of fate. And I've blamed myself for it ever since.'

'Oh God.' Cathy put her hand to her mouth. 'I'm sorry – I never thought – that you'd still be so upset about it.'

A sob heaved from Frank's chest. It came right from his ribs and seemed to shake him all over. It was awful. Cathy wanted to curl up in her chair just as Frank had done earlier.

'You'd – just been born. You were premature.' Frank stopped and drew in a deep breath. 'I'd fallen out with your mother. We'd never – bonded. She was a perplexing woman, I told you. You were in that little incubator. She wasn't fit to drive, but she was driving. You see, I'd bought her that car. I'd bought it, so I felt responsible.' Frank shuddered. 'And then—'

Cathy nodded, her eyes welling.

'And then you never saw her again.'

'Yes.' Frank nodded vehemently.

Cathy waited. She was stirred, but she had to know more. Part of her wanted to sneak away at this point and leave him in peace, but her more dominant side could smell a lead like a tabloid journalist. It was just too important to let go. She'd tried to pretend that it affected nothing, but the truth was it affected everything. Now, when Frank was vulnerable, was the best time to get facts from him.

'And – and my grandmother? Your wife? I don't know anything about her. She must have been devastated.'

'Oh – she got over it,' Frank said, 'and she wasn't around for long. I'm sorry to tell you this, but that's the truth. I was never one to settle for long. We weren't married, which was a bit of a scandal back then. But you wanted the truth and you've got it.'

'But she's – she's dead, my grandmother?'

'Oh yes.' Frank nodded, his fingers over his eyes. 'Yes, she's very dead. Dead for years, I'm sorry to tell you.'

'That's okay. I did guess that much.'

'Yes.' Frank took a slurp of his Red Bull.

'And—' Cathy winced, wondering if she was

pushing her luck. 'And my father. You must have known him for a while before the . . . the . . .'

'The accident. Just say it and stop wimping about,' Frank snapped without looking up.

'My father.' Cathy swallowed, determined to push a little bit further. 'What did he do? What was he like?'

Frank leaned back on the bench and pulled his hand from his eyes. He gazed up into the umbrella of leaves.

'I didn't know your father very well.'

Cathy bent forward intensely, her elbows resting on her knees.

'What do you mean?'

'I've just told you.'

'Tell me more,' Cathy persevered firmly.

'Look, Catherine, I don't know how else to phrase it. How can I put this delicately? I can't. So I won't. Your mother was a bastard child of a passionate affair. Is that clear? We never had a good relationship. I hardly knew her. I knew your father' – he paused, stroking the white stumps of stubble on his gaunt chin – 'even less well. In fact, it's an understatement to say that I didn't know your father very well. I didn't know your father at all. I never met him. So I can't tell you anything about him. All I know is that I bought the car, your mother took off in it and I never saw her again. Is that clear? *Capisce? Comprends? Versteht?*'

Cathy pulled away. She got up and walked round the grass staring back at Frank. He was now extremely agitated.

'Catherine, I can't tell you what you want to hear. Do you understand?'

Cathy fought down the threat of tears as she stepped over Beefy, who was on his back with the bottle of

Frank's pills fixed between his four paws and was wrestling with the top with his fangs. She took a swig of Red Bull, this time draining the glass, and slammed it back on the table. Frank flinched, but she pretended she hadn't noticed.

'At least tell me what my father did,' she said raggedly. 'You must, just *must*, have known that.'

'Oh no.' Frank rocked on the bench. 'This is so painful. But you don't care. You don't care a bit about me. You want to go on and on, dredging up things that are helpful to you. Even if it kills me.'

Cathy stopped and put her hands on her hips. She eyed Frank sceptically.

'It's going to kill you to tell me what my father did for a living?'

'You really want to know?'

'Of course I bloody want to know.'

Cathy waited while the crows cawed in the evergreens, the slight breeze sent a hush over the flimsy branches of the willows and even a gurgle of water could be heard from the foot of the long garden.

'He was a mortuary technician,' Frank said and his face fell to the table where he slapped his hands over his skull.

Chapter Fourteen

It is better to travel in hope than to arrive. Cathy realised this after she had settled Frank back in his room, in his chair, with a cup of tea and told him she was going upstairs to talk to Barry. They'd been in the garden for two hours and he looked exhausted.

Cathy mounted the stairs slowly, stopping halfway up to gather herself, then continued. The landing was long, like the corridor on the ground floor. Four uneven carpeted steps led to a door at the far end. She realised in passing that it was a wonderful house, full of character. One you could imagine being populated by an army of children, family friends and garrulous aunts and uncles at Christmas time. She guessed it had never happened in Frank's time there.

She knocked on Barry's door and waited for him to let her in. He was playing music, quite loudly, although she hadn't been able to hear it anywhere in the house and he'd obviously been lying on his bed staring at the television. There was a half-full ashtray by the bed and a car magazine. He turned the television off, the music down and grinned at her raffishly.

'How'd it go?'

Cathy sat down on the edge of the bed. There was an armchair-shaped heap of clothes in the room, but nowhere else to sit. She didn't think Barry, devilish as he seemed to be, would read too much into her perching on his bed.

'Barry, I'm more confused than before. I'd had images, pictures in my head of my parents that I've carried round for years. They're all wrong.'

'Ah. In which case you'll need one of these.' Barry twisted a can of beer from a four-pack on his dressing table and handed her one. She hesitated, then took it. 'How's Frank?'

Cathy was touched to note that Barry was seriously concerned. If she'd bumped into him in the pub, the last thing she'd imagine was that he'd have the time, or energy, or patience to care about a withering old man. But he obviously did.

'He's all right now. And sitting outside did him good.'

'I saw that.' Barry laughed. 'I didn't like to interfere. It seemed as if you were bonding.' Barry jerked his head towards the latticed window at the end of the room. 'That looks over the garden.'

'Oh.' Cathy allowed herself a smile. 'Could you hear what we said too?'

Barry shook his head. 'I closed the window at that point. Promise.'

'Thanks.' Cathy pulled the ring of her can and a creamy spume of beer edged out. She took a small sip. It made her feel better. 'I'm going to stay the night.'

A look of joy spread over Barry's face. 'Great!'

'I want to keep an eye on things. And I want to see Frank eat properly tonight.'

Barry looked even more ecstatic.

'Double great! You can cook as well?'

'Only if you class toast as cooking. My boyfriend's the cook at home.' Cathy stopped suddenly. Her statement had come out naturally, out of habit. She looked down as the dismay surged in the pit of her stomach. All it took was a mention of Jason for all the pain of missing him to return. 'I mean, no, I can't really, but we'll rustle something up.'

'Oh. The B word.' Barry shrugged at her cheerfully. 'I guessed as much. A babe like you wouldn't be on her own for long. Never mind. He's not here now, is he?' He gave her a cheery wink. Cathy tried to smile. She didn't feel robust enough to talk about Jason. Barry winked again, even more comically and Cathy laughed at him.

'Don't you start.'

'All right, promise. Though with you in the room next door, I'll toss and turn all night. Just so's you know. Anyway, did you find out what you wanted to know from Frank?'

Cathy leant back on her elbows and gazed up at the ceiling. Melinda Messenger in a thong gazed back at her from a poster fixed there. She sighed.

'Well, I almost wish I hadn't asked. But I did and now I know. It's like reading the end of a book. You can't unknow what you know, even if you try to reread it and get that feeling of suspense back again.'

'Uh-huh.' Barry opened a beer for himself and drank from it. He flopped on to the armchair, regardless of the mound of clothes.

'My father', she said, looking at Barry flatly, 'was a mortuary technician.'

Barry pursed his lips.

'Oh dear.'

'Exactly. All my life, when I did think about my true parents, I pictured him as brilliant. In a surgical mask and green gown, performing life-saving operations.

Don't ask me why. I just thought he must have been a brain surgeon.'

'Well, he worked in a hospital, that's quite close.'

'It's not very close, is it?'

Barry shook his head.

'No, not really. Although he must have done funny hours. He probably knew a few brain surgeons. Must have sat with them in the canteen or something.'

Cathy heaved another deep sigh. 'And my mother was illegitimate. Born of a fling. Frank hardly knew her. He says he's got no photos, nothing. It explains everything. Why he's so isolated. Why there's no granny to go with the grandad. It's no surprise that I was always just an abstract thing to him. Even his own daughter was just an abstract thing. It's certainly not the treasure chest I thought it would be. It's Frank and no real information.'

'Apart from the job thing.'

'Yes.' Cathy sighed.

'It could be worse.' Barry sat up and pulled an optimistic face. 'My dad was a dickhead. And the even sadder thing is that he's still alive.'

Cathy snorted, half her mouthful of beer flying up her nose. Barry was laughing at her from his chair.

'So think yourself lucky!' he added.

'Yes,' agreed Cathy, wiping her streaming nose. 'Although my dad might have been a dickhead too. I'll never know.'

'Impossible.' Barry shook his head firmly. 'No dickhead could produce such a tremendous woman for a daughter. He must have been a very nice, well-balanced mortuary technician.'

'Is that possible?' Cathy rolled over on the bed so that

she was lying on her front. She studied Barry seriously. 'Don't you think you've got to be a bit barmy to go into a job like that?'

'A bit embalmy, maybe,' Barry suggested and Cathy giggled. 'No seriously, I don't. It's a service to the community. Somebody's got to do it. He was probably very . . . very. . .' Barry struggled, 'good at it.'

Cathy tried to keep a straight face, but couldn't.

'I wonder what my mum saw in him. He must have had something about him that she liked.'

'Well,' Barry pondered. 'He wouldn't have had any problem getting a stiff.'

Cathy stared at Barry for a moment, wondering whether she should be offended, but then couldn't help laughing.

'Now show some respect for the dead.' She waved a finger at him.

'As your dad would have said. Every day.'

'But why would you want to do that? Spend your life round dead things.' Cathy shuddered. 'I can't think why anyone would. I'd rather be a – a dustman.'

'Steady on. My dad was a dustman.' Barry pulled a reprimanding face.

'Was he really?'

'Yep. For about three months. It was the only job I ever remember him having, but he lost it because he kept going through the rubbish and saving things he thought might come in handy later. He used to bring these things home. Like rugs. And empty bottles. And an old cricket bat once. My mum said, "What in the bleedin' blazes is that for?" And he said, "It's to knock you about with, you old cow." But at least that was my introduction to cricket, so something good came out of it.'

'Oh Barry, I'm sorry.' Cathy propped herself up and looked at him sympathetically. He shrugged.

'It was years ago. He was taken away when I was a kid.' Barry fingered the top of his beer can, then when he looked at Cathy again he was filled with smiles. 'You know, holding down a good job's not so bad. Even if it is being a mortuary technician. I mean, I'm a car salesman. How do you think that feels? But I do well at it.'

'No, you're right. You're absolutely right. I should be proud of him.'

'Yes.' Barry nodded too. 'He was probably well-known for his ability. And his – his tact. Just think. It's not just about pushing dead people in and out of drawers. You've got to deal with all the relatives too. I mean, you couldn't possibly be a dickhead and work in a job like that. You'd have to be nice to grieving people.'

Cathy listened and bit her lip severely, her eyes suddenly filling with tears.

'Oh, don't say that,' she whispered. 'The bit about grieving relatives. I was only a baby. I couldn't even grieve.'

'Oh, sweetheart. I'm so sorry.' Barry was suddenly across the room, his arm round Cathy, holding her to him.

She curled against him, sniffing, all her tensions flowing out.

'It's okay.'

'I know.' He rocked her gently, smoothing her hair away from her hot forehead. 'It's a shock. You poor thing. There you are, living your life, and suddenly gitface appears out of nowhere and turns it all upside down.'

'Yes.' Cathy felt better for being held. Barry wasn't big, but he was strong for his size and it was so lovely to be cuddled. And it was all right for Barry to call Frank 'gitface'. When Jason had insulted Frank he'd known nothing about him. Barry cared about Frank. He knew Frank was a git; Jason had only been speculating.

'I'm glad you came here.' Barry dropped a comforting kiss on the top of Cathy's head. 'I'm glad you care. You're full of heart and Frank must be so proud of you.'

That made Cathy cry even more.

'I hope he cares about me. I – I care about Frank. I didn't want to, but I do.'

'I know you do.' Barry squeezed her. 'And so do I. So if we can't have rampant sex – which I assure you I would dearly love – then at least we're allies in this, aren't we?'

'Y-yes.'

Cathy gave Barry a grateful look. Her mascara must have been down to her chin and she probably looked like she'd just crawled out of a chimney. But Barry didn't seem to care. He gave her a broad smile, full of warmth, and she hugged him back.

'We'll look after him,' he stated.

'Yes. We will,' Cathy agreed and knew in her heart that from this point on that was exactly what she was going to do.

Barbara hardly recognised herself in the mirror. Her skin was white, her eyes dark with shadows. But she saw a firmness in her bearing. There was no going back from this position. It wasn't one she'd have chosen. She'd been forced into it, much against her will. But if

267

this was how it was going to be she would deal with it.

She took herself from her small, dark hall, where the gilt-edged mirror hung, to her study. There were only two sizeable rooms downstairs in her house and she had no call for a dining room. The back room had been a study since she'd moved in.

Now she had retrieved the word processor, the files, the books, the papers and the notes. Everything that Frank might, in another fit of madness, seek to destroy. Getting the word processor out of the house had been a struggle, but she'd done it, piece by piece. Frank still had his stupid new computer which was more of a Fisher Price Activity Centre as far as she could see. When he did notice that their key research tools had been removed he wouldn't miss them. Not if it was true that he didn't care any more.

Barbara sat at her desk. In the background, Radio 4 murmured. Barbara liked to hear quiet conversation while she worked. It was one thing she missed in the Bodleian Library. Her colleagues would have been surprised at that. While they dived on every rustle and suppressed giggle like the Gestapo, Barbara showed no reaction. She wanted the students to show respect for the books, but she didn't relish the stagnant silence that some of the librarians seemed to strive for. It was important to absorb thoughts. But it was also important to express thoughts. She was only just realising for herself how important it was to express them.

It was Sunday and she was listening to *The World This Weekend*. Soothed by the hum of voices, she addressed the heap of papers in front of her and set about organising them. In time, she would submit her draft chapters back to Frank. He'd only have to nod and she could get them off to the publisher. Barbara knew Frank's mind so well that she was sure of the angle he would take on each and every detail. And she had her own thoughts too, from years of extensive research. She would enter those along the way and it would be up to Frank to edit them out if he decided they were ludicrous. After all, the book would be in his name.

It was clear that Frank didn't want to work on *Alfred* any more. But somebody had to. Barbara would make sure the job was done.

She set her reading glasses on her nose and concentrated on the pile of paper. The doorbell shrilled through the house. She heaved an impatient breath. If she sat still, whoever it was would go away. She had a lot of work to do and very little time to do it in. Days at home were precious.

The doorbell rang again.

Barbara yanked off her glasses and in exasperation laid them on the desk. She walked out, through the hall and pulled open the front door.

The red hair and sharp blue eyes hit her first. Barbara leant against the hall wall, the door only partially open, and stared. How on earth had the woman got her address? It was a violation.

'Barbara,' Catherine said. 'I'm so sorry to come to your house like this. I know it's an intrusion and I'm sorry for that. I didn't mean to take you by surprise. But I'd like to talk to you about Frank.'

Barbara was silent. Responses powered through her head like ball lightning. She squashed her lips together, feeling her mouth grow dry.

'Really, I'm sorry just to pitch up on your doorstep like this. But there was no phone number for you and I could only find your address. Frank doesn't know I'm here, you see. Nobody does. I would have rung you and asked, but I couldn't. I'm in Oxford this weekend. I've seen Frank. I stayed over last night. He's in a terrible state.'

Barbara cleared her throat. She meant it to be authoritative, but she sounded like a piglet trying to cough. It was annoying. The girl, again, had no make-up on, was fresh-faced, and normally Barbara might even have tried to like her. But to like this girl was impossible. She had ruined Barbara's life.

'It is unspeakable of you to come here, to my private home,' she heard herself say.

But the red-headed girl didn't bolt, or cower. She squared her body and looked Barbara straight in the eye. Her eyes were a dark shade of blue, much as Frank's had once been. It sent a further arrow of fear through Barbara's body.

'I do need to talk to you, Barbara. I have to go home again today. I've got work to do in London. So I can't be here to take care of Frank. I'm so worried about him.'

Barbara stood up now, to her full height, pleased that she towered over Catherine.

'After all this time. Years, months, days, hours that I have been his . . . his everything, you dare to come here and tell *me* that *you* can't be here next week, so will I pop in?' Barbara issued. 'For thirty years I have been his secretary, his assistant, his student, his mentor, his companion, his friend, his nurse, his counsellor, his—' Barbara gasped. 'His—'

'Punchbag?'

Barbara swallowed. She was breathing so quickly she was going dizzy.

'I beg your pardon?'

270

'His punchbag. I saw it. Or rather, I got a sense of it last time I was here. He treats you appallingly, Barbara. I've picked that much up.'

'You think, do you, that you can make these insulting generalisations about how he behaves towards me after – what is it – two visits? What makes you so sure that I'm the sole object of his bad-tempered outbursts?' Pride dug at Barbara's chest.

'I – I actually think that he doesn't know how to treat anyone any differently.' Catherine wiped her hand across her face. Barbara peered at her. She wasn't crying, was she? Oh God, what next?

'You don't know him. At all,' Barbara bit.

'No, I don't. I don't. But you do. And I wish that you'd talk to me.'

'No.' Barbara edged the door closed. Just a bit, so that she felt safer.

'I just . . . I just need some help here.' Catherine pleaded. Barbara flinched.

'Ring the Samaritans.'

Then, to Barbara's complete horror, Catherine sank down on to the doorstep and put her head in her hands.

Barbara closed the door quickly. She bolted it and put the chain on. She ran away from the door, through the hall, into her study and closed that door too.

She stood still in the small room. The papers seemed solid and unreadable. All she could see in front of her eyes was the girl on the doorstep, in her jeans and cotton top, with tears in her eyes.

'I don't believe this.'

Barbara swallowed uncomfortably. She went back to the hall and unbolted the door. She took the chain off and opened it again.

Catherine was still there. She wasn't crying. Just sitting, with her arms loosely resting on her knees and staring into space. She glanced over her shoulder as the door opened again and looked up into Barbara's face. She looked like a very puzzled little girl.

'Catherine, it's not your fault. It's his,' Barbara said harshly. She hadn't expected to say that.

'Please,' Catherine said in a small voice. 'You have to understand. There's nobody else. When he dies, that's it. He's a complete shit, but he's all I've got.'

Barbara knew how that felt. She could have nodded till her head fell off. But like hell would she give herself away. She stared at Catherine with greater interest.

'You have talked to him about your – relationship with him?'

Catherine nodded.

'And he's told you what he knows?'

'Yes.' Catherine produced a tissue and dabbed it carelessly on her face. 'I know all about my mother being illegitimate and my father being a—' She gave a deep sigh. 'A mortuary technician.'

'Oh.' Barbara's lips twitched. There was always some pleasure in someone else's pain. 'Well, I'm sorry you had to find out. Maybe it would have been better if you didn't know.'

Catherine nodded. 'But it was a good, solid job. And he must have been a nice man.'

'Oh yes, I'm sure he was a nice man. Even if you wouldn't think so on the evidence.'

Barbara squatted awkwardly and found herself patting Catherine on the back. It was an awkward pat such as you might inflict on someone's dog when you hated the creatures. It was a quiet street, thank heavens, and Catherine was fortunately one to make her sniffles very subdued. Mercifully she hadn't demanded to be asked in. There was no way that Barbara was letting her over the threshold.

'Thank you.' Catherine stood up, and Barbara stepped back. 'Thank you for those kind words. I'm glad you don't hate me. Frank said you did, but I couldn't really believe it. And the thing is—' Catherine fumbled with a stringy knot of tissue. 'The thing is that I know Frank cares about me in a funny way because I'm the last bit of genetic material he's got floating round the planet. But he cares about you, because you're you.'

'What do you mean?' Barbara was sharp again. Nobody could lecture her about her relationship with Frank. Nobody.

'I mean, he's a shadow now. He needs you.'

A sound came out of Barbara's throat. Disbelieving, facetious, like a 'huh!'.

'I don't know if he's ever loved anybody in his life,' Catherine went on, looking more composed and more like a woman than a girl again. 'But whatever his definition of love is, I'd say it's to do with needing somebody. And he's fallen apart without you.'

Barbara was gratified to hear it. Something stirred in the pit of her stomach. But she knew the answer to Catherine's rhetorical question and she spat it out.

'He loved somebody once. Only once. That was your mother.'

Catherine's eyes were hopeful.

'Did he?' She looked dazed. 'He said they never really got along. I didn't know he'd cared about her so much. Thank you for telling me that. It makes me feel a lot better.'

273

The bitterness filled Barbara again. She couldn't help herself.

'Oh yes. I've been round him all this time and I know. So don't kid yourself, young woman, that he really cares for you. He looks for a sign in you, a memory of the thing he once loved. You're a ghost to him. Don't fool yourself into thinking it's more personal than that.'

Barbara saw Catherine's mouth gape open, but at that point she slammed the door. She bolted it, put the chain on and went back to her study. There was no ring on the bell. No insistence. This time she felt no compunction to go back and see if Catherine was still there. She put on her reading glasses and stared at her pile of papers, waiting for her breath to steady so that she could get back to work.

When Cathy returned to the house, Frank and Barry were sitting together in the living room, watching Italian football.

Her walk back – a long one, but she'd needed it – had been helpful. Barry let her in and she waved him off to the football so that she could sort herself out.

Cathy went upstairs to the bedroom she'd slept in and pushed everything back in her leather bag. It was a nice room, old-fashioned and clean, in a fifties bed-and-breakfast kind of way, with a wonky lamp with a low-wattage bulb, a few bits of solid furniture and some old pictures on the wall. The curtains had squeaked and struggled as she'd tried to draw them the night before – plastic hooks attached to a long, bendy bit of aluminium.

*

Her attempt at dinner the night before had been amateurish, but she was glad she'd tried. Falling back on that old friend, spaghetti bolognese, she'd gone out with Barry to get some basic ingredients and while Frank sat firmly in his chair, she and Barry had got the giggles putting it together.

Cathy's clumsy attempt at dinner for three had taken her vaulting back to Jason's fabulous culinary efforts. She'd felt maudlin when Barry pulled a tin of treacle out of one of the cupboards and said, 'Shall we stick this in it too?' Her days of being treated to gourmet meals were over. Just as everything wonderful that she and Jason had shared was over. But Frank's house was a different world and, once Barry had thrust another glass of Valpolicella her way and she'd drunk it happily, she'd managed to push her unhappy thoughts away.

Frank had eaten a little, but not much, making a fuss about Cathy's decision to stay over. He'd claimed it was all too complicated to work out which were the clean sheets and towels, but with Barry's help she'd shut him up. By nine, Frank was asleep in front of the television, so Barry and Cathy had stirred him.

Cathy had wanted to help him up to bed, but he'd squealed at her that he could make his own sodding way to bed. She left him to find his feet, seeing that he could walk well, if hesitantly, on his own. Barry and Cathy had sat still, their eyes raised to the ceiling as they heard Frank thumping about upstairs, until it had gone quiet.

Then Barry had taken her to the pub.

They'd met up with some of his friends there. Cathy

couldn't fail to notice that they'd all rolled their eyeballs at Barry when they thought she wasn't looking, but was pleased to note that he subtly shook his head in response. Whether that meant 'no' or 'no, not yet' she wasn't so sure.

They'd got home after closing time and, after a coffee and a chat in the kitchen, had tiptoed up the stairs to bed. Cathy had been relieved to hear carthorse snores coming from Frank's room. Then, at the door of the spare room, she'd turned to Barry to say goodnight.

'You haven't changed your mind I suppose.' He'd smiled at her drunkenly. 'About the rampant sex?'

'No.'

'All right. G'night then.'

She'd lain in bed for about an hour with a dull glimmer of light coming from the little lamp by the bed, listening to the trees rustling all round the house, her bedroom window nudged open for a breath of air, and wondering what on earth it would have been like to have known this house as a child. The long passages, the many rooms, the books, the outhouse, the gigantic garden and the little boat. Frank might have been a nicer person then. If only she'd had the chance to find out. For a moment the sheepshank knot threatened to form again, as she cursed Frank for never getting in touch with her before.

Then her bedroom door had been edged open. She'd sat bolt upright, ready to fend Barry off with the lamp, the pillow, anything she might be able playfully to thump him with. But, dropping her sights to carpet level, she saw Beefy striding purposefully towards her bed.

'C'mon then, Ragbag.'

He'd fallen on her chest in a contented heap, and she'd flicked the light off and sunk back into the lumpy pillows before sleep carried her away.

Now she swept her eyes over the bedroom, secretly hoping that it wouldn't be long before she was back again, hoisted her bag over her shoulder and went downstairs to say goodbye.

As she entered the living room, Barry jumped up.

'I've got to do something. Somewhere else. For a while,' he said and, grinning at Cathy, left her to talk to Frank alone. She made her way to the sofa and sat down.

'So, Frank. I have to be on my way.'

'Yes, yes.' Frank waved a hand in her direction. 'Go on, then. Don't make a fuss.'

Cathy bit her lip. Things had changed a lot since her first visit. Now Frank didn't have the ability to offend her so easily. She'd got over the shock of his rudeness – now that she expected it, she could almost deal with it. Frank wouldn't meet her eye. He could even be hiding his disappointment. She could hope.

'Thanks for telling me so much. I know it wasn't easy.'

Frank cackled. Cathy looked to the ceiling. If anyone had ever struck her as needing a gift voucher for 600 sessions with a psychiatrist, it was her own grandfather. Why couldn't he ever react like a normal person?

'I'm saying thank you,' she insisted. 'That's a nice thing for me to say. Just in case you didn't realise.'

'I'm overawed by your munificence. Now go away. Go on.'

'There's just one thing we didn't cover, and I need to talk to you about it.'

That wasn't precisely true. There were a lot of things they still hadn't covered properly, but Cathy knew she could only do so much at a time. She'd have more to say when she'd had time to think. But for now, she had to find out about Nick.

'Oh God,' Frank croaked, slapping a hand over his eyes. He peeped at her through it. 'What is it now?'

'Nick,' Cathy said curtly.

Frank dropped his hand from his eyes and stared at her aggressively.

'What about him?'

Cathy sighed.

'Why do you make everything so difficult? I want you to tell me why you bought us seats together. It was a strange thing to do. Neither of us could understand it.'

'But you talked.' Frank brightened, hauling himself up to look at Cathy properly. 'You got to know each other. You saw what it was like for him. How much he cared and how much he knew. And – he's good fun.'

'Good fun . . . ?' Cathy struggled. 'But I don't understand why you did it.'

Frank was exasperated again. He rubbed his hands all over his face, his mouth turning into a wavy line.

'My God, woman, what did you think I'd do to you? Send you out there, all on your own, to a game you had no interest in? How long would you have stayed? You had to have an incentive. You see? It's simple. Why can't you understand? How on earth did you get that first-class degree? Bribe the examiners?'

Cathy stood up. She wanted to leave on a sweet note, but it was so hard to do.

'You set us up and – and neither of us appreciated it.'

Frank pulled his mouth into an oval and pouted the shape at her. He looked like Kenneth Williams waiting for the audience to laugh at a smutty remark.

'Well, Catherine, I think Nick might have appreciated it.'

'He – he contacted you?'

Cathy put a hand on her hip just to show that she was more cross than curious, but her stomach had suddenly done a little jump and a plunge, like going over a hump-backed bridge.

'Yes, of course.'

'And . . . ?' Cathy hated herself for probing. Frank was obviously relishing it.

'And he obviously enjoyed meeting you. What more is there to say? I knew you two would spark off each other. I just knew it. It's perfect. I was right.'

Cathy opened her mouth to argue, but the fact was that she and Nick *had* sparked off each other. There had been a fizzing chemistry there. She didn't know why. He was everything she usually avoided in a man and she could guess that she herself was not what he was looking for in a woman. But there it was.

'Well, you shouldn't have done it,' she offered lamely.

'Nonetheless, Nick is looking forward to Old Trafford. You'll find your ticket over there, on the sideboard.'

'Oh no.' Cathy shook her head vehemently. 'Oh, no, no, no. You can't do this to me again.'

Frank retreated into his chair. He looked tiny again and once more she was reminded how frail he was.

'Catherine,' he said quietly. 'I'm asking you to go. Not for yourself, but for me. The series is one all. You

279

gave me such a good account of Lord's. I know you're really feeling the atmosphere now, not with your head, but through your senses. Please go. And tell me what it was like.'

'Who do you think you are, Cilla Black?' Cathy blazed at him as he cowered behind his blanket. 'Cathy from London and Nick from Birmingham, will you come back next week and tell us how you got on? I've got a personal life already, Frank. I can't just drop everything and go swanning off to . . . to . . .' Cathy frowned. 'Where the hell is Old Trafford anyway?'

'Manchester.' Frank sighed as if he were reciting the obvious to a dimwit. 'And of course you can drop everything. It's a Saturday. Even you can take a day away from your concerns. The world won't stop turning.'

'I won't do it.' Cathy stated, wondering how long it would take her to get to Manchester and back in a day. 'Apart from anything, it's just too far away from London.'

'Got that covered. You're booked into a hotel overnight.'

'You're manipulating me. Every step of the way. It's like squeezing toothpaste out of a tube for you, isn't it? Just like Barbara. Well, hello, Frank, time to wake up. Barbara's buggered off because she won't take it and I'm not going to be pushed round by you either. What do you say to that?'

Frank seemed to crumple, like a ball of paper. He went horribly quiet. He never went quiet for very long. After a few uncomfortably silent moments Cathy took a step towards him.

'Frank?'

'Life is short, Catherine. My life is even shorter.'

'That's emotional blackmail,' Cathy muttered.

'Yes. But it's true. Look at me.' Frank pulled his hands away from his chin and let Cathy rest her eyes on his small head, balanced on a thin neck. He looked like a cotton bud.

'So,' Cathy said, biting back the lump that had risen in her throat. 'What exactly is it that you want me to do?'

'Go to the match. Enjoy it. Come here again and tell me about it. That's all. I don't want you to do that alone. I thought Nick would be good company for you. I'm sorry if you found it intrusive.'

Cathy was taken aback. Frank seemed completely genuine in that instant.

'I'll think about it. Where's the ticket?'

'Over there.' Frank shot up in his chair and pointed. His energy had returned as suddenly as if he'd just been shot through with a thousand volts. But she couldn't change her mind simply because he looked demonic again. She'd committed herself.

'I'll go.' Cathy found the ticket in an envelope on the sideboard and stuck it into her bag. 'But only for you. And on one condition.'

'Which is?' Frank rubbed his hands together. He evidently felt triumphant.

'That when I come back to see you, you tell me, without any bullshit, why it is that Barbara feels the need to be so unpleasant to me.'

Frank sucked in his cheeks. He glared at Cathy, as if he couldn't drag his eyes away from her while he was thinking so hard.

'Do you have to use words like "bullshit"?' he asked,

her, wrinkling his nose. But Cathy continued to face him challengingly so eventually he shrugged, saying, 'All right. But you may not like it.'

'I really don't care any more,' Cathy said. 'Goodbye, I'll see you in a couple of weeks.'

And she left, wondering how she could possibly like anything less than the knowledge that her father had spent his life surrounded by dead people.

Chapter Fifteen

As soon as Cathy had settled herself at her desk and was slipping her jacket on to the back of the chair, Lisa Spencer stalked across the goldfish bowl. Lisa was thin, with cropped dark hair, spiky nails and spiky shoes. For some reason Cathy had always had an aversion to her, but recently she'd been further ruffled by the fact that Lisa had been allocated the office that had become free. Cathy had never been churlish about status, but her paperwork was piled over her small desk space and she knew she had more work to juggle than Lisa did. The office would have been helpful.

'Cathy! How are you doing?'

Cathy cringed as Lisa's red lips split to reveal a crack of white teeth. It wasn't a sincere smile. In fact, Lisa looked slightly nervous. The heatwave was continuing and Lisa had two damp spots under the arms of her crisp white blouse.

'How are you, Lisa?' Cathy replied non-committally. Beyond Lisa, Cathy could see Fiona passing. She stopped and pulled a face behind Lisa's back. Cathy bit her lip to stop herself laughing.

'It's about Bill Havers. Just to let you know that Mark's asked me to take on that project. Can you arrange to hand over everything you've got on Bill to me this morning?'

Cathy stared at Lisa's round eyes and the way her nails curled into her palm.

'I'm sorry?' she replied calmly as adrenalin pumped into her system. 'I'm sure that can't be right, Lisa. I've got an excellent working relationship with Bill and the project's well in hand.'

'You'll have to talk to Mark about it. I'm just the messenger,' Lisa said curtly and walked away.

Cathy stared after her, stunned. Why on earth had Lisa suddenly been speaking to Cathy as if she were her employee? If anything, Cathy was the more senior manager, office or no office. But more important, it made no business sense at all to take Cathy off the Havers project when she was so involved in it. Why would Mark do it, when he had supported her efforts with Bill all along? Fiona wheeled herself round the low dividing wall in her chair, her blue eyes grave. She'd obviously overheard what had been said.

'Fuck, I can't stand that woman,' she whispered. 'Now what's going on?'

Cathy looked into Fiona's face while her brain turned over. Then she got up and put on her jacket.

'I don't know,' she told Fiona as she marched past her. 'But I'm going to find out.'

Mark was in his office, speaking on the phone. He beckoned Cathy in and waved at a spare seat, turning his back and gazing through the louvre blinds at the roofs beyond his window as he completed his call. Then he put the phone down and turned round.

'Cathy. I'm sorry I didn't catch you as you got in, but I've had several urgent calls in a row. Has Lisa spoken to you?'

Cathy supposed that Mark might be able to guess

that she'd already encountered Lisa by the spots of angry colour in her cheeks.

'Yes,' she said, trying to sound serene.

'I know that you've become very involved with Bill and I can understand you being a little put out. When one's formed a close relationship with a client it's always tempting to want to nanny them through every eventuality.'

Cathy nodded, holding her breath.

'But we feel that we've used your skills to the best advantage on Havers now and it's time to move you on to something more ambitious.'

Cathy swallowed.

'Most of what's left of the project is nuts and bolts. Frankly, Cathy, Lisa is more suited to that kind of work. We need you for your specialist skills. I discussed it with Ruth at the board meeting and she agrees.'

Cathy was silent. Mark's eyes were professionally pleasant, but not warm.

'Did Ruth see my report on Hellier's?' Cathy asked, keeping her voice light.

'Ah, yes. I'm sorry, I meant to get back to you on that. I discussed your ideas with her, but it's a no-go, as I thought. I did try to warn you.' Mark looked more sympathetically at Cathy. 'You know Ruth can be a bit mercurial and, to be frank, she wasn't best pleased that you'd spent so much time on an idea that isn't workable for us. I think the word she used was "fanciful". I'm sorry, Cathy. It's great that you're innovative, but it's just as well I mediated for you. I don't think Ruth would have been quite so diplomatic in her rebuttal if you'd talked to her about it personally.'

Cathy's cheeks smarted.

'I – I always thought Ruth understood my commitment to regeneration,' she defended.

'Oh, she does. We both do.' Mark nodded. 'If she weren't off at that damned international conference now, she'd tell you that herself. But maybe it's as well she's not here. It wouldn't have done you any good to go straight to her without thinking through your ideas very carefully indeed. I don't think she'd have considered your . . . emotional involvement . . . with Bill sufficient reason to take your report seriously.'

'Emotional involvement?' Cathy sat up straight in her chair, eyes blazing. 'What on earth do you mean?'

'Don't get me wrong.' Mark put out a placating hand. 'I'm not implying anything untoward is happening. But you have spent a lot of time with Bill, and socially too, and you know how careful we all have to be. Everyone knows you like Bill and how passionate you are about your work in east London. But it's better that Ruth sees you're making decisions with your head, not your heart. It's pragmatic to let it drop.'

'Mark.' Cathy paused to choose her words carefully. 'Can I be blunt? Are you saying that you're taking me off the Havers project because you suspect that my good relationship with Bill is compromising my judgement?'

'Not at all.' Mark gave a quiet laugh and twiddled with the knob on the louvre blinds to open them fully. He turned back to Cathy. 'I'm actually paying you a compliment. I want your skills put to better use. It's time we challenged you further and put you on something more ambitious. Lisa can take Havers from here. You've got specialist skills which we need to use in other areas.'

Cathy sat motionless, her cheeks still glowing. She was being admonished and her ideas for developing Bill's company had apparently been rubbished at the top level. At the same time Mark seemed to be paying her a backhanded compliment. But she wasn't being asked how she felt about anything, including leaving the project with Bill just at a time when they'd established an excellent bond. Cathy's stomach turned over. She felt nauseous and unsettled.

'I'll have to explain to Bill myself, of course,' she said.

'Naturally,' Mark agreed. 'But Lisa's already set up a meeting with him this afternoon where she'll go over everything, so you needn't go into too much detail.'

Cathy shot Mark an unhappy look. He cleared his throat.

'Remember, Cathy,' he said with a laugh in his voice, although his eyes were unsmiling. 'You work for us, not for yourself.'

Back in her chair, Cathy stared unseeingly at her computer screen, tapping a pen in agitation on her desk.

Why would they whisk her away from Bill Havers at such short notice? There was something that wasn't right about the situation, although she couldn't put her finger on it. She wanted to speak to Bill herself, but now wasn't the right time. Not with Mark's words ringing in her ears. She worked for the company, not for herself.

She felt a pang of guilt for introducing Bill to Troy Vickers without higher authority. Could Mark possibly have got wind of that? If so, how? Was Bill right – that Mark wanted to broker a deal between Cooper's and Troy, not because it was the right thing to do, but because there was more money in it for the company?

On the other hand, the projects that Mark had asked Cathy to work on before they'd finished their conversation could only be seen as a great compliment. They were important to the company and they would establish Cathy as a key player. There was a logic to using Cathy's skills elsewhere, now that Bill's project was largely in hand. Perhaps she was reading far too much into everything? But she had been relishing the opportunity to see Bill's project through to completion and having it all taken away from her was deflating, to say the least. It seemed she simply had no say in it.

Tying herself up in knots, Cathy gazed at her list of new e-mails while her brain ticked over. A name jumped out at her, making her look more closely.

It was an e-mail from Nick. They'd exchanged business cards, but it was strange to be contacted by him. It gave her butterflies in her stomach. Especially now Frank had hinted that Nick had professed a liking for her.

'Cathy, as we're both headed the same way on Saturday, how about meeting at Birmingham Station and getting the train up to Manchester from there? Give me your ETA in Brum. Rgds, Nick.'

Cathy blinked at the screen, feeling her skin growing warmer. She'd put all thoughts of Old Trafford out of her mind, but the sudden reminder of the weekend ahead with Nick sent a flicker of electricity through her.

She'd heard nothing from Jason at all. But the facts were there. She'd asked Jason to marry her and Jason had told her to go away. Cathy reckoned she could take that as a no. She didn't have the heart to contact Jason herself, merely to have his rejection repeated. He knew where she was. He hadn't been in touch. The signal was clear.

Maybe Frank's callous assertion, 'the boyfriend who won't marry you', was the most astute thing anybody had said about their relationship. Perhaps it had been a split waiting to happen?

But it hadn't stopped Cathy missing Jason so badly that she had a constant nagging ache inside her. To make herself feel better, she'd propped up the '6' and '4' card that Nick had insisted she bring back from Edgbaston against the wardrobe in her bedroom and put her letter of apology from the England captain on her bedside table. She looked at them every night before she went to sleep, trying not to picture what Jason might be doing to Candida.

'You know what we should do?' Fiona's lowered voice cut through Cathy's musings. She gazed at her friend blankly and shook her head. Fiona jerked hers in the direction of Mark's office. 'We should give them all two fingers and take off on our own.'

'Hmn.' Cathy smiled at Fiona. 'Be nice, wouldn't it?'

'And in the meantime,' Fiona insisted,' what about that night on the town we promised ourselves? Next week some time?'

Cathy thought about it. 'Yes,' she said firmly. 'Yes, let's go for it.'

As Fiona rolled away to answer her phone, Cathy was left to gaze at the computer screen, conflicting thoughts swirling round her head and a ripple of anticipation in her stomach as Nick's e-mail danced in front of her eyes.

*

The sky was doing strange things as Cathy's train nosed into Birmingham New Street Station on Saturday morning. The air was close and warm, and a sheet of grey-green cloud had formed. It hung over Birmingham with a metallic glimmer, making everything look surreal. Cathy wondered if for the first time in weeks it might actually rain.

Nick was waiting for Cathy on the platform. That meant no time to dive off to the loos and practise a suitably nonchalant smile of welcome. He grinned at her and her chest tightened. He seemed so tall, so broad and so cheerful today. It was quite a shock to see him in the flesh again and be reminded of how masculine he was.

'Heya!' He immediately took her bag from her and put it over his own shoulder.

'Hi. What are you doing with my bag?'

'I'll carry this.'

'It's all right, I can manage it.'

'I've got it now.' Looking like an overgrown caddy with a hold-all of his own on one shoulder and her big leather bag on the other, he led the way through the concourse and towards the platform of their train to Manchester. Cathy kept pace with him, wondering why she felt ruffled that he'd kidnapped her bag. It was a nice thing to do, wasn't it? She tried to relax.

They boarded a small train, which was practically empty, and found seats either side of a flimsy table. Nick tossed the bags into the luggage rack overhead as if he were swinging a couple of conkers on a string. Cathy couldn't help peeking at his arms as they flexed. He was in a black cotton T-shirt and it looked rather good on him. The thought leapt in and out of her head again – how many rooms had Frank booked in the hotel?

The train had only just set off when a refreshments trolley came round, wheeled by an elderly man who looked as if he might rather be spending his Saturday morning banging on his front window at the kids playing football outside than being in a service industry. In a perky little outfit he looked strangely misused. Feeling sorry for him, Cathy bought them both coffee and he crashed away, swearing loudly as his trolley veered into the door at the end of the carriage.

Now Cathy had a chance to look at Nick properly, face to face. Her nerves were starting to settle a bit. He looked even blonder-haired, more golden-skinned and piercingly blue-eyed than she'd remembered.

She wondered why she hadn't realised on first sight that he was handsome. He was most definitely hand-some, though not in a knitting-pattern kind of way. His nose was too long and strong for anyone to call him cute, but he was manly. She fluttered her eyelashes over the rim of her paper cup, allowing herself for a moment to wonder what it might be like . . .

'So, you spoke to Frank, then.' Nick raised his eyebrows quizzically.

'Oh. Yes.'

Cathy blushed. She couldn't let on that Frank had told her he'd had some feedback from Nick. Although the fact that she now knew Nick liked her definitely made him much more attractive.

'So did I,' Nick said enigmatically.

'Oh. Good.'

'You were right, of course. He wasn't trying to set us up in *that* way at all.'

'Oh, no. No, of course he wasn't.'

'He's a funny bugger, isn't he?' Nick rested his head back on his seat and chuckled. 'Beefy. Who'd have thought it.'

'You like him a lot, don't you?' Cathy ventured.

'Oh yes. Always have. We've been talking to each other for – well, must be nearly two years on and off I reckon, on the newsgroup. He's sound. He knows his stuff. I respect him.' Nick sipped his coffee and shook his head thoughtfully. 'It's funny. I always assumed he thought I was public school, something along those lines. "The right sort", as they say at Lord's. You can't tell on a newsgroup, of course. You can't look at someone, or hear his accent. But I set him straight in an e-mail. Made it clear I wasn't posh at all.'

'Why did you tell him?' Cathy leant forward curiously.

'Why? I don't know. Just to get it out of the way, I suppose. He said I was a good, solid bloke.' Nick laughed. 'Then he said something a bit cryptic about me being the right man for the job.'

Cathy stared, shifting in her linen trousers as the seat began to prickle through the thin material.

'What job?'

'Chaperoning you round cricket grounds, I guess.' Nick grinned again and Cathy sat back.

Being grinned at by Nick was like being hit by a shaft of sunlight. It made her feel good all over, but was probably better appreciated wearing sunglasses. He did have very white teeth. The phrase 'good breeding stock' did a fast canter round her brain and she shooed it away quickly. Was it her age? Good grief.

'Well,' she said, 'he seems to think you'll make it all bearable for me, so that I can report back to him. Bizarre as it all still seems, I suppose I can understand it. In a Frank sort of way.' Cathy took several big gulps of coffee.

'You like him too, don't you?' Nick probed.

'Despite everything, yes,' she said.

'Hmn.' Nick smiled. Then he straightened his face. 'Right then.' It came out as 'royt then' and unaccountably Cathy squirmed with pleasure. Nick stood up, lifted his bag down and zipped it open. He pulled out a sheaf of newspapers. 'Frank seems to want you to follow things, so have a read of the sports pages.'

'Oh no,' Cathy groaned. This was as bad as being given physics homework.

'Nothing too taxing,' Nick teased. 'There you go. The *Mirror*, the *Sun*, the *Mail* and just for good measure, the *Guardian*. I take it you haven't been following this match up until today.'

'Well, I did have a peep at the news,' Cathy confessed, pouting down at the pile of papers. 'I think I know enough, honestly.'

'Look upon it as a project.' Nick sat down again and crossed his arms.

'What are you going to do? Test me afterwards?' Nick smiled.

'Yes.'

'Oh God,' she groaned.

'It'll take your mind off the fact that you're heading up to dragon country. You've never been this far north before, have you?'

In fact, it was true. In an England sense anyway. But Cathy had been secretly thrilled that she was going to visit another city she'd never seen.

'I've been to Scotland,' she defended.

'Doesn't count.' Nick shook his head. 'And as you're likely to start freaking out and demanding oxygen once we get fifty miles north of Birmingham, I thought it'd be better if you were distracted.'

Cathy scrutinised Nick's expression. It was drily humorous, but there was also a glint in his eye. Of satisfaction, perhaps. Or bolshiness. One of the two.

'I promise you I'm not going to get the bends or anything,' she assured him tartly.

'Read,' Nick instructed.

After one long, petulant look at him, she turned her attention to the newspapers.

Cathy had thought Manchester would be several hours from Birmingham. It was just a southerner's vague view of the north of England, based on lack of knowledge, more than anything else. But, in fact, by the time she was settling herself into the idea of a long journey they'd arrived.

As they rolled into Manchester Piccadilly Station, she could see craggy red buildings from the train. Plenty of high chimneys, echoing the era of feverish industrial activity. She was jettisoned back to a novel they'd all read at school, by Elizabeth Gaskell. Something about young women working in mills. Then she clicked. Of course, that had been set in Victorian Manchester. It made the city instantly more interesting to her. It set her thinking about regeneration and her own projects again.

She was going to make an observation aloud to Nick, but he was already lifting their bags on to his shoulders and heading off through the compartment. And he'd only tease her for being a softy southerner, so she held her tongue.

294

Once in the station, Nick hesitated before striding off down into a sloping tunnel. Cathy trotted along.

'Is this the way, then?'

'Has to be,' Nick said simply.

'You have been here before, haven't you?' she quizzed him, watching his profile.

Nick shrugged. 'Man with cool box headed this way. We follow.'

'So you've never been to Manchester before,' Cathy exclaimed.

'I've been through it. In a car. Not by train.'

Even so, Cathy felt less silly. And at least that meant he wouldn't be swinging her round like an extra bag all day as he raced from one familiar location to another.

But at the end of the corridor was a barrier which seemed to head into an underground system. The man with the cool box did a U-turn and retraced his steps back up the slope again.

'Now what?' Cathy's lips twitched. Nick was taking this very seriously. It was as if he had the responsibility of leading the tribe to new territory.

'We follow him.' Nick flashed Cathy a smile.

'You know, it's okay to get lost,' she puffed as she jogged alongside him. 'I won't think you're a failure or anything.'

'Cathy, we're looking for the tram. It's not difficult. I'll find it.'

'Okay.'

It was a bit like the moment he'd kidnapped her bag. Part of Cathy felt strangely protected, as if this big man would sort everything out. If anyone had appeared in that dark passageway and even scratched his head in a vaguely threatening way she felt sure Nick would just

295

bop him on the nose on his way past without even slowing his pace.

But another part of Cathy wanted to say, 'All right, I've got the message, now will you stop the he-man act and consult with me?' Between them they'd have worked out where the tram stop was. For a start, Cathy would have asked the guard at the end of the tunnel. But no, off they zoomed, round the station several times, having lost sight of the man with the cool box, until finally they chanced upon a sign.

'There you go.' Nick nodded at it. 'That's the way.'

'Oo Nick, you're so butch.' Cathy couldn't help it. She put on a Sandra Dickinson voice and batted her eyelashes at him. He stopped in his tracks.

'Do you think you'd have found it any quicker?' There was, fortunately, a spark of humour in his eyes.

The answer was patently 'yes', but Cathy shook her head.

'I'd probably have been deported from Manchester the minute I opened my mouth to ask somebody and revealed the fact that I hadn't got a visa.'

Nick's lips curled into a smile.

'All right, then. Shall we go? We're running late as it is.'

The tram was a complete squash: narrower than an underground train, with smaller compartments. Cathy was wedged in the middle of a crowd of Elvis Presleys; there must have been about fifteen of them, all with slick black wigs and painted-on eyebrows. Every so often they'd break into a chant, filling the airless carriage with loud male exuberance. Cathy twisted round to Nick, who seemed to be squeezed into a long, thin shape behind her.

'What are they chanting?' she hissed at him. 'I've heard that at the other grounds too.'

'Barmy Army,' Nick replied flatly. 'It's their anthem. They follow England everywhere. And I mean *everywhere.*'

'Oh,' she mouthed. Nick didn't seem entirely to approve. But they appeared friendly enough and at least four of them gave her broad winks, which she countered suitably with arched eyebrows.

There were several stops before Old Trafford. Cathy was fascinated by the way the tram wove over roads and on to rail, before mercifully the doors opened and, as people spilled off, her ribcage expanded to its normal size again.

With the tram gone, the platform seemed strangely isolated. They were in the outskirts of the city. Behind them, beyond the trees, was evidently a very built-up area. But ahead the view seemed open and uncluttered. Cathy could see the tops of two big arenas. But there was an odd feel about the station. Despite being in what was clearly a very populous area, it felt a little as if they'd suddenly arrived in the American Midwest.

The light had a lot to do with it. Everything had taken on an eerie, green tinge. Cathy glanced up at the sky. It was opaque and leaden, although the air was so hot that her skin had a sheen of sweat over it already.

'Football to the right, cricket to the left,' Nick said with some relish, nodding over at the tangle of spotlights, poles and towers of the grounds ahead. 'Let's go.'

They crossed the bridge over the track, followed a

narrow road and a wide path, and found themselves at the turnstiles.

Everything seemed smaller inside than the other grounds she'd seen. They stopped at a tea van to pick up a cup to take to their stand with them. Most of the spectators must have found their seats inside already. They were a bit late and play had started. The only real buzz outside was coming from the Elvises, who had made contact with the Crusaders and were waging a mock battle on the tarmac, meeting foil swords with long white scarves and a rendition of 'Don't be Cruel'.

'Twats,' Nick said.

'They're all right.' Cathy laughed. 'They're enjoying themselves. It's a far cry from football hooligans. I tell you, Nick' – she eyed him seriously – 'if this is the worst sort of supporter that cricket's got to offer I'll take it any day.'

'True. But I've loved this game since I was a small boy. When they start chanting in the stands, I just want to bang their heads together. It ruins my concentration.'

'But the players like it, don't they?' Cathy queried, determined to maintain her own view on this. She knew damn all about the game itself, but she had to be qualified to comment on the spectators and she was probably more objective than Nick. 'I'm sure I read something in one of those papers. Hussain had said that the crowd at Edgbaston was fantastic for getting behind the team and that they really urged the players on.'

'Well. Maybe. But as long as they don't overdo it.'

She realised once again how intense Nick's support for the game was. It wasn't that he didn't know how to enjoy himself, because he obviously did, but it was so important to him that he couldn't bear any distractions. She tried to think of something she felt the same way about to draw a parallel. It was a strain. She could remember getting really cross with Jason once for grinding spices incredibly loudly in the kitchen when she was watching *Anna and the King* on video. But it wasn't the same thing. When Cathy considered Nick's feelings for cricket she realised she was in the presence of a grand passion.

'Let's find our seats, then,' she said, making sure that Nick didn't see the grin she gave the Elvises, who were now feigning heart attacks en masse.

The ground seemed tiny. The pavilion was very smart, with the Lancashire rose on one flag fluttering high and the Australian flag on the other. Their seats were near the front and once again they were at an angle to the wicket. She could see now why that was better than being at either end of the stumps. You got a much better view from being slightly to the side.

The stands were lower all round than at Edgbaston, and particularly than at Lord's. The sky seemed more prominent, more oppressive than at the matches she'd been to before. The light really was very strange. Play was already in progress and, as they settled, Nick surveyed the scoreboard with a frown of concentration, sizing it up with what he could see happening on the pitch. He pulled a funny face.

'Oh dear,' Cathy whispered. 'Is it that bad?'

'Hmn? No, it's great. Flintoff's still in. He'd done well yesterday, but I thought he'd be gone by the time we arrived. Looks like we're just in time to see him get his first test hundred. About flipping time too.'

'Oh.'

'This is his home ground, by the way,' Nick murmured to her, his eyes smiling. 'So they'll be pleased about that.'

'Oh, jolly good.'

Nick gave her a funny look and Cathy realised that her 'jolly good' had sounded a bit Bertie Wooster. It had come out instinctively, like a reflex. It dated back to maybe two years ago when she and Jason had been forced to endure an evening with one of his colleagues who was a grotesque snob. They'd fled to the pub after the dinner and got the giggles doing impressions of him. Ever since, they'd lapse, every so often, into that silly voice just to make each other laugh. But how on earth could she explain all that to Nick? She couldn't.

'You could read the news, you know,' Nick said and, with a last curious look at her, turned his full attention to the game.

Cathy waited, trying desperately hard to understand what was going on. According to the papers England had bowled Australia out for very few runs on Thursday, had established a solid start to their batting on Friday and were now aiming to get a very high total of runs themselves. Cathy had, thankfully, got her head round the fact that in test matches each side was meant to bat twice and that there was a maximum of five days to get the job done. In the middle were Nasser Hussain, the one she recognised most easily and the huge blond England batsman she'd seen on the news before she'd even been to a match. Flintoff, not Flintstone.

The crowd whooped as his total drew nearer the magical hundred. Nick had explained that fifties and hundreds were as precious to batsmen as goals were to footballers. In-between scores all helped, but they weren't the benchmarks. So Cathy allowed the fizzing atmosphere to buffet her, fascinated to hear so many broad Lancashire accents in the stands bellowing 'Go'rn, Freddy!' and even allowed herself a polite 'Come on!' when his score went up to ninety-six and she realised that he was one boundary ball away from his dream.

'C'mon, you great bloody lump,' Nick issued through gritted teeth. 'Don't bugger it up now.'

'This really is exciting.' Cathy turned sparkling eyes to Nick. 'I mean, I'm really enjoying it. I'm glad I'm here.'

'Great.' Nick focused on the pitch, but then he looked at Cathy properly and smiled. 'Yes, I'm glad you're here too. Perhaps your grandfather's not demented after all.'

'I hope he's watching this.'

'He will be,' Nick stated.

'This is quite a big deal, this guy getting a hundred, isn't it? That's why everyone's so manic.'

Nick nodded very emphatically.

'Everyone's been waiting for him to show his potential. He's had enough chances. And this looks like his moment.'

'Great.' Cathy beamed back.

The bowler – a long, thin sliver of white with a goatee beard – raced along the ground and seemed to put his whole body into a spin as he hurled the ball. It flew like a bullet. The big batsman took a swing and the ball sailed off into the air.

Flintoff didn't even bother to run. Cathy jumped to her feet and clapped along with the others as they all watched the ball bounce on the roof of the pavilion. The crowd exploded, stamping and yelling themselves hoarse.

In the centre, Cathy saw the captain take off his helmet and go to slap Flintoff on the back. Flintoff wrenched off his helmet too, looked at the three lions on the crest and kissed it. Then he waved his bat in the air at each hollering stand in turn and at the pavilion where the entire England team seemed to have spilled out on the balcony to applaud him.

'Brilliant!' Cathy enthused, her spirits rising dramatically.

'Go, Freddy!' A chant began in the long stand where Cathy had seen the Elvises and the Crusaders. Almost everyone in the stadium took up the chant.

'Freddy?' Cathy quizzed Nick.

'Freddy Flintstone.' Nick grinned. 'Most cricketers acquire nicknames over time. You get used to them.'

'Like "Beefy"?' Cathy raised a humorous eyebrow.

'Exactly.'

Someone lobbed a stuffed kangaroo on to the pitch and everybody jeered in fun. A small group of Australians somewhere behind Cathy put on mockingly defiant faces as they waved a banner that read 'You've been Warne'd'.

The crowd wouldn't sit down. Flintoff had to do his bat-waving all over again. Eventually the clapping began to die out as excited conversation swamped the ground and people gradually sat down again.

Directly behind her Cathy heard a mature Lancashire voice say, ''Bout bloody time. What the 'eck did he think he was playing at?'

Nick gave Cathy an happy wink.

'That's what it's all about, lass,' he put on a Hovis voice.

'This game's not what I thought at all. It's actually really good fun,' Cathy breathed.

All of Cathy's tensions, her worries about work, her sorrow over losing Jason, her preoccupations and fears had evaporated for now. It didn't matter that she still didn't understand half of what was going on out there. (Earlier Nick had attempted to explain the laws of leg-before-wicket dismissals and she'd felt as if she were being given a crash course in superstring theory.) But she was there supporting England and an England player had done something to be happy about. It was a wonderful release. Something so different, and on so much bigger a scale than all her worries, that it was like being on holiday – a badly needed holiday, seeing as how she had accrued several weeks' leave from work during the year that she hadn't had time to take.

The energy flickered around the spectators right up until lunch. Cathy and Nick went off for a hamburger and strolled round the entire ground. Still high on the change of scene, or her new discovery, or whatever it was that had brought her alive that day, Cathy dragged Nick into the William Hill tent.

'I want to place a bet,' she declared.

'Why?' Nick seemed concerned.

'Because I've never done it before and this is turning out to be my summer of doing lots of things I've never done before.'

'Well, all right. As long as you're sure.'

'Don't worry about it.' Cathy was amused by Nick's caution. 'I know you're meant to be my chaperone, but

I am an adult.'

Nick responded with a quirky smile.

Cathy put five pounds on England to win.

'You know, that might not have been such a good idea,' Nick said ruefully as Cathy gathered her receipt, thanked the teller in the tent and they made their way outside.

'Why not? We've got to win now. We're miles ahead. Flintoff's still in and you said yourself, we've still got guys to come in who can bat.'

'It's not so much that. It's more *that*.' Nick jerked his head up at the sky.

'The weather? But if it rains we'll be ahead. That's got to be good. Then we'll definitely win.'

'Oh no.' Nick gave Cathy a kind look. 'That's not how it works. If both sides don't get a chance to bat through to a definite result because of rain, it's a draw.'

'No!' Cathy clutched her betting slip, aghast. 'After all this effort?'

'Yep. If that bastard sky does what I think it's going to do, they'll draw this and the series will be wide open.'

'But we've got to win. It's one all. We need to win this one.'

Nick gave a soft chuckle as they moseyed back around the ground to find their stand. 'You're getting it.'

'But that's really mean,' Cathy insisted indignantly. 'Then all those brilliant scores will be wasted. And the Ozzies will get away with it.'

Nick laughed again.

'That's why test cricket's so interesting. There are a million factors that come into it at any time. The captain's not just thinking about who's going to bowl next and where they should all stand. He's got to be working it out, several moves ahead, all the time. That includes the pitch conditions at every different ground and' – Nick glanced up and pulled a face – 'the weather.'

'Blimey, you make it sound like chess.'

Nick grinned at Cathy happily.

'You're getting it,' he said again and led her back to their seats.

Chapter Sixteen

When the players emerged after lunch, Nick told Cathy that the England captain had declared on the runs they'd already got.

'Declared?'

'It's a tactical move. The captain can decide to stop his own team batting and the other side comes in. He's looked at the weather forecast.' Nick nodded towards the England captain as, in his floppy cap, he led the team out into the middle to field while the Australians had another go at batting. 'About time, really. I think they'll be lucky to get a result out of this.'

The afternoon started brilliantly. The Australians seemed to be on a back foot. Within an hour they had already lost two batsmen and the crowd were boisterous again. The Australians with the banner several seats back from Cathy were holding it rather limply.

And then Cathy looked up and realised that that last rumble she'd heard had not come from the crowd but from the sky.

She had loved storms ever since she'd been a child. The awe of something so huge and unpredictable had always given her a cold chill of pleasure. In places, the sky was now almost black.

Nick touched her arm and pointed over at a row of lights.

'See that? Three on now. Another one and they'll come off anyway.'

'I can't believe it's suddenly gone so dark,' Cathy said in a hushed voice.

They sat still, waiting. If anything, the air was hotter and damper than before. Every small sound echoed around the ground. And in a space of only a few minutes it seemed as if they were sitting in twilight.

'Wow,' Cathy breathed.

'Ey-oop,' she heard. She'd thought it was Nick putting on his Hovis voice to amuse her again, but realised it had come from behind. 'Here's trouble.'

Simultaneously a crash of thunder banged around them, making everybody jump. There were a few squeals. A dry storm? Maybe the team would get away with it. In the centre of the pitch the two umpires had met and were comparing the readings on their light meters.

A blinding flash of light had everybody blinking like confused rabbits and was followed immediately by another deafening crash. Cathy laughed aloud.

'This day just gets better and—'

A jagged streak of forked lightning split the sky. There was a collective gasp of awe. By now nobody was looking at the pitch. The thunder boomed. It was as if a bomb had gone off above their heads. Everybody jumped again, some people leapt up and began to race away from the open stands. There was sudden activity all round, as if they were all on video and somebody had decided to press 'fast forward'.

The rain came. Not in spatters, but in a sudden cascade of stair rods, driving down as if hurled from a furious weather god sitting up there having a tantrum.

Cathy was vaguely aware of the little white figures sprinting towards the pavilion and of a frenetic burst of activity as people dashed back on to the pitch with huge tarpaulins.

She couldn't move. She blinked heavenwards, the angry battering of the rain stinging her face. Within seconds she was drenched from head to foot.

'Jee-sus!' she heard Nick exclaim next to her, getting to his feet and grabbing their bags. 'Come on.'

'No.' She shook her head, laughing back at him. 'I love it.'

Nick was soaked. Even though he was only a yard or so away, her vision of him was skewed by the sheet of water being thrust at them from the sky. His T-shirt was sopping wet, his jeans spattered with water, as if a circus clown had just run at him and doused him with a bucketful. She threw back her head and laughed again. 'It's fantastic!'

'Come on!' he said more assertively and took her arm. 'It's forked lightning. You don't want to be out in this.'

'Yes! I do!'

'No, you don't!'

Cathy allowed herself to be guided along the row of seats to the aisle. Already everyone else had scarpered. The thunder banged at them again and Cathy leapt in the air too. It had to be directly overheard. She'd never heard such a noise.

'Bloody heck,' Nick yelled. 'Let's get into one of the bars.'

'They weren't expecting this, were they?' Cathy giggled, even higher on atmosphere than before.

'I think', Nick called back as he pulled her up the

steps by the hand, 'that this might even have taken the weather forecasters by surprise. I've never seen a storm like it. Look at this bloody rain!'

They stopped at the top of the stand before they left the ground and looked back over the pitch. Already there were ponds of water forming on the flat grass. The groundsmen were racing round, their bodies hunched. Cathy's bare shoulders and arms were stinging. If she hadn't been able to see it was rain, she'd have sworn it was hail.

She gasped in awe, 'It looks like a flash flood.'

'You know,' Nick panted, with a firm grasp on Cathy's hand as he edged her towards the closest exit from the stand, 'I think that's exactly what it is.'

Cathy froze as she watched another fearsome band of light pelt from sky to earth, her heart thumping. The thunder cracked like a celestial firearm.

'Oo shit.' She giggled nervously at Nick. 'I think we'd better get out of here.'

Nick dragged her down the steps and they left the stand. The concourse was alive with spray, a shallow stream swirling round the tarmac. They reached the foot of the covered stairs.

'We've got to make a dash for it. Which way was the bar?' Nick called.

'That way.' Cathy and Nick pointed in opposite directions. Cathy, all her tensions released and her spirits as high as a comet, doubled over in a belly laugh.

'You.' Nick shook his head at her. A host of droplets flew away from his hair. 'I just can't work you out.'

Cathy grinned back, her face running with water. 'Stuffy southerner or okay kind of chick. You just don't know, do you?'

'And you just think I'm a northern git.'

Cathy opened her mouth in mock indignation, but ended up laughing again.

'One thing I do know, Nick. I've never had a summer like this before.'

'And neither have I.'

They paused, both shrinking into their wet clothes as another clatter of thunder shook the ground. They looked at each other again. Cathy's adrenalin was wooshing round her body as if it were coming straight from a hosepipe.

'Let's run to the bar,' Nick said.

He grasped her hand again. Cathy didn't resist. It seemed completely natural. So much for her hopes of not being swung round. She felt like a kite as he trailed her out of the little alcove at the foot of the steps, through what felt like a power shower, along the tarmac and into a dark, crowded bar where they pushed themselves in along with a mass of other bodies. The muggy heat of the room instantly hit Cathy, as did the crash of voices, laughter, exhilaration and the regular 'hooray!' every time the thunder boomed.

They aimed for the bar. It was nice to be in such a robustly cheerful crowd with Nick grasping her hand. It was like being dragged along by Superman. Cathy could pretend, for now, that nothing else mattered.

There were grins everywhere. Cathy stopped to giggle at a handful of England supporters whose white faces with red painted crosses had now merged into huge smears of pink.

'The Impressionists!' she pointed out.

One of them did an impression of Edna Everidge in

response, earning playful boos from the Australians wedged up against them.

'Another wet T-shirt! Yipee!'

Cathy pulled a face at the Elvis. His wig was skew-whiff and his painted-on eyebrows had washed right down his face. He looked like Alice Cooper. Everybody seemed heady. If you'd taken a hundred people, made them all smoke grass for two hours and stuck them in a bar together, Cathy didn't think you could have a more giddy group in one place.

At the bar, she collided with Nick's back, enjoying herself so much that she forgot to stop.

'What would you like?' he called over his shoulder.

'I'm not sure I need anything. I feel drunk already.'

His eyes softened towards her.

'I'll get you a pint, shall I?'

She nodded.

'And by the way, you really would win a Miss Wet T-Shirt competition at the moment. Just to warn you.'

'Oh.'

Cathy looked down. She was wearing a bra under her top, of course. She always did. But it wasn't made of iron and, given the fact that she'd effectively been taking a bath in her clothes, it probably wasn't surprising that the bra seemed to have melted away, her thin top was sticking to her every curve and it looked as if she wasn't wearing anything apart from papier mâché above the waist. Her breasts were sticking out like balloons.

'Oh my God!' Cathy yanked the soggy material away from her body instantly.

'I don't mind if you don't.'

Nick gave Cathy a saucy look, as if he'd suddenly

decided to treat her like a woman he fancied. As she was flushing, he turned to the bar to get the drinks.

Another pelt of thunder overhead had the whole bar yelling. Nick pulled away with two pints in plastic glasses and nodded towards the side of the room.

'We can lean over there.'

They pushed through the damp throng of people. Cathy dissolved into the atmosphere. It was as if for the moment she had stopped being Cathy, with all her individual failings and triumphs, and had become subsumed in something big, carefree, loud and happy.

They squashed against a wall behind a bunch of Crusaders, Cathy ducking to avoid a cardboard sword on the head.

'This is quite an experience,' she called to Nick as they both took long sips of their drinks. Nick grinned back. His face was still wet.

'Yeah.'

'I'm so glad I'm here.' Cathy couldn't stop smiling. Her spirits were free to flutter about at will, even if it was only for a day. It was a desperately needed break. 'I don't want to think about anything else, or anyone else. It's just here, now, this moment.'

A ferocious boom shook the bar into more cheers and laughs and a few pale squeals.

'It's like Bonfire Night!' Nick laughed down at Cathy.

'That makes me the Catherine wheel.'

'Well – I'm the one who's spinning,' Nick said.

Cathy looked up at Nick shyly. He hadn't taken his eyes off hers. His cheeks, with raindrops still rolling down them from his hair, were flushed. But he stuck his gaze on her and wouldn't let go. She swallowed.

312

She couldn't say anything due to the bubble in her throat.

'I was—' Nick began. 'I was looking forward to seeing you again.' He took a mouthful of beer and looked at her as if it was a very big statement.

Cathy paused, only for a minute, before she decided to let the petals open a little.

'I was looking forward to seeing you too,' she admitted quietly.

'You're very pretty,' Nick said, apropos of nothing.

What sort of conversation was this? It would never make any sense to anyone, Cathy decided, unless they could also feel the lump in her throat, the buzz on her skin, the sensation of delving into Nick's pale-blue eyes, the sexual chemistry between them that was so thick you'd have to cut through it with a chainsaw.

Around them, the crowded bar jostled and jumped, but to Cathy it was white noise. She seemed alone with Nick, conscious that he was swallowing hard, as she was.

'I'm going to kiss you. So hang on to your hat.'

'Okay,' she whispered.

Nick drew her to him and lowered his head to hers. He kissed her, and didn't stop kissing her for about three and a half years. In fact, it was probably more like three and a half minutes. But she was in no doubt that he would have let it go on for three and a half years if he could have done. And so would she.

'Oh dear,' she gasped, as they pulled apart again.

'Oh dear?' Nick cleared his throat, a smile playing round his lips. 'You say oh dear? You realise men get visible evidence from a situation like this.'

'Oh!' Cathy blushed.

'I can't kiss you again. I'm already glad it's a crowded bar.'

Nick shifted awkwardly against the wall, jiggling the bags on his shoulders. He hadn't even thought to put them down. He was like a walking crane. He pulled his wallet out of his jeans.

'Let me give you a tenner and you get us another beer. That'll give me time to compose myself.'

'It's okay, I'll get the beers in. No problem. It's my shout.'

'No, I want to get them.'

'It's my shout,' Cathy persisted.

'It's not the point,' Nick said, pulling out a ten-pound note and handing it to Cathy. 'I want to buy you a drink. The pleasure is all in the giving. See? And now I'd like to buy you a drink. On me. To you. Because it's what I want to do.'

'All right.' Cathy smiled into Nick's eyes. 'I'll get them.'

'Just go to the bar and let me get rid of this stiffy,' Nick said in a strained voice.

Cathy blushed again, her body on fire, and headed for the bar.

The phone trilled.

Cathy pulled herself from the sheets. She threw out a hand and patted it along the bedside table until it landed on the cool plastic of the receiver. She pulled it up to her ear.

'Hello?'

'Madam.' The male voice was a strangled combination of Hyacinth Bouquet and Graham Norton. 'I'm afraid we've had a complaint from room ninety-six.'

Cathy sat up on her knees, tugging at the damp sheet entwined round her body.

'Room ninety-six?'

'Yes indeed.'

She put her hand over the receiver and whispered to Nick, 'Room ninety-six has complained.'

'Oh no!' Nick mouthed back.

'I'm terribly sorry, what is the complaint?'

'Well,' the voice said awkwardly. 'It is gone two in the morning, madam. Room ninety-six is not happy about the time.'

Cathy clumsily took the refreshed glass of Baileys that Nick offered her.

'Let's have a look.' She grappled with the watch lying on the bedside cabinet. 'Oh yes, it is. You're quite right. And room ninety-six would rather we all revert to Greenwich Mean Time?'

'The noise,' the voice said discreetly. 'A little too much noise.'

'Ah.'

'The room is directly above yours, madam. Obviously this is a delicate matter and we don't like to interfere, but we must act on a complaint.'

'Oh yes. I see. I do see. I'm so sorry.' Cathy smothered a smile. 'We'll – we'll turn the – the television down, then.'

'Yes, madam. It would be a good idea if you turned the television down just a little bit.'

'We'll do that.'

'And do enjoy the rest of your stay, madam.'

'Yes, we will.' Cathy tried to wave Nick away as he flung himself on the bed and beckoned her to give him the phone. 'No,' she mouthed at him. 'It's sorted.'

'Give it to me. I've just had an idea.' He wrestled the phone away from Cathy, falling on top of her. She shrieked with laughter as her Baileys went all over her chest.

'Hello?' Nick said, forcing Cathy down as she struggled up and put a finger to his lips. 'You have an adult channel available on the television, don't you?'

Cathy slapped her free hand over her mouth and stared up at the ceiling in amazement. That was a first. Definitely, none of this had ever happened to her before.

'Well,' Nick continued, trailing a finger over the Baileys trickling over Cathy's collarbone and licking his fingertip. 'If we promise to be quiet, would you be so good as to feed the adult channel into our set and stick it on the bill?'

Cathy gasped into Nick's face. He nodded back at her, grinning.

'Yes and we promise we'll be really, really quiet. Yes, when we put the television on we'll keep it really low as well. Yes, promise. Thanks so much, mate.'

Nick put down the receiver and launched himself at Cathy, scooping up the Baileys from her neck with his tongue.

'I don't believe you did that!'

'Right. Into the shower with you.'

'No!'

'Yes!'

Nick hoisted her up in his arms and carried her across the hotel bedroom. They staggered from wall to wall.

'You!' She waved a finger at him, but he bit the end.

'What?'

'You're drunk,' she claimed.

'Into the shower!'

Nick stood Cathy up in the shower and turned the jet on. Hot water blasted them both. Cathy closed her eyes and pushed her head up into the warm spray.

'What you need is a good soaping,' Nick declared.

'If I do, you do.'

They had a battle with the soap. Nick won, so Cathy hopped away to the bath where she found a miniature bottle of shampoo. She slid back into the shower cubicle and squirted it over Nick's chest. Although she was very tipsy indeed, she didn't feel in the slightest bit tired.

They made love again in the shower. Cathy felt wonderful. Like the object of all Nick's desire. He seemed to be able to push and pull her around, like a piece of plasticine.

Nick pulled away, leaving Cathy aching and blinked at her through the shower.

'Let's see what's on the telly!' he grinned.

He grabbed her hand and hauled her back into the bedroom. She threw herself on the bed, sopping wet, warm and alive. Nick balanced on the edge of the bed and fiddled with the remote control until a blaze of contorted images shone from the screen.

Cathy's mouth dropped open. It was, most definitely, an adult channel.

'This is outrageous!' she exclaimed, but even as she did, she was giggling. She peered at Nick's body again. It was spectacular. Muscular, strong, solid and softened with dark-gold hairs in all the right places. She'd never felt such a physical drive as this.

'Now, now,' Nick teased her, wagging a finger. 'Give me that look and you're asking for trouble.'

Cathy flopped on the bed, gazing at Nick through a fog. She was aware that yet another dramatic reaction in his body had ensued.

'What is it with you?' she pleaded to the ceiling as Nick dived on the bed and crushed her again.

'What is it with *you*?' he breathed into her ear.

'At the moment,' she mumbled, 'I just don't care.'

'And neither do I. So let's not talk about it.'

'I know!' Nick exclaimed.

Cathy sat up, pushing her bedraggled hair out of her eyes.

'What?'

'Carpet. We haven't done that.'

'You're joking.' Cathy pulled a face at Nick. 'What are you, a man or a beast?'

'Have another glass of Baileys. Then you'll see what a great idea it is.'

Cathy struggled out of bed and found the bottle of Baileys again. They'd bought it at an off-licence on their way to the hotel. A very good investment, she decided, tripping over her shoes. She sloshed another drop into their water glasses and handed one to Nick. He took it and sipped delicately. She watched his lips. He really did have very nice lips. It was probably what made him such a good kisser.

'Oh God!' Nick groaned, his eyes raking over Cathy's body. 'You're like a rampaging disease, do you know that?'

'Oh, thank you so much.'

'No, it's like, I had food poisoning once and it was just like this. The feeling just got more and more persistent as the night went on.'

Nick feathered kisses over Cathy's neck, arms and breasts. She pulled herself up and gave him a wonky look.

'What's up?' he asked.

'You wanted carpet? You've got carpet.'

The slamming of doors in the corridor woke Cathy up. She opened her eyes blearily. Beyond the curtains, traffic was growling. Rain hammered at the windows. She tried to close her eyes again. What was she doing, waking up in the middle of the night anyway?

But then she realised it was daylight outside. A dim light was slanting through a gap where they hadn't quite closed the curtains properly. And she had goose-pimples on her skin. For the first time in weeks and weeks, she was actually a bit cold.

She struggled to sit up. Where was she? What was going on? Her body felt as if it had been turned inside out. So did her head. Everything was throbbing. The skin on her legs was itching and one arm was completely numb. She waved it about.

Next to her, on the carpet, was Nick, completely naked, with his head thrown back, snoring loudly.

Chapter Seventeen

At the reception desk Nick and Cathy wrestled with each other over the bill.

'Let me.' Nick stared at Cathy assertively. She guessed that at times that might have been quite a scary look, but his eyes were still pink from no sleep and a shower, and it was hard to be daunted by him. It was like being threatened by a mutant *Babe*.

'Don't be ridiculous. Frank only booked one room, for me. He obviously expected you to make it back to Birmingham last night. My room, my bill.'

'Nope. I ordered a few . . . additional extras. It's on me.'

'No way.' Cathy swiped the flimsy bit of paper back from him.

'Now, you listen to me.' Nick drew himself up to his full height and almost disappeared into the ceiling. Cathy peered up equally adamantly. It was hard to stay focused. The hotel lobby was very dark and cavernous. It was dotted with an odd combination of chrome, brass, gigantic mirrors and stale dark-green carpets. On no sleep and a few too many slurps of Baileys, it felt like she was making a guest appearance in a Douglas Adams novel.

'There's only room for one control freak here,' Nick stated. 'And I've decided that it's going to be me.'

Cathy prodded Nick in the chest.

'That's it! You are a control freak! That's a very penetrating piece of self-analysis.'

'Nothing compared with you. You really are a control freak.'

Cathy gasped.

'I'm not a control freak! I just know what's best. All of the time.'

Nick put on a deep voice.

'There can be only one!' His words resonated around the lobby and, as Cathy looked confused, he went on limply, 'It's from *Highlander*.'

'There can only be one control freak in *Highlander*?'

'No, immortal. There can be only one immortal. The others get their heads chopped off.'

'How is that relevant to our bill?'

Nick sighed and put out his hand. He looked as if he wasn't going to take no for an answer.

'Give it here.'

'No.'

'Excuse me, sir, madam?' The clerk leant over the desk and beckoned them closer. 'The bill is for your information. The expenses have been covered by Mr Harland. That was arranged before you arrived.'

Both Cathy and Nick stood stock still and stared at the young clerk. They must have stared for a long time, because he became very self-conscious and scratched at a spot on his neck with the end of his pen.

Cathy found her voice first.

'Mr Harland . . . he won't receive an itemised account of what we ordered, will he?'

'We're used to providing receipts to companies who cover their employees' expenses, madam. Of course we'll send Mr Harland a receipt.'

Cathy blanched.

Nick stepped forward and leant on the desk. The clerk backed away a few steps. Cathy guessed Nick was doing the scary look and perhaps the clerk, who hadn't seen Nick prancing around completely naked with a soggy T-shirt on his head the previous night, actually found him menacing.

'We would very much rather that you didn't send an itemised bill to Mr Harland,' he said in a low but firm voice.

'I'm afraid it's policy, sir,' the clerk squeaked back.

'No, no, you don't understand,' Cathy soothed, wondering if a bit of feminine diplomacy might get the job done. 'Mr Harland isn't my employer, he's my grandad. And he's treated me to this weekend away in – in your lovely city. And the truth is, he has a life-threatening heart condition and he is very shockable.' She ended with a tremulous attempt at a smile that probably looked as if she'd spent a day in a wind tunnel. 'So it would be very helpful if you would perhaps fail to send him a fully itemised bill for our stay. You do see my point, don't you?'

'If – if you would care to look at your bill' – the clerk quailed – 'I think you'll find that the word "porn" isn't even mentioned.'

Cathy blinked. Nick seemed to do a double-take too. But they crowded round the bill and examined it closely. There wasn't any mention of X-rated films. Just that they had watched 'films'. Even now, Cathy couldn't believe that they'd done that. She clutched her chest with relief.

'Oh, that's good. My grandfather is very frail.'

'But I don't see why he should cover that.' Nick was

still frowning. 'I wish I'd known. Can't we pay for all the extras beyond the cost of the room?'

'I'm afraid not, sir.' The clerk shook his head. 'Mr Harland has stayed at this hotel often during the cricket season. He is a highly respected customer and we agreed that he would collect the tab completely. Although he did say there might be a struggle.' The clerk offered a weak smile.

'Did he?' Cathy's dismay gave way to a flicker of amusement. 'Well, that's that, then. I think it's a *fait accompli*.'

'I would certainly say so, madam. Would you like to keep your copy of the bill for information?'

Cathy hesitated, a faint blush spreading over her face. Then she took the bill and tucked it into her bag.

'Yes, why not? Now come on, Nick. I'm starving. You promised to show me somewhere that does a proper breakfast, complete with mushy peas.'

It was still pelting down outside. The air was mild, but there was a thick film of water over the roads and pavements.

Nick and Cathy jogged through the rain, a little half-heartedly due to a deficit of energy and after roaming a few blocks close to the station, found a greasy spoon. Nick dived into the adjacent newsagent and emerged with a wodge of Sunday papers. Then they found a table inside the café.

It was the perfect hangover-no-sleep breakfast. A waitress staggered to their table under the weight of two plates of eggs, sausages, bacon, chips, baked beans and mushy peas. They drank huge mugs of tea. Cathy could only blink at the portion of the paper

323

Nick handed her as he devoured the sports section. Her brain was already trying to go back to sleep again.

Then they headed off to Manchester Piccadilly and took another small train back to Birmingham, sitting side by side but not talking much as the dismal view of rain descending beyond the windows preoccupied them. It was coming down so thickly it was like a low fog.

'No play today,' Nick said, gazing out at a lake that only yesterday had probably been a field.

'Unless they do it in rubber rings and armbands.'

'Or tomorrow, I bet.' Nick looked rueful. 'So that's that, then. Third match drawn. We're still one all.'

Cathy nodded. 'Is it my imagination,' she commented, as she spotted a herd of cows balancing on a hill as if they were waiting for Noah's Ark to drop by and pick them up, 'or is the rain actually getting heavier as we go south?'

'It's getting heavier,' Nick confirmed.

'I'm glad I'm travelling by train, then,' Cathy said. 'I bet loads of the roads are closed by now.'

They arrived at Birmingham New Street. Cathy looked at her timetable.

'Well, I guess I'd better make my way back to London.'

They stood on the brightly lit concourse, the same one Cathy had arrived at weeks ago for her very first cricket experience. It seemed more functional today and much less exciting. It was Sunday, of course, and people seemed to be drifting round in slow motion. But then, her brain felt like it had been taken out, zapped with a ray gun and slotted back in again. Cathy glanced at Nick.

'Mind you,' she went on, 'it's still fairly early afternoon. But you've probably got plans.'

'No,' Nick said instantly.

'Oh. Well. I've got a few trains I could get back to London. I guess I don't have to race away right this second.'

'In which case I could always take you to a pub close by and we could have a very gentle hair of the dog before you take off.'

Cathy nodded. 'That'd be nice. As long as it's very gentle. My body feels as if it's been through a car crusher.'

Nick grinned, the first grin he'd produced all day.

'Follow me, then.'

Nick led Cathy away from the station and along a convoluted mesh of pavements until she realised she was in Birmingham's shopping centre. The rain had eased off a little so they didn't need to run. After traversing the length of what Cathy assumed must be the main pedestrian precinct, with large branches of familiar chain stores ranged around them, Nick pulled her off down a side street.

'There's one down here,' he said. 'Not that any of them are really any good in the middle of town, but if you like more traditional pubs, it's probably the closest you'll get.'

The pub was thankfully dark and quiet inside. The sudden force of the weather seemed to have kept most visitors away from the centre of the city that day and it was just as well. Cathy was still feeling fragile and it was nice not to have to jostle with a crowd.

Nick bought them both a beer – Cathy decided not to argue about whose round it might be at this juncture – and they headed to the back of the pub where there were several deserted tables.

'So.' Cathy took the froth off her beer delicately.

'So?' Nick queried.

'So.' Cathy ransacked her brain. It was a chance to say something meaningful. They'd just had a romping weekend of fun and passion. At the moment nobody else existed. She'd deliberately pushed Jason as far from her mind as possible. She knew that her uncharacteristic abandon this weekend might have something to do with rebound, but she couldn't think about any of that. It was too abstract. Even London seemed to be a theoretical destination. But was she going to part company with Nick without either of them voicing any thoughts at all? She would have to get a train soon and it would be nice just to get a gauge. A very slight gauge, at least.

'So,' she struggled on womanfully. 'So here we are!'

'Yep.'

'Here we are. Here in Birmingham.'

'Yes indeed.' Nick nodded.

'And – well, who'd have thought it?'

Nick took a sip of beer, stopped to shudder as it went down and smacked his lips.

'Well, I live here. So I'd have thought it.' He grinned.

'But I don't,' she parried.

There was a pause between them. Both of them were too physically weary, in the nicest possible way, for there to be any awkwardness. But Cathy wondered if one of them should say something about what they'd done, what they might do. Or perhaps there was no need.

'I've had a brilliant weekend.' He flashed her a smile. 'It's been a real blast.'

Cathy nodded. 'Yes, it has. It made me forget about everything else. Just what I needed. I feel like someone's taken a Dyson to all of my cobwebs.'

Nick's eyebrows rose.

'I feel like someone's taken a hoover to me too.'

Cathy tutted at him playfully. She took another sip of beer. They fell silent again, the hum of conversation from the front of the pub wafting peacefully over them.

'Where is it that you live?' Cathy asked, random questions drifting through her mind. 'Tell me about it.'

Nick sat back. He didn't only do that, he leaned right back in his chair, as if he was retreating from the question.

'I told you. I share a house. On the outskirts of Brum. It's a laugh. I like the set-up there.'

'Right, yes, you did. Sorry.'

'Believe me, Cathy, I've told you more about myself than I've ever shared with any woman before. You're . . . different. I've wanted to tell you things.'

Cathy absorbed this information. She nearly smiled. She knew practically nothing about Nick. If he'd never divulged to any woman more than he'd divulged to her, he must have gone through his romantic life acting like the Scarlet Pimpernel. On the other hand, Nick had actually been to Cathy's house. He'd even met her ex-boyfriend. And at the thought of Jason, Cathy felt a horrible swell of guilt. She hadn't slept with Nick before, but she most certainly had now. She excused herself.

'I just need to find the Ladies.'

In the tiny upstairs toilet Cathy put on a little more

make-up and fluffed up her hair. A small window was wedged open. She was fascinated to hear how heavy the rain had become again. It was battering furiously against the roof and gushing along the drainpipe.

She decided that thinking about Jason at this point was not a good option. She'd had a wild and reckless weekend. The memory of it made her want to laugh out loud again. She would go back to Nick, have fun with him and then get her train. Any contemplation could be done later. After all, she and Nick knew how to contact each other. Far better not to make any grand statements now. It was much too soon to know what to say, if anything.

She went back to the bar full of smiles.

'My round,' she declared.

'I thought you wanted to take it gently?' Nick blinked at her, but there was a twinkle in his eyes.

'Stuff it. It's Sunday afternoon, I've got the journey to sober up, I feel like I'm having a weekend on Pluto, now is not the time to start being sensible. I'll get us another drink.'

'All righty.' Nick laughed under his breath. 'But I've only got to pour myself into a taxi. You've got a long way to go, so you watch yourself.'

They sat in the pub for hours. Every hour, on the hour, Cathy pulled out her timetable and stated that she'd missed the imminent train and would have to aim for the next one. Eventually Nick put a hand over hers.

'Cathy? Why don't you decide to get the last train? It doesn't leave that late anyway and that way we both know where we are.'

'Oh,' Cathy pondered for a second or two. 'Okay then.'

Finally it was definitely time to move for the train. Cathy felt wonderfully high and dizzy. They'd chatted about all sorts of things and Nick had given her a few further pointers on cricket. They'd laughed a lot. It had been fun and she was glad she'd stayed on. She gathered her bags and they both wandered from the back of the pub towards the door. It was wedged open, and they both stopped and stared outside.

The sky was firing machine-gun bullets. The sloped street was like a river. Buried at the back of the pub, Cathy hadn't realised that it had got so much worse. Other drinkers around them were guffawing and exclaiming about the outburst.

'Oh, blimey,' she said.

'Let's run for it.'

They did. It was a mad dash. Water swam over Cathy's sandals and she skidded more than once. Nick clutched her hand firmly. He dragged her along some sort of back route and they made it into the bowels of the station.

'We have to rush,' he called. 'Your train goes in a couple of minutes.'

'This isn't rushing?' Cathy shouted back, clattering with Nick up endless flights of stairs until, miraculously, they were back at the concourse. They gauged the platform quickly and headed that way.

'Just in time!' Cathy panted. The train was already alongside the platform. A few latecomers struggled on and doors were slamming.

'Go!' Nick grabbed her briefly and planted a kiss on her sopping wet forehead. 'Take care of yourself. I'll be in touch.'

Be in touch? Like, to let you know if I want to buy your insurance policy once I've checked out what's available? Even in her panic, Cathy was slightly bemused by his choice of words.

'I'll be in touch with you,' she answered, wrestling with the train door.

'Whatever. Get on, before it goes without you.'

''Bye!'

It was a fairly bizarre end to a fairly bizarre weekend, Cathy decided as she pushed her way into a warm, brightly lit carriage which, like the rest of the train, seemed only sparsely dotted with passengers. She stuffed her bag in the overhead compartment and sank into a seat. Then she peered out of the window to see if Nick was still on the platform. But she hadn't thought he would hang about to wave her off. It just didn't seem his style. And he hadn't. He'd gone.

She fell into tipsy, mellow thought. After a long weekend of all manner of exertion, her body seemed happy to flop. She'd probably stay in this position all the way to London. There were plenty of mental images to sustain her without the need to fiddle around with a paper, or a book. A check of her watch confirmed that it was well after nine. There was a vague mechanical hum surrounding her and any moment now she would probably close her eyes and drift off.

Time passed. The train didn't move. Cathy started to feel more awake. An announcement crackled over the speakers:

'Ladies and gentlemen, we apologise for the late running of this train, which is due to water on the line.

330

We will keep you informed of developments as soon as we get them.'

Cathy shifted in her seat. She gazed out again at the alien sights of the station. She began to feel a nibble of anxiety in her stomach.

More time passed. A guy who looked like a student wandered down the carriage. He turned to Cathy and addressed her in a broad Birmingham accent.

'What's going on? We've been here forty minutes. If I don't make it down to London tonight I'm going to miss all my connections!'

'Oh dear,' Cathy said with genuine sympathy, but he'd already wandered off again, looking harassed.

Now Cathy felt very awake. More time went by and before long she realised she'd been sitting on the train, waiting for something to happen, for an hour. She slid her St Christopher round on its chain. Then a further announcement was made.

'Ladies and gentlemen, I'm sorry to say that this train is cancelled. The line on our route is flooded and the rain is so heavy that there is no chance of us clearing it tonight. We would like to apologise—'

Cathy mentally switched off from the announcement at that point. She stood up, along with a handful of others who sprang up from the anonymity of the seats like grasshoppers, and joined in the general burst of indignation.

It was fortunate that she'd gone for a hair of the dog with Nick. As Cathy grappled with her bags and left the train to stand exactly on the spot on the platform where they'd said goodbye over an hour earlier, Cathy decided that being stranded in Birmingham on a Sunday night would be a terrible thing to contemplate with a hangover.

She didn't know anybody. The city was completely foreign to her. And it was far too distant from London to think about getting a bus or a taxi. Now it was gone ten o' clock. If the trains couldn't make it, she had no doubt that the coaches would be having trouble. And she had no idea how she'd go about getting a coach anyway.

She trudged up the stairs with her fellow thwarted travellers.

'What are we all going to do?' a couple she recognised from her carriage exclaimed at her, but more into the air than at anyone in particular. 'We're stuffed. We don't know anyone here. We'll have to book into a hotel and try again tomorrow.'

'Yes, I think I will as well.' Cathy pulled a rueful face. 'It's grim, isn't it?'

Cathy got to the top of the stairs leading up from her platform and stared at a row of public telephones. She stopped and put her bag down by her feet.

She didn't know anybody. Except . . .

No, it was a terrible idea. It was quite clear from Nick's relaxed attitude today that he wanted to be very casual about things. That was fine. She needed much more space to think anyway.

But the telephones had given her the idea. She reached into her handbag and pulled out her mobile phone. She stared at it.

What if Nick had gone out again by now, with some other woman? What if he'd got home and thought 'Thank God, I managed to get shot of her'? What if he already had a girlfriend and was just being cagey about it? It would be an appalling imposition. She didn't know enough about him to make any assumptions.

But on the other hand she was stranded in Birmingham and he was the only individual she knew who lived there.

They had just spent a weekend exploring each other in the most intimate manner. And yet Cathy was stuck in the city where Nick was the only soul she knew and she felt it would be a presumption to call him. She was being stupid. Of course she should call him.

Her heart thumping, Cathy found Nick's business card. There was a home phone number. Taking a deep breath for sustenance, she switched on her mobile phone.

It was dead. She stabbed at the 'on' button several times, but there was no response. The batteries were obviously low. She'd brought the phone with her, but hadn't thought to recharge it, not expecting anyone to need to get in touch with her urgently.

'Damn.'

Cathy tossed the phone back into her bag. Was it a sign? Even if it was, what else was she going to do?

Making a decision, Cathy crossed the concourse to the payphones and glanced at Nick's card again. She pressed out his home number on the metallic buttons and held her breath.

'Hello?' It was definitely Nick's voice that answered.

Cathy breathed again. She'd dreaded one of his housemates answering, taking a message and leaving something for Nick like, 'Cathy rang. She was still in Birmingham and wanted to come here but I told her you were out.' Ugh. Oh, ugh ugh.

'Nick. You're not going to believe this. I'm still in Birmingham. My train's been cancelled. The line's flooded. I'm stranded.'

There was a momentary pause. So slight that Cathy almost didn't notice it. Then Nick's voice was warm.

'Get yourself in a cab and come here. You can stay over.'

'Are you sure? I'm so sorry. If I could get back any other way—'

'Don't worry about it. Even my cab home had to go some really weird route to avoid flooded roads. Everything's underwater tonight. I did wonder if your train would make it all the way down.'

Cathy almost collapsed with relief. He really didn't seem to mind.

'I'm sorry, it's an imposition.'

'Don't be silly. Get a cab, come here, I'll drop you off at the station in the morning.'

'All right, I will. And thank you.'

Cathy put down the phone, churned up inside with an odd mixture of glee and angst, and trooped off through the station, only stopping to go back and phone Nick again when she realised she'd forgotten to ask him where he lived.

Chapter Eighteen

There were pizza boxes all over the living-room floor and a set of foil takeaway containers arranged into a ziggurat on the coffee table. Empty beer cans were dotted about like punctuation. There was one on the radiator, one on the telly, several next to the sofa and each armchair, and one next to the toilet in the bathroom.

The toilet roll itself – the thickness of tracing paper – was balanced on the holder where there was a used cardboard roll. Why was it that men were unable to put toilet rolls on holders? Even Jason had never apparently been dextrous enough to manage that job.

There was a pile of crockery in the sink, which had spread out to the draining board and all the other units. Everything, clean or unclean, seemed to be within grabbing distance. It was as if somebody had glued all the cupboard doors closed so that they couldn't be used. Over the fridge hung a *Playboy* calendar. Stuck to the fridge with a magnet was a glossy leaflet giving details of a stripping event coming soon to Birmingham.

On the living-room floor was an issue of *Loaded*, a video of *South Park*; *Botham's Ashes*, which Cathy guessed was Nick's, and a soft-porn video, which Cathy would have tutted at if she weren't on rather shaky ground. Next to the phone was a teetering pile of takeaway menus and a ripped-out page from a newspaper listing 0898 chat-up numbers.

There were no pictures, no lamps, no cushions, no rugs, no photos, no ornaments, no plants. The bulb hung starkly from the ceiling. And the living-room curtain rail was hanging off at the end, giving the impression that even the heavy dralon curtains were sliding down on their way to slump on the carpet with a sigh of despair.

Cathy took all this in, having arrived, been given a cup of tea, used the loo and come back to sit with Nick in his living room.

Nick seemed perfectly relaxed. He lounged on the sofa with one knee crossed over the other, his arm along the back, cradling his mug of tea. Cathy perched in an armchair and peered over at him curiously.

'You didn't say you'd been burgled,' she quipped. 'Left the place in a right state, didn't they?'

Nick gave her a look of dry amusement.

'Oh, I know. It's not very grown-up. Nothing matches, no home comforts. We don't really worry about things like that.'

Cathy felt slightly admonished for noticing the mess. But even when she'd been a student, her house had never been this bad.

'Don't tell me,' she joked. 'You all clear up on a rota system and it's your turn next year?'

Nick chuckled. 'No Vera this weekend. Vera sorts us out.'

'Lucky Vera.'

Cathy raised her eyebrows at Nick, trying not to laugh. It could have been really funny. But she couldn't help remembering that Nick was nearly thirty and,

336

from what she'd gathered, his housemates were of the same sort of age. There was something a bit regressive about the state of the house, as if they were all under the impression that they were still students. Or was it that she was too grown-up herself?

'It suits me, for now,' Nick said with an easy shrug.

Cathy nodded. 'How long have you lived here?'

Nick paused before answering.

'Four years,' he said.

'Right. Well, I bet it's . . . um . . .' Cathy tried to think of something positive to say. 'I bet the rent's nice and cheap.'

'Yep. It is.'

They both sipped their tea.

'Where are the others?' Cathy asked, wondering if they were going to have company at some point.

'Graham's away this weekend. Terry's out, I think. Steve's not here very often. D'you fancy watching something on the telly?'

'Oh. Yes, why not?'

Nick flicked the television on from a remote control and settled back into the sofa to watch. Cathy turned her eyes to the screen. She'd thought they might just chat, but then, it wasn't so easy to sit and make jovial small talk with someone you hardly knew, when you'd been doing exactly that all day and had already said your goodbyes.

And although it was a long time since Cathy had shared a house, she remembered that the living room, television and video were usually the social focus. There'd probably be a string of friends passing through, all piling on to the sofa, joining in with what was already going on, on any given evening. It was the normal thing to do.

'Ah, you've got cable as well,' she noted as Nick channel-hopped. 'For the sport, I assume?'

'Forced into it.' Nick nodded. 'Half the cricket's on satellite now and it's the only chance you've got of following any matches that don't involve England.'

'You follow the other teams as well, then?'

Nick gave Cathy a slightly puzzled look.

'Yes, of course. Everyone's playing everyone else all the time. It's good to know what form the other sides are in, for when we get to them. And besides that, it's cricket and any cricket's good to watch.' He looked at Cathy wryly. 'So what's your excuse for giving Murdoch thirty quid a month, then?'

'Oh, I don't know.' Cathy thought about what she watched when she was at home. 'Discovery. The History Channel. Some things on Sky One.' But her memories were enmeshed with visions of herself and Jason linked on her sofa, discussing what they were watching, getting animated with each other over a bottle of red. Often, she'd lie with her head in his lap and he'd stroke her hair while they talked. She shoved the images away quickly.

'*Thin Blue Line* do you?' Nick quizzed, stopping at a channel.

Cathy nodded.

They both relaxed, laughing over Rowan Atkinson's pronunciation of Hab-eeb. When the programme finished Cathy suppressed a yawn.

'Bed?' Nick asked.

She glanced at him. His eyes were warm, but not burning with passion. Which was just as well, as she was totally bushed.

'To sleep?' he added, laughing at her expression.

'Yes, please,' Cathy said.

Nick's bedroom was clean, but completely dis-organised. Cathy found it quite endearing. He had stacks of CDs, a pile of technical equipment next to a computer, floppy disks everywhere, a Hi-Fi system which was very black and looked quite new, and some incongruously well-ironed shirts hanging from the back of his wardrobe door. Cathy also noticed a Pirelli calendar still open at Miss April, but chose not to comment on it. She was exhausted and still somewhat tipsy from their afternoon in the pub.

Nick climbed into bed first, unabashed as he stripped off his clothes and she followed suit. She slid between his sheets, relieved to feel that they were smooth and clean, and he settled against her. It was arousing to feel his big, hard body against her back, but sleep was already claiming her. Nick wound an arm round her waist and she curled against him. An image flew into her head of Jason, winding an arm round Candida and falling into a contented sleep miles away from Birmingham. But then she was asleep.

The morning was a blur of tea, toast, a shower of tepid water, throwing on her crumpled linen trousers and, as the cotton top was horribly cold and damp from the rain, the silky shirt Cathy had brought as evening wear. Cathy went off to loiter in the living room to give Nick the privacy of changing into his work clothes without her staring at him. He appeared moments later in a crisp white shirt, a dark tie and dark trousers. She felt a pulse of attraction again. His hair was sticking up in tiny spikes, still wet from the shower. He smiled at her. She gathered her things ready to go.

There was a brief glimpse of a wiry person with cropped hair who gave her a brief wave on his way out of the door – who apparently was Terry – and then they were on the drive.

'My baby,' Nick said.

'You have a sports car?' Cathy peered at the red thing. It was low, flat and looked fast. She'd been too pummelled by rain the previous evening to notice anything but the lights inside the house and the doorbell.

'Yeppie.' Nick threw his briefcase inside.

Cathy climbed in. Nick pressed a couple of buttons on the CD player and Metallica blasted at them from several speakers. The car strained in the drive, then shot off into the road. She grabbed her seat belt.

Well, at least it saved them both from trying to think of something to say, Cathy thought, as she was whisked around Birmingham at high speed. It was energising, even if she did feel like a bit of an old fogey, drumming her fingers on her knee not quite in time to the music. But it was fun and not the way she usually launched herself into a Monday morning. Perhaps she should always start her week in this way? She cast Nick a glance. He was humming, tapping his fingers on the steering wheel. Cathy found herself thinking how nice it would be if she could enjoy herself as much as he did, most of the time. She'd always lived her life so safely – or at least until this astonishing summer. And there was Nick, swinging his sports car round corners, seemingly not planning his life more than about an hour ahead. She laughed quietly to herself.

They veered round several roundabouts and suddenly Cathy could see the station. Nick swept the car into the covered arches near the taxi rank and pulled over. He stilled the engine and turned in his seat.

'There you go,' he called above the sound of clashing guitars.

Cathy was about to grab her bag and dance away in a cool and feisty way, but then she changed her mind.

'Could you turn the music down for a sec?' she yelled.

Nick obliged.

'Sorry,' he muttered.

'I just wanted to say goodbye and thanks for a great weekend.' She gave Nick a bright smile.

Nick's eyes softened towards her. For a moment, she thought she saw confusion on his face, but then he grinned.

'I had a great time. Thanks, Cathy.'

'Me too.'

And realising that neither of them could really say anything else at this point, Cathy took her bag, climbed out of the car and waved at Nick. As she turned to walk briskly into the station, she heard the engine revving, a final toot of the horn and the car screeching away.

Thankfully, there was a Virgin train running. Cathy grabbed a strong coffee and took it with her. She found a quiet seat and settled into it.

She was going to be late for work. There wasn't much she could do about that. But she certainly didn't have time to go home to Walthamstow first, change into something smarter and then go to the office. She

341

smoothed her hands over the creases in her trousers. Hopefully, if she sat down a lot, people wouldn't notice. It was a little worrying, though, to have to turn up late looking weary and dishevelled. Especially as Mark had only just appointed her the leader of two new projects. Others would be looking to her to be professional.

But aware that she was getting anxious about something she couldn't change, Cathy sipped her coffee and tried to be philosophical.

The train crawled back to London with all the speed of a tortoise stalking a lettuce. It was as if someone with a broom was walking in front of it and sweeping the water off the track as they went. Staring out at the endless fields glazed over with water, Cathy fell into a daze. Scenes from the weekend replayed themselves in her head. Her lips curled into a smile.

It had been amazing. Fun. Euphoric. Uplifting. Exhausting. Brilliant. She'd escaped from everything that was the reality of her life. It was like kicking off your shoes and having a go in a bouncy castle, and forgetting you were an adult. The release had been tremendous and she realised now that it was something that she'd badly needed. Work concerns aside, Cathy still felt as if she was floating on a happy cloud somewhere above the intracacies of her normal life.

She let her head loll back against the seat and closed her eyes. She felt herself drifting into a doze, but as her body relaxed, a vision of Jason appeared to haunt her.

What might Jason have been doing this weekend while Cathy was off having a passionate encounter? Would he have been sitting in his flat, depressed and lonely, replaying his favourite Stanley Kubrick videos?

Or out with his friends, trying hard to forget his girlfriend's betrayal, getting drunk and maudlin before wandering home alone? Or away, in a miserable and impersonal hotel room, working himself to the point of exhaustion? Or had he been romping with Candida?

Cathy opened her eyes again. Would it have been anything like her own romp?

In fact, Cathy could guess how it might have happened.

First, Jason would make Candida laugh. He was good at that. And Candida would notice that his dark eyes were luminous when he laughed. Then he'd produce a few abstract facts, not to impress but because he couldn't help it. And all this with the delicious waft of whatever he was preparing in the sparklingly clean kitchenette of his flat floating over them. He might have played music, but he wasn't big on music. He preferred to talk. After a while, Candida would stop trying to bowl him over with her hair swings, her hip sways, or her model poses on his sofa and she'd start listening. She'd forget herself because he was an interesting man and listening to him talk was fun. He'd talk about films, or cooking, or tell her about his trips away, complete with plenty of amusing anecdotes. Maybe he'd mimic some of the people he'd met that week. He was good at that.

And then Jason would wander off to the kitchen to stir, or prod, or chop, or baste whatever it was he was getting ready. And she'd follow him to the door and pose there, watching him, fascinated by him because he himself was so fascinated by what he was doing.

But – aha! Cathy took a sip of her coffee. What

343

Candida wouldn't know was that Jason liked to be very private when he cooked.

Cathy knew Jason intimately. Candida didn't. Her first mistake would be to watch him in the kitchen. For Jason that was like a complete stranger walking in on him when he was on the loo, or tweezing his nasal hairs, or washing his undercarriage in the bath. Cooking, for Jason, was not only an activity that gave pleasure to other people, it was a very sensual pleasure. He took pride in buying the very best ingredients for what he cooked. It was the quality time that he spent with himself.

So. Cathy had got as far as Candida lounging in the door. She'd sense that Jason was uncomfortable. It would take her a while, because she was obviously thick. She couldn't be rich, beautiful, cultured, slim *and* brainy. Something had to give. Cathy decided it was brainy.

So Candida would go back to the sofa and recline. Jason would appear with a meal. He'd maybe even light candles at the table. They'd sit, eat and talk, and drink. After a while, Jason would realise that his funny asides weren't being returned. He'd see that this woman was a Barbie doll. He'd watch her poking and prodding at her meal – because she was obviously watching her figure. He'd be disappointed that she wasn't enjoying what he'd cooked.

But Jason was on the rebound. Cathy reasoned it through. So he'd love every minute of Candida's adoration and forgive her for leaving the food. And she would adore him. Of course she would. Apparently, all sorts of women were after Jason. Why would Candida be any different? And after the meal they'd go back to the sofa and play a game. She'd pretend she hadn't decided to sleep with him and he'd pretend that he didn't desperately want to sleep with her.

She'd pull up her dress a little every time she crossed her legs – it had to be the same dress Cathy had seen her in, with the enticing splits up the side, because Cathy didn't know what she had in her wardrobe and couldn't picture her in anything else. But Jason, Cathy knew, had an endearing streak of shyness. It would make him even more attractive.

After a while, and a few more glasses of red, she'd start touching his arm. And he'd start touching hers back. Then she'd allow her hand to rest on his. And bit by bit they'd establish that it was perfectly all right to invade each other's space. Not only all right, but a bloody good idea. And then they'd go to bed.

Cathy choked on the dregs of her coffee, her eyes stinging.

In bed, Jason would take things very gently. It would be a very sensual experience, which built up slowly, into passion. And Candida, being Candida, would writhe about, being tanned and showing off her meagre proportions. Jason would think at some point that being with model-like Candida was much more exciting than being with cuddly Cathy. Candida probably oozed expensive scent. And she'd be wearing a little silky thong. Jason would be out of his mind.

Ah – but! Cathy sat up again, heaving such a loud sigh that several heads turned. She cleared her throat quickly.

But – the thing was, after they'd had sex, Jason would want to talk for a while. Just a quiet murmur of conversation maybe. But Candida would have run out of things to say by then.

So – once Jason was high on Candida's perfume and her slippery body and her dazzling legs and smile and glossy black hair, he'd feel disappointed and unfulfilled. Perhaps that would be the moment when he'd miss Cathy the most.

As the months passed and as it became common knowledge that Jason was going out with Candida, she'd be dragging him out to fashionable restaurants and soulless, trendy wine bars on evenings when he would rather go to the cinema, or chat with friends in the pub, or watch a documentary, or even read a book. Because she'd need constant stimulation beyond him and, although he was stimulated by her physically, he would never, ever click with her mentally.

By the time he and Candida were married, Jason would be crying secretly to himself because he wanted somebody to share his interests with and, although Candida was gorgeous, he'd be ringing Cathy up, about five years from now, saying, 'What happened to us? I'm so lonely without you. You were my soulmate.'

And Cathy would say, 'It was that bitch. She came between us.'

'Bitch?'

'Bitch.'

Cathy looked up. All heads were turned towards her. Opposite her a man in a suit was staring.

'Did I say "bitch" out loud?' she asked faintly.

He nodded and from a seat across the aisle somebody said, 'Yes.'

'I'm so sorry.'

As Cathy had anticipated, turning up at work was embarrassing. She was late and crumpled. She'd tried

346

to smarten herself up in the Ladies at Euston, brushing her hair and clipping it back, and dabbing more blusher on to her wan cheeks, but she was sure she looked as drained as she felt.

Fiona widened her eyes suggestively as Cathy crept past and ducked into her seat. She stuck her head round the cubicle.

'Good weekend?'

Cathy gave her an expressive look. 'Eventful, that's for sure.'

'Oo, tell me more!'

Cathy glanced at her watch guiltily. 'Perhaps not just now. Let's do that night out this week.'

'That had better be Friday if we're going to paint the town red. I'm not waiting that long. Lunch?' Fiona pressed.

'Tomorrow? I'm not sure I'll get away with a long lunch out today.'

'Okay, tomorrow,' Fiona agreed. 'And feel free to drop hints in the meantime.'

'I promise to tell you all about it.' Cathy smiled. 'But now I've really got to catch up on what's happened this morning.'

'Well, Ruth was looking for you, Mark's off today, some sort of stomach bug. I answered your phone and spoke to Bill Havers. He wanted you to call him. There's a note on your desk.'

'Lovely.' Cathy slid her chair up to her desk to hide her creased trousers.

'And there were a few other things,' Fiona said, pulling a rueful face. 'But I tell you what, I'll get us both coffee and you can read the notes I've left you.'

'Thanks so much, Fi.' Cathy smiled at Fiona warmly.

'You are great. You're wasted here, you know.'

'And so are you,' Fiona said meaningfully before she disappeared.

First things first, Cathy thought, smoothing her hair away from her face and skim-reading the Post-Its that Fiona had stuck all over her computer. She was very curious to know what Bill had to say, but Ruth was the boss, so she was the top priority. Lisa Spencer marched past as Cathy was hurriedly applying her lipstick and rebuttoning her shirt. Her sharp eyes opened in surprise. Well, perhaps they were all used to Cathy being the first one in and the last to leave, looking pristine and jumping to every order – but today was something of an exception. It wouldn't become a habit.

Cathy took herself to Ruth's office and tapped on the door. She entered in response to the monosyllabic 'Come'.

Ruth Hodges was in her late forties, with short, dry hair and cool grey eyes. She was the managing director of the company – a company that she had created herself some years ago. Cathy had always held her in very high esteem. She was concentrating on a report, half-moon glasses on her nose. She looked up at Cathy's entrance.

'Ah, Cathy.' There was a slight pause as Ruth ran her eyes down Cathy's form. No doubt noticing that the silky top wasn't quite appropriate and that the linen trousers were full of wrinkles. But Ruth, like Lisa, looked more surprised than dismayed, which was probably good. Ruth raised a fine eyebrow. 'Are you all right, Cathy? You seem a bit breathless.'

'I'm – I really am quite all right,' Cathy reassured swiftly. 'I had a terrible problem with the . . . boiler this morning, I'm afraid. It was quite dangerous and I had to make sure it was dealt with urgently.'

'I'm sorry to hear it,' Ruth said passively, her focus switching instantly to some papers on her desk, which ensured that Cathy felt that she hadn't believed a word. And who could blame her? Cathy could easily convince herself that Ruth's X-ray vision had detected the carpet burns on her knees and elbows. But now that Cathy was in Ruth's presence, she remembered all too vividly how humiliated she'd felt when Mark had passed on Ruth's disdain for her idea of fixing Bill Havers up with Troy Vickers to build the new Hellier's offices.

'Do sit down.' Ruth indicated a chair and Cathy sank into it. 'It appears we have a problem. Mark is incapacitated today and I have to address the Chamber of Commerce, but I need somebody to represent us at an important meeting. I'm not going to ask you to do it, I'm afraid.'

'Oh,' Cathy breathed.

'No, I'm going to have to tell you to do it.' Ruth handed Cathy the papers she had been sifting through. 'Next to Mark, you're the only person here I would trust to speak for us at a senior level. The brief is all there. Perhaps you could run your eyes over it now while you're sitting here and come back to me with any immediate questions. It's important we get this right.'

Cathy felt a flush run through her. It would be today, of course, that she would be presented with such a unique opportunity. But she would do it. She wouldn't let herself, or Ruth, down. She pulled herself up straight.

'Of course.'

Cathy read the the covering page of the brief. She

read it again, blinking to clear her eyes, unsure of her own understanding.

There could be no doubt. It was a meeting between Cooper's Construction and Troy Vickers – a *second* meeting, according to the brief. The aim was to broker a deal between them to work on the Hellier's offices.

A second meeting. It confirmed that Bill's rumour had been correct. Cooper's and Troy Vickers had already been brought together. By whom?

By Mark.

Tensely Cathy read each page of the report. She read it all again to make sure. Her pulse slowed. This was Mark's report. There was a reference to an attachment, where Mark's ideas were apparently worked out and presented in full.

Cathy leafed through the folios to find the attachment. It was almost word for word the report that she'd given to Mark. It even included the appendices she'd worked so hard on. The only thing Mark had done was substituted Cooper's for Bill Havers and reworked some of the logic. Instead of this being an opportunity to boost an east London company and bring employment to the area, it had been presented to Ruth as a chance to make money for her company – by using Cooper's. Havers Construction hadn't even been mentioned.

Cathy looked up at Ruth. She was dumbstruck. Ruth raised her eyes and peered over her glasses.

'Any questions?'

'Yes,' Cathy said in a pale voice. 'Quite a few.'

'We don't have much time.' Ruth looked at the gold watch on her wrist to make the point. 'Mark feels that Troy is wavering. I need you to go in very strongly and give it all you've got. I don't need to tell you how influential both Vickers and Cooper's are. If we can marry them I will be extremely happy.'

Cathy's eyes smarted.

'Ruth, I'm afraid I still feel that Havers Construction are the right company to press with Troy. I know that you weren't impressed by my report, but if I can only explain—'

Ruth squinted at Cathy with a hint of impatience.

'I don't know what you mean, Cathy. I've never seen any such report from you.'

'My report on bringing Havers and Vickers together, with a view to working on the Hellier's building?' Cathy pleaded. 'You thought it was "fanciful"?' And as Ruth merely frowned, Cathy went on, 'The one where I put the case for Havers being the ideal company to develop at this time, given the subsidies and the need for local employment?'

Ruth shook her head, her eyes clouding.

'Cathy, I just don't know what you're talking about. This idea was put to me by Mark. He made the link between Hellier's, London and Troy Vickers. He added Cooper's to that and now we have a deal to negotiate.'

'But—'

'I'd be curious to know what you think a medium-sized firm like Havers might have to offer Troy Vickers, but the fact is the meeting is already set up and we're committed to presenting Cooper's to Vickers now. We just don't have time to argue.' Ruth stood up, gathering papers and placing them in a folder. 'I have a presentation to give in precisely one hour. If you don't think you can handle this meeting you'd better tell me now.'

Cathy gaped at Ruth, words not coming. As Ruth's grey eyes regarded her seriously, there was a sharp knock at the door.

'Come!' Ruth called.

Mark Lyme, red-faced and puffing, launched himself into the room.

'Ruth, Cathy,' he greeted them. 'I apologise profusely for being out of action earlier this morning, but as you can see, I'm here and well.'

'Are you sure you're fit?' Ruth quizzed, as Cathy merely stared at Mark in horror.

'Dosed up on Immodium.' Mark gave a hearty laugh and patted his stomach. 'I know, too much detail, but let's say I had an awful night, but I'm fit as a fiddle now.'

'Well.' Ruth looked cautiously from Mark to Cathy. 'I think you'd better pass this back to Mark, Cathy. I'm sorry to take up your time, but obviously Mark will want to handle the meeting himself now.'

Cathy stood up, still failing to find words. She stared straight into Mark's eyes. He looked away, wiping the back of his hand across his damp forehead. Cathy thrust the sheaf of papers at Mark's chest and he took them. His eyelids fluttered when he saw what she had been reading.

'Good, so we're all sorted,' Ruth said. 'You'd better get back to what you were doing, Cathy. I believe Mark has put you on some important contracts.'

'Yes,' Cathy said, moving out of the office and stopping next to Mark. 'Yes, Mark has been making sure that I'm being put to good use.'

Ruth ushered them both out of her office and they were left standing in the corridor. Cathy touched Mark's arm.

'Hmn?' He made the noise a little too brightly.

'You're unbelievable,' Cathy said and walked away.

'Coffee's on your desk,' Fiona called as Cathy squeezed herself back into her desk chair.

Cathy's blood was boiling. But she had to be very careful. To accuse a senior colleague of plagiarism was extremely serious. And she would be on shifting ground. It would be Mark's word against Cathy's. Cathy could re-present her report, but Mark could merely say that they had both had similar ideas at the same time. They'd discussed it. The rumours of Hellier's move to London had been mere whispers, but only Cathy knew that she had picked up on them and made a connection that could be valuable to the company, while Mark hadn't. Why should Ruth believe that? Why would plagiarism even come into it as far as Ruth was concerned?

But the fact that Mark had patently stolen Cathy's ideas was only one issue. It seemed obvious, now, that Mark had chosen to ignore Cathy's reasoning for a social conscience to play a rational part in the deal, but was eager to go for the money-making option. It was also clear why Mark had taken her off the Havers project. Mark hadn't wanted Cathy to mess things up for him by pushing Bill towards Troy Vickers.

Cathy jumped as Fiona's hand landed softly on her shoulder.

'Something's up. I just know it,' Fiona said quietly. 'This isn't just about your weekend, is it? It's something to do with work.'

'Fi,' Cathy breathed, appealing to her friend with soulful eyes. 'I can't really talk about it right now. Not here.'

353

'I know. You're not a whinger. You're professional through and through. But I just want to say I'm here if you need to yell. We'll do that lunch tomorrow. Promise me.'

Cathy took several deep breaths. She managed a smile.

'Promise. And thanks so much for the coffee. I'll do a run later. I'd better ring Bill Havers now.'

'Okay.' Fi slipped away.

Steadying herself, Cathy dialled Bill's number.

Bill was ebullient.

'Cathy, you're a diamond. I don't know what's going to happen yet, but that introduction you gave me was knockout. I think we might really be on our way now.'

Cathy felt horrendously torn. She was at work, representing the company which was this afternoon going out with all guns blazing to try to persuade Troy to work with Cooper's Construction. She had no choice. She had to be completely neutral.

'I'm really glad you were at the club meeting, Bill. You'd have spoken to everyone there, whether I was there or not. I know that.'

There was a pause. Cathy prayed that Bill would understand her position.

'Too right,' Bill said. 'It was nice to see you there socially, but I should probably tell you that I happened to meet up with some bloke who might have done my business some good.'

Despite the knot in her stomach, Cathy managed a smile.

'I'm very glad to hear it, Bill. I know that you'd only ever want to be judged on merit and I'm sure that's the way things will be done. I've got every confidence in Lisa Spencer to help you forward from here. I hope things are going smoothly.'

In fact, Cathy had no confidence in Lisa's ability to push Bill's company to its full potential, but it was true that she hoped things were going smoothly.

'Between you and me, gel.' Bill lowered his voice, although Cathy thought it was a bit bizarre, seeing as how she was the one who needed to be discreet. 'Lisa's actually a cyborg. Just thought you should know.'

Cathy pressed her lips together.

'Thanks very much. I'll bear it in mind.'

'You just tell me when you take off on your own.'

Cathy absorbed Bill's confidence, feeling warmer.

'Call me if you've got anything you want to talk through,' she ended diplomatically.

When Cathy got home she dumped her bags, headed for the kitchen and put a frozen pizza in the oven. She found a half-full bottle of Chardonnay in the fridge and poured herself a glass. She took a small sip. At least it was a nice white. She looked at the label of the bottle again. She couldn't even remember buying an Australian Chardonnay and leaving it in the fridge. It just proved how blitzed she'd been recently.

She leant heavily against her kitchen sink and gazed through the window. It was still light outside. A turquoise twilight was starting to drape itself over the gardens of the terraced row.

What had happened to that fabulous feeling of release that she'd experienced over the weekend? Since she'd arrived at the office, she'd felt as if a crackling fire had been put out by a heavy blanket. All the optimism, the expansion, the freedom she'd felt had been over-powered by other issues.

She vowed to herself that she would look for a way, somehow, of finding those feelings again.

It had been a hell of a day. Cathy hadn't seen Mark again after their tense encounter in the corridor. She'd been bombarded with immediate work issues after she'd spoken to Bill, so the day had passed in a blur. She could remember Fiona sticking a Danish pastry under her nose at about four o' clock, then waving to say that she was leaving some time later. When Cathy had looked at her watch again it was nearly seven o'clock.

Now Cathy wished she could ring somebody and talk about her day, about Mark, about Bill, about the betrayal she felt, about the confusion that filled her. Normally, she would have rung Jason. But she also wanted to remember the sensuality of being around Nick and explore the reasons for Jason's big brown eyes still hovering around her. She might have rung Fiona, but Fiona was visiting her sister this evening, she'd said, and they were having lunch tomorrow. The heart-to-heart would have to wait.

Cathy was so tired that she merely leant on her sink and stared unseeingly through her kitchen window, until she realised that Mrs Ali was at her own kitchen sink opposite and was waving at her. How long Mrs Ali had been waving while Cathy had been in her own world she had no idea.

Mrs Ali was holding something up and proffering it to Cathy. It was a plant. Cathy nodded. Mrs Ali mouthed something. Cathy could make out as Mrs Ali repeated it several times, 'For you!'

Being offered a plant was a big thing. It meant that she and the Alis were taking a tentative step towards friendship. Cathy welcomed it. She liked the family very much. She put up her hands in a 'wait a sec' gesture and fiddled with her kitchen window. Mrs Ali opened her own kitchen window and waited, the plant held aloft.

Cathy's window wouldn't open. She tried again. It was stuck fast. That was odd. There had never been anything wrong with it. It was a normal kitchen window that opened normally and closed normally. She pushed it and pulled it, wrenched the handle and still nothing happened.

Then Cathy realised that there were little white cylindrical lumps on the window frames that definitely hadn't been there when she'd taken off for her weekend. She examined them closely. They were window locks. They could only have been put in by someone who had access to her house. Only one person other than herself had a full set of keys and that was Jason.

Cathy retrieved the plant from Mrs Ali. They met, in the end, in the garden, leaning over the fence. Even though Cathy's windows were now all effectively superglued stuck, at least she could get the back door open.

'It's a cutting,' Mrs Ali explained. 'I was thinking of you being so upset about your house being bleak and empty. And I thought you would like a variegated tradescantia. This has little pink bits in the leaves, see?'

'That's so kind of you.' Cathy took it gratefully, shivering slightly as darkness was now falling and she still hadn't eaten the pizza that was roasting in the oven.

'Yes,' Mrs Ali went on. 'Because I know that when I first moved here my garden was a bombsite, like yours, and it all takes time. So I thought this might cheer you up while you decide what to do with your garden.'

'Thank you.' Cathy gave a wobbly smile. 'You're so nice.'

'Maybe your house will not seem so empty now.' Mrs Ali gave Cathy a warm look.

'No, I'm sure it won't,' Cathy said. She didn't have the heart to explain that the emptiness of her house was due to a deficit of suitable partners rather than a lack of house plants, which she had in abundance. She took the tradescantia inside and placed it prominently on the kitchen windowsill so that Mrs Ali would see that she valued it.

Then, once it was decent to do so, Cathy pulled down the blind on her kitchen window to block out her neighbours and allowed herself several moments of walking around her kitchen in confusion.

Jason had come to her house and fitted window locks. Nobody else could have done it. The thought turned Cathy's stomach upside down.

It was Melissa and Brian who had initially been so anxious about Cathy's safety. But Cathy had passed that concern on to Jason and Jason had made it his business to put the chain on the door for her. He'd shown that he cared about her security and now the window locks had appeared.

Why had Jason done such a considerate thing? It brought a lump to Cathy's throat. She'd been off having wild and crazy sex, and had come to the conclusion that he'd probably been doing the same. She'd thought of Jason at times over the weekend, but he must have been thinking of her too. Even more, perhaps. Enough to turn up with his DIY kit.

Had he arrived thinking that Cathy would be in? Had he wanted to talk? Or had he deliberately made sure she was out before doing her a practical favour? The sort of favour that you could easily do for a platonic friend without it meaning anything? After all, they'd been together for four years. Perhaps they weren't in a relationship any more, but they weren't enemies.

Cathy poured herself another glass of wine while she thought about it. She looked at the label on the bottle again. She wasn't going mad after all. She definitely *hadn't* bought this bottle of wine herself. It was one of Jason's favourites. He must have brought it with him. Thinking – what? That he and Cathy might drink it together? Or? No, it was much more likely that he knew the third test match was already under way and, given the pattern of that summer so far, the chances would be that Cathy was away watching it over the weekend. He'd had a glass or two himself and he'd left the bottle for her. It was a nice thing to do, but Cathy realised, feeling deflated, that she couldn't read anything into it at all. None of it meant that Jason wanted to talk things through with her. He was treating her kindly. He would – he was like that. But she realised that it probably meant nothing more than that.

Then she noticed that the smell of something burning was coming from her oven and when she pulled out her pizza it was brown.

'Balls.'

Cathy took herself to the sofa and sat down. She contemplated her glass of wine again. She was so tired.

She knew that what she must do, as soon as she'd organised her thoughts, was to ring Jason, maturely and politely, as that seemed to be the way he was behaving towards her now. She should ring him and thank him for putting locks on her windows.

But the thought of ringing Jason made Cathy's stomach buckle. It would be emotional. How could it not be? They hadn't spoken to each other since she'd proposed to him through the letter box. She'd end up in tears again, she knew it. Besides, how could she ring Jason and speak to him when only last night she'd shared a bed with Nick and, while sharing the bed, had enjoyed being held by him?

Aware that she was contorting herself into a series of emotional knots, Cathy stretched herself out on the sofa. She tried to get comfortable so that she could think a little more clearly.

She fell asleep there.

The mobile was bleeping insistently. Cathy stirred on the sofa and rolled over. She was stiff and cold. A pale light was filtering through the living-room curtains.

The ringing stopped before she could move, so she sat up slowly, rubbed at her arms and yawned. She looked at her watch. It was seven o' clock.

She'd plugged in her phone to recharge it overnight. It was probably telling her that she had some messages. She'd deal with it later. First, she had to become a human being again.

She soaked in a hot bath. While she was immersed in water, she heard her mobile going off again. She sighed. A work call, undoubtedly, which she would answer when she was ready. It was still very early. She dressed for work. Then she took the time to make herself a hot breakfast. After she'd eaten, Cathy felt a lot better.

She didn't rush to prepare herself for the office. She'd be on time, but Mark's betrayal had left her feeling highly jaded. Somehow she had to find a way to prove herself to Ruth and make her point about the Havers project; if need be, without mentioning Mark at all. But Mark was still supposed to be Cathy's immediate boss. Working for him was going to be horrible. She'd have to find a way to deal with it.

Her mobile rang again as she was about to leave for work. Cathy scooped it up from the living-room carpet.

'Hello?'

'Oh, thank God you're there! It's Barry. I've been trying to reach you.'

'Barry?' Cathy frowned. 'What's up?'

'Cathy. Please get here. They've wheeled him off. Please, please, please, please come up. I can't cope with this. There's nobody here but me.'

The living room dissolved around Cathy. Her blood froze in her veins. She could hear the panic in Barry's voice.

'What do you mean? Who's been wheeled off? Where?'

'Frank's had a heart attack,' Barry blurted. 'He's—'

They lost the connection.

Clutching her mobile, Cathy raced up the stairs to her bedroom. She tossed her mangled clothes from the weekend on the floor and put a heap of clean things in her bag. She had a jacket halfway up her arms and was sprinting down the stairs when the mobile rang again.

'Hello?' she panted.

It was Barry. In tears.

'Thank God. You've got to—'

'Is he alive?' Cathy barked. Terror enclosed her like ice.

'I – I think so, but I don't think he's going to make it,' Barry sobbed. 'I need you to be here. You've got to—'

'I'm on my way,' she said.

Chapter Nineteen

What was the best way to get to Oxford? A taxi would have to take the same route as the coach. The coach took about the same time as the train, given timetables and tube routes.

But her grandfather was critically ill, possibly dying. For all Cathy knew, he might be already dead. Every minute was precious. At a time like this there was no such thing as a sensible way to do things. There was only time. She got a taxi.

In the back of the minicab Cathy practised some deep-breathing exercises and tried to stay calm. Even though at this moment all she wanted was to be fired up the M40 hanging on to an exocet missile.

'So – what's all the hurry, then?' her cab driver asked her pleasantly.

'My grandfather. Heart attack,' Cathy issued.

The driver absorbed this information, then he put his foot on the accelerator.

'Message received and understood. I'll get you there as fast as I can without being nicked. What d'you want me to do – M25 or North Circular?'

'I'll leave it up to you. Just get me there fast, please.'

Convinced that her cabbie was doing his level best, Cathy went for her mobile. First she punched out Ruth's number. She prayed that Ruth would be in her office. The last thing she wanted was to leave a message and for there to be any misunderstandings. And she had no intention of talking to Mark.

Ruth answered the phone. Cathy swiftly explained her situation.

There was a pause. Ruth's voice was kind when she spoke again.

'How awful for you, Cathy. Of course I understand. Take a day to see him and sort yourself out.'

Cathy's pulse stuttered. A day? Would this take a day? What if he was dead? What if he wasn't?

'I've accrued quite a lot of leave,' Cathy said, trying desperately to keep a logical head while her emotions were fluctuating wildly. 'And I haven't had any plans for a holiday – I hope it can come off that.'

'Of course,' Ruth reassured her. 'Will you be on your mobile number?'

'Yes,' Cathy replied faintly.

'I know this is a difficult time for you, Cathy, but you understand how busy we are. Obviously you'll have a lot to deal with today, but if I can refer urgent problems to your mobile?'

'Oh, of course.' Cathy swallowed back her dismay. What if Frank was dead? Her only living relative? Whom she hadn't had a chance to get to know? Would she still be available on her mobile? When *was* it acceptable for family concerns to take precedence over work issues? Would Ruth be trying to get her on the mobile when she was standing at Frank's graveside, about to cast a handful of dry earth on to the coffin? Tears stung in her eyes, but she kept her voice even. 'I'll speak to Fiona myself and ask her what she can cover.'

'Fiona?' Ruth queried.

'Fiona's exceptionally capable. I've got every confidence in her.'

Ruth rang off, after making sure that they had
covered any immediate work problems and assuring
Cathy of her sympathy.

Cathy phoned Fiona next, not wanting to stop and
think. All the time that she could beat down the scream
of denial that was fighting its way through her chest,
she had momentum. She explained breathlessly what
had happened and went on, 'I'm sorry, Fi. We'll have to
postpone that lunch. I'll have to catch up with you
when I call. But I promise I'll let you know what's
happening.'

Fi's voice softened.

'Don't worry about lunch – we can do that any time.
But, bloody hell, Cathy, are you all right? Can I do
anything?'

Cathy drew in a noisy breath. Tears were threatening
to erupt at any moment.

'I'm fine. No, I'm not fine. But thanks, Fi. Can you do
a bit of covering for me, just for today?'

'Today?' Fiona quizzed, her voice rising. 'It's going
to take you longer than one flipping day to get yourself
straight.'

'I just don't know. We're so busy and I'm meant to be
moving the projects forward.'

'Projects schmojects.' Fiona tutted. 'All right, I'm
talking to Cathy Gordon here so I know you won't
listen, but we can deal with it. I know most of what
you're working on and I can field your calls. So don't
you worry about it. I'll talk to Ruth.'

Thanking Fiona profusely and feeling a little better,
Cathy rang off.

What now? She sat back on the cushioned seat. The cab driver, probably sensing that she was over-wrought, decided not to make small talk. She gazed weakly out of the window. Whom should she be calling? Whom did she *want* to call?

She wanted to call Jason. They had four years of history. He would understand what it meant. They cared for each other. Even if the relationship was wrecked, Cathy was sure Jason would care. She would want to know, if he were in trouble. Her fingers twitched towards her mobile.

But she had so recently been passionate with another man. Would it be using Jason for comfort when she needed it? Nick flew into her mind again.

Nick knew Frank – although only in an abstract way. Should he be told that Frank was desperately ill? What could he do about it, even if she told him? Part of Cathy wanted to ring Nick and talk to him – but would he think she was trying to lean on him? Especially in Jason's absence? Would he find it an imposition? Their weekend had been so happy and carefree – did Cathy really want to land such a heavy situation on Nick?

Cathy wavered. She put her head back on the seat and stared up at the pimples lining the car roof. She was shattered by Frank's heart attack. She had more than enough to cope with emotionally, without chasing either Nick or Jason on the phone. She wouldn't ring either of them. Not now.

But something was nagging at her. Somebody needed to know about this.

'Oh, my God,' she whispered to herself.

She needed to tell Melissa and Brian. The last time she'd talked to Melissa about Frank, Cathy had shied away from the subject. Perhaps it was because certain things were clear in Cathy's mind. Melissa and Brian were her parents. She didn't think of them in any other way. They weren't *like* her parents, they weren't parent *substitutes*. They *were* her parents and she was their daughter, just as much as any home-grown natural daughter would have been. She loved them both dearly and they'd both been there for her, so many times, when she'd been lost, or confused, or upset. So recently Melissa had let Cathy sob herself into exhaustion on the phone over her break-up with Jason. She had been fantastic. But what questions might have been in Melissa's mind? Or Brian's, while they continued to offer their unqualified love and support?

Neither Melissa nor Brian had pursued any questioning as far as Frank was concerned. That was their way – to live and let live. To do the right thing and show respect for the feelings of other people. But Cathy realised, as the taxi sped along, that her parents might have needed to hear more from her. Some further reassurance, perhaps. Some explanation. She should have offered them much more information, so that they could see for themselves how much she valued them, but all she'd given them were crumbs and half-sentences. Now she should call them. She should tell them what was happening. They would both be at work, but Cathy dialled the home number immediately. As the phone rang, she remembered too that Melissa had been in touch with Frank, on and off, over the years. It was all on Cathy's behalf. Of course they should know.

How must they have felt to know that Cathy was off exploring a family that was nothing to do with either of them, after all the love and care they had lavished on

367

her? She would have to show them, soon, how much she treasured them both. Their affection was constant, unselfish and unchanging. The thought nearly brought the looming tears to spilling point.

'Hello, you two,' she said softly to the answerphone. 'You both know I love you.' Cathy cleared her throat. 'I'm on my way to Oxford to see Frank – he's had a heart attack. I – I guess it's so long since we've talked about this, you'll be wondering why I give a damn about him. Let's talk about it properly soon. I've got my mobile with me, so you can get me on that. I have to follow this through, I hope you understand. But it doesn't change anything I feel for you. 'Bye for now.'

Then Cathy heaved a ragged breath, slipped her mobile back into her bag, sat like a stone in the back seat and spent the rest of the journey thinking of all the things she had wanted to say to Frank.

'Where's this hospital, then?' the cabbie asked after they'd left the M40 and were speeding towards Oxford.

What had Barry said? It was on the outskirts of Oxford. What was the name of the area? 'It's Headington. That's what my friend said.'

'Sign there for Headington. I'll follow that.'

It felt like an army of gerbils were gnawing away at Cathy's stomach. The tension grew as the taxi faltered, sped up again, slowed down in an effort to find a sign.

'We should just ask somebody.' Cathy was sitting so far forward she was gripping the headrest of the passenger seat.

'Ah, there you go, love. John Radcliffe Hospital. Is that it?'

'Must be. JR. Yes, go there.'

'Right you are.'

They careered round a roundabout and down a residential stretch of road. All the time Cathy was chanting in her head, *This can't be the right way. We'll have to turn round. We're not going to make it. He's gone already. I know he's gone and I didn't say goodbye.*

'There!' The driver threw out his hand in triumph as a huge sign appeared and a long drive presented itself which led up to a cluster of big white buildings. At least the hospital looked modern. And big. With any luck they'd know what they were doing.

'Oh, thank God.' Cathy collapsed back on her seat as they drove up the slope. She gathered her bag and found her purse ready to pay. Her purse? As the car swept up to one of the porched entrances, she realised she didn't walk round with hundreds of pounds of cash in her purse. It'd have to be a cheque, obviously.

The driver gave her a sum total for the journey. It was much lower than she expected.

'Are you being kind to me?' she asked him.

'I lost my old dad last year, love. Just bang out the cheque and we'll say no more about it.'

'Thank you.' Feeling very emotional, Cathy added ten pounds that she couldn't afford to the amount to show her appreciation.

'Now go on!' The driver urged. 'Go and give your gramps a hug.'

Cathy got out of the car and legged it into the hospital. She had no idea which entrance she was throwing herself at, but she knew Frank was in intensive care. She'd get in and ask, and do it all at great speed. If the gods were smiling down on her today they would give her a chance to say goodbye.

Cathy found Barry in the corridor, outside the intensive care ward. She rushed at him and he threw out his arms and hugged her hard. She could feel his entire body trembling.

What was he doing in the corridor? And why wasn't he speaking? It was too late. She began to tremble too. Barry held her even tighter.

'Oh, God,' he said into her neck at last.

Cathy pulled away from him and searched his face.

'He's dead. Isn't he.' It was statement more than a question.

'No,' Barry managed. 'But he's in surgery.'

'He's alive?' Cathy's spirits shot up to the ceiling like the Nimble balloon. 'You mean, I'm not too late? Oh, thank God! Thank God.'

'Oh, Cathy, he was blue. His face, his lips, everything went blue. I've never seen anything like that before. I tell you, Cathy, he may be alive for now, but—' Barry didn't finish his sentence.'

'You can tell me all about it now.'

Cathy gradually began to realise just how shaken up Barry was. He looked like a little boy who'd just fallen over, his lips wobbling, his eyes bright with tears he knew he wasn't allowed to shed.

'Let's sit down and you tell me,' she said.

Barry allowed himself to be guided to a bench and they sat together. Cathy clasped his hand. It was freezing cold. She rubbed it to get the circulation back.

'It was this morning.' Barry gulped. 'I was just having a quick cuppa and toast before work and I went into his room with a mug of tea for him, just to say cheerio, like I always do. And he wasn't moving.'

'Okay.'

'And he was blue and white and purple. His hands were just reaching out, like thin sticks. And he murmured something but he couldn't even speak.'

Cathy squeezed Barry's fingers. 'But you did the right thing. It's okay.'

'I just got straight on the phone. I could see that it was . . . it was desperate. So I rang 999. And an ambulance came. And they jammed this huge needle into his hand and pumped stuff into him, and took him off on a drip, in a stretcher thing, with an oxygen mask on.'

'Well done,' Cathy reassured Barry quickly. 'You saved his life.'

Barry seemed astounded.

'Last night. He wasn't well. He said he had a headache, and aches and pains in his arms. I should have known.'

'No, you shouldn't. I wouldn't have known either. Nobody would have done. So you went with the ambulance?'

Barry nodded.

'He didn't have anyone else. And – the thing is – he's been like a father to me. I never had a father. I'm sorry.' Barry laughed at himself as he wiped the back of his hand over his eyes. 'Reach for the sick bucket. I know.'

'No, I know what you mean. I can see how you two are. He's very important to you.'

'He's brilliant, Cathy.' Barry entreated her: 'I wish you could see how brilliant he is.'

Cathy nodded, squeezing Barry's hand so hard that he winced.

'Ouch.'

'Sorry.'

'So when we got here,' Barry went on, 'it was all confusing. They asked me to wait in the day room, but I couldn't stand sitting down, so I paced about a lot. And he disappeared for ages. And then they wheeled him away, off to surgery.'

'Right.' Cathy chewed on her lip nervously. This was the bit she was dreading. 'And what are they doing?'

'I'm not sure. Exploratory and possible bypass is what they said.'

'Oh! Well, that's good!' Cathy sat up and forced a bright smile.

'It is?'

'Oh, yes. Lots of people have bypasses and go on for years and years afterwards. It was probably just what he needed anyway.'

Barry looked completely unconvinced.

'He's old. And he isn't strong. And he's been gone for hours.'

Cathy squeezed Barry's knee. Someone had to be upbeat here.

'Well, what do you expect? It's not like having your legs waxed, is it? Course he'll be gone for ages. That's so they get it right. I'd much rather they didn't rush it, wouldn't you?'

'I guess.'

'Course you would. Do you want him to rattle round ever afterwards because they left the forceps and the knitting needles in there?'

Barry stared at Cathy in confusion, then gave her an exhausted smile.

'God, I'm so glad you're here.'

'And I'm so bloody glad you rang me. You've done a wonderful job.'

Barry rested his elbows on his knees and gazed wearily at the floor. He was in smart trousers, a shirt and tie. Obviously he'd been ready to dash off to work. But his tie was pulled away from the collar, the first three buttons undone. He must have had a hell of a time dealing with all this on his own.

But Cathy knew there was something missing. It nagged at her, then, suddenly she realised. She tried to broach the subject gently. The last thing she wanted was Barry reproaching himself for things that weren't his fault.

'Did – er – have you heard from Barbara at all?'

Barry looked up bleakly. Even his brown eyes seemed paler today.

'No,' he murmured. 'Haven't seen her for ages. She's given up on Frank. Like I told you.'

'Right.'

Cathy frowned to herself. Carefully she took Barry's hand again.

'Barbara – she works, doesn't she? On weekdays?'

'Er, yes. She does part-time. Or maybe some full days. I'm not sure of her exact hours.'

'Okay. And you said she works in a library somewhere?'

Barry scratched his head. His hair stuck out in mahogany tufts. He looked like an unkempt spaniel.

'At the Bodleian.'

'The Bodleian. And that's like – a big library here?'

'Right in the middle of Oxford. Huge, grand thing. She works in there, somewhere.'

Cathy nodded.

'Why?' Barry looked stressed, his brow crumpling.

'It's okay,' Cathy soothed. 'First I want to chat to the

ward sister and see if we can find out anything else. Then we'll take it from there.'

'You think Barbara would care about this?'

Cathy took a deep breath. Men. They just didn't get it. But she looked at Barry very kindly.

'Yes,' she stated.

'But she's – she's buggered off. I tell you, she doesn't give a damn any more.'

'Oh, yes, she does,' Cathy said. 'But you sit right here, I'll find out what I can, then we'll see if we've got time to go and get a coffee or something. You look as if you need one.'

Barry nodded obediently. He seemed very happy for Cathy to take charge.

She pushed her way tentatively into the ward and was directed to the sister, who was filling in reports in a small office. The sister responded immediately to Cathy's introduction from one of the nurses as Mr Harland's granddaughter. She pushed her office door closed so that they were private.

'I'm very pleased a relative has arrived,' she said. 'Are there any other family members who can be contacted?'

'I'm – I'm it,' Cathy said.

In that second, Cathy realised the stark truth. Frank wasn't just all she'd got. She was all he'd got.

She must have looked very shocked, because the sister's eyes became deeply compassionate.

'If there are any close friends, anybody else, now would be a good time to let them know.'

Cathy nodded, the lump rising in her throat again.

'I see. Yes, I'll take care of that.'

'Good. Obviously visiting hours don't apply. You

should feel free to be here as much as possible.'

'So – is he going to make it through surgery?'

'He's had a major attack. We've got his medical history. He's been treated for a severe heart condition for some time, but it seemed to be under control. Now the surgeons are trying to perform a bypass. The chances of success in somebody of your grandfather's age, with his general state of health and with the condition he has, are . . .' The sister's voice was sympathetic. 'I'm afraid they're slim. It is best to prepare yourself for the worst.'

'It's all right. I understand.'

'It seems very likely that he'll survive surgery. But the question is for how long. I hope you understand.'

'Yes. And I'm grateful for your honesty.'

The sister nodded.

'But we are doing our very best. And his lodger, Barry? He's told me that Frank's a tough cookie.'

At last the sister was using Frank's name. It made his chances of survival somehow seem greater. He wasn't a statistic yet. He was alive, with a personality, a spirit, a pulse and a name.

'Oh, yes.' Cathy tried to laugh. 'He's an obstinate, obnoxious bastard. I don't believe he'll give up without an almighty fight.'

'That's good.' The sister smiled. 'Just what I wanted to hear. Now he won't be back in the ward for at least another hour, possibly longer. So why don't you take Barry and get something to eat and drink and come back when you're ready?'

'And Barry,' Cathy said. 'He's not just the lodger. He and Frank are very great friends. Please, could you treat Barry as you would a relative?'

'Of course.'

'And there is another friend. Barbara. Please don't let on that I've said this but . . . Well, she is very close. Closer than anybody.'

The sister looked concerned.

'Barry didn't mention anybody called Barbara. We would have made sure she was contacted. I'm very sorry.'

'No, don't worry.' Cathy gave a rueful smile. 'She and Frank had a blow-out not long ago and Barry thought it might be a permanent rift. He didn't sense . . . quite what I sensed between them.'

'Ah, I see.' There was a flicker of humour in the sister's eyes.

'Exactly,' Cathy said with relief. 'I'm going to contact Barbara now. She's – she's the closest he's ever had to' – she hesitated over her choice of words – 'to a partner. I'd be grateful if she could be given that respect.'

'Yes, of course.' The sister nodded emphatically.

Cathy left the office feeling unburdened. At least now everything should be handled delicately. She hoped she had said all the right things.

Barry was still sitting on the bench in the corridor, staring into space, looking bushed.

'Now, you!' Cathy sat down and grabbed Barry's hand again. 'It's all fine. They're doing a bypass and everything looks good. All we can do now is hope. He's in very good hands. So why don't you go off and find a canteen and grab something to eat? We've got at least an hour, maybe more, before he'll be back on the ward.'

'And what are you going to do?' Barry peered at Cathy with tired eyes.

She considered not telling him. But it was silly to be mysterious.

'I'm going to get Barbara.'

Barry looked amazed.

'To *get* her?'

'Yep. I'll find her and I'll bring her back here.'

Barry shook his head slowly, pursing his lips.

'I'm just not sure that's a good idea, Cathy. You should have seen Frank ranting about her the last few weeks. It might just kill him off. He's been so . . . so livid about their row. I've never seen him so furious. About anything.'

'You silly.' Cathy patted his hand and stood up, already trying to remember where the taxi rank was. 'That's because he loves her.'

Cathy found a taxi and threw herself into it.

'Where to?' The driver was already pulling away. Cathy thought hard. She looked at her watch.

'What time does the Bodleian Library close?'

The driver caught her eyes in his mirror. He already looked pissed off.

'Dunno.'

'Can we get to it in a taxi?'

The driver sniffed.

'I can pull up in Broad Street.'

'Okay, yes, please. Then if you could please wait for me while I go and get somebody.'

The driver muttered under his breath. Cathy tried to ignore it. The important thing was to get the job done. At this moment Barbara thought that she was punishing Frank. Cathy could guess that she was wondering, daily, how long it would take before he apologised to

377

her. It would be eating her up. Perhaps it took a woman to know that. But poor Barbara had no idea that time was about to run out on her.

The taxi crawled through the narrow streets. Cathy realised that they must be hitting the beginning of the rush hour. Great. Eventually the driver pulled the cab into a herringbone mesh of parking places in the middle of a road, ranged either side with craggy colleges and small shops. He stopped the car and sat, tapping his fingers on the wheel.

'Where is the Bodleian, please?' Cathy asked politely.

The driver stuck out a hand. Ahead, Cathy could see a domed building, with a fence and bizarre gargoyles round it.

'That's it, there?'

'Behind it. And over the road too. It's all over the place.'

'Where's the main entrance?'

The driver paused, just long enough to let Cathy know he was in a very bad mood.

'Do I look like a student?'

Cathy was about to crawl out, but she stopped and thought better of it. She needed this man to be here when she got back. She didn't have time to romp around Oxford wondering where she might find another taxi.

'My grandfather is having heart surgery in the JR at this very moment. His . . . wife doesn't know. I'm going to get her now, so that he's not dead by the time she finds out. Then we need to go back to the JR again. So if you would be patient, I would appreciate it very much. Money isn't the issue. But saying goodbye to somebody you love who's about to die is. I hope that clarifies things.'

'Sure,' the driver said defensively. He shifted in his seat. 'I'll put the meter on waiting time.'

'Thank you,' Cathy clipped icily at him.

And off she sped. To the left was Blackwell's bookshop. To the right was the domed building. Was the Bodleian a student library? Was that why the taxi driver was being so arsy? She stopped a teenager who was loping past in a college scarf and demanded to know where the main entrance was. He pointed her round the corner, opposite the King's Arms pub.

'Thank you.' Cathy clutched his arm. 'Thanks so much.'

She rounded the corner and pushed open the paned glass doors. Instantly a man in a suit, looking grim, stopped her.

'Card, please.'

'Pardon?'

'Your card?'

'I don't have a card.' Cathy wanted to yell at him. *More haste, less speed*, she preached to herself mentally. 'I mean, I'm sorry, I don't have a card.' She tried a smile. 'There is a very urgent situation and I need to contact Barbara.'

'You can wait for your friend outside. We don't take messages,' he replied with a countenance like a cliff face.

'No, I'm sorry, I haven't explained it very well. Barbara works here.' He didn't snap back at her instantly, so Cathy guessed she'd got his attention. 'It's about Frank Harland, her friend. Professor Harland. There's something she must know straight away.'

'Frank?' A voice drifted over from inside the lobby. It was a birdlike woman who scuttled over with staccato steps. 'What about Frank Harland?'

Cathy turned to the woman.

'I'm Frank Harland's granddaughter. He's having emergency heart surgery in the JR. Barbara doesn't know. I need to—'

She got no further. The bird woman had skipped over to a long desk and had picked up the phone. She glanced over her shoulder at Cathy.

'Barbara's in the Radcliffe Camera. She might still be there. Let me see.'

'Thank you.' Cathy felt her shoulders relax again. They'd been up somewhere by her ears for the last twenty minutes. She had no idea what the Radcliffe Camera was, but it didn't matter as long as Barbara was still there.

'Well, I wish you'd said,' the doorman mumbled gruffly and gave her an apologetic look. 'We all know Frank. I hope it's nothing serious.'

Cathy could only pull a regretful face in reply and the doorman's became grave.

'Please tell him Vince says hello.'

'I will.'

'Anne?' The bird woman said in a polished voice, much more polished than the one she'd just used with Cathy. 'Is Barbara still there? Oh, she is? That's great. Can you get her on the phone, please? It's very urgent.'

Cathy waited. A few students wandered out. Others wandered in. She hardly noticed.

'Barbara? It's Geraldine.' The bird woman paused. She turned to look at Cathy again. Cathy pulled an anxious face, hoping Geraldine would be gentle. How much did these people know? Was Geraldine the sparrow just going to blurt it all out?

Then Geraldine seemed to think better of second-

380

hand news and held the receiver out to Cathy.

Cathy trotted forward and took it immediately.

'Barbara? It's Cathy. Please don't say anything, just listen. Frank's in the JR and I've come to get you.'

She squashed the receiver to her ear until it hurt. Were they still connected?

'Hello, Barbara? I've got a taxi waiting in the street.'

The silence continued. Whether Barbara was in shock, or in disgust that Cathy had come to her place of work, or had actually fainted clean away Cathy couldn't know, but she added assertively just in case:

'I'm not leaving without you. I'll be outside the thing with the gargoyles. If I have to stand there all night, I will.'

'The Sheldonian,' Geraldine whispered.

'The Sheldonian!' Cathy declared. 'I'll be standing there until you turn up. My taxi's right next to it.'

Cathy looked at Geraldine in despair.

'I think we've been cut off,' she said plaintively. 'There's nobody there.'

'Give me five minutes,' Barbara barked and the line went dead.

Barbara approached Cathy with an upright, noble demeanour. Cathy's first thought was that she looked no different in her work clothes from in the home clothes she'd seen her in. But her face was pale, and her fingers were curling and uncurling into her palms. Cathy noticed all this, but she moved towards Barbara the moment she saw her.

'Come on,' she said and motioned her towards the taxi.

They both climbed awkwardly into the back of the

381

cab. The driver was silent, but Cathy no longer cared whether he was having the day from hell, or had won the lottery that morning. She was more worried about Barbara's tense, mute presence. Barbara hadn't even asked how it had happened.

As they left the town behind and roamed off towards Headington again, Cathy decided that she should speak first.

'Barry rang me first thing this morning,' she said. And as Barbara offered no reply, she decided that Barbara was aching to know what had happened, but was too proud to ask. Cathy took a deep breath and began again.

'Apparently Barry found Frank this morning and he was – he was having a heart attack. So Barry rang an ambulance, they came and got him and now he's in the JR.'

Cathy glanced at Barbara. She was looking out of the window, but Cathy knew she was absorbing every word. It was like watching a cactus drink in rain and hoping that somehow, somewhere, it was going to produce a flower.

'When I got here I realised that Barry hadn't contacted you. He meant to, but he was panicking too much to think straight. And – um – at the moment Frank's in surgery.'

At this point Barbara's body jerked, like a sleeper unconsciously twitching in the night. Cathy wanted to put her hand on Barbara's, but she knew she couldn't. So she went on soothingly:

'He's having bypass surgery and by the time we get there hopefully they'll have finished. I spoke to the ward sister and she said the signs are . . . are really good.'

Barbara cleared her throat loudly. She still couldn't look Cathy in the eye. They both swung to the left as the taxi took a corner, apparently on two wheels. Not, Cathy could imagine, out of any sympathy for their haste, but because the driver wanted to see them both hit the floor. She gritted her teeth.

'I'm sorry I imposed on your privacy at work,' Cathy said. She let out a huge sigh. She hadn't meant it to be audible, but she couldn't help it. 'I knew you'd want to be there. I want to tell you everything I know before we arrive. I think that's it. Barry's still there. He's very upset. That's because his own father let him down badly and he was put in some sort of cheap boarding school. He's never had a real family and he's come to look upon Frank as a father figure. So—'

Cathy paused insouciantly. Had Barbara ever known anything about Barry? Somehow she doubted it. Barry had told Cathy, cheerfully as ever, that Barbara hated his guts. But Cathy hoped she'd imparted some information that might, on this occasion, sink in. She didn't want Barbara to belittle Barry to his face at the hospital. Not when he was so fragile.

'So it's . . . um . . .' Cathy paused to fall all over Barbara as the driver sadistically took the mini roundabout just before the hospital as if he were auditioning for the army. 'So it's just the three of us.'

Barbara shook her head in some private, no doubt disparaging, line of thought.

The taxi screeched to a halt. Both women were catapulted forward and bounced back into their seats again. The driver yanked open the dividing window.

'How much? Cathy snapped, niceties no longer an issue.

The driver threw an inflated figure at her.

'That can't be right.' Surprisingly it was Barbara who spoke.

'Forget it, Barbara,' Cathy muttered quietly. 'Life's too bloody short. Let's just pay and get out of here.'

'I'll pay.'

Cathy didn't argue. Barbara had already opened a sleek leather wallet and was handing notes to the driver. They piled out on to the concrete and the taxi shot away, only just giving them time to close the doors.

'Wanker,' Cathy emitted before she could stop herself.

'So, where is he?' Barbara smoothed down her skirt and gave Cathy a cagey look. Oh, she was hating every minute of this, Cathy knew. But at least once they'd got to the ward, Barbara could be independent of Cathy's knowledge.

'Follow me.'

They strode off through a series of corridors and stairs until they had reached the ward where Cathy had last left Barry. Barry was nowhere to be seen.

Cathy stopped just before the swing doors. Suddenly she didn't want to go any further. She had done what her instincts had bellowed at her to do. She had brought Barbara back to Frank.

Now she suddenly felt weak. Frank might be out of surgery. He might not be out of surgery. He might not have survived surgery. Or if he had, he might be taking his last tremulous breaths somewhere beyond those doors. Cathy hadn't even realised she'd done it. She'd reached the doors and she'd started to back away, step by step. She was reversing down the corridor.

384

Barbara stood at the doors and stared at her. Cathy was aware that she was retreating, but couldn't stop herself.

'What's the matter?' Barbara issued in a brittle voice.

'I – I.' Cathy shook her head. 'I don't want to know.'

'Yes, you do,' Barbara stated. 'Of course you do.'

'No.' Cathy put up her hands. 'No, I don't.'

Barbara seemed frozen herself. The doors stood between the two women and knowledge.

But the one thing Cathy had learned recently was that you cannot unknow things that you would rather not know. She felt the tears that she had been biting back surge up into her throat, right up, until her eyes bulged.

'Barbara,' she pleaded in a tight voice. 'Please will you go and find out. And then come and tell me.'

Barbara clenched her jaw. Cathy could see through exhausted, misty vision that Barbara's face had gained a determination that made her look fearsomely strong.

'I thought you had more guts than this.'

Barbara only said it, but to Cathy it was as if she'd shouted it. She smeared her fingers over her face and took a big breath. At some point she would understand that Barbara's statement was a compliment. For the moment she felt as if she'd been slapped. It did the job.

'Right.' Cathy walked to the ward doors so that she and Barbara could enter together. 'I'm ready.'

Chapter Twenty

Frank was in a room off to the side of the main ward and he had the place all to himself. Not that he was appreciating the rare NHS luxury of it, as he was totally out for the count.

He had wires attached to every visible part of his body. A metal cage held the sheets high above him, so that his chest, neck and head appeared to be poking out of a huge, white tent. An oxygen mask was clamped over his face and a tube snaked from his arm up to a drip. There was a jagged green line running across a monitor and a regular 'bleep' coming from another machine. It was like a scene from *ER*.

One thing was for sure. Frank was very firmly anchored down. He wouldn't be able to run away when he woke up without taking the bed, the machines and the walls with him. That was a relief.

It was a small, square room. Several chairs were dotted about for visitors. Barry was seated on one, at the back of the room, as if he had to sit as far away as possible for fear of doing anything to worsen Frank's delicate state. He had his hands cupped over his face.

Barry looked round as the two women slipped into the room. His eyes widened at the sight of Barbara, who was standing stock still, staring at Frank.

He stood up and walked to Cathy, took her hand and squeezed it.

'Have you spoken to the sister?' Cathy whispered to him. He shook his head. 'Okay, come on, then. Let's go and get a progress report.'

Barry glanced over at Frank.

'What if the things stop bleeping while we're not here?' He looked very scared.

'They won't,' Cathy told him. 'And if there's any sudden change Barbara will tell us. Won't you, Barbara?'

Barbara's eyes had lost all the defensive energy that had been there before. She nodded. As they left the room, Cathy saw her move closer to the bed. As she'd thought, Barbara needed some private time with this new situation.

They found the ward sister again and she seemed very upbeat.

'It's gone well,' she told them both. 'He's a tough old bird, isn't he?'

'Yes,' Cathy affirmed.

'Will you be able to stay close by for a while?' the sister asked Cathy.

Cathy hesitated. Ruth had given her a day. She had to check her mobile messages – and it was worrying her. There was work to do. There was always work to do. She'd have to juggle things somehow. But she knew that she couldn't leave Frank now. What if he came round, only for a few minutes, and then faded away for ever? She had to be here. But how was she going to manage it all? How long would it take?

'You know,' the sister mused, 'nobody ever dies leaving an empty in-tray. It's a thought that often occurs to me. Especially on this ward.'

'I'm off work,' Barry interjected. 'I've phoned them.

I'm on leave until things have settled down, so I'll be around.'

Cathy looked at Barry's face, at the urgency in his eyes. Frank was her grandfather, the only blood relative she had. Emotion clawed at her throat. She could picture Ruth's disapproving grey eyes, but this was Cathy's life. Nobody had any right to interfere with it. It was too important.

'I'm here too,' Cathy said decisively. 'For the duration. However long that is.'

'I'm pleased to hear it.' The sister looked at Cathy kindly. 'Now he's stable, so there's no immediate cause for concern. He's had a big anaesthetic, so he's likely to sleep through the night. It's better that he does. Obviously, when he wakes up he's going to be extremely weak. I'd suggest none of you tires him out by trying to make him talk. He'll be happy just to know that you're all around. If you get a sign that he's strained at all, you'll know to leave.'

'Is there anything we can actually do?' Cathy asked, feeling increasingly helpless.

'Your grandad's chosen a very good place to be ill.' The sister put a hand on Cathy's arm. 'This is an excellent, modern hospital and he's in extremely good hands.'

Barry nodded emphatically.

'I know that's true. All the nurses I've been out with from here say the same thing.'

The sister's lips twitched and even Cathy managed a slight smile.

'What?' said Barry innocently.

'C'mon, Casanova.' Cathy took his arm. 'Let's pop in once more, then I'm going to take you home and make us both some dinner.'

Cathy ensured that the sister had phone numbers for herself and Barry. The sister promised they would both be contacted instantly if there was any change in Frank's condition. Otherwise, it was as well if they got a good night's sleep and returned the next day.

They slid quietly back into Frank's room. Barbara had pulled a chair up to the side of the bed. She had taken Frank's hand and was stroking it gently, taking care not to disturb the thick needle strapped into the top of his hand and the tube which ran from it. She was looking intently at Frank's face and seemed unaware that anybody had come into the room.

Cathy glanced at Barry and jerked her head to indicate that they should leave.

They took a taxi home to north Oxford. They murmured reassurances to each other in the back seat.

'He didn't look so bad, did he?' Barry said.

'No. He looked fine.'

'He might come out of this after all. He is tough, really.'

'Yes, he's tough and bloody-minded. He'll be home soon.'

Barry let them both into the house. They headed for the kitchen. Cathy, doing what everyone does when they don't know what to do, put the kettle on.

'I can't believe it. You were right.' Barry lolled against the fridge door.

'Hmn? About what?' Cathy asked, vaguely searching for mugs in the cupboards. She had been going into a daze herself. She still wasn't quite sure if she was in Birmingham, London or Oxford. It had all been so frenetic.

'Barbara. She thinks a lot of Frank, doesn't she?'

'I think I'm beginning to get the gist of their story at last,' Cathy said, finding coffee and making a mugful for them both. 'Do you want to sit in the sitting room?'

Barry shook his head.

'Reminds me too much of finding Frank this morning. Let's stay in here instead.'

They pulled up chairs at a scrubbed pine table set against the wall. Cathy sipped her coffee, her eyes feeling more and more like kaleidoscopes.

'My guess is that Barbara's disappearance brought on Frank's attack,' she speculated.

'I think the cricket was the clincher.' Barry rubbed his eyes. 'You should have seen him when it started raining on Saturday. Yelling at the telly, clinging on to the chair, downing his pills. I really should have known. I'm such an idiot.'

'No, you're not,' Cathy said firmly. 'It can't possibly just have been the cricket.'

'You don't know what this Ashes series means to him. He keeps saying it's his last chance.'

'*His* last chance?'

'To see England win, before he goes off to the big pavilion in the sky.' Barry managed a weak smile. 'I've been hoping England lose, just so that he hangs on for another test series. I've got a horrible feeling that if they win he'll give up. He'll be able to slip away feeling happy.'

'For once in his life,' Cathy murmured.

Barry pulled at his tie and rolled it up. He put it on the table, frowning.

'Why do you say that?'

'I don't know.' Cathy was surprised herself. 'I just get

the impression that he's a troubled man. Don't you?'

'Hmn. I've always thought he was at his happiest when he was shouting at Barbara.'

A comfortable silence fell between them. It was odd that Cathy felt so at home in this house, with Barry beside her at the table. It wasn't like being a visitor in a stranger's house any more. In some ways she felt even more at home here than she did at the home she'd been brought up in, with Melissa and Brian quietly going about their business. There was something in the air that made her feel she belonged and maybe even Frank's outbursts triggered a flow of recognition inside her. She had always been a bit volatile herself, although in recent years she'd managed to control it better. In Frank's house, she actually felt as if she fitted in.

A plaintive yowl from her feet disturbed her musings.

'Oh, Beefy!' she whispered, leaning down to pick him up. He settled into her lap, purring back at her like a drum and headbutting her chin.

'I think he wants you to adopt him,' Barry said. Then he pulled a rueful face. 'Sorry, didn't mean to touch on a delicate subject.'

'Nothing delicate about it.' Cathy rubbed the ginger head and Beefy closed his eyes in rapture. 'Of course I'll look after him. Until Frank comes home and claims his baby.'

'Bugger, bugger, bugger.' Nick fiddled with the computer in his bedroom, frustrated.

No e-mails from Frank. Not even any contribution to the cricket newsgroup from Frank in his alias as 'Beefy'. And not a word from Cathy.

Nick didn't like being left up in the air. He was the one who was usually enigmatic – especially with women. He wanted Cathy to talk to him, but he didn't want to make the first move. She might get the wrong signals and take it all too seriously. He didn't want to be serious about things – not yet. He wasn't ready.

But he'd been turning it all over in his mind since the weekend. In some ways Cathy was ideal. She didn't live on his doorstep. Geography dictated that things had to be distant. As far as Nick was concerned, distance was good. It gave him time to think. There was no way they could invade each other's space, even if they wanted to. Cathy would never turn up unexpectedly in one of his local pubs, when he was having a fun night out with the lads. In fact, when he thought about it, he wondered if Cathy would ever have done that, even if she'd lived next door.

He leaned back in his chair and sipped from his tea as he read through the messages on the cricket newsgroup. The Ashes series was in the balance. His emotional life was in the balance. It made him uneasy.

In a matter of days, England would be taking on Australia again at Headingley. Would Cathy be there once more? Nick assumed so. His own ticket had arrived in the post on Monday. It would be a crucial match. There was still the Oval to come, but Headingley could decide the series. He wanted to enjoy it with Cathy. Perhaps even have another night in a hotel. There was plenty of time for Cathy to get in touch and make an arrangement for them to travel up to Leeds together. But this time he found himself wanting to be sure that they were on for that weekend. It would give him something to look forward to.

He'd been secretly thrilled when Cathy had rung to say that she was stranded in Birmingham on Sunday night. It had been a bit of a shock, knowing that she'd be able to see the way he lived, warts and all. But the reality had been less stressful than he'd thought. She obviously hadn't been greatly impressed – Nick guessed that was fair enough. But she'd taken it in her stride.

With Cathy he'd felt sexy, likeable, funny, accepted. The physical side of things had been truly amazing. Last night Nick had got home late from work, feeling shattered, and had gone to bed early. In the night he'd reached for Cathy's warm body in bed, only to find an empty space. He'd been surprised that he'd done that.

His attention wandering from the computer screen, Nick let his mind drift back to their night in the Manchester hotel. The memory of it aroused him.

There was a knock at his door and Terry walked in without waiting for a reply.

Nick turned round irritably. Was there no flipping privacy in this house?

'What is it?'

'Phone call for you. Didn't you hear it ringing?'

Nick frowned.

'Anything important?'

'Someone called Hannah.' Terry raised his eyebrows teasingly.

'Hannah?' Nick searched his memory. Then the image came back to him, of dark fluffy hair and a sweet face. From the night he'd been out on the town with Graham. She'd given him her number – but he hadn't called her. He'd clean forgotten about it. 'Oh my God. *That* Hannah.'

'Want me to say you're out?' Terry grinned.

'Yes. No. Hang on a sec, how did she get this number?'

'I think Graham went out for a drink with her mate. What's her name? Mel?'

'Mel?' Of course. The two women had said they shared a house. So Graham had thought highly enough of Mel to give her his home number? That was a first. And it would be natural enough for Mel to pass it on to Hannah.

'Well? Are you in or out?'

'Erm . . .' Nick clicked his tongue. He felt as if he'd been hunted down. It was irksome. But there was an aspect of it which was quite flattering. He'd still got Cathy on his mind, but it was nice to be fancied.

'Is she fit?' Terry quizzed, relaxing against the door frame.

'Who?'

'Hannah.' Terry rolled his eyes. 'How many have you got on the go at the moment?'

Nick gave a low laugh. But Hannah was waiting on the other end of the line. If Terry told her Nick was out, she'd probably only ring back another time. It was better to talk to her now and take control of the situation. He'd make an excuse about seeing her. He wasn't particularly interested in pursuing it, but she had been nice. Nick strode into the living room and sat down on the sofa, disconcerted to find himself sitting on Terry's jacket.

'Oi. Hang this up, will you, mate?' Nick picked up the jacket and thrust it at Terry, who looked surprised.

'All right, Mary Poppins.'

'Bugger off.'

Nick picked up the phone.

Cathy took herself off to the little old-fashioned bedroom at the top of Frank's house, which she was rapidly claiming as her own, switched on the tatty lamp and sat down in the soft glow of the bulb to collect her phone messages. She found that she had had nine calls – all of them connected with work.

She listened to them, making rough notes for herself. Her stomach twisted with anxiety. It was as if nobody knew she had an urgent situation to deal with. What had Ruth told them? They were acting as if nothing had happened.

How on earth was Cathy going to explain to Ruth that she needed more time? That a frail old man that she cared about passionately was lying in a hospital bed, his life dangling by a slender thread, and that she couldn't leave him?

Cathy hung her head and closed her eyes, her thoughts spinning like mice in a wheel. Tears climbed up her throat again. They would just have to understand. She couldn't desert Frank. He was her grandfather. He needed her. She needed him. There was so much she wanted to ask him, to tell him, to talk about with him. She might not get that chance, but if she left without having even tried, she would never, ever forgive herself.

Ruth's last message, left only an hour previously, had said that she would be working late. Taking a shaky breath, Cathy sat up straighter and pressed out Ruth's number.

'Yes?' Ruth said briskly.

'It's Cathy.' Cathy gathered herself, ready to be firm. She must not be swayed. She knew what she had to do.

'Cathy, how are things?'

'I'm still in Oxford,' Cathy began. 'My grandfather's in a very bad way. He's had heart surgery today and he still hasn't come round. I'm very worried about him.'

'I'm sorry to hear that.'

'I – I do understand how very busy we are – but I must ask you for some more time.' Cathy cleared her throat to keep her voice steady.

'Cathy.' Ruth sighed. 'I realise you are in a terrible predicament, but we have meetings scheduled for the rest of the week. Do you think your grandfather has stabilised?'

Cathy opened her mouth to protest. She couldn't find the words.

'I know this must be a worrying time,' Ruth went on. 'Don't think me hard, but I have a company to run here and we can't afford to carry anybody, especially at the moment.'

'I do understand.' Cathy gazed at the dusty pictures on the wall, at the rickety wardrobe in the corner, the shelf stacked with battered orange Penguin classics. The sights and smells of the old house.

'I know I can rely on you to keep a cool head,' Ruth said more warmly. 'Why don't you stay up in Oxford tonight and make your way in to the office tomorrow? It would be good if you could be here by early afternoon. And you need to continue to field the calls that are coming your way. Obviously, you can't just disappear, however urgent your situation is.'

And then, quite suddenly and without warning

396

Cathy was overpowered by emotion. Her eyes filled up and spilled over with hot tears. Her voice came out as a wrenched sob.

'I can't do that, Ruth.'

She put a hand over her mouth. She was shaking. The tears fell from her chin into her lap.

'I'm sorry? I'm saying that we need you here, Cathy. I understand this is difficult for you, but you can't make an emotional decision.'

'I've *got* to make an emotional decision. I have no choice. I have to be here for my grandfather and I'm afraid that if you can't take the time I need from my leave then I will have to offer you my resignation.'

There was a silence. A band of iron clamped itself round Cathy's chest as the tears continued to stream down her face.

'I'm very sorry to hear that.'

There was an awkward silence. Cathy wiped her wet cheeks with unsteady fingers.

'I've got enough leave to cover my period of notice.' She took an uneven breath. 'And obviously I'll be willing to come in and do a proper handover. But I can't do that until the situation has stabilised here.'

Ruth was very subdued.

'Think it over, Cathy. Ring me again as soon as you're sure.'

After Ruth had rung off, Cathy stared at her mobile in disbelief.

Had she really just had that conversation? Had she been told to be back at work tomorrow, while her grandfather lay dying? Had she really, in return, handed in her notice?

'Oh my God.'

'Brandy's what you need,' Barry said, helpfully producing a bottle from somewhere beneath his pile of laundry and waving it. He poured a decent measure into two tumblers and handed her one.

Cathy, lying on her stomach on Barry's bed, took the glass distractedly. Beefy had followed her in and had curled up happily on the rumpled duvet beside her. Cathy stroked his head. She wasn't tearful any more. In fact, she felt an odd sense of release. But she still couldn't believe what was happening.

'What have I done?' She took a sip of her brandy, shuddered and peered at Barry. He gave her a quirky smile.

'The right thing?' he suggested.

'God, I don't know about that. I mean, six months ago I had everything mapped out in my head. There was my job, my house and Jason. It was all coming together. Moving forward logically. But then Frank turned up and . . . well, it's as if everything's changed since then.'

'Ah.' Barry put up a finger. 'You made the fatal mistake.'

'Which was?'

'Planning.' Barry grinned. 'Such a waste of time. I don't know why anyone ever does it.'

Cathy turned her glass round in her hands.

'I'm going to have to plan now,' she mused. 'I haven't got a job.'

'Look, I don't like to pry, but if you need a loan or anything, just to tide you over, I can help you.'

'Thanks.' Cathy smiled at his weary face. 'I really appreciate that. But I'll be fine. I was earning quite good money and I didn't have much chance to spend it. I've got a bit of a safety net.'

But not for long, Cathy realised. And what would she do next? It would take time to find another job. And she was too bewildered to work out what else she might do.

'You're lucky,' Barry announced. 'You're free. You can do anything you like.'

'Well, yes.' Cathy allowed that thought to sink in. It made her feel happier. In fact, it made her feel very relieved. 'Yes, I am. You're right. Thank you. But you're free too, Barry. If you really dislike your job as much as you say, you could do something different.'

'Don't tell me you're going to persuade everyone else to resign now,' Barry teased her. 'No, it's harder when you're still on the treadmill. You tell yourself you'll get off one day, do something you really enjoy, and before you know it they're handing you the carriage clock.'

It reminded Cathy of something Nick had said about his own job.

'But you're in a good position, although you can't see it now,' Barry went on. 'It's a question of whether the cup's half full or half empty. Like the horse shit story. You know that one?'

'No?' Cathy wriggled up on to her elbows. 'Tell me.'

'A man has two young sons. One's an awful pessimist, the other's a great optimist. On Christmas morning he delivers the presents to their rooms and waits for them to wake up to see their reactions.'

'Go on.'

'Well, he goes to the pessimist's bedroom first. He's got all the toys money can buy, but he finds fault with everything he's got.'

Cathy pulled a face.

'So then the father goes to the optimist's bedroom. He's been given a great pile of horse shit. But he's dancing round the room and clapping his hands with glee.'

'Why?' Cathy laughed.

'Because, the optimistic son says, "If there's shit, there's got to be a pony."'

'That's brilliant.' Cathy laughed. 'Thank you. I'll remember it.'

'So it seems to me', Barry said, 'that you've just got to work out where your pony is.'

Barry was right. Cathy gazed up at Melinda Messenger on the ceiling and thought about it. Now was the right time to make good things happen. She was free. She couldn't think too far ahead, not while she had the painful image of Frank's body fighting for life in the strange hospital bed. But she would make sure that this was a turning point in her life. And hadn't Bill Havers always told her that she was a girl who could go places? With or without Ruth's or Mark's backing? What if he was right?

'It's great to be able to talk to you like this,' Barry went on. 'I've never had a female friend. I've slept with all of them.'

'You've slept with *all* the women you know?' Cathy peered at Barry curiously.

He nodded sheepishly.

'Even the receptionist and the accounts assistant at the garage. And I can't go into a single pub in Oxford without banging into an old flame. It's quite wearing.'

'And all those nurses too – was that true?'

Barry thought about it.

'Yep.'

'No wonder you looked so freaked out at the hospital. You must have been expecting to bang into an ex at every corner.'

'Well, the thing was, after my wife kicked me out and before I came to live with Frank I tried to run a place on my own. But I needed a lodger. So I advertised in the nurses' home.'

'You devil!'

'I suppose it was a bit unsubtle, really. But I did get to meet a lot of them. Ah well, I'm thirty-three now and I guess it will soon be time for me to calm down. It's tough, though.'

'God, yes,' Cathy teased him. 'I've never known such a sex monster.'

'It's not about sex. Sex is fine, but I like the company. I just want to be loved. I couldn't say that to any of my mates.' Barry looked at Cathy haplessly. 'I don't think Penny really did love me. But one day maybe I'll meet someone right for me. Anyway. It's been so great chatting to you tonight, Cathy. I was really strung out about Frank. I know I wouldn't have slept.'

Cathy ruffled Beefy's fur and smiled at Barry. He looked so young with his eyes bleary, like charcoal smudges in the middle of his face.

'You've helped me relax too. Thanks for everything you've done today. Now we should go to bed,' Cathy said, pulling herself up and yawning. 'It'll be a long day tomorrow and we need to be ready.'

Barry put his head to one side, straining to hear something.

'Is that the phone?'

Cathy opened Barry's bedroom door. The telephone

was ringing downstairs. Not a change in Frank for the worse? No, please, not tonight, not now.

Cathy dived out of the door, raced along the corridor and down the stairs two at a time. She reached the hall. The ringing was coming from Frank's room. Cathy burst in, put the light on and ran to the desk. She yanked the receiver up. Barry was only two steps behind her.

'Yes?'

'Catherine?' It was Barbara's voice. Cathy held on to Barry's arm. She nodded. Which was stupid, because Barbara couldn't see her. Mind you, it was a bit stupid of Barbara to have asked if it was Cathy. Who else would it be? Cathy waited for dreadful news.

'I'm at home,' Barbara said abruptly. 'I've just left Frank. He's still sleeping.'

She seemed to yank back on her words and there was silence.

'Oh. Oh, that's great news. Good,' Cathy panted. 'I thought for a horrible minute there things had got . . . got worse.'

'No,' Barbara said. 'No change.'

More silence. Cathy swallowed.

'Great, well, that's great. Thank you. Barry and I were just – we had something to eat earlier, which was horrible because I cooked it, but Barry didn't seem to mind – and oh, we've fed Beefy. So he's all right. And we'll make sure he's well looked after while Frank's away. So we're just a bit tired. And you must be very tired too. So—'

'There's no need for you to make small talk with me. You don't have to like me, Catherine,' Barbara said.

Cathy floundered for words. Barry was holding her

hand. She turned away from him for a second so that he couldn't see her face and lowered her voice.

'I know I don't, Barbara. But I do like you.'

There was a further tense silence.

'I can't imagine why,' Barbara said. But it wasn't said in a way that invited a string of compliments. And Cathy couldn't think of any compliments anyway. She just liked Barbara. She'd only just realised that she did, but there it was.

'Well – I'm – will you be there tomorrow?' Cathy asked.

'Yes.'

Cathy chewed her lip. She didn't want to ring off first.

'Good,' she said meekly.

'I spoke to the ward sister, but it seemed she already knew about me. From you.'

It was hard to tell from Barbara's tone whether it was an accusation or a gesture of appreciation. Cathy felt awful. She'd had no right to barge in and speak on Barbara's behalf. After all these decades with Frank . . . it was no wonder that Barbara felt Cathy was a usurper.

'I – I only mentioned that you were . . . important. I'm sorry, I didn't mean to say anything out of turn. I just – Barbara, I'm sorry.'

'Thank you,' Barbara interrupted her curtly. 'For what you did today.'

Cathy squeezed Barry's hand. He was trying to peer over her shoulder to see her face, but she curled herself round. This was private. Woman to woman.

'I hope I did the right thing,' Cathy whispered back.

'You seem to have a certain amount of perception.'

403

Cathy's jaw dropped. Barbara had thanked her and almost said something nice. It was amazing. And what a wonderful note to end a fraught day on. She was speechless.

'Goodnight,' Barbara said in a clipped voice and put the phone down.

Cathy replaced the receiver slowly and turned to Barry. His face was a picture of concern. She threw her arms round him and he hugged her back.

'Blimey, what was that for? Is everything all right?'

'It's all fine,' she breathed into his neck. 'Everything is going to be fine.'

Snuggled up in bed at nearly midnight, with Beefy under her arm and her mobile in the other hand, Cathy looked up as Barry delivered her a cup of hot chocolate. It had brown lumps floating in it and he seemed to have forgotten to add any milk, but Cathy was deeply touched.

'You look dead on your feet,' Cathy said softly. 'Go to bed now.'

'Only if you give me your phone,' Barry said seriously. 'You can't sort anything else out tonight.'

'I know,' she agreed. 'But I just want to check my messages. We've been downstairs for a while and I wouldn't have heard my phone if it rang.'

Barry perched on the side of the bed and stroked Beefy's back gently. The instant rattle of a purr made them both smile.

'Who is it you're so desperate to hear from?' Barry asked.

Cathy turned the question over in her mind. After Barbara had phoned they'd both talked downstairs for a while. Somehow her weekend with Nick and her torn feelings about Jason had come out.

'I don't know,' she said honestly.

'You know, you don't have to solve everything before you go to sleep. You look exhausted.'

'I am exhausted.'

'Then give me your phone and close your eyes.' Cathy made a noise of resistance as Barry reached for her mobile. He gave her a resigned smile. 'All right, then, you check the messages, but I'm going to stay with you to make sure there's nothing to churn you up.'

'Would you? That's really sweet.'

Cathy dialled into her message line and listened. Barry took a sip of the hot chocolate he'd brought her and shuddered.

'Whatever you do, don't drink that.'

'Okay.'

Then she concentrated.

There was one message. Melissa had phoned:

'Cathy, dear. We're both thinking of you. Please do let me know what's happening. I – I understand completely how attached you are to Frank. Please don't worry about it. But let us know if there's anything at all we can do to help you. Do you need any money? 'Bye for now, darling, and take care of yourself.'

'Melissa,' Cathy whispered, comforted by the message. She turned her phone off. Barry prised it from her and placed it on the bedside table.

'Better now?' he asked, full of concern.

'Yes.' Cathy slid down between the sheets. 'I think so.'

'Just remember what you said to me earlier,' Barry

said, switching off Cathy's bedside light for her and standing up. 'Everything's going to be fine.'

'Yes. Yes, it is,' Cathy murmured as she began to drift off.

Chapter Twenty-one

It took several days for Cathy to feel that everything might be fine after all. In that time she visited Frank constantly. At times she went with Barry, at other times they staggered their visits so they could each get some rest.

Barbara was there all the time. Judging by the cards and flowers that poured into Frank's room on a daily basis, it seemed that everybody at Oxford University knew about his illness. Cathy had been amazed to read the thoughts on the cards and the labels on the flowers. So many people, it seemed, knew of her grandfather and admired him. It was a revelation. One card even read 'To Frank and Barbara, thinking of you both'. Cathy had noted wryly that Barbara had edged that card to the front of Frank's bedside cabinet.

Initially, Frank had been lying in his bed, completely oblivious to all the attention. He had opened weak eyes several times, looked startled and closed them again. Once or twice he'd attempted to speak, but his words had been incoherent and stifled by his oxygen mask.

On one occasion Cathy was sitting in the chair at the back of the room, keeping a quiet vigil, while Barbara took a coffee break in the canteen, when one of the nurses put her head round the door.

'Peter and Hilary Benson to see Frank. Is it okay if they just pop in briefly and talk to you?'

The Peter and Hilary Benson?

Cathy had been stunned to recognise the famous academics, peeping delicately into the room. She'd seen Peter Benson on television many times. His wife was a well-known critic in her own right. Cathy had read some of her book reviews. And they'd come to visit her very own grandfather. Not sure whether to curtsy or simply prostrate herself on the floor, Cathy had stuttered something about Frank's condition. They left quickly, having made sympathetic comments. Cathy sank back into her chair and gazed at the tiny form sleeping under the heap of hospital sheets, the bleeps of his machines providing oddly comforting background music. How little she really knew about Frank. If only he would get better, and tell her more about his life.

But it wasn't until Friday, as Cathy entered the ward on her own – Barry having gone in to work that day to clear up as much paperwork as he could – that she knew for sure that it was going to be all right.

She heard the yells even before she'd pushed open the door to his side room. She had never heard such a welcome noise in her life.

Frank was sitting up in bed. The oxygen mask was off. He had a newspaper over his knees and a nurse was patiently refilling his water jug and listening.

'The bastards! I mean, the presumption of it!'

'Frank!'

His face was pink instead of white. He was small and frail and was still bound up to his machines, but he looked like her grandfather again. Cathy threw herself at him in relief and stuck a huge kiss on his cheek. Frank stared back at Cathy without comprehension. He slapped his hand on the opened broadsheet. He obviously had far more important things on his mind already.

'Have you seen this?' he demanded.

'Seen what? *The Times*? Nope, haven't had a chance to review the British press this morning.' Cathy smiled at the nurse as she raised her eyebrows and left the room.

Cathy pulled up a chair, her spirits soaring. He was cross. That meant he was well. She'd never expected Frank to say, 'Hello, thanks so much for coming.' That would have been worrying. Her grin spread from ear to ear.

'It's my bloody obituary!' Frank shouted, his voice hoarse.

He thrust the newspaper out for Cathy. She read the page he was indicating.

'Oh God!' She put her hand to her mouth.

She was caught between the horror and the humour of it. What on earth would it feel like to read your own obituary while you were still alive? How on earth had they got the wrong end of the stick?

But as she scanned the lines, she also realised that there was so very much she didn't know about her own grandfather. Had he really written so many books? And been so prominent – even revered – in circles she knew nothing about? Enough for *The Times* to consider him worthy of an obituary, even if it was a little premature.

'Oh, Frank!' She put her hand over his. 'How awful for you.'

'I'll say it's bloody awful. A third of a page? A "difficult but brilliant man"? Is that all I get? I tell you,

I want half a page when I go. And a decent photograph too.'

Her stomach untwisting for the first time in days, Cathy's head began to clear. What else was going on, out there in the real world beyond hospitals, heart monitors and anxieties?

Cathy had kept in touch with Melissa assiduously. Their nightly phone calls had been a great comfort, when she'd been tucked up in the wonky bed in Frank's house, fraught with worries. She hadn't told Melissa that she'd resigned – not yet. Melissa was such a believer in 'safety first', something she'd instilled into Cathy all her life and Cathy knew that the news would only alarm her.

'Have you talked to Jason recently?' Melissa had asked carefully.

'No.' Cathy had released a long breath. 'No, I haven't told him about this. I really can't lean on him, Melissa. It'd be like emotional blackmail. We haven't spoken to each other for ages. I think we've both assumed it's over. And he's so busy. I don't know what he could do, even if he knew. I just – just can't tell him now.'

'I understand how you feel, dear,' Melissa said. 'But don't you think he'd want to know if you were in trouble?'

'He'd only feel obligated to me and that's the last thing I'd want. I don't know what I think about Jason, but I don't want to impose on him. It's all been a bit complicated and I think we've both found . . . other distractions.'

'If only you hadn't both been so busy,' Melissa had mused.

410

'Yes.' Cathy had allowed herself some time to wonder how things might have been if she and Jason hadn't been so busy. But the thought made her feel miserable and she hadn't wanted Melissa to make her think about complicated matters that only made her feel even more confused, so she had turned the conversation to other things.

Cathy had phoned Ruth in the week and confirmed her resignation in writing. Ruth had expressed her deep regret, which had given Cathy a slight pang. But Cathy only had to think back to the disappointment she'd felt in the company, in Mark, in Ruth's treatment of her, in not being able to explore her ideas freely to realise that she was hugely relieved. And not only relieved, but excited about what the future might bring.

Fiona had been dismayed when Cathy had told her about her resignation. 'You bloody what?' she'd said. 'Oh, thank you so much. Leave me here without a friend, why don't you.' But Fiona had reassured Cathy that in all seriousness, she understood her reasoning. And Cathy, in return, had reassured Fiona that they would stay good friends, wherever they worked. So far they'd only managed a few snatched conversations between hospital visits, where Cathy was obliged to turn her mobile phone off, but Fiona phoned again, when Cathy had just got back to the house after Frank's obituary crisis. She was breathless.

'Listen, I'm in Dom's so nobody can overhear me. You'll never guess what's happened!'

'What?'

'Mark's resigned. But the rumour is he didn't jump, he was pushed. You know all the Cooper's Construction stuff? Apparently Harry Cooper had been doing Mark one or two rather large favours – including building a huge conservatory on the back of Mark's poxy house. For free.'

Cathy's eyebrows shot up.

'My God. Are you sure? How do you know?'

'Believe me, I know. You know Mark's been knobbing Lisa for months without his wife knowing? Well, he dumped Lisa like a sack of bricks and she's distraught. So she's gone for the kill.'

Cathy's mouth dropped open in shock.

'No!'

'Yes.'

'Oh God.' Cathy couldn't help laughing.

'So Ruth's come by your report on Bill Havers and the Hellier's project. And she thinks it's brilliant. And that you're a complete star.'

'Hang on.' Cathy put a hand to her head. 'This is too fast. How did she "come by" my report?'

'Well, it was a bit of Lisa and a bit of me, but we tracked it down. So Ruth's seen it, and the upshot of it is that I'm pretty sure you've got all the time you want to spend with your grandfather and Ruth's still going to be begging you to come back.'

'Bugger me,' Cathy breathed.

'Got to go. They'll miss me. Talk to you soon. And you didn't hear this from me, okay?'

It was ten days after Frank's attack when Cathy entered his room to find Barbara sitting at his bedside, reading aloud an article from the *Guardian* to him. Cathy noticed that Frank's hand had rested over Barbara's but that he pulled it away as he saw Cathy. She took a seat quietly at the back of the room while Barbara finished reading.

As Cathy's eyes roamed the room, she saw that the small magiboard above Frank's head had been defaced. It was a white oblong, that read 'Nurse looking after this shift'. Some days, when they remembered, one of the nurses would write a name in marker pen in the gap. But the 'f' in shift had been struck through. It now read 'Nurse looking after this shit'.

Cathy buried a smile. The nurses had to express themselves somehow and it assured her that Frank was getting back to his normal self.

Once Barbara had finished reading, Frank concentrated on Cathy.

'Have you spoken to Nick? He'll wonder why I'm not posting on the group.'

Cathy sat up straight.

'Er, no, I haven't. Not for a while.'

'You haven't checked my e-mail?' Frank struggled up in bed. 'Why not?'

Cathy blinked back.

'I wouldn't dream of going anywhere near your computer without your permission and anyway, I don't know your password.'

'My password's "Beefy",' Frank stated. 'It wouldn't take a rocket scientist to work that out, would it? Please turn on the computer, check my messages and tell Nick I am temporarily indisposed. He will tell the cricket group and they'll realise that I haven't been kidnapped. And besides which, you'll have to tell him that you can't make it to Headingley.'

Cathy had forgotten completely about the coming test match. Not that she had forgotten about Nick –

413

she'd often thought about him and wondered if she should call him, but she hadn't acted on it. Just as she'd often thought of calling Jason, but hadn't done so. It had all seemed too complicated. But she was startled to realise that the next test match was already upon them. Where had the time gone?

'Did you get me a ticket, then?' she asked.

'Of course. It's in the house. But you can't go to Headingley,' Frank emphasised. 'I need you here.'

'But – will you be able to follow what's going on? This is a crucial match.'

Frank pulled a strange face. If Cathy hadn't known him better she might have thought he was smiling. But if he was, it was very crooked.

'Crucial, is it, eh? And what would you care? Don't tell me you've got to like the stuffy old game after all?'

'It's not stuffy at all.' Cathy sat forward on her chair. 'I've grown to like it very much. Of course I'd love to go and watch the match. But I don't want to leave you, Frank. And I wouldn't go, even if you begged me to.'

'Well, there's no need to get hysterical,' Frank blustered. 'Nick's got his ticket and he should go. You tell him that from me. But he'll be wondering what's going on and you need to tell him you're not going. That's all there is to it.'

Barbara quietly folded the paper on her lap. Until Frank's hospitalisation the two women had never observed each other around Frank. But now a quiet understanding had developed between them. Cathy even thought that Barbara might be gratified to know that Frank was rude to Cathy too. Perhaps she'd thought that his granddaughter would get special treatment? It seemed, for the moment at least, that they were allies.

'When can I get out of this bloody place?' Frank exclaimed to the whitewashed ceiling.

'When they let you out.' Barbara calmly turned the paper over and read the back page.

'Catherine.' Frank fixed her with a glare. 'I need some answers from you. You know both Barry and Nick well, now. How would you have felt if they were your colleagues? Are they the sort of men you could have worked with?'

Cathy opened her mouth to answer, confused.

'Meaning – theoretically? I'm not with you.'

Frank threw himself back on the bed, jiggling his tubes around in the process. Cathy stared at the bleeping monitor in alarm.

'Why am I surrounded by difficult people? I ask simple questions, I get convoluted answers.' He glared at Barbara, then Cathy. 'To say you two have the brain of a plant between you would be an insult to dahlias.'

Cathy and Barbara exchanged silent glances, then Barbara stood up and laid the newspaper on the seat of her chair.

'I think it's time for a coffee break, don't you, Catherine?'

'Yes,' Cathy said.

They both left the room, leaving Frank glowering under his sea of sheets.

Cathy turned to Barbara as they walked in the direction of the canteen.

'What the hell was that all about?'

Barbara didn't answer immediately. Cathy had been

playing her hand very tentatively with Barbara, not rushing things, not being too friendly. At times Barbara seemed much at peace with Cathy's presence. At other times she seemed to want to flinch away from her. *Softly softly*, Cathy was constantly chanting to herself.

'I don't know,' Barbara said. 'But Frank likes to play God.'

Barbara's answer didn't help much. Cathy rewound her conversation with Frank, but she still couldn't make sense of it. Barbara went on:

'Has it occurred to you that Frank has a large estate?'

For a moment Cathy's confused brain could only picture Broadwater Farm. What did she mean, large estate?

'No. I'd never thought about it.'

'Royalties from his work, amassed income. A house worth a packet. Little things like that, perhaps? Not to mention the fact that he had family wealth long before he set out on a distinguished academic career,' Barbara said simply. Or was there an edge in her voice that was very well disguised?

'I – I don't see how that affects me, Barbara. It'd never even crossed my mind.'

'Well, perhaps it should.'

They reached the swing doors leading to the canteen. Cathy stopped and gave Barbara a puzzled look. Barbara's face revealed no emotion.

'Why?'

'Because Frank has never married,' Barbara explained with exaggerated patience. 'And in the absence of a spouse, you're his next of kin.'

*

Cathy decided to bite the bullet and phone Nick. The Headingley test match was upon them and she realised that he must have been wondering what they were going to do.

It felt odd, dialling Nick's mobile number. She wasn't sure how she was going to feel when she heard his voice again.

'Hello?' He sounded energetic, as ever.

'Nick, it's Cathy.'

His voice softened instantly.

'Oh. Cathy. I was wondering where you'd got to. How are you?'

It was surprisingly nice to hear him again. Cathy told Nick everything that had happened, going right back to when she'd got Barry's panicked call and shot up to Oxford in a taxi. It seemed like months ago, when in reality it was only a week and a half. In that time she hadn't heard from Nick. But she hadn't contacted him either. However, Nick needed to know what had been happening to Frank, so Cathy explained it all, Nick cutting in every so often with noises of dismay. Then, as she'd covered Frank's bypass operation and the fact that he was recovering, she felt she might be overwhelming Nick with detail, so she ground to a halt.

'I'm so sorry to hear all that.' Nick was genuinely concerned. 'You know, I think a lot of Frank. It's not just the love of cricket – he's been really supportive when I've moaned about my job. Please give him my very best regards. If there's anything I can do, anything at all, you just let me know.'

'Well, Frank says you must go to Headingley, even though I can't be there.'

'You can't?' Nick protested. He sounded very put out.

'I'm sorry, no. I can't leave him.'

'That's such a shame.' Nick paused. 'I don't suppose you could just slip away? Do you think he'd notice?'

'Nick!' Cathy was flattered, but at the same time her heart was here, in Oxford, with Frank. There was no question of sneaking off when he wasn't looking.

'I'm sorry. Forget I said that. I – I'm disappointed you can't make it, though. I was looking forward to it.'

'I know, Nick.' Cathy lowered her voice to be more intimate. 'It would have been fun. But I'm needed here.'

'I understand. Of course I do.'

'So—'

'So – what about your ticket?' Nick's voice gained more life. 'Did Frank buy you one?'

'Er, yes. He did, apparently. It's here, in the house somewhere.'

'Right.' Nick paused. 'I was just wondering, if you're not going to use your ticket and if you can't think of anyone else to hand it on to, you wouldn't send it to me, would you? It's just, I could go with Graham. He's going to be around this weekend and it'd be a shame for the seat to be empty. There's still time for it to get here in the post.'

'Oh. Yes. I could send it to you.'

'You've got my address?' Nick repeated it for Cathy and she jotted it down, complete with the post code.

'Yes, no reason why it shouldn't be used,' she said brightly.

'Well, hopefully I'll talk to you soon, Cathy. And thanks for letting me know about Frank. I'll tell the newsgroup. Everyone was wondering where he'd got to. And I hope you get to see some of the match anyway. Look out for two ugly blokes in the stands, won't you? I'll let you know how it goes. You take care of yourself.'

After Nick had rung off Cathy felt very odd. She walked round the house, frowning at Beefy. It was reasonable, she supposed, that Nick would want to go to the Headingley test match with somebody, rather than nobody. But somehow these test matches had been a bit special. She and Nick had been seated together at every one so far. Now he was going to go with someone else.

But it was a rational, if rather pragmatic request on Nick's behalf. She shouldn't feel so ruffled. All she had to do now was find the ticket.

Cathy sat herself at Frank's desk. It was solid, old and crowned with the incongruously modern computer. A low lamp cast an arc of pale light across the scuffed oak surface.

Barry had gone to the hospital to take Frank a portable television. With the Headingley test about to start, Frank was getting agitated. He was missing all the preamble, he'd complained, and he could only get Kylie Minogue on the hospital radio. Barry should be gone for a couple of hours, and for the moment Cathy was glad that she and Beefy had the house to themselves.

She'd promised Frank that she would download his e-mails and print them off for him to read. And she had to find the ticket.

Cathy switched on the computer and sipped her tea as it whined into action. She found her way into Frank's e-mail folder, typed in Frank's password and read through his messages. There was a smattering of junk mail, several cricket-focused e-mails. Two further messages appeared to be ongoing academic discussions about Anglo-Saxon inflections. They made as much sense to her as Nick's analysis of the bowling at Old Trafford.

And there was one from Nick. Cathy hovered over it as the modem clicked itself off. What if Nick had said something about her? It was like going through someone's trouser pockets. Uncomfortably, she clicked on the message.

'Frank,' she read. 'Thank you for Old Trafford. You must let me repay you somehow.'

Cathy heaved a sigh of relief as she slowly scrolled down. It was fine. Nothing personal. He was talking about the team, the play, giving details that Cathy hadn't been able to report back to Frank. What was an off-cutter, for heaven's sake? She got to the end.

'Kind regards, Nick. PS Thanks for introducing me to Cathy. How do you know when you're in love?'

'Oh, heck!'

Cathy got up and paced round. Where was Beefy? She needed someone to talk to about this. She found the cat playing with a frog in the kitchen. He didn't seem to be interested in eating it, but was batting it on the head softly with his paw to make it squeak.

'Beefy!'

Gingerly Cathy edged the frog into the empty washing-up bowl and threw a tea towel over the top to stop it hopping out again. Beefy sat on his hind legs and watched contentedly. Cathy tutted at him. It was just as well she had no phobias in that direction. If Beefy wanted to play 'fetch' with big spiders it would have been another matter.

Cathy twisted the key in the back door, let herself out and set off down into the garden with the frog thumping up and down under the tea towel. Beefy trotted beside her, all the way down to the river in the gloom of twilight. Cathy slipped the frog on to the river bank and Beefy followed her back up the lawn.

She stopped halfway up the garden and looked at the house. It was so peaceful. So beautiful. So *big*. With craggy eaves on either side and draped with Virginia creeper, which was now a luscious green but would no doubt be a stunning red in a couple of months, it really was a dream of a house. Lights winked from the windows, a warm glow coming from the living room where Cathy had been at the desk.

What memories must Barbara have of her time here with Frank? She could imagine them sitting out under the laburnum, sipping tea, perhaps, Frank carping about something that had provoked his intellect, Barbara fobbing him off. It was a romance, of sorts.

Romances, of sorts, seemed to be the reality of most people's lives. Look at Melissa and Brian – comfortable together and very happy, but never madly in love. And Frank's one passionate affair, with her grandmother, what had that been all about? Cathy had been in love with Jason and he with her, once. She could remember when she'd felt sick with excitement at the thought of seeing him. And in time, he'd confessed to feeling as nervous as a teenager every time he'd seen her. They'd never really seen the relationship develop.

But Nick had speculated that he was in love with *her*. What did he mean? What had they shared together? Lust? Passion? A chemical imbalance? A biological fire had certainly sprung up between them – but was that what being in love was all about? When Cathy thought of Nick, she remembered his smooth skin, his blue eyes, his gorgeous body, the way he lowered his voice when he laughed. It sent a tingle over her. But had she ever speculated that she might be in love with him? Should she have done?

Bemused, Cathy went back to the computer. She tried to push Nick's comment to the back of her mind and concentrate on what she'd been intending to do. She had to print off Frank's messages. There had to be a printer somewhere. It was tucked under the desk. She switched it on. The paper slid through the printer, the messages stacking themselves neatly in the tray.

'Right, then. Now, ticket,' Cathy muttered, standing up and looking around. Beefy yawned at her unhelpfully. 'Ticket?' she asked him. He gazed back, unwilling to do anything constructive, seeing as how Cathy had robbed him of his frog.

Cathy considered. The desk had several wide, deep drawers. She perched on the chair and yanked each one open in turn. The bottom drawer was the deepest. It was full of folders and letters. She rummaged through them. 'Aha! Got it, Beefy.'

Inside a flat envelope Cathy found the ticket to the match. Somewhat reluctantly she put it on the desk, ready to send to Nick. What if she had been intending to go to Headingley and had read Nick's e-mail before she saw him again? She'd found him very attractive anyway – even more attractive when Frank had hinted that Nick had confessed to liking her. How might she have felt to see him again, knowing that he'd speculated that he might even be in love with her? But it had been a very throwaway remark. He might have been drunk when he wrote it. Or he might have thought it in a moment of impulse and changed his mind later. Or he might have been feeling aroused and confused lust with being in love. 'Hmn.'

Cathy was about to close the desk drawer again, when the label on the top folder caught her eye. It was handwritten, in Frank's distinctive ink pen, looping and swirling. It read 'Catherine'.

Cathy stared at it.

It would be the simplest thing in the world to take the folder out, open it and look at everything that was inside. But it was private. It was none of her business. It would be like burglary. Except that the folder had her name on it and everything in it somehow had to be relevant to her.

She glanced over her shoulder at Beefy. He was washing his paws. Why was she looking at him? To get his permission? To check that he didn't have a microscopic camera lodged in one of his teeth that was recording her every move?

Cathy closed the drawer firmly. She drummed her fingers on her knees. She opened the drawer again. She was on her own. Nobody would ever, ever know she had seen it. She pulled the thick folder out, holding her breath, and laid it carefully on the desk top. Then she angled the lamp so that it shone directly on the centre of the desk like a spotlight. She opened the folder.

There was a wodge of letters; some large, buff envelopes; the edges of photographs; a mass of things. She slid the papers out so that they were under the light. The postmarks dated back for years. She saw photographs of herself as a baby, a child, an adolescent, a young woman. She recognised Melissa's neat handwriting from the envelopes and from the letters she could see.

So it was all true. Melissa had been updating Frank on her progress for years and years. And he had been keeping everything safely, in this folder, in his desk, next to him. Cathy was moved. He had cared, much more than she'd realised.

But what had Melissa told him? With crazed momentum Cathy scrambled her way through the letters. Where should she start? At the beginning. Her eyes darted hurriedly over the dates of the letters, shuffling them and finding her way back to the start of the story. Frank was methodical. They were kept in date order and it was easy for her to set about her job.

She began to read hungrily. At times she wanted to laugh, as Melissa reported something funny she'd said, or something stupid she'd done. At other times Melissa's affection for her shone through so powerfully that Cathy felt her eyes brimming. So much love for her adopted daughter. Melissa had never shown Cathy just how strong it was. But it had always been there.

'Melissa,' Cathy breathed.

Melissa had been keen to assure Frank that Cathy was like him. In her looks, her mannerisms, her temperament. Cathy read voraciously on, until she reached a very recent letter, dated some time in May of that year. She skimmed through it excitedly, then frowned. She read it through again.

She stood up and walked round Beefy, who had settled himself with his paws tucked under his body in the middle of the carpet. He served as a mini roundabout while Cathy wove circles round him. She read the paragraph that was confusing her aloud.

'If you wish to meet Cathy after all this time, you must allow me to put the idea to her first. But I think the truth would be too much for her to cope with at this point. I think that getting to know a grandfather will be challenging enough.'

Then Melissa had signed off.

Cathy let the hand holding the letter fall to her side and stood very still. The house seemed eerily silent. Then she turned back to the desk and quickly read the last few letters that Melissa had sent.

Nothing. No further reference to that cryptic comment. No acknowledgement of it. What Frank had written in return was anybody's guess.

What was Frank hiding from her that would be so difficult for her to cope with? What *was* the truth?

Cathy swept all the other letters to one side and concentrated again on Melissa's one paragraph. She stared and stared at the stark white paper and the neat black letters that Melissa had written. A chill swept over her body.

'Ah, there you are!'

'Argh!'

Cathy leapt at the sudden sound of a human voice. Barry, in the doorway, jumped in the air.

'My God!' he exclaimed. 'Don't do that.'

Cathy scooped up the letters and began to stuff them back into the folder.

'Everything all right?' Barry quizzed.

'What? Oh, yes. Fine. No, not fine. But I can't talk about it yet. I need to think.'

'Er, right. Well, I dumped the telly there for Frank and he's in good spirits, for him. We sat around pretending to be England selectors for a bit, but then I left him alone.' Barry paused. 'Are you sure you're all right?'

Cathy stared at Barry blankly. Someone, somewhere, was telling her something. But it was like trying to hear a whisper when you had wax earplugs in, a blanket over your head and were locked in a soundproof room.

Barry ran a hand through his soft hair. He peered at Cathy in bewilderment.

'Is there anything I can do, Cathy? You've gone white.'

'Oh my God,' Cathy breathed, realisation hitting her. She made for the door. Barry touched her arm and she looked him in the eye. 'There is something you can do, Barry. You can drive me to the hospital. Now.'

'Now?' Barry's eyebrows rose.

'Now.'

Cathy ran through the corridors. Barry chased after her, trying to catch her arm.

'Calm down,' he called, as sweetly as possible for someone who was out of breath.

'Calm's got bugger all to do with it,' Cathy yelled back.

They reached the entrance to the ward. Beyond, in a room just off to the right, Frank would be heaped up in his bed.

Cathy stopped in the corridor in front of the double doors. It was the second time she'd defaulted at this particular fence. Beyond the artificial barrier was something that she didn't want to know. She wasn't ready.

'Cathy!' Barry clutched her arm. 'I don't think you

should race in there like this. It won't be good for your blood pressure. And it certainly won't be good for Frank's. I don't know what's going on, but you really need to stop and take a breath.'

'Barry,' Cathy panted back at him. 'Please do me a huge favour. Please wait here for me until I come out again.'

'Of course.' Barry gave her a confused look. 'I'll be right here. On the bench. As soon as you need me.'

'Thank you, thank you so much.'

Feeling more alone than she ever had in her life, Cathy pushed her way into the ward. She stopped outside Frank's door. It was closed. She couldn't see much through the glass. She walked straight in.

Frank's body was hunched under the sheets. His eyes flickered open at the intrusion. Cathy strode to the bed and stared down at him angrily.

'Why did you lie to me?' she seethed.

Frank tried to pull himself up, but only managed to crawl an inch further up his pillows.

Cathy could see, by the guilt that dripped from his eyes, that she was right.

'You're *not* my grandfather. I want you to tell me exactly who you are, just as you should have done months ago.'

'You know who I am,' Frank said weakly.

'I want to hear it. From your own lips.'

'Catherine . . .'

'Say it!'

'I – I am your father,' Frank whispered.

Chapter Twenty-two

'A mortuary technician?' Cathy hurled the words at Frank. It was an odd thing to come out with at the moment your very own father had just confirmed his identity to you, but it was what arrived on her lips. 'Why did you say my father did *that*?'

'I . . .' Frank's face was like an iceberg. 'I've spent my life around dead things. Analysing them. Preserving them. It seemed . . . apt.'

'But all that crap you gave me about buying my mother a car and her going off in it and never seeing her again? Why did you tell me that?'

'That was true.' Frank fixed his eyes on his sheets.

'Just tell me. What happened. The truth.'

Frank's head fell back against his pillows. He took a long, audible breath.

'I hadn't known your mother was . . . expecting you,' Frank said raggedly. 'You were born very prematurely. Your mother was ill in hospital for a while, then released, while you stayed in an incubator. She drove to see me. It was a car I'd bought for her when – when we'd been together.'

Frank stopped. His eyes filled with tears. Cathy hardened her heart. She stood motionless, waiting for him to continue.

'We – we argued.' His voice was a whisper. His eyes wandered, as if he were reliving the experience. 'I said

I couldn't cope with a child. I hadn't known. It was a shock. I needed time to adjust. She drove away in anger. She had an accident.'

Frank's jaw trembled.

'I see,' Cathy murmured.

The room had become completely silent, apart from the hum of the air-conditioning and the soft bleeping of Frank's machinery.

'You were left,' Frank croaked. 'Helpless, plugged into machines, alone.'

'And . . .' She could hardly hear her own voice.

'And I knew I had nothing to offer you. Not on my own. Not me being – me. So you – you were adopted.'

A hot tear squeezed from the corner of Cathy's eye. She let it run down her face.

'But I visited you. Often. In your little incubator. And one day when I was there I met Melissa Gordon.'

'Yes.' Cathy fought with the pain in her chest. Her heart felt as if it wanted to explode.

'And' – Frank appealed to Cathy with weak, wet eyes – 'when they took you away, something died inside me. Again.'

Compassion stirred in Cathy's soul, but her blood was still warm with anger. There were so many things she wanted to know. Too many things. As a result, her mind crashed like a computer and she was left with a blank screen.

'I'll talk to you again when I'm ready,' she said.

'Catherine?' Frank's anxious voice apprehended her. 'I want you to know. You are as beautiful as your mother was.'

Cathy swallowed. 'What was her name?'

Frank's shoulders heaved.

'Annette.'

Cathy stared at Frank, too numb to speak. Then she left the room and closed the door quietly behind her.

Barry drove Cathy home. She sat as motionless as a statue, gazing ahead at the road. She was aware that Barry was glancing at her all the time and that he was worried, but for a while she couldn't tell him anything at all.

Once they were inside the house, he produced his bottle of brandy again. Cathy drifted through into the living room – Frank's room – and settled on the sofa. She took the glass that Barry offered. He perched himself on the cushions next to her and took her hand.

'Whenever you're ready, Cathy.'

She sipped the brandy.

'It's simple, really,' she said at last, the words tumbling out. 'Frank isn't my grandfather after all. He's my father.'

Barry's stunned silence gave Cathy more time to think. She went to the desk and retrieved the folder of papers she'd left there. She took them back to the sofa and sat with them cradled on her lap. Here she held everything that her own father had ever known about her, until she'd turned up at his house and he'd met her properly for the first time.

So Frank had respected Melissa's wish not to startle Cathy with any dramatic revelations. But had it suited him to be known as her grandfather? Perhaps he hadn't been ready to acknowledge his closeness to his own daughter? He would have been obliged to tell her the painful story he'd stuttered out to her when she confronted him tonight, off his guard, tired, ill and alarmed, in his hospital room. The truth was that he'd let her mother – Annette – down. And she'd stormed away, and died in an accident that same night.

No wonder he'd been trying to distance himself from it. And no wonder he'd been such a troubled man. He'd turned his back on his lover and then turned his back on their daughter. He'd had many years to be troubled by it.

But the image haunted Cathy, of herself as a tiny baby, encased in an incubator, Frank standing somewhere, out of reach, watching. How must Frank have felt, to see his own daughter helpless and vulnerable, wired up to machines, her life in the hands of the hospital staff? Was it much how Cathy had felt to see Frank, small and frail, his life dependent on the technology that surrounded him?

She rubbed her hands over her face. The tears had receded. She was too dazed.

'Well, bugger me sideways,' Barry said, after a considerable lapse of time.

The doorbell chimed. Cathy's eyes glazed over. She looked at Barry.

'I'll deal with that.' He got up straight away. 'You sit tight.'

While Barry was busy in the hall, Cathy looked around the room. At the lofty bookcases edging the walls. The books crammed into every available space, some with hard covers, others with cracked, faded spines. At the heavy lamps, the faded rugs, the solid chairs. The television that brought Frank cricket. The computer where he'd spewed out ideas. All the details of the room – her father's room.

From the hall she could hear low, male voices, but

they washed over her. Until the living-room door opened and she looked up again to smile at Barry. Except it wasn't Barry's face that was peering down at her.

It was Jason's.

'Oh!' Cathy shot to her feet, her heart leaping. The folder of cuttings and letters slid on to the sofa. 'Oh my God! Jason!' She burst into tears. 'Oh my God! It's you!'

He looked unkempt. His black hair was a mess, his eyes dark and tired, and he was wearing a suit, the tie loosened. He crossed the room in three bounds and grabbed Cathy in a bear hug.

'You're here.' Cathy let the words tumble out, sniffing her emotional outburst away. The force of it had surprised her. Jason brushed a tear from her face with his finger and devoured her with his gaze. She found herself laughing, as suddenly as she'd cried. 'It really is you. Here. What the hell are you doing here?'

'Cathy.' He drew her to him and held her tightly. 'I flew back as soon as Melissa told me about Frank's heart attack. I'm so sorry I haven't been here to help you through this.'

'Melissa told you?' Cathy pulled away to study Jason's face. 'Why? What's been going on?'

'She left a message at work and finally they got it through to me. I was in Brussels this week, but as soon as I heard the news I wriggled out of the meetings and got a flight back. I've driven straight up from Heathrow.' Then his expression clouded. 'I hope you don't mind.'

'Mind?' Cathy half laughed and half cried. She was so overwhelmed with relief, joy and excitement to see him that she didn't know which to do first. 'Why would I mind? I just can't believe it.'

Jason looked as if a weight had been lifted from him.

'I tried to ring you, but I couldn't get through. Melissa had given me this address, so all I could do was turn up and hope it wouldn't be an intrusion. I just want to help, if I can.'

Cathy closed her eyes and buried her head against Jason's chest. The sight of him, the smell of him, the feel of him, the sound of him were so welcome to her heart that she couldn't find the words to express it.

'Jason, you – you have no idea how glad I am to see you.'

'Is Frank all right?' Jason took Cathy's hand and squeezed it. 'Barry said out in the hall that you'd had a shock this evening, but that you'd want to tell me yourself. Is he out of danger yet?'

'Oh, Jason.' Cathy sighed. 'Frank's out of danger for now, but there's so much else.'

Jason held Cathy's eyes with his. In the mahogany depths she could see just how much he cared. He looked as if he might kiss her, but then gently ruffled her hair instead.

'You can tell me all about it.'

'And Barry.' Cathy gathered herself and looked around for him. 'You've met him now? He's been so wonderful. Where did he go?'

'He said there was a documentary on breasts on Channel 4 which he just couldn't miss and that he'd be in his room.' Jason gave Cathy a gentle smile. 'I think it was a timely exit to allow you to talk to me. But he said we could drink the brandy if we needed to.'

'In which case', Cathy said, 'we'd better get comfortable on the sofa. I've got a hell of a lot to tell you.'

*

'Well, you are a sight for sore eyes,' Barbara under-stated deftly.

Frank's eyes were red-rimmed, his skin pale and drawn. He'd been wiping at his face with a hand-kerchief as Barbara had walked in.

Barbara hadn't been intending to drop in again so late, but she'd found a copy of *The Cricketer* with an interesting article in it and she'd thought just to slip it on his bedside table if he was sleeping, and say a quiet goodnight if he was awake.

But she hadn't expected to see Frank lying in his bed *crying*. Barbara wasn't sure that she had ever seen Frank in tears. The shock of it had prompted the harsh observation.

Frank screwed up his face in frustration. Annoyance apparently won over sorrow.

'Doesn't anybody know how to *knock* in this place?'

'So what's the matter?' Barbara barked out the question. The truth was she was deeply unnerved. Frank's anger was a sign of his defiance. To see him collapsed and weeping whispered of resignation – something she dreaded with all of her heart. She clutched *The Cricketer* to her side.

'Catherine was here. She knows the truth,' Frank announced with a tremor in his voice.

Barbara raised both eyebrows. The information sank in. A distant feeling of neglect needled at her, until it was prominent.

'Does she, indeed? So your little joke about mortuary technicians didn't make her laugh after all?'

'She was very angry,' Frank muttered.

'Was she?' Barbara bit her tongue as she could have said more.

Frank stared at Barbara, perplexed.

'Is that all you can say?'

'What on earth do you expect me to say? Frank, I'm so sorry for you?' Barbara took a breath, her eyes narrowing. 'Or did you want sympathy for the fact that you once had a love affair that you've taken out on everybody else ever since?'

'Don't talk about Annette to me. Ever,' Frank ejected strongly.

'Oh, God, why not?' Sarcasm came to Barbara's aid. 'Because I actually knew her? Because I'd burst the bubble of your fantasy? Because she's been dead for twenty-eight years but we're not permitted to talk about her just in case we might all be allowed to bury the past and move on? What is your reasoning exactly?'

Frank crawled up his pillows, his face white. He struggled for words, then said, 'Why is everyone having a go at me tonight?'

'Maybe because you deserve it?' A rush of heat swamped Barbara's body.

Frank stared back, his eyes like Venn Diagrams. 'Anybody else about to fly in and get me all worked up, I wonder? Jeremy Paxman? David Starkey? I'm sure my blood pressure could go up a few more notches. Let's go for the world record and be damned.'

'Oh, shut up, you selfish man!' Barbara snapped.

She marched across the room and slapped his cricket magazine on his bedside table for him. Frank stared at Barbara's outburst in amazement.

'Yes, you might well look surprised,' Barbara seethed. 'I've had enough. Of you, of this, of being taken for granted. Walking in here and finding you weeping over the memory of *her* is just the final straw.'

'Look, now hang on,' Frank said faintly.

'No, you look. You think you are the centre of every-thing. You love the idea that we all revolve around you and your stupid, childish tantrums. You lost Annette because you were a self-centred egomaniac and you've been nursing your poor little wounds ever since. It really is about time', she finished, looking at the shocked, wizened face, 'that you grew up.'

'I – I had a dream of love,' Frank spluttered. It was odd hearing the word 'love' coming from his dry lips.

Barbara's nostrils flared.

'You had a dream? Who do you think you are? Martin Luther King? You're a bad-tempered little old man. Come to terms with it.'

'Barbara!' Frank shrank back into his sheets.

'What?' she bit back at him. She was already on her way to the door.

'Barbara, don't go. Don't leave me. We have to talk.'

Barbara swivelled at the door.

'About what? You? Your feelings? Your sensitivities? Your ego? We've been talking about nothing else for the last thirty years. I think we could say that the subject has been done to death, don't you?'

She twisted the door handle roughly.

'No – about you – about us.' Frank's voice was strange. It was high-pitched, almost like a woman's, and he sounded as if he were choking on a fishbone.

Barbara flashed him a quick look to make sure he wasn't dying on the spot.

'You'll be fine, Frank. You always are. You don't need me.'

'Barbara!'

'Frank, just – piss off.'

Barbara threw herself at the double doors, out into the corridor and marched quickly away. She needed to get home and be on her own, as fast as possible.

'I can't believe what you've been going through,' Jason said, kissing the tips of Cathy's fingers. 'And your job too. So many profound changes in your life.'

'I can't really believe it myself.'

Cny was lying comfortably on Jason. They were on the sofa, her head in his lap, and it was nearing three o'clock in the morning. She'd talked for hours and Jason had listened. Now she was tired, but soothed by the warmth of his body, his hand gently stroking her hair and the knowledge that he was with her.

'I've been so neglectful,' Jason said softly. 'And I've been selfish. You told me I was never there for you and you were dead right. I've only come to realise how true that was over the last couple of weeks. When Melissa told me about Frank's heart attack it hit me very hard. Even if you'd tried to get hold of me, I'd have been away.'

'Don't be hard on yourself, Jace.' Cathy took his hand. 'I haven't been very sympathetic about your trips away, or your long hours. And we haven't exactly been an item recently, have we?'

'That's another thing.' Jason leant forward and retrieved his brandy glass. He took a sip. 'I read that situation all wrong. You and Nick. I thought it was just a fling.'

Cathy stiffened. It was very strange to hear Jason talking about her liaison with Nick so calmly. She wasn't sure that she felt so calm about him herself. But there was no point in denying that she'd slept with Nick. Not when Jason seemed to be sure of it himself.

'Well, I suppose we've both had little flings. For whatever reason,' she said quietly.

'Yes.' Jason sat back against the cushions and gazed into space.

So Jason had also been physical with Candida. As Cathy had thought. Momentarily, it needled at her. She sat up straight and considered Jason's profile. But he looked very peaceful and she realised that she had no right whatsoever to be upset.

'The thing is,' Jason continued, 'I thought your affair with Nick was a phase. Compensating for me being away so much. Even punishing me for it. But it wasn't that at all.'

'It wasn't?' Cathy was curious to hear Jason's reasoning.

He shook his head. 'No. It was because you were changing. But I was too short-sighted to realise it.'

'Do you think so?' Had she been changing? Perhaps she had. But she'd been too involved in the process to notice.

'Ever since Frank arrived on the scene your outlook on things, everything about you, has been on the move. And that Nick bloke – well, I guess he's been a part of that too. I could see he was nothing like me. I don't know – of course – what he had to offer you. But I was standing still, carrying on as if nothing had happened, thinking you'd get over it. And all the time, you were moving on.'

Cathy noted that Jason was talking about Nick in the past tense. Did he assume that her 'affair', as he put it, with Nick was over, then? Was it over?

438

'And your job.' Jason shook his head, smiling to himself. 'I'm not actually surprised that you've resigned, that's the funny thing. I was half expecting you to do it.'

'Really? Good God, I wish you'd have warned me, then. It took me completely by surprise.'

'That's the whole point.' Jason studied her face intently. Cathy was stirred. He had that 'Italian' look about him again, the one she'd noticed when they first met. 'You were never particularly impulsive. You used to act on reason rather than emotion. But it's as if your true character's coming out now. Nothing you do could surprise me any more.'

Cathy laughed under her breath.

'Well, you surprised me tonight. You were the last person I'd expected to tip up at my grandfather's house.' She sat up with a jolt. 'My God, I mean, my *father*'s house.'

She fell silent, her brain flooded with thoughts again.

'Let's get you to bed, young lady. You're going to have a lot to deal with in the next few days. You need your sleep.'

Cathy nodded. At last she felt tired enough to shut down her brain for the night.

'And Jason?' she asked uncertainly. 'How long are you going to be here?'

Jason looked rueful. 'I'm not surprised you're expecting me to dash away again, given my track record. But I've got them to cover for me for the next two days, so I'm taking those as leave. Then it's the weekend and I can work it out from there. I'm here for as long as you need me. Is that all right?'

His long black lashes flickered unsteadily as he assessed her reaction.

439

When Cathy was a little girl, Melissa used to put her to bed. She'd stroke her forehead and say, 'God's in his heaven and all is right with the world.' Cathy hadn't experienced that feeling of deep contentment for many years. The world had interposed and reality had shaken her security. But she felt it now. Jason was beside her and all was right with the world. She reached out for him. 'Yes. That's all right,' she said softly.

Nick was feeling upbeat.

There was only one thing better than England wiping the floor with the opposition and that was a really close, tense match. Headingley was turning out to be a stormer.

It was a glorious Saturday. The sun blazed over Leeds and Nick had driven up early to make sure they were there on time. Now he was settled in his seat, the heat intensifying on his face as the sun crept higher in the clear sky, his Test Match Special hat perched on his head, so that he could plug an earphone into his ear and catch up on the commentary at any crucial point in the game.

And next to him was not Graham, as he'd planned, but Hannah.

Nick had had every intention of taking Graham to Headingley with him. The ticket had arrived from Cathy on Friday and he was all set up. As much as he regretted Cathy not being able to make it, Nick had been looking forward to a boys' day out. He and Graham always jogged along well and they made each other laugh.

Then Graham had pulled out on Friday evening,

called away to some family gathering that he couldn't get out of. That left Nick with a spare ticket, the prospect of a long drive to Leeds and a day out at an exciting match with an empty seat beside him. Lost for ideas, Nick had called several of his friends and tried to entice them along, but they'd already got plans for the weekend. That was when the thought had occurred to him.

Hannah had been light-hearted when they'd talked on the phone, not heavy at all, and she hadn't even hinted that they should meet up. She'd just been touching base, she'd said, so they'd bantered instead about all sorts of things and Nick had hung up feeling good about it. Maybe he'd call her again, maybe he wouldn't.

But as he was left with a spare ticket and nobody to take to the test match, he'd found himself thinking that Hannah would be good company. There was no reason to be worried that she might read too much into it. She seemed too easygoing for that. So he'd rung her, explained that Graham had left him in the lurch and asked her along. She didn't complain about not being his first choice – she merely laughed and said she didn't know anything about cricket at all, but if he wanted a complete ignoramus sitting next to him she was up for it.

Nick had picked Hannah up from her house early in the morning. She'd danced out, in a light cotton dress and sandals, her hair soft and smelling of apple shampoo, and climbed into the passenger seat of his Toyota. He'd wondered if she'd exclaim on his sports car, and be impressed – but she wasn't at all. She'd chosen a CD from his stack that she particularly liked, and throughout the journey they'd chatted easily about life, work, Birmingham and cricket.

Now they were seated together in the stand, soaking up the sun, sipping from polystyrene cups full of tea and Nick was enjoying himself.

England were bowling. Caddick was on fine form, although Gough wasn't his usual dynamic self. The pitch was hard, dry and baked by the sun. There were cracks in the crease that Nick hoped the spin bowlers might make good use of later in the day. Greg Blewett was settling himself in with the bat and there had been a few close edges. One dropped catch in the slips early in the day had ensured the crowd remained on edge and there was a lively buzz round the ground.

A magnificent catch at square leg from Hussain had brought them all to life only minutes earlier. Nick had found himself explaining some background to Hannah, so that she understood the significance. And it had struck him: here he was again, with a woman for company, outlining the laws of the game – something he'd never have pictured himself doing several months ago. He'd even found himself comparing Hannah's reactions with Cathy's.

Hannah was less ascerbic than Cathy and Nick was missing Cathy's sharp asides. But she was very relaxed and was proving to be good fun to be with. She often laughed, made a few jokes of her own and seemed to find everything that Nick explained interesting. She seemed more haphazard in the way she talked about her life, what she'd done and what she might do next. More like Nick was himself, in fact. And Nick had found out some curious facts about her. For example, when he'd told her that the England captain was born in Madras, her response had surprised him. 'Intriguing place. So busy, so colourful. I had a smashing time there,' she'd said.

'You've been to India?'

'Sure. Did a trip round the world a few years ago. I'd dropped out of the academic scene to be a hippy, so while all my friends went off to university I travelled instead. It was great.'

'On your own?' Nick had quizzed.

'Sometimes. Other times I met up with people I knew who were travelling. We had a three-week-long party in Thailand and at one point I stayed with a cousin who was working on a sheep farm in Oz.'

'You've been to Australia too?'

'Yep.' She'd grinned at him impishly. 'Why? Did you think I was a stay-at-home girl with a boring job who'd be impressed by your fast car?'

'God, no.' Nick had run his hand over his hair, wondering if he had actually assumed some of those things. 'I've never been to Oz. Keep meaning to go down there for the return Ashes matches, but I've never got my act together to do it.'

'You should,' she'd said simply.

At lunchtime they wandered around the concourse and found a hot-dog stand. By this point they were chatting very comfortably and Nick wasn't even embarrassed when he ended up with a strand of onion dangling from his chin. Hannah laughed and mopped at it with her paper napkin. Then, later in the afternoon, Hannah shot off to find the Ladies during a bowling change and came back with two frothy plastic cups of lager.

'I know you're driving,' she said, handing him one.

'But it's a scorcher today and you must be working up a thirst. Hours to go before we have to hit the road.'

Nick glanced at her. She really was quite pretty. Not in the same way as Cathy at all. Hannah had nothing of Cathy's colouring, or verve about her, but she was feminine in an understated way. Her eyes were wide and gentle, and often alive with humour. They lacked the fiercely intense blue of Cathy's. Which was probably why he didn't sense the powerful stirring of sexual chemistry which he felt around Cathy. But he found himself thinking he could get to like Hannah.

The afternoon wore on, England's bowlers working their hearts out in the dusty heat to strive for wickets. Nick bought himself and Hannah another cold lager, and they drank them leisurely. Blewett and Waugh had formed a strong partnership and stuck to their guns, firing fours off to the boundary. Then, suddenly, there was a breakthrough.

Craig White, one of England's fast bowlers, trapped Blewett leg before wicket and the crowd erupted. From there on Australia began to crumble.

'This is great fun.' Hannah smiled, as another wicket tumbled to a diving catch from Thorpe in the slips and Union Jacks were hoisted aloft all around them.

'It puts the match right back in the balance again,' Nick enthused. 'If Blewett and Waugh had carried on for much longer, we'd have been out of the picture.'

'So what does this mean, then?' Hannah peered at Nick over her lager.

'It means we have a game on our hands. One that we stand a damned fine chance of winning if we use our heads.' Nick grinned. 'As long as our batsmen do their bit when they come out to bat again.'

'And if they don't?' Hannah asked.

'It's only Saturday. They've got all day Sunday and even Monday to bat if necessary. All they have to do is take their time.' The thought made Nick feel tense. 'That's all they have to do. Not rush things. It's not much to ask when the Ashes are at stake.'

'You care a lot about this, don't you?' Hannah said. She was studying Nick's face with open curiosity.

'I've loved this game since I was a little boy. I knew all the statistics of all the matches off by heart. I could have told you the batting or bowling average of any England player you could name. I don't have time to absorb so many stats these days, but I get more emotional about it now than I did when I was a kid. And that's saying something.'

She smiled at him.

'It's nice to be passionate about something. It shows you've got a big heart.'

Surprised by the casual compliment, Nick looked straight into Hannah's eyes. There was a muted light in the tawny depths, of something: perhaps admiration, perhaps liking. Perhaps it was even attraction. In return, he felt a pulse in his groin.

'Come here,' he muttered and, pushing his hand gently into her mass of soft hair, he lowered his lips to hers and brushed a kiss there. He pulled away again. Hannah's eyelashes fluttered unsteadily. He'd obviously taken her by surprise. But he'd taken himself by surprise too. And the odd thing was, of all the sensations that were mingling in his body at that moment the most prominent one was guilt. He'd kissed another woman, yet recently he'd been totally preoccupied with thoughts of Cathy. Daily, nightly, enough to mention in an e-mail to Frank that he might be in love with her. It should really have been Cathy sitting right there beside him.

Nick pulled himself back in his seat, feeling awkward. He shouldn't have kissed Hannah. That was an impulsive gesture. It was probably a mistake.

'Thanks,' Hannah said, with a light laugh. 'You didn't have to do that, but I liked it. Now, let's concentrate on the match, shall we?'

Chapter Twenty-three

Cathy waited until Sunday morning to visit Frank again. She knew that he would be obsessed with the action from Headingley, even if his brain was still churning, as was hers, with the aftershocks of their showdown. Cathy wanted Frank's full attention when she saw him. But she also needed time on her own to think.

Barry brought back news of Frank's progress from the hospital on a daily basis, which confirmed Cathy's predictions. He was making progress, but he was glued to the portable television. Although Cathy had very important business to do with Frank, she knew how much this Ashes series meant to him and how key this test match was to the outcome of the series. In a funny kind of way she was beginning to understand him.

She'd stayed up at the house in Oxford, though, reluctant to leave it. Every so often she'd wander around it, running her hands over a table, or fingering a book, gazing at the majestic garden, sliding around the wooden floor on the rugs, absorbing the evidence of Frank's life. Everything around her told a tale of his personality and she drank in every detail.

Jason had stayed in the house with her. Somehow they both managed to cram into the old single bed. There was no question of Jason sleeping anywhere else. On the night that he had arrived, when they'd found

447

their way to bed as dawn was breaking, they'd been aroused by the closeness of each other's bodies, much as they used to be, and had made love. It had been a wonderful experience. Slow, sensual and breathtaking. Their bodies had fitted together like two pieces of a puzzle. It wasn't the violent passion Cathy had experienced with Nick, but it was in every way more tantalising and erotic.

And the atmosphere in the house since Jason had turned up was excellent. Barry and Jason had taken to each other easily. Barry was delighted to have someone staying who could actually cook and Jason had been entertaining them with some of his most successful recipes. They'd spent several evenings chatting and drinking wine as a threesome. Cathy was intrigued to observe the banter that flowed between Jason and Barry, and she was relieved that Barry didn't feel like a gooseberry. She already felt that he was a special friend – even an unexpected addition to her small family – and she sensed that he felt the same.

But now Cathy wanted to go back to her London house. There were things she was putting off, important things to do with her career, and she needed to go home to give them her full concentration. She was also feeling a strong pull to return to her own surroundings and an environment where everything was familiar. It would help her to balance her old identity with her new one.

So, on Sunday morning, she went with Jason to the hospital. She had to tell Frank that she was leaving for a short while and there were a few things they needed to say to each other.

Frank seemed astonished to see Cathy walk in. He

pulled himself up on his pillows, his eyes widening. Behind Cathy, Jason entered.

'Frank, I want you to meet Jason. Jason, this is my father.'

Frank put out a thin hand. Cathy's stomach curled to see how small it looked in comparison to Jason's sturdy, tanned hand which he extended too. The two men shook hands over the sheets.

'I – I've heard a fair bit about you,' Frank said, then clamped his mouth shut. He peered at Cathy uncertainly. It was as if he expected to be lambasted at any moment. Or perhaps he wondered if Jason had been recruited to punch him on the nose.

'And I've heard a fair bit about you too,' Jason replied with good humour, allowing Frank's arm to drape back on his blankets.

'As you know,' Cathy went on briskly by way of explanation, 'Jason's been my boyfriend for four years. He's important to me. And you're important to me too. So it made sense that you should meet each other.'

Frank nodded obediently. He seemed incredibly docile today. Had they put him on tranquilisers? Or could it be that he'd found their confrontation of a few days ago sobering? Something had changed in him.

'I'll just nip off and see if I can get us both some coffee, Cathy.' Jason nodded at Frank and made for the door, leaving father and daughter alone.

Frank stared at the door as it swung shut.

'Diplomatic, isn't he?' He rolled his head on the pillow so that he could look at Cathy properly. 'Your Jason is a nice man. I shouldn't have been so rude about him. Handsome too. You've obviously got substantial pulling power.'

449

Cathy sifted the comment through for sarcasm, but there wasn't any. Frank looked surprisingly unsure of himself.

'I told you. You shouldn't have made assumptions. We're good together.'

'I didn't think I'd ever see you again,' Frank said.

Cathy knew that wasn't true, as Barry had specifically told Frank on her behalf that she was taking time to think, but would visit him when she was ready. But perhaps Frank was voicing a fear. She was touched by it.

'We have a lot to talk about, Frank, but you're still fragile and so am I. When we're both stronger we'll get together again and do things properly.'

'Are you leaving Oxford?' Frank looked agitated.

'I have to go back to London just for a few days,' Cathy told him gently.

Then her veneer of brusqueness gave way to affection. She pulled up a chair and sat down, leaning her elbows on the edge of the bed. Tentatively she put out a hand to Frank's. He let her touch him and his fingers twitched. He turned his head to gaze at her. She assessed him. He was quieter than she'd ever seen him.

'I need to sort out some work issues, collect my post, that sort of thing. But I'll be back again soon.'

'You will come back, though,' Frank asserted, his eyebrows knitting anxiously. 'Won't you?'

'Frank, you can be sure I'll be back before you've even noticed I'm gone. I'm not letting you go now.'

'Your mother,' Frank blurted. 'You wanted to know what she was like. She looked just like you. Red hair and blazing eyes. You should know that. She was a beauty.'

'Thank you,' Cathy breathed at him.

'I couldn't let her go. For a long, long time. If you'd met her you'd understand why. I had no say in the matter. She was enchanting.'

Cathy was stirred. Her mother was enchanting. Her father was a respected man. In her dreams she'd woven such a fairy tale. She'd just omitted the fact that they were both loose cannons who apparently caused chaos wherever they went.

'But she's very dead. Yes, very, very dead. And we all have to move on.' Frank let out a harrowed sigh. 'I've been preserving the dead for far too long. Now it's time to live.'

'I'm – I'm very pleased to hear you say that.'

'Have you seen Barbara?' Frank croaked hoarsely.

Cathy shook her head. 'Not for a couple of days. Have you?'

'No.' Frank's head drooped.

'You haven't scared her off again, have you?' Cathy tried to joke.

Frank closed his eyes. He put one hand over his face. He looked as if he was trying not to cry.

'I've been an idiot,' he gasped. 'Such an idiot.'

Cathy took his fingers and laid them in her palm. She stroked his hand carefully, flinching at the feel of the huge needle threaded into the skinny hand. This had all been horribly frightening for Frank. Never mind how stressed she'd been, he was obviously completely overwhelmed.

'There's nothing that can't be put right,' Cathy soothed. Then, wondering if she was overstepping the mark, went on, 'Barbara loves you very much.'

'I know,' Frank's voice came out as a whisper.

451

Cathy shuffled closer. There were tears dribbling down his waxy skin. She put out a finger and delicately wiped them away.

'You love her too, don't you?' she coaxed.

There was a long silence, then Frank heaved a sob.

'Yes.'

Cathy's smile spread. Frank, with his hand smothering his eyes, couldn't see it.

'Well.' She took a big breath. 'I think perhaps you should tell her.'

'I don't think I'm going to get the chance. She's left me.'

'Again?' Hopefully Frank could cope with a bit of teasing.

'Yes. I haven't seen her for several days. She came here, just after you'd left, the other night. She told me to piss off. Can you believe it? Barbara? Using language like that?'

Cathy thought about it.

'She's probably felt a lot better since then.'

'Do you think so?' Frank uncovered his eyes. 'I've been so cruel to Barbara. I wouldn't blame her for holding a party on my grave.'

'I don't think parties are Barbara's style. I'll bet she's just taking a couple of days to cool off and she'll be in to see you.'

'Yes. She'll be in to see me just so that she can tell me to piss off again.' Frank's eyes rounded in alarm.

'If she does tell you to piss off again, you'll just have to put up with it,' Cathy reasoned. 'You deserve a lot worse from her and you know it.'

Frank accepted this without complaint.

'Catherine.' He wriggled himself into a sitting

position. 'What do you think I should do? About Barbara? I mean, what do you really think?'

Cathy hesitated.

'I think you know the answer to that yourself.'

Nick had found the John Radcliffe without any trouble. He'd cannoned down the M40 and from there he'd followed signs to the suburb and to the hospital.

He was feeling energised today. Yesterday had been a superb break from the routine and Hannah had been terrific company, right up until the moment when he'd dropped her off at her house, late at night. There hadn't been any awkwardness, or any expectation of another impulsive kiss. In fact, Nick could almost convince himself that she'd forgotten about the kiss completely. So, feeling relieved and in good humour, Nick had taken himself home, slept like a baby and got up early so that he could drive down to visit Frank before the match started again.

He strode into the building, a bunch of flowers and a souvenir T-shirt from Headingley in his grasp. He found an enquiry desk and before long had directions to the ward that Frank was in.

As he made his way down the corridor, Nick admonished himself for not visiting Frank before. He'd sent a card, but given the esteem he held Frank in and the fact that he'd been given free tickets to every Ashes test match so far that year, he should really have visited. He'd just been uncertain of his right to be there and unsure of how it would feel to meet Cathy over the cardiograms. And the fact remained, also, that as much as he felt that he and Frank knew each other well over the Internet, they'd never actually met before. He hadn't been sure that Frank would have wanted Nick's first impression to be of him ill in hospital.

But Nick was sure now that a personal visit was the right action. Apart from anything, Frank would need an eyewitness report of Saturday's play before the teams got stuck in again today. Nick would provide that.

Feeling chirpy, Nick turned towards the intensive care ward, pushed through two swinging double doors and found a nurse. He asked which bed Frank Harland was in and she nodded back down the ward.

'In that little room off to the side, down there, to your left.'

'Lovely.' He grinned at her. 'Thank you.'

He reached the door to the side room and pushed it open. He was inside before he'd had a chance to stop and think about whether anybody else might be there. He halted in his tracks, just inside the door, his bunch of flowers clutched to his chest.

Cathy was leaning over the bed, pulling on a jacket at the same time as she kissed the old man on the cheek – the old man who was obviously Frank. Seeing her again gave Nick a jolt. She was lovely. He kicked himself for even thinking about flirting with Hannah.

But then Nick realised there was another visitor in the room. A slim, swarthy, good-looking man whom he recognised. He was standing at the back of the room, draining a cup of coffee. Then he turned and met Nick's eye. It was Jason.

Nick froze. Cathy hadn't seen him enter. She still had her back to him. Frank was obscured by Cathy, so he hadn't seen Nick either. So far, only Jason's dark eyes were probing him.

Then Cathy turned to face Jason and Nick could see her face. As she looked at her boyfriend her eyes softened. It was a look of such depth, of such love, that Nick felt awed by it.

'We'd better be on our way now, Jace,' she said.

Nick began to back out of the room. But Jason had glanced back at him, and now Cathy had turned round too and seen him. Momentarily, her face paled. But it was Jason who stepped in.

'Come on, then, Cathy. Frank's got another visitor and I'm sure they've got lots to talk about.'

'Nick,' she said.

'Hello, Cathy,' he replied.

There was a pause in which nobody spoke. But then Cathy swung round to Frank. If she was at all flustered to see him, Nick thought she disguised it admirably.

'Frank? This is Nick. He'll be able to give you the lowdown from Headingley. No doubt you two have got a load to talk about, so we'll slip away.'

'Nick?' Frank struggled up in bed. 'Are you Nick? Well come in, man. Sit yourself down. I need your opinion on Blewett's LBW. Martin-Jenkins is saying he thought it was too high and we were lucky to get away with it. What did you think?'

Nick chuckled, but glanced at Cathy uneasily. She picked up her bag, slung it over her shoulder and moved towards the door. Nick stood aside to let her and Jason pass.

'I'll see you soon, Frank,' Cathy called. As they both walked past, Jason with his eyes fixed ahead, Cathy gave Nick a warm smile and touched his arm. 'Take care of yourself, won't you?'

'And you,' Nick said quietly.

Then the door swung and they'd both gone, leaving Nick alone with Frank. He stood dazed for a moment, wondering what to think.

The way that Cathy had looked at Jason said it all. Even if Nick and Cathy had explored a relationship, would she have ever looked at him in that way? She loved Jason. That was probably all there was to it.

Was he upset by that revelation? Nick was put out, certainly. But had he really been in love with Cathy? He wasn't so sure. He'd have to think about it, but he was surprised that he wasn't more hurt than he was.

'Come on, then, man. Sit yourself down.' Frank Harland's face was tinged with pink. He seemed very excited to have Nick as a visitor and Nick grinned at him. At last, the two men were face to face.

'Got you a present,' Nick said, walking towards the bed and holding out the T-shirt.

It was wonderful to get home. The house seemed much prettier after having spent time away and it felt good to get back to the ungainly scramble of east London. Cathy had been starting to overdose on beautiful buildings and leafy roads in Oxford. It was nice to be caught up in the gritty bustle of Walthamstow again.

On the way down she had noted the time and mused that play at Headingley would have started again. Jason had been very quiet as he drove – no doubt due to the sudden encounter with Nick in Frank's room. He hadn't passed any comment, though, and for the first half of the journey they'd both been dwelling on private thoughts.

Cathy had been startled to see Nick. He was as big, solid and attractive as ever. But now that she and Jason

456

had rekindled the fire in their own relationship, Nick seemed more of an abstract entity. She would never forget the glorious abandon of their time together and what it had done for her. But she'd realised on seeing Nick again, if she hadn't already known before, that it was an experience she didn't want to relive with him over and over again. Nick had been an integral part of a key chapter in her life, one she would always remember. It had been fantastic, but her life had moved on and now it seemed like a delicious memory. But Jason was her soulmate. She needed him like she needed air.

Jason had switched the car radio on to long wave and *Test Match Special* flowed through the speakers.

'You don't mind listening to it?' Cathy had asked, intrigued that Jason was showing so much of an interest in cricket. When they'd been staying at Frank's house, with Barry enthusing about the match, it had been natural for them all to sit and watch the highlights together. But she hadn't thought of Jason as a cricket fan.

Jason had given her an ironic smile.

'I went to an all-boys' grammar school, don't forget. Cricket and rugby were pumped into our blood. And this is the Ashes. Of course I'm interested.'

Cathy had been amused by the interaction of the BBC commentators. As they pulled off the M25 and headed homewards on the network of London roads, Henry Blofeld had been blustering something about home-made cakes, and Jonathon Agnew had been teasing him. It had made Cathy laugh. There was something about following cricket, she realised, that was more than just knowing the score. It was an institution and the characters who were attached to it were very much a part of that.

When they got in, Jason turned on the television so that they could follow the match. Cathy made them coffee and darted about, watering her wilting plants. Mrs Ali must have been distraught to see the tradescantia panting on the kitchen shelf. She swamped it with water.

'How are we doing?' She stopped to glance at the TV screen.

'Tense stuff,' Jason said. 'Very much neck and neck.'

Cathy looked at Jason for a moment. He seemed very relaxed, sitting there on the sofa. It was a relief that he didn't seem to be associating the test match with Cathy's excursions with Nick. On the other hand, she reasoned, as Jason had strayed himself, perhaps he felt even-handed about it. And it seemed that their time apart, and perhaps even the knowledge that another man was interested in Cathy, had prompted Jason radically to change his approach to their relationship. Just as Cathy's outlook had been changing, almost weekly, throughout this giddy summer.

'I need to go upstairs to make some calls,' she said. 'I must talk to Melissa properly now and Sunday after-noon's a good time to have a long chat with her.'

'Give her my love.' Jason smiled at Cathy.

'I will.' She regarded him warmly. 'I've got her to thank for getting in touch with you.'

'My guess is that she realised it couldn't be long before the truth about Frank came out. She must have known how important it'd be for you to have the support of someone who loves you. Loves you very much, at that.' He eyed her intently. 'And you won't be

458

too hard on her, will you, Cathy? She couldn't have told you who Frank really was. It wasn't for her to do and she was only trying to protect you.'

'I know.' A wave of happiness washed over Cathy as she studied Jason's familiar, lovely face. 'I couldn't have done without your support these last few days, Jason. I can't thank you enough.'

'There's no need to thank me for something I should have been doing anyway.' Jason got up, took Cathy in his arms and gave her a lingering kiss. As he reluctantly pulled his lips away, she was left with a warm glow. 'And it's what you deserve. You're a very special woman, you know. I'm very lucky to have another chance to prove myself to you.'

'And I'm lucky to have you back.' She kissed him again, then dragged herself from him and made her way to the door.

'I heard on *The World This Weekend* that the match was a nail-biter,' Barbara exclaimed as she swept into Frank's room so that he couldn't make any comment on her sudden arrival. 'So that's why I'm here. I've brought you a radio with long wave so that you can tune in to *Test Match Special*. I know sometimes you like to listen to them analysing the match while you're watching the television and it just struck me, this morning, that you hadn't got a long-wave radio. So here you are.'

Frank was still as a stone in bed. He stared at Barbara as she flounced around his room.

'I've brought you some fresh mint tea bags – all you have to do is ask for a cup of boiling water when they bring the tea round. And another dressing gown. It won't be long before you'll be getting up and walking around.'

Barbara removed the dressing gown from the Debenhams bag and shook it out so that Frank could see it.

'It was in a sale, so don't think I've gone mad. I thought your other one, being wool, was probably too warm. This is lighter, so it won't make you sweat.'

She dumped it over a chair, slapped the box of tea bags on to his bedside table and almost threw the radio at him.

'Oh, and earphones.'

She tossed those over the radio.

'But as it's a beautiful Sunday, I'm not going to hang around in this morbid little room. I'm going to have lunch outside in my garden and look at the first draft of *Alfred* which, despite your utter indifference, I have finished. When you're out of here I'll bring it round to the house and you can rip it to shreds.'

On her way back to the door again she paused, breathless. Frank was staring at her open-mouthed.

'And', she finished, 'if you think I'm going to apologise for telling you to piss off, you'd better not hold your breath. I won't.'

She grabbed the door handle.

'*Barbara*!' Frank's voice was a shout more than a roar, but it was probably the best he could manage under the circumstances.

'What?' she snapped.

'Will you bloody come here, you impossible, difficult, kind, wonderful woman?'

Barbara froze with her hand on the handle.

'I'm going to have lunch,' she repeated.

'Come *here*!'

'I'm not a border collie. If you want me, you'd better ask me nicely.'

'Will you come here, *please*?'

Barbara pursed her lips, but she took two steps towards the bed.

'All right. I'm here. What is it?'

Frank struggled with himself until he was upright, wrestling with his miles of tubing.

'You really finished *Alfred*?'

'I've put it together. I've had to add some sections, where we'd done research but not written drafts, and I've made the whole thing read fluently. It still needs some work, but it's closer to being finished than it's ever been.'

'Well I'll be goddamned.' Frank shook his head in disbelief.

'What did you expect?' Barbara said. 'That I'd abandon my life's work with you, just because you weren't in the mood any more? Now I'm going to leave you to watch the match. Don't get overexcited.'

Frank let out a long breath.

'Don't go yet. I've got something to show you.'

Barbara waited. Frank didn't move.

'I need you to pass it to me,' he went on. 'Please? It's in my cupboard, but I can't reach down that far without all these needles falling out.'

Barbara cleared her throat loudly to make the point that this was all very tiresome, but she stepped around the bed, ducked down to the bedside cupboard and opened it. There were all the spare pyjamas, towels and washing things that she'd made sure he'd got in there. And there was a plastic bag wrapped round something.

461

'What? This?' she asked ungraciously, pulling out the bag. There was something small and solid inside.

'Yes, that's it. Can you give it to me?'

Barbara handed him the bag.

'No, no. Come and sit down here.' Frank indicated the chair near the bed on the other side.

'How long is this going to take?' Barbara checked her watch ostentatiously. She wasn't going to be pushed about by Frank again. Not ever.

'Just – please sit down. Let me unwrap this. I want your opinion on it.'

Barbara let out a loud sigh, stalked round the bed and sat in the chair. Frank pulled off the plastic bag and produced a small wooden box, with a hand-painted lid. It looked very old. It instantly teased at Barbara's love of antiquity.

'I've never seen that before,' she exclaimed. 'What is it?'

'This', Frank said thoughtfully, brushing his finger-tips over the top of the box, 'is my grandmother's jewellery box. There isn't much that came down to me, but one or two things in here are rather lovely.'

'Oh.' Barbara leant forward for a better look. It was a beautiful box. It should probably have been displayed somewhere in the house, but Frank had kept it secretly somewhere. Presumably because it meant a great deal to him. From within, Frank produced a much smaller box, covered in a deep-red velvet. It had worn thin and looked equally old.

'Take a look at this.'

He pressed the catch to open the box, then turned it round and showed Barbara. Inside was a ring. It was gold, with a huge raised ruby set in an exquisite star of

462

tiny diamonds. Barbara was captured by its beauty. But suppressing her emotional reaction to it, she gave Frank an admonishing look.

'That is far too precious to be left lying round the house. You should have kept it in a safe somewhere.'

'A safe? Why would I put it in a safe? I've decided to give it away.'

Barbara sat back in her chair, unsmiling. Frank was going to give this ring to Catherine. Of course. And he wanted her opinion. Now that Catherine knew Frank was her father, it would be the ideal time to offer her such a gift. She smoothed her hands carefully over her lap. She reminded herself that none of this was the girl's fault. Despite herself, she actually *liked* Catherine. Barbara was trying to be fair, but Frank was making it damned difficult.

'I'm sure Catherine will love it.'

'But the size.' Frank considered the ring thought-fully. 'I think it might be the wrong size. How big are Catherine's hands? About the same size as yours, do you think?'

Barbara glanced at her fingers.

'Well, it's difficult to say. Perhaps.'

'Try it on for me, will you? I want to see what it looks like.'

Barbara shrank back into her chair. He wanted to put a ring on her finger, something that when she was younger she had dreamt of every night, just so that he could see if it was suitable for another woman? What did he think she was, a mannequin?

'That's silly,' Barbara said. 'There's no point in me trying it on at all.'

'Please?' Frank took Barbara's hand. He slid the ring

carefully on to her finger, nudging it over her knuckle and twisting it into place. He had chosen her ring finger, on her left hand. She stared down at Frank's white fingers holding the ring in place. The symbolism of it was overpowering, but he was so blind that he wouldn't see it. She tried to pull away, but Frank gripped hold of her hand firmly.

'You know,' he said. 'I think it looks rather good on you.'

'Frank. Stop this,' she demanded.

'Barbara,' he said, raising his eyes to hers. She was perplexed. He seemed to want to say something else.

'What is it, Frank?'

'Will you please be my wife?'

Drowning men, she'd heard, saw their lives flash before their eyes. She saw her life with Frank whizz past, almost every day of it, on fast forward. It left her dizzy. But was he joking? Was he suddenly going to produce his cackle and fall back on the pillows, slapping his knee at the expression on her face? He looked completely serious.

'What do you mean?' Barbara asked, fairly point-lessly. But she was buying time and she needed him to explain himself.

Frank looked very confused.

'What do you think I mean? I've just asked you to marry me.'

Barbara drew in a silent breath. Her head was spinning. But a flame of anger flickered through her body.

'And what, after thirty years, has brought this on?' Frank's mouth dropped open. As he didn't speak, Barbara went on, 'Is it convenience, or just resignation to the fact that I've been a part of your life for longer than either of us can remember?'

'Is that yes or no?'

'I've never been proposed to before, Frank Harland, and I'm not about to accept the hand of a man who thinks of me as a cross between a housekeeper and a secretary, just because it suddenly suits him.'

'Is that—' Frank was almost cross-eyed with surprise, but Barbara didn't care. 'Is that piss off?'

'When I get married, if I ever do,' Barbara said, certain of herself and standing up, 'it will be to a man who loves me.'

'Barbara!'

'What?' She moved towards the door. 'Shocked that I still have feelings? That I have a romantic heart? That I'm not overwhelmed with gratitude?'

'No, look.' Frank was leaning so far over the edge of the bed, his arm outstretched towards her, that he almost tumbled off it. 'I meant to say that I love you, but I just forgot. I've never done this before.'

'Oh, Frank.' Barbara shook her head at him. 'What an amateur you are.'

'So that is piss off, then?' Frank's voice rose in anguish.

'Yes, Frank.' Barbara wrenched at the door handle. 'It most definitely is.'

Late on Sunday afternoon, after a long, satisfying talk with Melissa, Cathy was sitting in her upstairs bedroom, gazing into space and turning a multitude of thoughts over in her mind, when Jason yelled up to her:

'Cathy? You should come down and catch the end of this match. It's amazing.'

She trotted down and found Jason in the living room, literally on the edge of his seat. He pointed at the television.

'Caddick and Gough batting, only just holding on. They need five runs to win. Can you believe it? Five more runs and we'll be two-one up in the Ashes with only one match to go. I never thought I'd get so excited about cricket. This match is a belter.'

Cathy settled on the sofa with Jason. She picked at the tortilla chips in the bowl and helped herself to a glass of red wine. Jason's Beaujolais, that he loved so much. It was so good to taste it again, with Jason beside her. He took her hand, raised it to his lips and kissed it, while giving her a devilish look.

'If this match weren't so good I'd have other things on my mind.' He raised his eyebrows at her suggestively, before they both turned their attention back to the cricket.

'So what's – oh, no!' Cathy's heart jumped. Gough was caught out.

'Bugger,' Jason ejected.

'Damn. He shouldn't swipe at it like that.'

'You're quite an expert on it now, aren't you?' Jason said.

'Well, I did get my finger fractured by the England captain,' Cathy swaggered. 'You've seen the letter he wrote me. We're practically best mates.'

'Still five runs to get, then.' Jason fixed his eyes on the screen. 'And here comes our number eleven.'

They sipped their wine tensely as Schofield, the last England batsman, traipsed out to the crease.

'I've got a very bad feeling about this,' Jason said ruefully. 'Schofield's on strike.'

'On strike?'

Meaning, he's the one who's got to face the next ball. But Caddy's the better batsman.' Jason shook his head ominously.

'God knows what this is doing to Frank's blood pressure,' Cathy murmured. She felt her nerves stretching. Who'd have ever thought that she'd care one way or another whether England won a cricket match? But she thought of Frank, desperately wanting to see England recapture the Ashes before he died. And now she was involved too. If only England could pull it off.

'Go on,' she urged the batsman, who looked like a rabbit stuck in a headlight.

'Phew!' Jason splashed refills into their glasses as the over finished and everyone scampered around changing ends. 'We live to see another over. Now it's Caddick on strike. Just a single and a four. That'll do it.'

They watched. Andy Caddick whacked the ball away to the boundary. The crowd roared. She knew exactly how they would feel, being there, lapping up the electric atmosphere. She wished she were there too. But not with Nick. With Jason? Maybe one day they'd actually go to a match together.

'Four!' Jason yelled. 'Great. We can't lose this match any more.'

'We can't? How come?'

'The scores are even now. That means that if nothing else happens, we're drawn. All we need is one more run and we've secured this match.' Jason shuffled even further forward on his seat. 'Good news.'

Cathy laughed at him.

'I never knew how much you cared, darling.'

'It's the Ashes, girl,' Jason stated.

The camera swept around the Headingley crowd. Everyone was on their feet, waving banners, brandishing beer glasses, sticking the 'four' cards into the air. The clamour was incredible.

'One run.' Cathy held on to her glass tightly. 'Just one measly run.'

'Come on!' Jason slapped his knees.

The lanky Australian bowler who Cathy now knew was Glenn McGrath pelted in. He let rip with the ball. It hit Caddick's stumps with such force that they flew in all directions and clattered to the ground.

The Australians congratulated each other in glee. Caddick's shoulders drooped as he stared at the mess behind him. The cheers of the crowd were replaced by an air of deflation. The batsmen jogged away quickly to avoid any stray fans mobbing them and headed for the pavilion. The match was over.

'Oh.' Cathy sighed. 'What a horrible anticlimax.'

Jason cast himself back on the sofa, musing, 'A draw isn't so bad. At one point we looked as if we were going to lose it. And it's the Oval next.'

'So we've got to go through this all over again.' Cathy wondered if Frank's heart would take it. She even wondered if her own heart would take it.

'But', Jason said, sounding a little brighter, 'the fact that the Oval's the decider is probably good news.'

'Why's that?' Cathy asked curiously.

'Because, my darling, we have a tendency to play well at the Oval. It's tradition.'

'Nick, are you all right?'

Nick peered up blearily. He'd had his fingers over

468

his eyes for the last five minutes. He couldn't stand the tension. But England hadn't lost. That was the main thing.

The pub had been alive with shouts one minute and full of disgruntled murmurs the next. But many of these guys watching, late on a Sunday afternoon with no football on and no better excuse for a day out boozing, were not ardent cricket fans. They couldn't be. Because if they were, they'd realise that today's result was a reprieve.

Nick had driven back to Birmingham, after a very long talk with Frank that had been interesting, enlightening and at the same time uplifting. Not only could Nick understand completely why Cathy's frustration with Frank was tempered with affection, he could also place the personality that he'd been bonding with over the Internet for so long. Everything made more sense now. And in addition, Frank had voiced some ideas that were very thought-provoking. All in all, it had been a hell of a morning. The whole way home Nick had been dwelling on his brief meeting with Cathy. He was still waiting for the thunderbolt of despair to hit him. Dismay, yes. Despair, no. Nick was relieved that his reaction hadn't been stronger.

When he'd got home, Nick had found Graham on the sofa with Mel. They were watching the match.

'Right,' he had stated. 'I'm going to watch this up the pub. Are you with me or against me?'

'With you,' they'd decided.

As they'd piled out of the house, Nick had realised that it would be a bit off, given that they were going as a group, not to ask Hannah along as well. So he'd phoned her and she'd met them at the pub. It wasn't a date. Nick wasn't sure if he was ready to go that far yet. But he'd felt that it would be nice for Hannah join in.

Now, Hannah was cradling her drink and watching him with genuine concern.

'Are you all right, Nick? I know this game meant a lot to you.'

'I'm fine.'

'That's a relief.' She smiled at him. 'Sorry England lost, though. That's a bummer.'

'We didn't lose,' Nick explained. 'We drew. And we've got one match left to play.'

'Oh. I get it. So we've just got to win the last one?'

'Correct.'

'And then what?'

'And then', Nick said, breaking into a grin, 'we reclaim the Ashes.'

'Ah, I see.' Hannah examined Nick's expression. 'What are you so happy about, then? Aren't we going to have our nerves ripped to shreds all over again?'

'Very possibly,' Nick reasoned. 'However, there is another factor. The final match is at the Oval. And England win at the Oval.'

'Always?' Hannah looked surprised.

'No. Not always. But often enough for me to be absurdly optimistic about it. Fancy another drink?'

On Monday morning Cathy woke up to find the sun blazing through her yellow curtains. The whole room was washed with golden light. She could hear Jason in the shower, getting ready for work, and the birds were cheeping manically. A bubble of happiness rose in her throat, so she lay there, remembering the passion of the previous night. If anything, the physicality between herself and Jason was getting better by the day. A smile spread across her face.

Cathy rolled over and switched on her radio. It was the sports news and Garry Richardson was talking about the cricket. She propped herself up on her elbows and listened. Nasser Hussain was being asked about the last match in the series, to be played at the Oval. The Australian captain had said, apparently, that he was out for blood.

'Well, if they want blood,' the England Captain said grittily, 'they've got it.'

'You go for it,' Cathy urged the radio. 'Fracture as many fingers as you have to. Everyone will understand.'

Feeling buoyant, Cathy bounced out of bed and pulled on a loose T-shirt. Today, she would start putting her ideas for her new career into motion. She'd talked it through with Jason the night before and he'd backed her to the hilt. 'Whatever you do, Cathy,' he'd said, 'you'll be fantastic and I'll back you all the way.'

The phone rang. Cathy cantered into her study, humming to herself, and picked it up.

'Ruth!' Cathy was stalled by the sound of her ex-boss's voice on the line. 'I was going to ring you today to tell you I've just got back to London and I can arrange a handover to suit you.'

'Thank you, Cathy,' Ruth said. 'But I've actually called for a different reason.' Ruth paused. 'I'd like to offer you a senior partnership in the company. You'll want to take some time to think about it, but I'd be delighted if you would accept. I think you're exactly the right woman for the job.'

After she'd put the phone down Cathy went to find Jason.

He was still lathering himself in the shower, singing 'Mambo Number Five' at the top of his voice.

'Come on in.' He gave Cathy an inviting smile. 'The water's lovely.'

'Ruth's just offered me a senior partnership,' Cathy blurted out.

Jason turned off the taps instantly and stood there dripping, the dark hairs on his chest matted with soap. He studied Cathy intensely.

'And?'

Cathy thought about it hard.

'I know what I've got to do,' she said.

'I thought you would,' Jason grinned soapily and pulled her into the shower.

Chapter Twenty-four

'I always thought this one had your name on it.' Bill Havers winked at Cathy as they stood in the compact business unit of the Docklands complex, contemplating the view over the Thames.

Cathy watched the river, tiny crests peaking on the brown water as the barges edged their way past. She propped open the window and took a deep breath.

'It's perfect.'

The seagulls squealed overhead. A low horn sounded somewhere along the river and drifted towards them on the warm air. All around them there was activity. Cathy was stirred.

'I know you needed thinking time and all that, but I'm so chuffed for you, Cathy.' Bill's cheeks glowed. 'If there was ever a gel to set up on her own, it's you.'

'Thanks, Bill.' Cathy was cheered by Bill's unrestrained enthusiasm. 'It took me a while to realise it myself, but I know you're right now.'

She wandered around the office, touching the table, the chairs, the solid cabinets, already visualising what she would do with them.

'You know, Ruth's come up trumps for me,' Bill said. 'When she started to move on the Hellier's deal, all those discussions with me and Troy, all those brilliant things she suggested to make sure my bid was a good one – well, she went right up in my estimation. You don't mind me saying that, do you?'

'Of course not.' Cathy shook her head emphatically. 'I've always admired Ruth a great deal and for now she's the perfect person to help you clinch the Hellier's contract. Time is crucial and it's going to take me a while to establish myself. It's right for you, Bill, and that's the most important thing.'

'Although you introduced me to Troy.' Bill looked awkward. 'And I know it was your brainwork what pushed it all forward.'

Cathy raised an eyebrow cryptically, but she didn't comment. Besides, the work that she'd done under the umbrella of her old company remained work that she had done for them. She would rethink her role now. And start afresh. She had plenty of ideas, plenty of contacts and a huge amount of motivation. She didn't need to carry old projects forward with her and run the risk of being accused of unprofessional behaviour. Now she could concentrate on her true love – the development of small companies, here, in east London, where her background and enthusiasm were needed – and appreciated.

'But in the future, Cathy. Once this Hellier's business is under way. You know if I ever need expert advice – and I will, I'm sure of it – you'll be the one I come to.'

'Thank you.' Cathy was warmed.

'That Mark, though.' Bill pulled a face at Cathy.

She kept her expression neutral in response, although a smile pulled at the corners of her lips.

'What about Mark?'

'Wanker.' Bill grimaced. ''Scuse my French. I wasn't

sorry he went off to work for someone else. I couldn't stand dealing with him.'

Yes, Cathy mused to herself. She'd been hoodwinked by Mark. A naive lack of judgement on her part. She could hardly believe that she'd originally thought he was on her side. How wrong she'd been.

'But Mark's not in the picture any more,' she said brightly. 'And it looks as if we both have an exciting time ahead of us.'

Bill rubbed his hands together. 'So, where are you going to sit, then?' He chuckled as Cathy tried out the four chairs that were positioned round the wide table in the centre of the room. 'As the boss, you've got the pick of the lot.'

'Well, I could sit in a different one every day, I suppose.' Cathy grinned back at Bill. 'It would help me to keep a broad perspective.'

'It will just be you, will it? I wondered if you was going to employ anyone else.'

'Just me at the moment,' Cathy confirmed. 'Although I could use a bit of IT expertise. I'll have to think about it.'

'Can't help you there, I'm afraid,' Bill said ruefully. 'But I can help you in all other areas. I've got three of my mates already lined up to meet you. They're just like I was, need the whole works. So I've told them, I know just the right woman for the job. And you'll have to give me a shout if you need any additional stuff for this office. I can get you anything you want at knock-down prices.'

'Great.' New customers, cheap office equipment and Bill as her ally – and her friend. Moment by moment, Cathy was growing more excited about getting the business started.

'Listen, gel, I'll be downstairs. There's a shop unit down there I need to talk to about some extra shelving. Get the feel of the place for yourself and you can meet me down there when you're ready. We can grab a nice cuppa before you take off to see your bank bloke.'

Bill disappeared, leaving Cathy to drift around the office on her own. A little incubation unit for her very own business. The thrill rose in her throat again and she went to the window, her heart thumping, and pulled out her mobile.

Fiona answered immediately.

'Fi?' Cathy couldn't keep the smile from her voice. 'Guess what? You know you talked about giving them all two fingers and going it alone? Well, I've done it. I'm taking one of Bill's Docklands business units and setting up on my own. Cathy Gordon, business development consultant. Who'd have thought it?'

Fiona let out a long whistle. 'Well done, that woman. After being tempted with a senior partnership as well. Good for you, Cathy! That's completely fantastic.'

'It's a bit scary,' Cathy breezed on. 'But I'm so excited that I haven't really got time to be scared. There's so much to do and just myself to rely on. But that's part of the challenge.'

'Cathy,' Fiona said more seriously, 'you haven't really thought this through, have you?'

Cathy's smile dropped a little.

'I – yes, I have. I've got an appointment with the bank right after this and I'm organising start-up funding as well. One thing I do know, after years of working in development, is how to get a company up and running. I've been in touch with all the relevant people.' Cathy stopped as Fiona didn't interrupt with any reassuring noises. 'Fi, what do you mean? I thought you'd be right behind me.'

'I am, you twit.' Fiona laughed and lowered her voice. 'What I mean is you haven't got yourself a brilliant assistant who also happens to be superb designer of web pages. Someone who'd be prepared to work for a modest wage until the company was beating all the competition hollow. At which point this person would naturally expect to earn masses, but that would take time.'

Cathy stared at the thick swell of the river.

'And this person would also do the coffee run quite willingly,' Fiona added.

'You mean—'

'I mean me,' Fiona stated. 'If you don't let me come and work for you I'll never speak to you again.'

There was a first time for everything and this had been a summer of first times. The thought brought a smile to Cathy's lips as she strolled from the Oval tube station towards the ground on the Sunday of the last Ashes test match. She was caught up in a cavalcade of boaters, shorts, vest tops, summer dresses, cool boxes and hampers, as had happened before. But this time Jason was beside her. Jason, who in fact seemed to be finding it difficult to spend any time away from her ever since their wonderful reunion at her father's house.

Everywhere Cathy could see Draculas. They out-numbered the Queen Mothers by about ten to one. Vampires abounded. The England captain's assurance that they were out for blood seemed to have taken hold in the imagination.

Cathy was thrilled that Frank had bought them

tickets. He'd got Barry to send them down to her, with an apology that he couldn't get any for the Saturday – they'd been sold out months in advance. But as play had gone over into Sunday and it looked like being the decisive day, it was a piece of luck.

'It could be', Frank had written, 'the most memorable day in English cricket for a very long time.'

He'd apologised for only being able to get seats in the Gover stand, but when Cathy got there, she loved it. It was low, open to the air and strong sun, and full of atmosphere. Quite a few of the Draculas were ranged around them and they were having a lovely time. By the time play started at eleven the crowd was already cheerfully boisterous.

It had been a tight final match so far. Cathy had followed it, in the newspapers, on the television when she had the time, or on her long-wave radio. With every run scored, or every wicket that had fallen, her heart had jumped. Now that the prospect of a historic victory was within England's grasp, Cathy had noticed that most people were taking an interest. Even Fiona had been plying Cathy with questions about it and musing that she might go to a match next year, just to see what it was like.

Cathy took Jason's hand and squeezed it. He winked at her.

'Got the valium, just in case?'

She laughed.

'Here they come. We'd better keep everything crossed now.'

They concentrated on the players prancing out to the crease.

The previous night they'd both gone down to

478

Woking to have dinner with Melissa and Brian. Although Cathy's parents already knew about her reunion with Jason, and she had thanked Melissa warmly for her part in bringing them back together, Melissa and Brin had greeted Jason like a long-lost son. Cathy had been moved to see that Melissa had even had tears in her eyes.

She and Melissa had had a long talk, on their own in the kitchen, while Brian had tried to show Jason how to play 'Penny Lane' from his *Simple Songs for the Guitar Novice* book. Ignoring the twanging and caterwauling coming from the next room, Cathy had hugged Melissa. And Melissa had reassured Cathy, once again, that her only concern had been for Cathy's happiness. Everything I did', she told Cathy softly, 'with Jason and with Frank over the years, was driven by love for you, darling.'

Although Melissa had initially had serious qualms about maintaining contact with Cathy's true father, she explained that Frank had been happier for Cathy to know nothing about him at all. Perhaps, Melissa had mused, it was because he always intended at some point to let Cathy know who he was. Then, over the years, he'd apparently got cold feet and let time pass without doing anything about it. Until suddenly, with a deep sense of his own mortality, he'd decided to act. By that time Melissa was worried that it was too late for the real facts to come out without turning her daughter's life upside down. She'd suggested that Frank present himself as her grandfather. He was of an age where it would be credible. She'd been deeply uncomfortable with a white lie, Melissa had said, her usually steady grey eyes misty, but she had hoped and prayed that Cathy would one day understand.

479

Cathy had much to think about. But the shock waves were already starting to subside. She knew that little by little she'd start to get used to all the revelations that had been foisted on her that summer. And with Jason beside her the process would be easier.

She gave Jason a hopelessly romantic look as he leant forward to focus on the play. He had such a lovely profile and she could see the soft arrow of black hair that teased its way down the nape of his neck. Perhaps she'd never feel the explosive sexual chemistry that she'd experienced with Nick again. But she and Jason had rediscovered the passion that had once sizzled between them and being with Nick had somehow left Cathy feeling as if she were balancing on a knife edge. Who wanted to go to Alton Towers every day of their life?

Cathy was growing to know herself a lot better – and that summer had been a steep learning curve. She didn't want constant thrills. Excitement, yes. Impulsive moments, certainly. Jason brought her those things. But he also offered her a strong, loving relationship, one which stimulated her physically, emotionally and mentally. With Jason she could do exactly what Fiona had advised her to do – be happy being Cathy Gordon. And he loved her for it. Somebody, no doubt, with softer hands than hers would come along and mould Nick into shape. But it wasn't to be Cathy's job. She was far too in love with her boyfriend.

Cathy felt a warm rush of contentment. Who might have thought that she and Jason would be sitting together at the decisive Ashes test match, both excited about the game, about the new ideas they were sharing and about each other?

She smiled and concentrated her mind on following the rest of the match.

After the lunch interval the anticipation of the crowd built up into a crescendo. England were batting. Nasser Hussain, the captain, was holding the fort at one end, but with the loss of three quick wickets the other senior batsmen had been dismissed, and it was down to Hussain and Flintoff to battle on and keep England's hopes alive.

With every close call for an LBW, every ball edged within the reach of the slip fielders, every missed swipe the crowd yelled.

Then Flintoff caught the edge of the ball with his bat and it flew into the hands of Ricky Ponting, the skilful Australian fielder.

Around Cathy, grown men were hiding their faces. There were cries of dismay. Her ribcage felt as if it were held in a truss. She could hardly breathe. The shouts from the crowd were so overpowering they could probably be heard right across London. With every replay shown on the huge screens at either side of the ground she could see the tenseness in the face of the England captain. So near and yet such a mountain to climb.

Too big a mountain, now. Flintoff had been the last England player who could bat well and they were down to the bowlers who could bat a bit. Cathy sensed with dread that this could be the start of a collapse.

'We're not going to do it,' she whispered to Jason, her voice choked. She could feel tears of disappointment rising in her throat.

'Hang on in there.' Jason held her hand tightly. 'It's not over yet.'

'But – poor Frank.' Cathy swallowed painfully. 'He's watching this. He'll be distraught.'

Jason considered Cathy.

'You know, Cathy, there have been so many great things that have happened this year. Perhaps wanting to win the Ashes as well is just asking too much.'

Cathy crammed her hands into her lap, her palms smarting with the bite of her nails, as Dominic Cork came out to the crease for England. He was swirling his bat and trotting. She closed her eyes and prayed.

He survived the first ball and the crowd went berserk. By this time everyone was calling comments to everyone else, regardless of whether they knew each other or not. Next to Cathy, an elegant, elderly man who had been exclaiming to her throughout the day, grabbed her arm.

'If anyone can do it, Dom can. He won us the centenary test match at Lord's. He can do it. I know he can do it. All he has to do is make sure Hussain gets the strike. He must realise that. Mustn't he?'

Noting the desperation in the man's voice, Cathy nodded reassuringly and leant forward again to watch.

They all held their breath as Hussain slowly added to the England score, every scampered, precious run provoking raucous shouts of encouragement from the entire stadium. When Dominic Cork hit a clean four, every individual in the ground leapt to his or her feet.

Now they were close. So close that nobody bothered to sit down again. All around Cathy, people were punching their arms into the air and yelling in agony.

'Do it,' the elderly man said, his voice breaking. 'Just do it. I can't take any more!'

A frantic single put Hussain back on strike. Shane

Warne, the blond spin bowler who Cathy knew was fearsomely good, flipped the ball around in his hands as he glared at the England captain aggressively.

'Four runs,' The elderly man ejected emotionally, his body hunched. Cathy took his arm quickly and held him up. 'That's all we need.' He choked. 'I can't watch.'

'Yes, you can,' Cathy urged him. Up in Oxford, in his hospital bed, Frank would be in exactly the same state. Cathy's throat was so tight she could hardly speak, but she croaked at her old man, 'You're not going to miss this. You just hang on to me.'

Warne bowled. The crowd stared.

Hussain dropped to his knees and hammered the ball. It flew behind his wicket. Two slip fielders dived on it – and missed. Steve Waugh, the Australian captain, sprinted after it. The grass was dry and flat. The ball raced away. Waugh ran. The ball hit the boundary rope.

England had won the Ashes.

Beside her the elderly man burst into tears of joy. The crowd went bananas. Cathy pogoed up and down with the rest of them and Jason engulfed her in an embrace that knocked the breath out of her.

'Fourteen years! Fourteen bloody years since the Ashes came home. It's brilliant.'

'God, how must Frank feel?' Cathy laughed back, as Jason lifted her into the air and put her down again.

And Nick. He'd be doing cartwheels.

'Even I didn't think I'd care this much,' Jason said. 'We won! And I was *here* on the day. Un-bloody-believable. Frank is an angel for getting these tickets.'

'We were here, we were here,' Cathy chanted, feeling as childishly euphoric as everybody else.

'Look at that.' Jason nudged Cathy and pointed.

In front of them a grandfather had hoisted his grandson on to his shoulder and was jiving with a stuffed kangaroo. Cathy laughed. Sun, a few slow beers in the early afternoon and England had won. She was filled with exuberance.

They danced around the stand with the Draculas. Nobody could stop grinning. Cathy would exchange glances with total strangers and they'd burst into smiles. Poeple talked to each other as if they were great friends and exclaimed to each other.

'Fourteen years!'

'We did it. We blimmin' well did it!'

'Hey, Primrose!'

Cathy spun round. There was her tasty nun, the one with the twinkly brown eyes. He was leading his troop down the steps from seats in the back tiers and they were passing by her row. He must have recognised her due to the yellow shorts, top and sunhat. Today he and his merry band were dressed as Master vampires, complete with silly plastic teeth.

She waved at him frantically.

'Hiya, guys! What a win!'

They all cheered madly, jumping around as they recognised her, then carried on their leaps and hops down the steps. Everybody was now flooding over the pitch.

'What happens now, Jace?'

'Presentations,' Jason said eagerly. 'And this is one I just can't wait for.'

They picked their way back along the row, grinning at everybody they saw, and down the steps to the boundary, where they vaulted over on to the smooth turf of the pitch.

It was amazing to walk on it. Cathy gazed at the soft, even surface in fascination. She'd never got this close to a cricket pitch in her life.

'It's more like a carpet than grass,' she mused to Jason, who had grabbed her arm to hurry her towards the pavilion.

'A lot of work to keep it in this condition. Spare a thought for the groundsman.'

Cathy did. 'Okay I've done that.' She jogged along-side Jason, beaming at him. 'Can I go back to being stupidly excited now?'

They surged forward with the crowd to the pavilion. England players spilt out on to the balcony of their dressing room to raise their arms and cheer back at the crowd. Dominic Cork appeared with a bottle of champagne and sprayed everybody with it. Nobody could shut up, even when a tall man with curly blond hair whom Cathy recognised as David Gower from *They Think It's All Over* tried to begin the presentations on the long balcony. He stopped and laughed at the crowd who gave him a resounding cheer in return.

Then he worked his way through the presentations, which Cathy could only remember afterwards as a blur. Some umpires were given medals, the Australian captain came out and said a few words, to a great many good-humoured heckles. Then the England captain appeared. The crowd gave him a reception of thunderous applause as they bounced up and down. The Draculas began to chant to the tune of 'Rupert the Bear'.

'Nasser, Nasser Hussain, everyone knows his name . . .'

Cathy stood beaming, like the proverbial Cheshire

485

Cat. Some sixty miles away Frank would be red-faced with joy, hopefully with Barbara by his side, patting his hand and smiling too. Perhaps Barry would be at the hospital, or maybe at home. No, more likely in the pub with his mates, laughing his infectious laugh. And Nick? He'd be walking on the ceiling by now.

And how many other people in England would care? Cathy had noticed that the tabloids had talked of 'Ashes Fever', due to the gripping finish at the last match. She knew Fiona had promised to watch – and if Fiona, a woman who thought that all sport was incredibly silly, was curious about what was happening, perhaps everybody was.

Maybe even if Frank hadn't given Cathy this crash course in a game she'd never bothered to think about before she'd be switching on the television and watching today herself. Certainly she would if Jason had encouraged her to. Possibly she'd have become intrigued by cricket then. Or perhaps, as the young Australian woman had told her way back in the taxi going to Edgbaston, it was just about understanding a basic few rules before a love affair with the game began to develop. Never again would Cathy be confused into thinking that all they did was stand around and scratch their crotches. It was a whole new world. A wonderfully exciting, stimulating, perplexing world and Cathy was now subsumed into it.

She threw her hands in the air and clapped until her palms stung as the England captain raised a tiny object to the crowd, his grin splitting his face. Somebody next to her erupted into loud sobs.

'I'm so happy,' the middle-aged man told her with tears rolling down his face. He handed her his bottle of champagne to hold while he found himself a hanky.

'Is that it?' Cathy hissed at Jason, indicating the tiny trophy the captain was waving ecstatically.

'The urn. I told you, little Ern.'

'Okay, okay.' Cathy took a swig from the champagne bottle without thinking, only to find that the middle-aged man told her and Jason to keep it, with his compliments, and handed them both plastic cups to drink it out of, as he produced another from his cool box and popped the cork. It flew into the air, along with the other champagne corks that were whizzing about like fireworks.

'Nasser's been awarded England's Man of the Series.' Jason grabbed Cathy's arm. 'The man who marmalised your finger. What do you think of that?'

'If he's responsible for making me feel as good as this, he can marmalise my toes as well. And I have got his letter to frame. Pride of place, over the mantelpiece,' Cathy enthused back to Jason. 'I can't believe what I've been missing all these years, and I'm so glad we're here together.'

'We were here, we were here,' Jason sang and grabbed Cathy to kiss her.

They stayed on the ground, lapping up the atmosphere, cheering at every opportunity. The England team loitered on the balcony, waving and having called conversations with the crowd at the front, sharing their euphoria. Until finally, people began to drift away.

'I don't want to go home yet,' Cathy told Jason. 'I'm buzzing.'

'Me too. Although' – Jason arched an eyebrow provocatively – 'I rather like the idea of being at home with you when you're buzzing.'

'Later, darling.'

'Shall we go and pile into the pub with the other drunken bastards, then? I do think the atmosphere will be' – Jason put on his overtly posh voice to make her laugh – 'fiendishly jolly. What say you?'

'I say we adjourn to a hostelry and stay there until we can't walk.'

'Great plan. Let's go.'

'I can't – I can't,' Nick sobbed all over Graham's shoulder. 'I can't speak.'

'The Lord is merciful,' Graham quipped, patting his big friend on the shoulder.

But Nick couldn't stop the tears. For the last fourteen years he'd been aching for this moment. He'd suffered the torture of seeing England lose, he'd withstood the taunts and the hackneyed jokes about the England cricket team, always defending them, always supporting them. But he'd prayed, urged them to show what they were made of. And they'd done it. They'd won against Australia, the best team in the world. Nick was totally overwhelmed.

He felt like a little boy again, gulping back the emotion, trying not to show it. But Graham didn't seem to mind. Around them the Australian bar was in utter chaos. People were singing and a conga had started across the room. Here, in a pub dedicated to sport and especially fond of cricket, he was among friends.

'This is magic, mate. I can't explain it.'

'You don't have to.'

Nick pulled away and dashed his hands over his eyes.

'I feel like such a prat. But I can't help it.'

488

'You know what you need?' Graham quirked his eyebrows.

'I know. Another beer. I'll get them in.'

'Nope.' Graham grinned. 'You need to kiss someone. But it ain't going to be me.'

'What I need', Nick said, his voice wavering, 'is to get utterly hammered. I have never been so happy in my entire goddamn life.'

Graham tutted.

'You're going to balls this one up as well if you're not careful.'

'This what?' Nick pulled an innocent face, but he knew what Graham was talking about. He was just amazed to hear Graham give him that sort of advice. Surely his mates were the ones to say, 'Forget her, mate, she's not worth it. Let's go and play pool.' But looking at Graham, it struck him that Graham was older too. They were both men now, not boys.

'Ring Hannah. Tell her how you feel. Share it with her. Then we can get hammered,' Graham said.

'Come on, man. You're joking. This is my big moment.'

'Exactly,' Graham agreed. 'And if you wait until tomorrow night when your lips actually function well enough to speak again before you bother to report back to her she'll feel completely left out. And it'll be your own bloody fault. You want to keep pushing them away? How long for?'

Nick put out his hands in appeal.

'Where's all this coming from? Why you, of all people?'

'Because' – Graham rolled his tongue around his cheek – 'it so happens that I want to give Mel a ring right now and see what she's up to. Listen, mate, we can't watch *The Simpsons* for the rest of our lives. I don't know about you, but I'm sick of it.'

'You can never be sick of *The Simpsons*.' Nick pointed his finger severely. 'That's sacrilege.'

'You can when you've seen every episode so many times that you can quote it off by heart.' Graham looked anguished. 'I want to move on, Nick, and so should you. I'm seeing someone now. Mel's nice. I like her. I don't want to mess it up. This fiction bubble we all live in, all lads together, it's been great, but it's got to burst some time. Nice as it was, it had its place.'

Nick laughed. The idea that Graham had been thinking the same things as him was incredible. Not that he'd have brought it up first. It would have seemed disloyal to criticise the way they all lived. But now Graham had been honest. It was a relief.

Perhaps Nick would even tell Graham that he'd already been to see some estate agents in the week and was thinking about buying a house. Just a small place, somewhere he could make a bit more homely. He'd been thinking that it would be nice to come home to a clean kitchen, perhaps a more comfortable sofa. Even a set of curtains that actually fitted the window. A few home comforts would be quite appealing.

'All right,' Nick conceded. 'I'll ring Hannah. Then we can get hammered, can't we?'

'Yep. But I'm going to ask Mel to meet us in here. Up to you if you want to play gooseberry.'

'Are you kidding?' The words came out on autopilot. But when Nick thought about it, he realised that it wasn't such a bad idea. In fact, if Hannah was free, it'd be fun. He wanted to see her again. He just didn't know how to juggle it all: mates, work, cricket, women. But perhaps it was more simple than he realised. Hannah could come to the bar and they could all enjoy the moment together. Hannah wouldn't mind if Nick got completely plastered. She knew this was a special occasion. There was, in fact, nothing to run away from.

He grinned at Graham.

'All right. I'll ask Hannah to join us. But that doesn't mean we make up a foursome and go round bloody Do-It-All next weekend. Is that quite clear?'

Graham looked totally horrified.

'God, no.'

'Fine, then. We understand each other.'

Nick leapt off to make his phone call.

Frank lay back in his hospital bed, the tears streaming down his face. Barbara was perched on the side of the bed, stroking his forehead.

'It's done.' Frank's breath whistled from his nostrils. 'The job is done.'

'Now you listen,' Barbara cut into his dramatic moment caustically. 'You once told me that I couldn't have your ashes until these Ashes had been won. But if you've got any thoughts of giving up now, I'm here to tell you straight that I won't have it.'

Frank opened one eye.

'You won't have it?'

'No.'

'Does that mean – are you going to be around for a while, then?'

Barbara narrowed her eyes.

'I'm certainly not going to commit myself yet.'

'But you did come back to me. You came here today,

to share this with me. You knew how much I'd want you here.'

'I think, Frank Harland, that you still have something to say to me.'

'Barbara.' Frank took her hand. 'You know that I love you, don't you?'

Barbara maintained a level gaze, but her heart began to soften. This was the culmination of all Frank's hopes. The Ashes had been won. The commentators were excitably showing replays and interviewing players. All this was coming from the small television in the corner. And yet, she had Frank's undivided attention. But he needed to *tell* her that he loved her. She had to hear it.

'That was a question, not a statement,' she said. 'Try again.'

Frank's face twitched emotionally. Then, to her utter shock, he reached for the remote control lying on the blankets and turned the television off. The room was suddenly quiet.

'Barbara.' He stroked her hand softly. 'I love you. I have done for a very long time and I'm so sorry I didn't tell you before.'

She curled her fingers round his hand. She knew now. She could hear it in his voice and see it in his face.

'I love you too, Frank,' she whispered.

'I know I'm old and ill and not the man I used to be. I know that I don't deserve the affection of such a fine woman as yourself. But will you do me the honour of becoming my wife?'

Now Barbara could allow happiness to swell in her chest. She looked back at Frank, her eyes shining.

'Yes, Frank, I will.'

'Then you have made me the happiest man alive.' Frank pulled her towards him with a sudden show of strength and they embraced.

'Now put that bloody television back on.' Barbara gently disentangled herself, blushing like a schoolgirl. 'You can't miss this moment. You've waited for it for fourteen years.'

Frank's eyes glistened. His thin lips stretched into a smile.

'You are a bossy old boot. When did you start being so bossy?'

'The minute', Barbara told him affectionately, 'that I realised it worked.'

'And this is what I've let myself in for?' Frank probed. 'Months of you telling me what to do?'

'Months?' Barbara kept a very straight face. 'You'd better think in terms of years, Frank.'

'Oh, all right, then,' Frank agreed, as they both settled, their hands locked together, to watch the match celebrations.

'I've got a surprise for you,' Jason said, once they'd stumbled into the house and Cathy was lying on the sofa, giggling at the ceiling for no reason at all.

'You have?'

'Yes. It's a present. But it's a surprise.'

Cathy tried to pull a sensible face.

'Then I promise I won't tell anyone.'

Jason disappeared into the kitchen. Cathy hung off the sofa trying to see round the door. He was scrambling around in the broom cupboard. Something clunked against the wall. Cathy snorted. What had he got her? A set of weights?

'Jason?'

'Coming. Now don't look. Close your eyes.'

'Okay.'

Cathy spread her fingers over her eyes, peering through the tiny gaps. Jason brought something into the living room and stood next to it.

'God, I'm a bit pissed so I'm not doing this properly. But, Cathy, here is your present. Tum tum tara!'

Cathy pulled her fingers away. Jason was very proudly pointing at her present. It was a cricket bat. With a little silver bow stuck on the top.

Her mouth dropped open in surprise and she started to laugh.

'Oh, God, now you think I should start playing? I'm not the next Rachel Heyhoe-Flint, you know. I'm far too unfit.'

Jason looked down at the bat in confusion.

'Ah, wrong side. No wonder.'

He spun the bat round so that Cathy could see the face. She got up and walked towards it curiously, dropping to her knees to examine it more closely.

'Oh, good grief! I don't believe it. Where did you get this?'

There, on the smooth willow surface of the bat were a series of squiggles in black pen. And as Cathy focused on them, she began to make out the names.

'Nasser Hussain, Alec Stewart, Mike Atherton,' she breathed, holding the bat at an angle to read them all. 'Andy Caddick. Trescothick. And Gough too. All of them! And here's Vaughan. Incredible.'

'A bat signed by the entire England team,' Jason said, glowing with pleasure as he watched Cathy's reaction. 'I'm going to put it on the wall for you. Next to your letter from the England captain. As a momento of this unique summer.'

'It's amazing.' Cathy stood up and laced her arms round Jason's neck. She kissed him, savouring the taste of his lips. 'You really are a special boyfriend. I love it. It's the most wonderful thing I've ever been given.'

'This has been an important year for you, Cathy. I want you to remember it always.'

'Yes,' she mused, sinking into the oaky depths of Jason's eyes. 'This has been a stunning year. Everything's changed. And to think we've been seeing each other for four years. I feel as if we've only just met.'

'In which case', Jason said, pulling her into his arms, 'we'd better get to know each other a whole lot better, hadn't we?'

Chapter Twenty-five

Frank and Barbara were married on a fine, breezy September afternoon, in the chapel of the college where Frank had taught and where Barbara had studied. It was where Barbara had first fallen in love with him.

Cathy had been astounded when Barbara had asked her to help her choose her wedding outfit. She'd asked with such hesitancy that Cathy, who knew as much about style and fashion as she did about Ugandan traffic by-laws, found herself enthusiastically agreeing to help.

Together they'd scoured the Oxford shops, a little awkwardly as they weren't familiar with each other's tastes, until Barbara admitted that she'd always hated shopping for clothes on the basis that she could be doing something much more interesting. They'd gone for some coffee and talked it over.

'I know!' Cathy had come up with a solution. 'Let's get you something made up. Then the dressmaker will have to worry about it. You'll just have to be measured and turn up for a fitting or two.'

'Oh, I'm not sure.' Barbara had looked concerned. 'It might be quite costly.'

'Who's paying?'

'Well, actually, Frank's insisted on paying for the frock.'

Frock? Cathy had horrifying images of sensible

navy-blue nylon, pulled in at the waist with a thin matching belt. No way, even in Cathy's wildest nightmares, was Barbara going to dance down the aisle on the happiest day of her life in a frock. She could tell that Barbara had never spoiled herself and she was going to make sure that this was one occasion when she did. Especially if Frank was footing the bill.

'There you go.' Cathy had grinned. 'He's paying. We're splashing out. Decided.'

So they had gone back to the streets and asked everywhere, including Pronuptia, whether they knew of any dressmakers in Oxford. They'd found a little shop, at the back of the main precinct, which Cathy was thrilled to see had some lovely designs in their display window.

Cathy had made sure they got to see the manageress straight away and had explained their predicament. They hated looking for clothes, but they needed something wonderful, and yet tasteful and mature. They were shown possible designs.

'That's it.' Cathy stuck her finger on one of the pages.

Barbara blinked at it.

'Are you sure? For me? It's a bit . . . well . . .'

'A bit what?'

'A bit sensual.'

Cathy had considered Barbara carefully.

'Do you want my father to look at you as you sweep towards him thinking, "Yes, that's my old Barbara," or do you want him to think, "Jesus wept. How could I not have seen how gorgeous Barbara was all these years?" Think about it.'

Barbara had blushed bright red.

'The latter. Yes, I'll have that one please.'

Barbara had been measured up, they'd chosen a beautiful material for the dress and Cathy had persuaded Barbara to go with her to a café where they could have a glass of wine to celebrate.

'Thank you,' Barbara had said. 'I – I want to say something to you, Cathy. I'm sorry that I was foul to you when I first met you. I didn't know what was going on and it was a considerable shock.'

'Now that I understand everything so much better I'm not surprised,' Cathy had assured her. 'We've all had a lot of shocks to deal with. But please don't worry about it any more.'

Barbara had smiled cautiously at Cathy. 'Actually, I've often thought that if you hadn't turned up, none of this ever would have happened.'

'What do you mean?' Cathy had sipped her wine in surprise.

'I think you were a – a kind of catalyst. In sorting things out that had long needed sorting out. It gave us all a jolt.'

'I'm just glad it's brought out the best in Frank. From what I can tell, it was about bloody time.'

'Well. You won't understand this I expect, but when you spend a very long time around an unreasonable person you start to become unreasonable yourself. I didn't even like myself any more. I was judgemental of Barry and yet I've found him to be a very kind man.' Barbara had laughed under her breath. 'I even hated the stupid cat. As if the cat ever did anything wrong.'

'Beefy really is a very sweet cat,' Cathy had interjected in Beefy's defence.

'I'd never have imagined that I'd finish *Alfred*. I'd always thought that I was just the one who supplied

Frank with information and ideas, and he was the genius who put it all together. But do you know, Cathy, I really enjoyed doing it. And I realised I could do it, I just hadn't had the confidence to make my own voice heard before.'

Cathy had raised an eyebrow. 'I'll be expecting to see your name splashed all over the history section of Waterstone's for years to come.'

'Oh, I don't know.' Barbara had looked down. 'But Frank is insisting that *Alfred* comes out under both our names. As joint authors. That made me very happy. It confirmed to me that he thinks of us as – as a team. It was very heartening.'

'Maybe next time you'll write a biography under your own name?'

'Well, I do have some inspiration. There was a man, Aelfric. He was quite an absorbing thinker. If it's viable I have several ideas for an unusual biography of him. But never mind that now.' Barbara had flapped her hands. 'Frank told me that you've got a new office in Docklands and that your business is blossoming.'

Cathy thought of the beautiful little office she'd set up. Soon, Fiona would be joining her. Now she had the freedom to work her heart out on projects she felt were worthwhile, and really make a difference.

'There's a lot to sort out, but I'm so glad I've done it.'

'I'm very happy for you.' Barbara nodded her approval. 'And there's one other thing I'd like to ask you. But I'm not sure what you'll say.'

Cathy and Barbara both took sips of their wine.

'Go on.'

'Well.' Barbara looked very uncomfortable. Her cheeks had turned pink. 'The thing is, it sounds somewhat adolescent and I know I'm a middle-aged woman and it's probably not appropriate. But . . . I wondered if you'd like to be my bridesmaid?' Cathy was deeply moved. Barbara went on, looking highly embarrassed, 'You see, I never thought I'd have a family. I'd given up on that idea years ago. Yet when I considered our situation, I realised that by marrying your father, I'd be . . . I'd be' – Barbara drank from her wine again – 'I'd be your stepmother. Only in one way of thinking, of course. I wouldn't want to impose at all. I know that Melissa and Brian will always be your parents. I only mean that—'

'Of course,' Cathy had breathed. 'How lovely!'

'Do you think so?' Barbara's eyes had brightened.

'Absolutely.' Cathy had laughed suddenly. 'And I'd be honoured to be your bridesmaid.'

So in late September Cathy found herself dolled up in a pretty pale-yellow dress, following Barbara down the aisle as she made her way towards Frank.

The outfit they'd had tailored for Barbara, a creamy coffee-coloured dress, down to the shins but with a scalloped edge, split up to the knee on one side, looked stunning. It was straight across the cleavage, but sleeveless and was made more formal by a delicate bolero top edged with pearls. Cathy had also managed to persuade Barbara to go for a tiny cap with cream net round it, which the hairdresser, having had the time of her life creating waves and puffs in Barbara's hair where they'd never existed, had perched on her head perfectly.

Cathy was eager not to miss Frank's expression when he saw Barbara like this and, as she caught sight of his face, she grinned in triumph. He was flabbergasted.

Frank had asked Barry to be his best man. Although Cathy was sure he had many old friends who might have served the purpose, she sensed he'd asked Barry because he knew that it would mean a lot to him. That had raised her father even further in her estimation.

Barry had now found himself a small flat, telling Cathy that as Frank and Barbara were getting married, it was time for him to move on. Staying with Frank had been wonderful and he'd be back, regularly, to see his 'old mate', but he needed to make some more solid plans for his own future.

He had a new girlfriend too: Stephie. She was one of the nurses he'd started chatting to during his regular visits to Frank in hospital. But she was different, he'd told Cathy. She had met Stephie when Barry had invited her and Jason up to Oxford so that they could go out for a drink as a group and she'd seen why Stephie might be a bit different from Barry's previous girlfriends. She was level-headed and didn't take any nonsense. Barry had spent the entire evening gazing at her like a love-sick puppy, his chirpy one-liners forgotten. Cathy had also caught Stephie looking at Barry affectionately when he was getting their drinks at the bar. It was possible that he'd hit the jackpot this time.

Cathy spotted Stephie in the chapel and mentally applauded Barry for asking her.

Jason was there too, in the front pew, as Frank had insisted.

'You might not be married, but he's your other half,' Frank had asserted. 'That's where he goes.'

And also in the front pew were the 'guests of

honour', as Frank had described them. Melissa and Brian – Melissa looking elegant in pale grey, Brian, with his endearing fly-away hair, looking slightly surprised to find himself in a suit. As they spotted Cathy, Melissa broke into a warm smile and Brian gave her an impulsive wave. Cathy beamed back at them, before concentrating on following Barbara, all the way up the aisle to where Frank waited.

After the wedding all the guests adjourned to Frank's house. The garden was full of people Cathy had never met. Then she spotted a familiar face, but couldn't place it.

'It's Vince. Remember me?' He held out a hand to Cathy.

Now she remembered. It was the man who'd almost wrestled her to the floor at the Bodleian Library, when she'd been desperately trying to reach Barbara. He was one of many friends and colleagues from Frank's university days who thronged in the garden now.

As twilight began to descend, Frank stood on the terrace and called for everyone's attention so that he could make a short speech. The garden lanterns that Cathy, Barbara and Barry had made sure were everywhere glowed around him. Frank looked pale after such a long day, but he sounded robust. He talked of Barbara and they toasted Barbara, who looked secretly delighted. Then Frank went on to say:

'And I'd like to propose a toast to Catherine.'

It gave Cathy a shock. Jason squeezed her arm and kissed her cheek. There was a bemused hush among the guests, many of whom hadn't even been introduced to her.

'Oh don't be so bloody surprised,' Frank said.

'Cathy, come up here. Let them all see you.'

Cathy threaded her way from the table where she'd been overseeing the buffet up to the terrace and stood next to Frank.

'Friends, colleagues, enemies, people whom we've invited so as not to offend. I would like to introduce you to my daughter Catherine,' Frank said, iterating his words slowly. He waited for this news to be absorbed. 'I consider myself the most fortunate man alive. Not only do I have a wonderful wife, I couldn't wish for a better daughter. I know that Melissa and Brian Gordon, who are my most honoured guests today, will understand me. I want to thank them both from the bottom of my heart for . . . for everything, and for their constant and generous understanding of my love for my daughter. I don't think there's anything more – anything more that a man could ask.'

He stopped, overcome.

Cathy put an arm round him. Barbara was there too, taking Frank's hand and holding it.

'No, no, don't fuss me.' Frank pulled away. 'I've got things I have to say.'

The guests shuffled forward on the lawn to hear better. A champagne cork popped and there was a collective 'sh'. Quiet descended on the small crowd. As night began to fall and the sky was streaked with violet, the willows on the river bank rustled and a handful of frogs croaked briefly.

'Barbara?' Frank appealed, looking at her. 'The paperwork? You know where it is. The summary. Of my plan.'

Barbara seemed stuck to the spot. Cathy glanced at her. What was this?

'Now?' Barbara queried softly.

'Yes,' Frank insisted. 'I want it to be now.'

Barbara nodded and, with a cryptic look at Cathy, disappeared through the french windows into the house. She reappeared moments later and handed a piece of paper to Frank. Frank stepped forward on the terrace and motioned Cathy to come closer. She took a couple of steps and stood nearer to Frank, while not wishing to share his spotlight.

'I wish to announce something.' Frank rocked on his heels, his chin up.

Now Cathy could see how he could have been a lecturer. His voice had risen, commanding attention without being shrill. It must have been a mode that, in his armchair, in front of his television, he had ceased to need. How long had it been since he addressed an enraptured audience? But Cathy was transfixed, as was every single wedding guest. They willed him to go on as he inhaled, reached for Barbara's hand and took his time about it.

'I had thought I wouldn't live beyond this summer. This wonderful Ashes summer. I made plans, thinking that they would have to be put into practice in my . . . absence,' Frank said. 'But it appears that the surgeons of the John Radcliffe Hospital, God bless their bony arses, have ensured that I will be around to torture you all for longer than I had anticipated.'

There were a few muted calls of 'shame', but Frank held up a hand.

'So I would like to announce now something I intended to be revealed in my will.'

Cathy shrank away to the back of the terrace. This was no time to talk ornaments and savings accounts, surely? What on earth would Barbara feel about this, on her wedding day? But Barbara seemed very calm. She glanced round to see where Cathy was, gave her a cautious smile and indicated that she should come closer. Cathy crept a step forward and stood still.

'So this is it,' Frank declared, his voice resonating. 'At least, this is the part I'm willing to share with you critical buggers.' Frank rustled the paper and squinted at it.

Cathy held her breath. Frank squared his shoulders.

'I am only Frank Harland, not Martin Luther King. Thank you, Barbara, for that astute observation. But I do have a dream.' Frank raised his eyes to his audience. 'I have bought a plot of land which will be built into a cricket academy, intended for the encouragement of young, disadvantaged enthusiasts. I'm not the first one to have such an idea, but I may be the first to stick to my principles. The academy will be a centre of hope for those youngsters who won't find it anywhere else. That, I won't negotiate. The building plans have been approved and I have provided the initial capital myself. All we have to do now is build it and make it work.'

Cathy listened, transfixed. There was a pause while this information drifted over the heads of the guests and then a ripple started, which became strong applause.

Frank waved his hands. 'No, no, no. I don't want your thanks. None of you privileged ponces is going to benefit from this and you're all too old anyway.' He let his hands drop to his sides and gazed out over his long lawn, over the heads of the gathering. 'It has always been my dream to do something to help. Something constructive. Something to inspire the young to feel optimistic about themselves. There are kids out there who never get the chance to see if they're good at anything. Playing fields are getting smaller. Schools run on tight budgets. Given the choice between a football field or a cricket pitch, most schools, especially in inner city areas, opt for football. I want to offer these kids something else and, although you may have thought I love the sound of my own bloody voice, that's actually why I adored teaching.'

There was an awed hush as Frank grappled with his paper again. Cathy took a deep breath. The scent of the river bank and late summer blossoms flooded her nostrils.

'The academy will be established from private resources, but from there it needs to gain status so that it can receive funding help from elsewhere. God knows, even the English Cricket Board might show a flicker of interest. But it will at first rely on sponsorship, my considerable (if I may say so) investment, and the hard work and dedication of those who will strive to make it a success.'

Frank folded his notes and took a long breath. Barbara, next to him, squeezed his hand. Cathy was entranced. She could never have imagined that Frank had been planning this, that he had such an ambitious vision. He'd seemed so self-obsessed. But all this time he'd been working it out. She was awed.

'And now, Barry, will you come up here?' Frank gestured to Barry.

Cathy located Barry, looking as dumbstruck as she was herself, standing just in front of the terrace. Earlier, he'd given a short but affectionate best man's speech in

Frank's honour and he looked as if he was still getting over it. He stumbled up the low steps to the terrace and stood next to Cathy, bewildered. Frank's voice demanded their attention again.

'This is my dream, as I've explained, and I know whom I want to work with me. They will have to tell me if they don't wish to be a part of it, but I hope that even if they reject my ideas, they will see my faith in them as a compliment. I would like my daughter, Catherine,' Frank continued fluently, as Cathy's eyes widened in alarm, 'to take the leading role in the development of the academy. She is ideally qualified. Most of you don't know Catherine, but she's a skilled economist and committed to providing opportunities for others. She is warm, intelligent and driven by humanitarian instincts.'

Frank paused for breath, his voice breaking emotionally. Then he gathered himself and stood straight again.

'Her track record proves this without any doubt. She has recently started her own business as a consultant and obviously I respect the fact that she has independent ideas to explore. However, I believe that my daughter is the right person to head the academy and I will be doing my best to persuade her to sell her consultancy skills to me. Perhaps, in time, she may think upon the academy as her major client. Especially now that she has a growing fascination with cricket.'

There was a whisper of subdued laughter. Cathy gaped at Frank in disbelief.

'My best man,' Frank continued without looking round, 'Barry Merrick, is a talented man, an excellent communicator and an ardent cricket fan. His talents are

507

not being fully explored in his current line of work and I know that he is looking to move on. I am offering Barry a full-time position in the academy, where he will use his considerable skills and his undeniable energy in sales and marketing.'

Cathy felt Barry take her hand. She was too stunned to do anything other than give it a light squeeze.

'It is also my wish that Nick Allen will be a part of the management team. Nick will provide Information Technology expertise and a passion for the game equal to my own. Nick isn't here today, but I have already spoken to him about this. Last week he confirmed his interest. He will work initially as a consultant. He is open to the idea that the position may become full-time in due course.'

Cathy was now encased in concrete. She couldn't have moved if she'd wanted to. Herself? Barry? Nick? Working together?

Frank stared intently at his notes for a moment longer, then ranged his eyes over his captive audience.

'That's it. That's my announcement. And now, as it's the first time I've ever got married, I'd like to get back to the wedding celebrations and I hope you all drink enough to feel very ill tomorrow. But first I have to thank my wife, Barbara, for continuing to put up with me and supporting me in all the decisions I've made about the academy. Right. That's it. Get on with it. Enjoy yourselves.'

Frank backed away towards Barbara and she took his arm. They spoke privately together in low murmurs. After a slight delay, in which everyone seemed to gather his or her breath, the guests burst into loud clapping.

Barry turned round to Cathy, his eyes like flying saucers.

'What the fuck? Did you know anything about this?'

Cathy shook her head mutely.

Jason appeared at her side. He rubbed Cathy's shoulder and grinned at her.

'Jesus, that's so exciting!'

Jason's expression said this was the best thing that could ever have happened to Cathy. She couldn't take it in.

'I don't understand. A cricket academy? I wouldn't know where to start.'

'Flipping heck,' Barry was saying to himself, rubbing his hair in disbelief. Frank had momentarily disappeared through the french windows with Barbara. Cathy pleaded to Barry.

'Did you know about this? Anything at all? I can't get my head round it.'

'No, me neither,' Barry said, his shock obviously developing into relish as his smile spread. 'But bloody hell, Cathy, this is a chance in a million. It's amazing. I can't believe it. Bloody good old Frank. I'm sick of selling cars. I know I can do much, much more. And he knows it too. If he weren't already married I'd marry him, brilliant bugger that he is.'

'I've just started a business.' Cathy looked at Jason for support. It was obvious Barry was already plunging into his wildest dreams with his wellies on. 'I've rented an office. Fiona's coming to work for me.'

Jason looked at her kindly.

'Yes, but you've got to think about what Frank said. He wants you to act as a consultant. You can do that. You've only just set up and you're looking for clients.

You've got to forget for a minute that Frank's your dad and think of it with a business head on. It's just up your street.'

'I . . . maybe you're right. But a cricket academy? I've only just been introduced to the whole thing.'

'Forget the cricket for a moment. If I offered you the chance to work on a project that provided opportunities for kids who needed them, what would you say?'

'I – I'd say that was interesting,' Cathy struggled.

'There you go.' Jason grinned. 'Once you've had a chance to think it through, you're going to agree with Barry. He's right, it *is* a chance in a million. You'll get to make your name, show your business head off and do some good. That's what you want to do, isn't it?'

'Of course,' Cathy replied, confused. 'That's why I work with developing companies. To help them see their potential. That's my calling. Not cricket.'

Jason raised his eyebrows and smiled. Barry, apparently eavesdropping while he was privately celebrating, had computed Cathy's words.

'Development? Encouragement? Did I hear a conflict somewhere? I don't think so.' Barry chuckled loudly. He turned to Jason. 'Bloody hell, have we got another bottle of champers somewhere? I think we need it.'

'Go grab one,' Jason urged him. 'I think Cathy could use a large glass of something.'

Barry bounded away like Tigger. Cathy stared after him. She appealed to Jason again.

'It's not what I've planned.'

'With all due respect to your mum, I think that's Melissa speaking,' Jason said gently. 'The Cathy I'm getting to know now is open to ideas. Especially exciting ones.'

Cathy studied Jason's expression and felt her confidence rise.

'You might well be right. This is so different from what I'd pictured myself doing, I should probably do it.'

'Cathy.' Jason laughed at her puzzled face. 'My incredibly capable, successful, lovable girlfriend. You'll do this standing on your head. But you still don't get it, do you?'

'What don't I get?'

'This is what Frank was doing. All summer. And I thought he was mad for sending you off to cricket matches. But he wasn't at all. It was the sanest, most imaginative thing he could have done. He was giving you a taster, because he wanted his only child to play a key role in his academy. He wanted you to get a feel for the game he's so passionate about. He wanted you to see it, taste it and love it first. And only then was he going to tell you about his plans. Do you see now?'

'Yes.'

Jason was right. All summer, this was what Frank had been doing. Sending his only daughter out there to experience the sensations for herself. He'd brought Nick into the equation because he respected Nick and thought he should be a part of the academy. Perhaps Frank, with his penchant for playing God, had also thought that Nick and Cathy would spark off each other. Well, he hadn't been wrong. They had. It had been an explosion. An irrational, exciting and ultimately meaningless explosion. But Frank had wanted Cathy and Nick to get to know each other for other reasons too. He wanted to see if they would be able to work together.

Maybe Frank had also been harking back to the days when he had last experienced an explosion. With Annette – Cathy's mother. Now he'd realised that the woman who had sustained him, nurtured him and loved him to the point where he was always strong was not the same woman who'd made him feel helpless with desire. It was Barbara who until this day had been his other half in all but the law.

At last, Cathy felt that she understood the intricacy of Frank's actions. The realisation was humbling. She'd misjudged him and now she felt nothing but admiration for him. Frank, the man she had initially avoided, then disliked and now loved profoundly: her father.

'I understand it now,' Cathy said to Jason. 'It's overwhelming.'

'I know.' Jason kissed her cheek.

Barry arrived with a full bottle of champagne and three glasses.

'Not interrupting, am I? We should have a toast.'

'Any sign of Frank and Barbara?' Jason peered around. 'Nope. And I can't see Melissa and Brian. But a few curious faces are looking at us.' He winked at Cathy. 'Let's keep this moment private for now.'

'But—' Cathy put out a hand to Jason's arm. She looked deeply into his eyes. 'Frank's wish. To see Nick involved. It's a shock to me, but there's a logic to it. I know why Frank's done this, but I really don't want you to be offended, Jace.'

Jason held his glass out to Barry, and then let him fill Cathy's before answering. Barry looked from one to the other of them cautiously.

'I know why Frank's brought Nick on board.' Jason

held Cathy's gaze confidently. 'It's because he thinks he's the right man for the job. I can't argue with that. From what I know, Frank's made a sound decision. We'll have to see how this works out between you all, but I can't foresee any problems. Certainly not for me. And' – he clinked glasses with Cathy – 'I trust you completely.'

'Thank you,' she mouthed back at him.

'To Frank's academy and to us,' Barry declared.

Cathy pushed her glass against Barry's and Jason's, and they all slugged a mouthful.

'To fresh beginnings,' Jason offered, and they all clinked glasses and drank again.

'To a whole new concept of family,' Cathy said, tears sticking in her throat. 'I've discovered so much this year. A father, a stepmother, Melissa and Brian being so fantastic, a great new friend and a wonderful boyfriend. We're all in this together now. Whether we like it or not.'

'I'm up for that,' Jason said, clinking his glass.

'We always were in it together.' Barry beamed, forgetting to clink glasses and clutching Cathy in a hug. Then he grabbed Jason in a manly clinch. Jason patted his shoulders.

'You're my besht friend, you are,' Jason teased. Barry laughed. Cathy had never seen either of them look so inspired and so carefree.

'You're a great bloke, Jason. I never thought I could approve of a guy who robbed me of Cathy's adoration, but I know she's in really good hands. Whoa!' Barry squinted out over the lawn. 'I see Stephie over there, looking for me. I'm off to give her a glass of bubbly and I'll catch you two later.'

He galloped away, leaving Jason and Cathy alone on the terrace. Cathy blushed to have Jason's sole attention, which was silly, as she'd known her boy-friend for four years. But it was as if they were very new and intriguing to each other again. And Jason was probing her with dark, intense eyes and her skin was warming under his gaze.

'I – I should probably go and find Frank,' she said. 'I should tell him that I understand and that I'll do everything I can to help. I really do want to be a part of his academy. The more I think about it, the more I'm convinced.'

'Have you made up your mind?'

'Yes.' Cathy nodded. 'I'm in.'

'In which case, may I venture to say that Frank's already assuming that you'll agree and that he's just got married.' Jason winked at Cathy. 'I think he might want some private time with his wife.'

'Oh. Yes, of course.'

'So Frank's all right. Let's give him some peace.'

Cathy nodded. 'And Barbara looked gorgeous, didn't she? I planned it with her, but even I didn't think she'd shine up so well. A real babe.'

'He's probably taken her off privately somewhere to tell her that.'

'Yes.' Cathy smiled at the thought.

'But you', Jason said, 'are the belle of the ball. I've never seen you looking so radiant.'

Jason put out a hand and stroked Cathy's hair.

The sensual look he gave her sent her temperature soaring.

'Really?'

'Look at you.' Jason took her hands and held her out

for inspection. 'Sumptuously tanned, with endearing little freckles all over your chest. Hair like fire. And with the candlelight flickering all around you, you're like a great big yellow and orange . . . thing.'

'A great big thing?' Cathy queried with dry humour.

'Let me rephrase it. You're like an exotic orchid. A tropical fruit. A wild red poppy in a sea of daisies. Something to be gasped at in wonderment.' Jason husked at her, 'You're the most beautiful thing I've ever seen in my life.'

'Thank you,' she breathed.

'I love you, Cathy, and I've never been so proud of you. And I wanted to ask you something.' Jason paused, his eyes dancing at her. 'Would you mind if I left a few things at your house sometimes?'

'What sort of things?'

'Things like boxer shorts?'

'Boxer shorts?' Cathy laughed loudly. 'Yes of course, if you want.'

'But I also wondered if I could leave a few other things there?'

'And what other things would they be?' Cathy's lips twitched into a smile.

'Well, things like bottles of wine, sumptuous delicacies, finely woven silk, exotic perfume.' Jason stopped to think. 'My stereo, television, Stanley Kubrick videos, double bed, which is a lot more comfortable than yours . . .'